1

Every Breath You Take

Every Breath You Take
Bayou Devils MC
Book Three

A.M. Myers

Every Breath You Take

A.M. Myers

The characters and events in this book are fictitious. Names, characters, places and plots are a product of the author's imagination. Any similarity to real persons, living or dead, is coincidental and not intended by the author.

Cover Design by Jay Aheer
Proofreading by Julie Deaton
Photography by Wander Aguiar
Cover Model: Jonny James

Every Breath You Take

Prologue
Lincoln

"Just perfect," I sneer, crossing my arms over my chest as I lean back in my chair and glare out of the picture window. Dark, ominous clouds peek over the snow-capped mountains on the outskirts of town and the air carries a hint of rain but that's just the cherry on top of this shitty day. When I woke up this morning, I had a plan and it certainly didn't include sitting in the office of my parents' charter plane business and fielding customer calls while Dad ran supplies out to one of the remote villages. I know Mom was up with Nora and Rowan all night long as they projectile vomited all over the house but I don't why that has to fuck with my day.

My girlfriend, Megan, called last night and asked if I wanted to take her dad's boat out since he was going out of town today. I was totally down for that and even planned a little picnic for us in the hopes that today just might be the day I finally get past second base with her but that's never going to happen with the summer storm quickly approaching town. Then again, I could always grab a couple scary movies and popcorn and show up on her doorstep. With her dad out of town, we'll have the house to ourselves and no matter how brave she tries to be, she'll be in my lap before the thirty-minute mark. It's not as romantic as I planned but I could still make it work.

Smirking, I spin in my chair to face the desk and reach for the office phone just as it rings. With a sigh, I scoop it up and press it to my ear.

"JP Charters, this is Lincoln. How can I help you?"

"Yeah, I was just wonderin' how much y'all charge for a sightseeing tour?" a man with a thick southern accent asks and I roll my eyes as I spin to face the list of our rates on the wall. Normally, I don't mind working with my parents since Dad usually lets me help him with the planes but dealing with customers is the one thing I hate. Tourist season here in Ketchikan, Alaska, makes me want to claw my damn eyes out. Every time a cruise ship docks, my otherwise quiet town is overrun with people who ever never stepped foot out of the city and don't understand some basic truths about this area of the country. If I had a nickel for every idiot who thought it was a great idea to pet a wild animal, my parents could retire.

"How long were you thinking?"

"Well, shit, I don't know. How long can we get?"

"We've got a couple Cessnas that can go for about two hours before needing to refuel but you can book it for as long as you'd like."

He sighs and I spin back around to stare out the window as I wait for his response, a headache brewing. Thank God, I'm not down at the docks today. Whenever I get in trouble, that's my go-to punishment because I hate standing there, waving our sign around as people disembark. On those days, when I have to interact with customers face-to-face, it's hard to keep my irritation in check.

"My wife really wants to see some animals. How long you figure that would take?"

I shake my head and scrub my hand over my face. It's always the same fucking story. I've been hiking in the woods around Ketchikan since the moment I learned to walk and I know it like the back of my hand but any native Alaskan will tell you there's no way to one hundred percent predict where the animals will be on any given day. But does that stop people from asking us to take their party right to them or demanding a refund when we can't? No, it doesn't. It got so bad that Dad had to put a warning on all our promotional stuff saying that we couldn't guarantee anything.

"This isn't a zoo, Sir. These are wild animals and we can't just make them appear."

"Sure, but you know about where they're at, right? We want to see some bears."

Of course.

"If you want to see bears, your best bet would be to go up to Neets Point."

"Okay, that sounds good. Let's do that. Y'all free tomorrow?"

I shake my head, glancing down at the schedule in front of me despite the fact that I couldn't take him to Neets Point even if we were available.

"No, Sir. To get to Neets Point, you need a boat or a floatplane. We have neither of those."

"I see. Well, do you know where I could find one?"

Nodding, I lean back in the chair and rattle off a couple of our competitors that I know could help him before hanging up and letting out a heavy sigh. I check my watch and glance out the window, scanning the sky. Dad should be back soon and I'm getting anxious to see Megan. Just as I reach for the phone to call her, the radio behind me squawks and I flick a glance over my shoulder.

"Linc?" Dad's voice crackles through the speakers and I push out of the chair, unhooking the microphone as I hold it close to my lips and press the button.

"Hey, Dad. You about home? You're never going to believe the phone call I just got from a customer."

"Lincoln," he says again and the pain in his voice catches my attention as my heart rate quickens.

Something's not right, a voice in my head screams and my hand shakes as I press the button again.

"You okay, Dad?"

Please say yes.

Please say yes.

Please say yes.

10

"Not exactly, kid," his voice echoes through the office and I suck in a breath, a roaring sound filling my ears. "The plane went down."

I collapse back into my chair, my mind recalling every image I've ever seen of a small plane crash as I stare out of the window like somehow, I might catch him landing on the runway instead of trapped in a mangled metal box.

"What do you mean it went down?" I whisper, holding the microphone close to my lips. "What happened?"

"I'm not sure. I had just come over the mountain when all the gauges started going crazy and I couldn't stop it. She went down hard."

I run through the mechanics of the plane in my mind, trying to figure out what could have possibly failed but it's impossible to think with my heart hammering in my chest and each breath punching out of my chest. Looking down at the microphone in my hand, I realize I need to get him some help. Nodding, I turn toward the desk and grab a pen.

"Give me your coordinates, Dad, and I'll get help out to you."

He rattles off some coordinates and I scribble them down before grabbing the phone and dialing nine-one-one. I relay all the information to the operator before setting the phone down and grabbing the microphone again.

"Okay, Dad. Help is on the way."

"Listen to me, Linc," he says, his voice growing weaker and chills blanket my skin. "They're not going to make it in time."

I recoil, staring down at the microphone in my hand with wide eyes before I press the button. "What are you talking about? They're coming right now. You've just got to hang on."

"I need you to listen, son. I'm losing a lot of blood and I'm pretty sure I nicked an artery in my leg. The crash site is fifteen miles out of town, at least. This is a body recovery, not a rescue."

"Don't say that," I hiss, tears burning my eyes. "Just hang on."

"Lincoln," he whispers, his voice trailing off at the end and my heart seizes.

"Dad!"

"I'm still here." His voice is even weaker than before and it hits me all at once, crashing down on me like an avalanche that this is the last time I'm ever going to speak to my father. Tears slips down my cheeks and I rest my head in my hand, struggling to breathe. I'm not ready for this. I'm only fifteen – how the hell am I supposed to go on without my dad? And Mom... Oh, God. I have to call Mom and tell her what's happening.

"Do me a favor, Kid?" he asks and I nod.

"Yeah, Dad. Anything."

"Take care of your mom and sisters for me, okay? You're all they have left now and they need you."

A sob rips its way through my lips and I pound my fist into the desk. Why? Why is this happening to him? To our family?

"I will. I promise." My voice cracks and I flick a few tears off my face.

"And tell them all how much I love them. If there was anyway out of this, I would be there with you all."

"I'll tell them."

"Good. It's time to be the man I've been raising you to be. I know it's not fair but you've already made me so proud, Lincoln. This is just the hand we've been dealt and I know I can count on you to step up."

"I won't let you down."

The silence stretches between us and my chest feels tight, my mind screaming as I wait for him to respond to me.

"I know you won't. You're a good kid and an even better son. Never forget how much I love you."

"I love you, too, Dad," I whisper, praying for more time but the only response is a haunting static.

Every Breath You Take

A.M. Myers

Chapter One
Tatum

A crash echoes through the empty streets and my heart slams into my ribs as I squint into the darkness, searching for any sign of danger. I quicken my steps when I find nothing. I would much prefer if the danger just jumped out at me because then, I could deal with it. The unknown drives me crazy. Ducking my head, I press onward and flex my fingers around the can of pepper spray in my hand. My pulse pounds in my ears and I suck in a breath, reminding myself that I only have one more block to go. One more block and I'll be home, safe and sound… or as safe as you can be in this part of town. There was a time, before I ever lived here, that this neighborhood was a desired place to live but drugs and crime started creeping in and everyone else left, dropping the property value. The only people left are the folks like me who can't afford to move anywhere else.

Thunder rumbles in the distance and I smile, lifting my face to the sky to breathe in the scent of rain temporarily masking the stench of stale beer and cigarettes that usually lingers in the air. A breeze blows through my hair and I consider opening the windows as soon as I get home so the fresh rain smell can fill my little apartment. I wouldn't even entertain the idea if I didn't live on the third floor of my building. Plus, the landlord hasn't fixed the fire escapes yet so anyone that tries to climb it will go crashing to their death before they reach me.

A car alarm wails behind me and I jump as I glance over my shoulder, my pulse spiking. The dark street at my back only intensifies the sense of foreboding that I've been carrying around all night. God, why can't I shake this feeling? My mother's voice pierces through my thoughts, once again nagging me to pack up and move somewhere safer. That's easy for her to say, though. Apartments in a nice part of town cost money and with the two jobs I already have, I'm barely making it. I just have to keep telling myself that someday all this struggle will pay off. I will finally save enough money to go to school and become a nurse, someday I'll make enough money to buy a house in a better part of town and then, all the shit I'm going through now will be a distant memory.

Hopefully.

Relief surges through me as my apartment building comes into view and I jog over to the door, eager to get inside and collapse into a heap on my bed. When I reach the door, I duck inside and check my mailbox before turning for the stairs. I take them two at a time, always keeping an eye on my surroundings as I march down the hallway with my head held high. One of the first things I learned when I moved here was that if you looked scared, people would only mess with you more so even when I'm feeling weak, I keep my head up and try to look as badass as I wish I felt. The light above me flickers as I stop at my door and jam my key into the first deadbolt and I blow out a breath, sending up a silent prayer to God or whatever deity is watching out for me that I don't get killed tonight. A shiver twists down my spine and I shake my head as I move to unlock the second deadbolt. Maybe my mother is right. What good will my sacrifices do if I don't live long enough to realize my dream?

Once inside, I shut the door and relock both deadbolts before securing the chain and turning with a sigh, letting the sense of security wash over me. I drop my keys onto the table with a clank and survey my small apartment, making sure everything is exactly as I left it earlier. There's a bowl next to the sink from my breakfast and the small pile of bills are stacked neatly on the dining room table – so far, so good. A blanket is strewn over the back of the couch from where I was watching a movie last night and as I scan over to the TV, I stop. The curtains are open and for the life of me, I can't remember if I left them closed or not. Squinting my eyes closed, I picture the living room last night as I got ready for bed but I still can't recall what position the curtains were in. My heart races as I scan the apartment again but it's silent and I shake my head as I blow out a breath.

This is ridiculous.

I'm a grown woman but I still play this stupid game that Mom made my twin brother, Theo, and I play every time we came back to wherever we were staying at the time. I can't help it, though. After all these years, she's trained me to notice every little thing and be hyper focused on my surroundings. In some ways, it's nice, especially as a woman living alone but right now, when I'm so tired I could just fall over right here and I can't remember how I left the damn curtains, it's a damn inconvenience.

Sighing, I push off the door and drag my tired body to the bedroom, still focused on everything around me no matter how stupid I think it is. In my bedroom, I plop down on the mattress and kick my shoes off, groaning at the ache that radiates up my calves. When my friend, Mia, called me yesterday and asked me to cover her shift at the diner, I jumped at the opportunity to make some more money but after sixteen hours on my feet, I'm not sure that it's worth it. It's not unusual to get home from a shift with every part of my body aching and sometimes, it feels like I'm killing myself and not getting anywhere.

Grabbing my phone out of my pocket, I pull up my bank account and let out a pained groan when I see the measly balance in my savings account. I doubt it's even enough to buy the books I would need for one year of classes. Sighing, I go back to the home screen and open my messages before firing off one to my mom to let her know I made it home safe and sound. It's just past two in the morning so she won't get it until she wakes up but it will put her mind at ease and save me a sunrise visit from her when all I want to do is fall face first in this bed and sleep for the next twenty-four hours.

Pushing myself to my feet, I toss my phone back on the bed and amble over to the window before pushing it up just enough to let the scent of rain fill the room. Closing my eyes, I breathe it in for a moment before stripping out of my uniform and tossing it in the hamper. I grab the XXL t-shirt off the chair in the corner and slip it over my head before crawling into bed. Grabbing my phone off the mattress, I plug it in and set it on the table next to my bed before opening the drawer and laying my fingers on the cold metal of my pistol. Just knowing it's there if I need it makes me feel more secure and I close the drawer again as I fluff up my pillow and lie down. The world goes dark as I pull the comforter up over my head and close my eyes, sleep already luring me into its warm embrace.

Bang!

Bang!

Bang!

I shoot up, flinging the blanket back as I stare down the dark hallway, every hair on my arm raised. My hand reaches for the pistol mindlessly as I suck in a breath and remind myself that it's probably Lonnie, the old drunk that lives down the hall. He's always going to the wrong door and when his key doesn't work, he'll make a ruckus until someone points him in the right direction. Another round of pounding reverberates through the apartment and I open the drawer, grabbing the gun, as I push the covers off my legs. Nothing good can come from someone pounding on your door at two in the morning – even if it is just Lonnie. I slip out of bed just as the person at my door knocks again and I set the pistol down on the bed as I grab a pair of mesh shorts and slip them on. Once I'm dressed, I grab the gun again and creep down the hallway, my heart pounding and my body poised to strike at a moment's notice.

A few feet from the door, my steps slow and I creep forward on tippy toes, trying to make as little noise as possible. When I reach the door, I glance in the peephole and my hand shakes as I watch the man in a suit on the other side who is clearly not Lonnie. He doesn't seem threatening but Mom always taught us that you can never be too careful. A nice suit could make the devil look like a saint.

"What do you want?" I yell through the door, my grip firm on the gun and my finger hovering over the trigger.

"I need to speak to Miss Tatum Carter."

I shake my head. "Not at two in the morning you don't."

"Please," he says, lowering his voice. "I'm from the Baton Rouge Police Department and it's urgent that I speak to Miss Carter."

Sinking my teeth into my lip, I take a step back and look around before sucking in a breath before moving back to the door.

"Let me see your badge," I order as I peer through the peephole again and he holds a badge and his ID up to the glass. I inspect it for a moment before stepping away from the door and setting the gun down on the table, away from me but still within reach. I unlock the deadbolt but leave the chain in place as I crack the door open and peer up at him.

"Let me see that badge again," I say and he presents it to me. It may seem ridiculous but it was only a few months ago that a man dressed up as a police officer to gain access to the apartments of a few of my neighbors. He raped them and left them for dead.

"What do you want?" I ask when I'm done inspecting his ID and he slips it back into his pocket.

"Miss Carter, I presume?" he asks and I nod. "I'm Detective Rodriguez. Do you mind if I come in and speak to you for a moment?"

"About?"

"I would really prefer to speak to you about that inside, ma'am."

I study him for another moment before nodding and closing the door to release the chain. When I open it again, he steps inside and scans the room, his gaze lingering on the pistol on the table before he turns to me with a quirked brow.

"It's registered," I assure him.

"You always keep it on the kitchen table?"

I shake my head. "No, but I'm a single woman living in one of the worst areas of town. It's never far from me. Besides, you're the one pounding on my door at two in the morning."

"I do apologize for that. The subject is… sensitive and I needed to speak to you before anyone else did."

I wrap my arms around myself. "Well, now you're worrying me. What's going on?"

"Please," he says, gesturing to the table. "Have a seat."

He sits at the head of the rectangular table and I choose the chair adjacent to him as he sets a folder down on the table. Sighing, he pulls a photo out of the folder and sets it down in front of me.

"Do you recognize this car?"

I nod, staring down at the dependable little Nissan she loves – now a mangled mess. "Yes, it's my mother's. What happened?"

Worry twists in my gut and it only gets worse when Detective Rodriguez looks uneasy. "At eleven fifty-three this evening, I was called to the scene of a hit and run accident involving this vehicle. When I arrived, they were loading a woman into the ambulance. They rushed her to the hospital and after all attempts to revive her, she was pronounced dead at twelve thirty-six a.m."

"Are-are you telling me my mother is dead?" I stutter, pressing a hand against my chest in an attempt to restart my stalled heart. A roaring sound fills my ears and my mind blanks as I wait for his answer. An answer that I somehow already know – like I can feel it deep down in my gut – but I can't believe it. Not until he says the words.

"That's the reason I'm here, ma'am. We need you to identify the body."

All the air rushes out of me and I nod. "Oh."

Detective Rodriguez pulls another photo out and places it face down on the table in front of me. "I know this is a difficult time for you, Miss Carter, but the sooner we confirm that it is your mother, the sooner we can shift our focus to figuring out what really happened."

The room spins as I stare at him, trying to process what he just said. How the hell am I supposed to do this? It can't be true. Not my mother. She's the strongest, bravest person I've ever met so there's no way she was taken out by a simple car accident. It's not possible. This doesn't feel real. Like any moment, I'll wake up and be back in my bed, under the covers. I set my shaking hand down on the table, my heart jumping into my throat as I try to convince myself to flip the photo over. My mind is screaming to do it but my hand won't move as it desperately tries to save me from discovering the truth.

Lightning streaks across the sky as I reach forward and gently turn the photo over as the world around me fades out of focus. A sob lodges in my throat and I stare down at the photo of my beautiful mother, laid out on a metal autopsy table with a pale blue sheet pulled up over her chest. Tears spill down my cheeks and the sob that I was barely holding back tears through my lips. Detective Rodriguez lays his hand on top of mine and another sob rips through me. He doesn't need me to say anything because the sound of my cries is all the evidence we both need. It's my mother lying on that cold metal table in a morgue somewhere across town and in her death, she's taking a chunk of my soul with her.

* * * *

My stomach sinks like a stone and my feet are rooted to the concrete as I sit on a park bench across from the Baton Rouge Police Department, staring up at the formidable building that holds answers. Answers that I'm not even sure I want.

"Ready to go?" Theo asks, sitting down next to me on the bench and I shrug my shoulders.

"Yes. No. I don't know."

"We'll go in whenever you're ready, T," he assures me and I turn to him with a raised brow.

"How the hell are you being so damn strong right now?"

He shakes his head. "I think I'm just in shock."

Turning back to the building, I nod. Shock is a good word for how this feels. Theo is stationed in Charleston with the Navy and after Detective Rodriguez left my apartment two days ago, I called him in tears. After five hours and several calls to his chief, he was on the road to help me process all of this and bury our mother. But none of it feels real.

"It doesn't seem possible…" I muse and Theo turns to me.

"What doesn't?"

"The car accident. I mean, this is the same woman who has a gun conveniently hidden in every room of her house, the one who built a panic room out of her bedroom closet, she made us train in at least three different martial arts, made us run drills for every disaster scenario and a car accident is what kills her? It doesn't fit."

"I know," he whispers. "I'm still trying to wrap my mind around it."

Shaking my head, I sigh. "I guess we won't get any answers out here."

"Ready to do this, then?" He holds his hand out to me and I grab it as I push to my feet.

"Yeah."

We cross the street in silence, hands clasped, and I can feel his nerves amplifying my own. Maybe it's because we're twins or maybe it's because growing up, we only had each other and Mom to lean on but this is the way it's always been for us. Sometimes, I swear I can hear his thoughts as loudly as my own.

"Relax," he whispers under his breath as he open the door to the police station and I shoot him a look. We're both on edge so he has no room to chastise me.

"Back at you, little brother."

He turns a glare on me and I smile. It's a fight we've had too many times to count and it's the fastest way to tick him off.

"By three minutes."

"Can I help you, folks?" the officer behind the front desk asks as we approach and Theo squares his shoulders as he nods.

"Yeah. We're here to talk to Detective Rodriguez."

"Name?"

"Theo and Tate Carter," Theo answers, authority in his voice.

The officer grabs the phone and glances up at us. "He expecting you?"

Theo nods and the officer dials Detective Rodriguez before instructing us to sit in the waiting area. We claim the last two chairs up against the wall and Theo crosses his arms over his chest, his gaze flicking over the room continuously. Even now, he can't stop himself from doing the things our mother ingrained in us.

"You know, the other night I couldn't remember how I had left the curtains in my apartment and it bothered me all night long."

He scoffs. "Try living with a roommate who doesn't understand your obsessive need to scan the room before you leave."

"Have you ever wondered why she was like that?"

"Every fucking day of my life," he replies, meeting my gaze and I nod. Our mother's strange behavior wasn't something either one of us noticed until we were teenagers because up until then, we didn't know any different. We thought all parents made their children practice at the gun range every weekend or act out what they would do if someone broke into the house.

"Miss Carter?" someone says from the doorway and we both turn as Detective Rodriguez steps out and extends his hand to Theo. "Hello, I'm Detective Rodriguez."

"Theo Carter."

Detective Rodriguez nods and motions toward the door he just came out of. "Why don't you follow me and we'll go over the case so far?"

We stand in unison and follow Detective Rodriguez back to an interview room with a table in the center. There are two chairs on one side so Theo and I sit there as Detective Rodriguez sits across from us and sets a thick folder down on the table. He pulls out several photos of our mother's mangled car and places them in front of us.

"First off, I just want to express my deepest condolences for your loss. This is my least favorite part of the job but I promise I will do everything I can to find who ran your mother off the road."

"You're sure that someone else was involved?" Theo asks, inspecting the photos in front of us and Rodriguez nods. He pulls out another photo and lays it in front of us, pointing to something in the shot.

"There was white paint found on the back bumper of your mother's car as well as tire marks indicating that a second vehicle was at the scene. It looks like whoever was driving that vehicle was very intoxicated."

Theo stares down at the photos before glancing up. "How can you tell that?"

Rodriguez pulls out more photos; these of the road leading up to the accident where you can see tire marks swerving all over the road. "We can't find anyone that witnessed the accident and unfortunately, traffic cameras in that part of town are down but based on the tire tracks, I would bet my career that the second driver was completely wasted."

"What part of town was she in?" I ask and he pulls out a map and lays it in front of us before pointing to the edge of town. "What was she doing out there?"

I turn to look at Theo and he shrugs.

"Your guess is as good as mine, Miss Carter," Detective Rodriguez says and my gaze flicks across the map to where her house is as my mind spins. What was she doing there? Not that she would have ever told me if I asked. My mother liked to keep her secrets.

"And you said there are no witnesses?" Theo asks, a scowl on his face as he inspects the evidence laid out in front of us.

"Not that we can find right now. We'll keep looking but in that neighborhood, the chances aren't high."

A feeling of hopelessness weighs down on me. "So, that's it, then?"

"No, ma'am. You have my word that I will keep searching for answers but just understand it's not going to be easy."

Theo meets my eyes and my heart breaks a little more knowing we may spend the rest of our lives searching for answers.

"Y'all can have your mother's body moved to a funeral home whenever you're ready. The medical examiner has finished everything he needs to do."

A sob wells up in my throat and Theo wraps an arm around my shoulders. "Okay, we'll take care of it and please keep in touch if you get any updates on the case."

Rodriguez nods and stands, holding his hand out toward Theo. "Of course."

They shake hands and he leads us back out to the waiting area before disappearing in the back. Theo leads me outside and I shiver as we cross the street and sit down on the park bench again.

"I hate not knowing," Theo whispers and I nod in agreement. Mom always taught us that knowledge is power so not having the answers we need only makes all this worse.

"What was she doing there?" I ask again, almost to myself and Theo sighs.

"Honestly, T, with Mom it could be anything."

I nod, watching the cars drive past us as I try to wrap my head around everything that's happened in the last forty-eight hours and everything that still needs to be done.

"Does Mom have life insurance?" I ask and Theo shrugs.

"I doubt it. She would have considered it an unnecessary expense."

I drop my head into my hands and suck in a breath. "How are we going to pay for a funeral, Theo? I don't have anything."

He wraps his arm around my shoulder and pulls me into his side. "We'll have to cremate her and spread her ashes. It's not like we have anyone to invite, anyway."

"We could do it at the beach she loved in Grand Isle," I suggest and he nods.

"Yeah, that sounds good. I'll take care of everything, okay?"

I nod, relieved that he's willing to take the lead because I'm barely hanging on at this point and I can't imagine adding anything else to my plate.

Every Breath You Take

Chapter Two
Lincoln

Aerosmith spills out of the bar's speakers as our waitress, Kelly, stops at our table and sets a bottle of beer down in front of Moose and me.

"Can I get you boys anything else?" she asks, flashing me a teasing smile that makes me want to pull her into my lap.

"What time you get off tonight, Kel?" I ask and her grin grows.

"Well, I suppose that depends on how good you are, biker boy. But I clock out at eleven."

With a wolfish grin, I reach for her and she slaps my hand away as she backs away from the table, shaking her finger at me. Kelly and I have been dancing around each other since the guys and I first started coming to this bar a couple weeks ago and I'm eager to make something finally happen between us.

"There's Smith," Moose says, nodding toward the door and I glance up as our brother weaves through the crowd toward our table. As soon as he sits down, Kelly is back with a beer for him and she flashes me a wink before returning to the bar.

"What a fuckin' day," Smith says as he grabs the bottle and raises it to his lips, chugging half of it. Two girls walk past him, makin' eyes, but he doesn't even notice them. With a sigh, he sets his beer bottle down and scrubs his hand over his face, looking exhausted.

"Keep that up and you'll be sleeping on the floor," I point out, glancing down at the dirty bar floor with a grimace. He scoffs.

"After all the shit I dealt with today, it might be an improvement." He casts and annoyed glance at a group of college aged girls giggling in the corner and I bite back a smirk. Smith is usually a pretty easygoing guy but he's had a lot on his plate lately and it's making him short-tempered.

Moose quirks a brow. "Your brother?"

"Who fucking else?" he snaps and I can see the stress plain as day on his face. Since they were little, Smith and his little brother, Clay, only had each other to lean on and they were as tight as two people could be. Clay has always been a bit of a troublemaker, though, and a few years ago, he started getting into drugs. Now, it seems like all Smith does is clean up after his brother and try to save him from himself.

"What did he do this time?" I ask and Smith shakes his head as he downs the rest of his beer and holds his empty bottle up in the air. Kelly nods in our direction and holds up a finger, indicating that it will be a minute. Sighing, he turns back to the table.

"Rodriguez called me this morning. Turns out my baby brother got arrested for harassing some poor young lady yesterday and spent last night in a jail cell sobering up. When I picked him up, we got into it and he ran off. I've spent all day trying to find him."

"No luck?" Moose asks and Smith shakes his head.

"Nope and I'm worried he's somewhere with a goddamn needle shoved in his arm."

My thoughts drift to my sisters, Nora and Rowan, and I feel a pang of guilt as I raise my beer bottle to my lips. I don't envy Smith's position but I sure as hell understand it. And I know the hell he'll be in if he isn't able to save his brother.

"Take a load off, brother, and tomorrow we'll help you find him."

Smith nods as Kelly stops at our table and drops his beer off. She meets my eyes and I grin as my cock jumps in my jeans. Goddamn, I'm excited for tonight. It's been a while since I've gotten a beautiful woman underneath me and I'm hungry for it. She turns and walks away, her hips hypnotizing me with their gentle sway and I lick my lips.

"Man, I wouldn't," Moose warns and I blink, glancing in his direction.

"Huh?"

He tilts his head toward the bar, where Kelly is filling a glass with beer. "That one is trouble."

"Kelly?" I scoff, shaking my head.

"Yeah, Kelly. A girl like that is old lady material."

"Careful, Brother," Smith teases, a smile on his face for the first time tonight. "You dip your wick in that and next thing you know, you'll be down on one knee with a ring in your hand just like Storm and Chance."

I shudder. Our brothers, Storm and Chance, both fell hard and got married recently and as much as I like their wives, I'm not about to make that mistake...again. Fool me once and all that.

"Yeah, that's not going to fucking happen."

"Pretty sure that's exactly what Storm said before he met Ali."

"Or Chance before he met Carly," Moose adds.

I shrug. "I've got more willpower than either one of them and I've already almost made that mistake once before."

"I don't know," Moose murmurs with a shrug. "They seem happy."

"They seem whipped," I quip and Smith snorts.

I watch Kelly as she works behind the bar and a smile teases my lips. "I think you're wrong about Kelly."

"Dun, dun, dun-dun," Smith hums and images of my first wedding rush back to me as I kick him under the table.

"Jackass."

I glance to the other corner of the bar, catching the eye of a pretty little thing in a denim mini skirt and tank top. She holds my gaze for a few seconds before smiling and looking away. I grin, grabbing my beer and taking another drink as I keep my gaze on her. She meets my eyes again and her pale cheeks turn pink. I picture her on her knees in front of me, pink still staining her cheeks as she wraps her lips around my cock and shift in my chair. My jeans feel tight and I swallow down some more beer but I can't even taste it anymore. If Kelly's off the table, I definitely have another option.

"Also, a bad idea," Moose says, and I turn to him with a frown.

"Why the hell are you trying to ruin all my fun?"

"Don't do it, man," Moose warns, shaking his head. "That girl's got stage five clinger written all over her. She'll have a tracker embedded in your nuts before you even realize what's happening."

"Thanks for the visual, asshole."

He shrugs and my gaze is drawn back to the corner as I think about risking it anyway. Fuck, I'm so goddamn horny that I might just take on a stalker. No, scratch that. I swing back toward the bar and Kelly smiles, tempting me once again. Damn. You know what, I'm not going to catch feelings for the girl after one wild night. Never going to happen. Smiling, I push my chair back and stand up just as my phone starts ringing.

Fuck.

Pulling it out of my pocket, I check the screen and sigh. It's our club president, Blaze, and I can't send his call to voice mail.

"Yeah, boss, what's up?" I answer as Smith and Moose stare up at me.

"I need your help with something," he answers, slurring his words and my brows pull up. I can't remember the last time I saw Blaze drunk but he sounds blitzed right now. "Can you come to the clubhouse?"

I nod, glancing down at my watch. "Yeah, give me fifteen."

He hangs up without another word and I shake my head as I pull the phone away from my ear.

"Everything okay?" Smith asks and I nod.

"Yeah. Blaze just needs to talk to me. I'll see you boys later."

Moose smirks. "You better thank him for saving you from matrimonial bliss."

"Fuck off, asshole," I shoot back with a laugh as I back away from the table and flip them off. "Oh, and thanks for paying my tab."

"Son of a bitch," he hisses and I turn around, ducking out of the front door. Headlights illuminate the front of the bar as a car swings into the lot and I zip up my leather jacket to fight off the chill in the air. When I reach my bike, I swing my leg over and I smile as she rumbles to life beneath me. I've been all over this country and no place feels like home like the back of my bike.

My phone rings again and I glance at the screen, silencing it when I see that it's Rowan, my baby sister. I'll just have to call her back later. The streets are quiet as I make my way to the clubhouse and it provides me with an easy ride to clear my thoughts. As I get closer, I start to wonder what Blaze could need my help with and why the hell he's drowning in a bottle tonight.

I first joined the Bayou Devils MC four years ago, right after I rolled into town. At that point, I'd been on the road for two years and I was tired of the nomadic lifestyle. The pain that had once driven me from my home was dulled and I was ready to build a life again somewhere. Blaze and the club had just undergone a major restructuring, getting out of guns and drugs after he was shot, and he didn't have a whole lot of people in his corner but he was determined to make the club legitimate. When I heard of the work they were doing to help those in need, it struck a chord with me and I found a new home for myself.

The clubhouse parking lot is empty except for Blaze's bike when I pull in and I park next to him, worry gnawing at me. We had a lot of drama go down with Ali and Carly, Storm and Chance's girls, a while back but things have been quiet lately. Still, I can't shake this feeling like something big is on the horizon. It's like I'm constantly poised, ready for an attack from any angle and I wish I could figure out why.

When I walk into the clubhouse, my gaze is drawn to the bar where Blaze is posted on a stool, a glass filled with amber liquid in his hand. He downs the rest of it and sets it on the bar as he grabs the bottle of bourbon and pours himself some more.

"Thanks for coming," he slurs, not meeting my eyes. I scan the room, looking for anyone else but it's empty.

"Where's everyone at?"

He turns, his bloodshot eyes flicking around the room like he's just now realizing no one is here before he shrugs and falls off his stool, somehow staying upright. He grabs his glass off the bar. "Follow me. There's something I need to show you."

I do as instructed, following behind him as he stumbles into his office. He shuts the door and motions for me to sit down as he ambles over to the filing cabinet and grabs another bottle of bourbon out of the top drawer. He carries it, with his glass, over to the desk and sinks into the chair, hopelessness and pain contorting his face. This isn't the same man that I've come to know over the past four years and I'm even more worried about why he's called me here tonight.

"What's going on, Blaze?"

He finishes off the liquor in his glass before tossing a thick file across the desk and it lands in front of me with a thump. "I need you to do something for me."

I rip my gaze away from him as he pours more bourbon in his glass and glance down at the folder in front of me, flipping it open. A photo of a young woman with dark red hair, pale skin, and amber eyes that seem to shred right through me lays on top and I meet his gaze again.

"Who is she?"

He shakes his head. "You don't need to know that."

What the fuck?

We're a pretty tight club and we don't keep secrets from each other, something that he insisted on when he turned everything around.

"What do you mean I don't need to know?"

Blaze shakes his head, finishing off another glass and reaching for the bottle again. "Don't worry about that. I just need you to follow her."

"Follow her?" I ask, standing up and snatching the bottle out of his hand. "And how much of this have you had tonight?"

"Not enough," he snarls, reaching for the bottle but I manage to keep it out of his grasp.

"I think you've had plenty."

"No," he moans, propping his elbows on the desk and dropping his head into his hands. "Just let me forget."

"Jesus Christ, Blaze. Forget what?"

He grabs his glass and throws it across the room. I flinch as it hits the wall and shatters.

"Just do what I asked you to do!"

I stare down at the photo again, running through reasons why Blaze might need me to follow this woman. I flip through some more pictures of her, looking for any clue as to why he would ask me to do this. "Why?"

"Just do it, Kodiak. Follow her and report back to me every day. I want to know what she's doing and who she's seeing. Everything. Every little detail."

I drop the photos and back away from the desk, shaking my head. The club has been dedicated to protecting people for the last five years and this doesn't feel right.

"I need to know why I'm doing this."

Blaze lets out a sardonic laugh. "No, you don't. I'm your president and I've given you an order."

I tense and meet his hard stare. "You know I respect the hell out of you, Blaze, but if you think I'm going to stalk some poor innocent woman without knowing why, you're out of your goddamn mind."

"Just do it!" he roars and I cross my arms over my chest, waiting for him to keep talking. Finally, he sighs. "You're not stalking her and I need you to trust that I have a damn good reason if I'm asking you to do this."

After studying him for a moment, I nod. He's right. I know what kind of man Blaze is so I don't really believe that he means this woman any harm but it's still weird for him to be so evasive.

"Are you in trouble, Blaze? Is she?"

"No more questions, Kodiak. I need your help. Will you do this for me?"

I glance down at the photos on the desk and sigh. "What am I looking for exactly?"

"Don't worry about that yet. Just record everything."

Without another word, he grabs the bottle of liquor out of my hand and storms out of the office. I stare down at the photo and wonder what the hell I'm getting myself into.

*   *   *   *

*Tatum Elizabeth Carter
Born on September 9, 1992 in Denver, Colorado,
to Sarah Rose Carter.*

*Moved to Baton Rouge in 1998 when Tatum and
her twin brother, Theodore, were six years old.
    She works as a waitress in a diner and a gas
station attendant on the rough side of town.
    He's a first class petty officer in the U.S. Navy
Their mother, Sarah, was killed in a car accident
            five days ago.*

I read through the information a few more times,
looking for any clue as to why Blaze asked me to do this
but I'm still in the same spot I was three days ago when
he first plopped this folder down in front of me. There
are no answers here but I can't stop reading, can't stop
searching. My phone starts beeping and I glance over at
it, straightening in my seat when I see the alert from the
tracker I put on Theodore's car a few days ago.

They pull into the parking lot and I slip my
sunglasses on despite the clouds blanketing the sky in an
attempt to remain unnoticed. I'm glad I thought to
borrow Smith's truck. Had I shown up in my matte black
Camaro there's no way I could remain anonymous. They
slip into a spot six spaces down from me and I grab my
phone, pretending to look at it as they climb out and Tate
grabs a plain looking urn from the back seat. Theo offers
his arm and she takes it as they start off down the path to
the beach.

Memories from my own father's funeral surface
and tears burn my eyes. Back then, I believed everyone
when they told me that time heals all wounds and that
things would get easier. In some ways, I suppose they
were right but grief is tricky. Something will remind me

of my dad and out of the blue, I'm overcome with pain like I'm that kid again, saying good-bye to my old man over a radio. Or I'll wake up one morning and I won't be able to think of anything else. That feeling will hang over me like a dark cloud all day long, assaulting me with pain.

There's so much in my life that my father missed out on and so much that I still needed him for but he was stolen from us. Watching Tate and Theo as they stop by the water, I know the anguish they're feeling for the loss of their mother. I understand the ache overwhelming them and it makes me feel connected to them in a way that only someone who's lost a parent can be. Especially her. I'm not sure what it is exactly – maybe the steely set of her amber gaze that tells the world she can handle herself or the broken look she's been wearing lately that reveals the soft side I suspect she keeps hidden most of the time but she is different than any other girl I've ever seen.

Rolling down the truck window, I shiver as cold air rushes into the cab and glance down at the parabolic microphone Blaze insisted I bring with me because when he said he wanted to know everything, he literally meant everything. It's also why I had to sneak cameras into their mother's house. I wonder how many Hail Marys I'd need to say to not feel like a creepy stalker when this is all over. Not that I even have a clue when it will end.

Up ahead, Tate and Theo turn to face each other as he unscrews the urn's lid. Even from two hundred yards away, I can still see her take a breath before she reaches in and pulls out a handful of ashes, sprinkling them in the water. A single tear slips down her cheek and I empathize with her even more. It doesn't matter what age it happens, losing a parent is always hard. A loss like that shakes your whole damn foundation and it takes time to find your footing again. Her brother is stoic and I wonder if he's trying to be strong for her or he's still too overwhelmed with shock to feel anything else. For me, it took weeks before the full magnitude of the loss of my father hit me.

I reach across the truck and grab the folder out of the passenger seat, flipping it open to read everything Blaze has about Tate's brother. I've been engrossed in this file for days, so fucking curious about all the damn holes in the story. Of course I can't get anything else out of Blaze and it's not the first time that I've wondered if this is really on the up and up. If this is really okay, why won't he tell me anything else and why am I not allowed to tell any of my brothers?

It makes no goddamn sense.

Glancing up, I watch them as they step toward the waves and sprinkle more of Sarah's ashes in the ocean before Tate discreetly wipes away another tear. I haven't even officially met this girl yet and she already has me reeling. I don't know if it's because she reminds me so much of my past but even standing on that beach at her mother's funeral, she has my full attention. She's sad, broken, and yet, still so fierce and strong. Beautiful but guarded.

In the past three days, I've spent most of my time parked outside of her house watching her on the video feed Streak, the club's resident tech expert, was able to hack into for me. I was surprised when I broke into her house and noticed the discreet cameras hiding throughout each room but add that to my growing list of questions. Besides, I'm secretly glad for them since they give me a whole new insight into this girl. Somehow, she's worming her way under my skin and I don't like it. Tossing the folder back to the passenger seat, I grab the microphone again and slip the headphones on before holding it out of the open window.

"When did Mom bring us down here for that vacation?" Tate asks, staring out at the ocean as the wind blows her hair all around her face.

"I don't know. It was shortly after we moved here."

She nods, pulling her sweater tighter and I barely resist the urge to climb out of the car and offer her my damn jacket. Jesus, what the fuck is wrong with me?

"Do you think we'll ever get any answers?" she asks and there's vulnerability in her voice but if Theo notices, he doesn't let on.

"No. I think Mom had more secrets than we can ever imagine."

Tate wipes away another tear and I want to wrap my arms around her and tell her that it will get easier. "It feels like I didn't even know her."

"I don't think we really did, T," he replies, wrapping an arm around her shoulders and pulling her closer.

"You have to promise that you'll never keep secrets from me, Theo."

He turns to her and wraps her up in a hug. "I promise. Besides, you'd know if I tried."

"Yeah, that's true," she agrees with a smile as she pulls away. "You ready to get out of here?"

He nods and they turn, disappearing behind one of the dunes as I pull the headphones off and toss the microphone in the passenger seat with a sigh. Pulling her photo from the folder, I let out an annoyed growl because despite the fact that I've never even met this girl, I'm eager to see her again.

Every Breath You Take

A.M. Myers

Chapter Three
Tatum

Standing at the entrance of the living room, I look around the space with a cup of coffee in my hand, memories flooding my mind. Mom's house is a classic southern cottage and one of the basic criteria of the design is its homey feel but Mom took it a step further. The light teal blue walls are welcoming but not overbearing or too bright and she managed to find white couches that don't feel sterile or untouchable. She coupled that with the wicker chairs that give it a coastal flair and two teal ottomans that are more like beanbags. Large windows allow the sunlight to flood the room and you can't take a step without the old hardwood floors creaking but, for me, that's always added to the charm of the place.

If I close my eyes, I can almost hear Mom moving around the kitchen, making dinner for Theo and me as a cool summer breeze blows through the house. Everything is exactly as she left it six days ago and it makes it so much harder to cope with the fact that she's gone. But she is. Her ashes are currently floating around in the Gulf of Mexico right now, seeing the rest of the world like she always wanted to.

Theo comes bounding down the stairs behind me and I quickly wipe a stray tear away and sniffle as I raise my coffee mug to my lips. He steps into the living room from the archway in the kitchen and I glance in his direction as he sips his own coffee.

"What are we going to do with this place?"

He peeks over at me before glancing around the room and shrugging. "I don't know. I suppose you could move in here."

Theo and I were born in Denver but as soon as we were released from the hospital, Mama loaded us up and hit the road. We always stayed in cheap, roadside hotels and we never stayed longer than three months before she would pack us up again and move to some other part of the country. First it was Arizona, then Iowa, North Carolina, North Dakota, Maine, Texas... We'd visited almost every state in the country before we landed in Baton Rouge when Theo and I were six. I have no idea what changed for her here but she decided to finally put down some roots and this place has been my home ever since. There isn't a single part of me that wants to lose it but I know I can't afford to keep it.

"And take over her mortgage payment?" I ask, shaking my head as tears build in my eyes. "I can't afford that, Theo."

Compassion fills his eyes. "I'll help you. I can send you money every month."

"I can't ask you to do that."

Setting his coffee down on the table, he walks over to me and wraps me up in a hug. "You didn't ask, I offered and I don't want to lose this place either. This is our house, the only one we've ever had."

Biting my bottom lip, I look up at him and mull it over. "Be honest with me. Can you really afford to send me money for the house?"

The moment of hesitation is all I need to see to know that as much as he wants to help, he's not in a much better position than I am.

"We have to sell it," I say before he can answer me and he shakes his head.

"Don't be stubborn," he growls. "This is our home."

"We can't afford it."

"I'll find a way, T. You need a better, safer place to live and Mom wouldn't want us to lose the house."

"Mom wouldn't want us to kill ourselves to keep it, either."

As he sighs again, I know that he's on the same page as me. Neither one of us *wants* to lose it but there's only so much we can do. Some things are just out of our control.

"If we're going to sell it, we need to start sorting through her things," Theo points out and I nod, gazing around the room.

"Where do we even start?"

He peeks over my shoulder to the storage closet in the hall. "There, I suppose."

I let out a groan. The last time I peeked in that particular closet, I was almost buried under a mountain of boxes.

"Oh, goody."

"Come on." He laughs, slinging his arm over my shoulder. "Let's finish our coffee and then we can get to work."

We sit across from each other at the kitchen table and start sharing memories of Mom as we finish off our coffee.

"Do you remember that hotel in Kansas City?" Theo asks and I start laughing.

"With the guy that would shout movie lines all night long? I thought Mom was gonna tear him a new one."

"For the love of God, it's three in the morning," Theo says, imitating Mom's voice and I start laughing but they quickly turn to tears as I realize I'll never hear that voice again.

"I miss her so much," I whisper and he nods.

"I wish I'd come home more these past few years." His voice breaks and a tear falls down his cheek. "The last time I saw her was almost a year ago."

Reaching across the table, I grab his hand. "You're all I have left now, Theo. We have to promise to not let so much time pass."

He nods. "I promise."

We finish our coffee as he tells me about what's going on in Charleston and after we rinse our mugs out in the sink, we walk over to the closet and stop in front of the closed door.

"If we don't make it through this, just know that I love you," I quip and glance over at Theo as he rolls his eyes.

"You're so goddamn dramatic."

I scoff, vividly remembering one time when we were younger when Theo was convinced a simple cold was going to kill him as I step forward and grip the door handle. "Whatever you say, kettle."

"Are you calling me dramatic?" he asks but I ignore him, opening the door and wincing. When nothing happens, I peek open my eyes and sigh. I half expected everything to just come pouring out of it like in cartoons. "Yes, clearly, I'm the dramatic one."

"Shut up," I say with a laugh, shoving him backward and he grabs onto my arm, almost sending us both crashing to the floor.

"Be serious. We have work to do," he scolds, his face serious but playfulness still in his tone. Smiling, I turn back to the closet and the pain of the last few days crashes down on me again. It's weird the way you can forget sometimes. Even though it just happened, there are still moments when I smile or something makes me laugh before I remember that my mother is gone and the guilt descends on me for daring to enjoy even a single moment of my life right now.

Sighing, I nod. "All right, let's do this."

We start gently pulling boxes out of the closet and setting them in various places around the room. When we run out of room to move around, we each go to a separate box and start digging through them.

"Do you remember these?" I ask, holding up the child-sized boxing gloves from when Mom made us start training.

"Shit, yeah. You hated it and Mom would drag us to class everyday."

I turn the gloves over in my hand, remembering the horrific fights Mom and I would have whenever it was time to go to class or practice.

"Oh, God, and then she bought that bag, set it up in the garage, and made me practice for hours a day."

Theo laughs. "Yeah, but look how good of a boxer you are now."

"I still hate it," I pout. Out of all the things our mother made us train in, boxing will always be my least favorite.

"You'll thank her when you get in a fight."

Arching a brow, I meet his gaze. "When am I ever going to get in a fight, Theo? When am I going to need to be able to reload a gun in two seconds or less? And yeah, sure, I can hit a target at fifteen hundred yards but who cares? I know all this useless stuff that I'm never going to need because I'm not a goddamn super spy or assassin."

"Come on, T. Some of that stuff she taught us is useful."

Sighing, I sink onto the ottoman and nod. "Yeah, it's useful and I guess, if it ever comes down to it, I'll be glad to have those skills but can you really say we had a childhood? As soon as we stopped bouncing from place to place every couple months, she started in with all this training. And for what? We may never know why she felt the need to teach us these things."

"I know," he says with a nod. "I'm not defending her choices but they aren't useless either. We both know how to defend ourselves better than most people should the need ever arise."

I press my fingers into my forehead. "I just want answers, Theo. I want to know what all of this was for and I want to know what happened to her. There's this nagging feeling, deep down in my gut, that her death wasn't just some random accident but as soon as I go down that rabbit hole, I start thinking that I'm losing my mind. Accidents happen all the time but she seemed invincible and it feels like I'm never going to get any peace."

"It hasn't even been a week, sis. Just give it time." He walks over and sits next to me on the ottoman, wrapping his arm around me as I lay my head on his shoulder.

"I think I'm losing my mind."

He laughs, giving me a squeeze. "Naw, T. You're just grieving."

"How are you holding it together so well?" I ask, lifting my head off his shoulder to study him.

"Honestly, I have no idea. I'm probably just going to break one day out of the blue and shock the shit out of everyone, including myself."

I want to tell him that's not healthy but who am I to talk? I'm over here dreaming up conspiracy theories.

"We better get back to it," I say, sighing. "I only have you for another day and a half."

The thought of Theo leaving so soon is upsetting and I suck in a breath as I stand up and walk over to another box.

"I'm sorry that I have to leave so soon."

I shrug. "I get it. I'm just going to miss you."

"I know. I miss you, too, and I missed so much time with Mom by being away. When my contract is up in a couple years, I don't think I'm going to reenlist."

"You know what you want to do once you're a free man again?"

He laughs, shaking his head as he stands up. "Nope. It'll be a fun adventure."

I giggle as I pull a taped up shoebox out one of the bigger boxes. Frowning, I inspect it before glancing up at Theo.

"Let me see your knife."

He flips the knife in his hand and holds the handle out to me. Taking it from him, I cut through the tape and sit down on the couch with the box in my lap.

"What is it?" Theo asks and I shake my head.

"I'm not sure yet." Carefully, I open the lid and scowl at the photo of a little boy sitting on top. Underneath that is a stack of handwritten letters that almost completely fill up the box. Grabbing the one on top, I unfold it and start to read before turning to Theo.

"I think these are love letters to Mom."

His eyes widen and he joins me on the couch. "What?"

He grabs another letter and unfolds it as I read through the one in my hand.

"Listen to this," I say, reading from the paper. "I understand your reason for leaving, baby, but it doesn't make this any easier. You leaving punched a hole right through the center of my heart and I know that I won't feel whole again until you're back in my arms."

"I have to believe that this is just part of our story, sweetheart," Theo says, reading from his letter. "Because if I think about this being the end, if I consider that you were never meant to be mine, I don't know how I'll go on."

"It's signed "Love, M"," I point out and he glances at the bottom of his letter.

"This one, too."

Reaching back into the box, I grab the photo of the boy and his bright blue eyes punch me in the gut. "Who do you think he is?"

"I have no idea," Theo replies, glancing down at the photo.

Reaching into the box, I pull out the letter on the very bottom and gasp as I read the date at the top. "Theo, these letters go all the way back to right around the time we were born."

He grabs the first letter I was reading. "The top letter is dated July 1998. That's right before we moved here."

Our eyes meet and I can hear all the questions running through his mind as they mix with mine. I can't help but feel like this is just one more thing that our mother took to her grave.

Every Breath You Take

*   *   *   *

Right before Mom moved Theo and me to Baton
Rouge, we were staying at this small motel right off the
interstate in Omaha, Nebraska. As six year olds, Theo
and I hated being cooped up in that room but Mom didn't
like for us to go outside, not with the kind of places we
were staying in but a couple days before we left, she took
us to the zoo. I can still remember it like it was
yesterday. We spent the whole day there – from the time
they opened until they ushered us out of the gates.
Looking back, it was one of the few times I saw Mom
looking carefree and I wish she were sitting across this
dining room table from me so I could ask her all of the
questions that have been swarming around in my head
for the past week.
A week.
Seven days.
It's such a short amount of time and somehow, it
still feels like forever when all I want to do is talk to my
mom. I sat in this exact chair three days before the
accident, telling her about how work was going at the
diner and talking about my plans to go to school
someday while she nagged me about moving back home
so she wouldn't have to worry about me so much. I wish
I had taken her up on that offer. Maybe things would be
different now if I had.

Theo stomps down the stairs and I quickly wipe away my tears before grabbing my coffee mug and raising it to my lips.

"Please tell me I'm not dreaming the smell of that coffee."

I laugh. "You're not. Did you sleep okay last night?"

He ambles over to the cupboard and grabs a mug. "Not really. I couldn't stop thinking about that damn shoebox we found."

"I know," I answer with a sigh. "I couldn't either."

We spent the rest of the evening reading through some of the letters in the box and trying to figure out who this mystery person in our mother's life was. Honestly, I think we're both more confused now than we were before we found that box. Did we even know our mother at all?

"Do you think this "M" guy is our dad?"

Theo sighs as he leans back against the counter and raises his cup to his lips. After he takes a sip, he runs his hand over his short hair.

"Anything is possible, T. But who says "M" is a man?"

My mouth pops open and I stare at him. "You think Mom was gay?"

He shrugs again. "Why not?"

"But she had us," I point out.

"Like I said, anything is possible."

Before I can say anything else, the doorbell rings and I glance over my shoulder, seeing a figure through the small windows at the top of the door.

"You expecting someone?" Theo asks and I shake my head.

"No, are you?"

My brother changes before my eyes, straightening his shoulders and setting his cup of coffee down on the counter. It's a look I know all too well – the same one I get anytime someone shows up at my apartment unannounced. Theo reaches into the hidden compartment next to the sink and pulls out Mom's 1911. He puts his finger to his lips, instructing me to be quiet before he starts creeping toward the door. Rolling my eyes, I circle around the other side of the kitchen and step into the living room as he opens the door.

"Can I help you?" he asks, his voice gruff and to the point.

"Yes, sir. I'm looking for Mr. Theodore Carter and Miss Tatum Carter."

Theo glances over at me with a raised brow before turning back to the man at the door. "And you are?"

"I'm Aaron Wiley, your mother's attorney." Mr. Wiley holds his hand out but Theo ignores it as he turns to me with wide eyes and sets the pistol down on the table next to the door. When he doesn't move or even look at Mr. Wiley again, I step forward, examining the tall, wiry man.

"You'll have to forgive us, Mr. Wiley. This week has been a bit of a whirlwind and we weren't aware that our mother had a lawyer."

He holds up a finger, nodding his head. "Ah, yes. Your mother did say that would be the case. Mind if I come in so we can talk?"

"Sure."

As Mr. Wiley steps inside, Theo regains some of his composure and grabs the gun off of the table, tucking it into his waist. He meets my gaze and I roll my eyes but his only response is a stern look meant to shut me up. Not that it's ever worked.

"Can I get you a cup of coffee, Mr. Wiley?" I ask as he sets his black leather briefcase on the dining room table. He nods.

"That would be nice. Thank you."

As I retreat into the kitchen, I can feel Theo behind me and I glance over my shoulder, meeting his intense stare.

"Before you ask, I don't have a clue what he's here about," I whisper.

He nods. "I know but why did Mom have a lawyer?"

"Just add it to the list of questions that have been building since her death."

"This is fucking insanity," he says under his breath as he grabs our coffee and heads back into the dining room. I pour coffee into a mug for Mr. Wiley and arrange sugar and cream on a tray before carrying both back into the dining room. After setting the tray down on the table, I sit next to Theo and sip my coffee as Mr. Wiley arranges papers in front of him.

"First off, let me just say that I'm so sorry for your loss."

"Thank you," Theo and I murmur at the same time.

"I don't mean to be rude, Mr. Wiley," Theo says, a frown etched onto his face. "But why are you here?"

"Your mother hired me to handle her estate."

"Estate?" My voice is filled with shock as I turn to look at Theo, who is as surprised as I am.

"May I?" he asks, holding up a sheet of paper and I nod. He flips it around and lays it down in front of us. The first thing I notice are the words "Last Will and Testament" printed boldly at the top of the page and then I see my mother's signature at the bottom.

"As soon as I learned of your mother's death, I started working on this because she stipulated that before either of you received any money, the house needed to be paid off."

"The house is paid off?" Theo asks, grabbing my hand under the table and I feel hope welling up in my chest.

"As of yesterday afternoon, it is. As soon as you sign everything today, I'll hand you the deed."

I clamp my free hand over my mouth, fighting back tears. Yesterday we were so sure that we'd lose the only home we've ever known and now, it's ours for as long as we want it.

"I'm sorry but did you say something about money?" Theo asks, glancing up from our mother's will. Mr. Wiley nods.

"Yes. As per her will, the two of you will equally split the rest of her estate which amounts to just shy of one million dollars."

A gasp fills the room and it takes me a moment to realize it slipped out of my own mouth. Theo stares at the dining room table, eyes wide and blank as I turn to Mr. Wiley, uncertain that I heard him correctly.

"I'm going to need you to say that again."

Mr. Wiley smiles. "In my briefcase, I have a check for each of you in the amount of four hundred ninety nine thousand, two hundred sixty two dollars and fifty cents."

"Oh my god," I breathe out as Theo squeezes my hand again and I glance over at him. His gaze is filled with questions.

Where did she get all that money?

Why didn't she ever tell us?

Who was this woman?

I shake my head, my answer the same for each one and he blows out a breath, dropping his head into his free hand.

"I apologize, Mr. Wiley. We're just…"

"…fucking shocked," Theo finishes for me and I can't stop the giggle that bubbles out of me. Mr. Wiley chuckles, nodding his head.

"I understand. If you'll point me in the direction of the restroom, I'll give you two a minute to talk."

"Through there, first door on your right," I answer, pointing to the hallway and he nods, pushing out of his chair. When he disappears around the corner, Theo turns to me.

"Where the fuck did she get that kind of money?" he hisses and I shake my head before shrugging. Truth is, I've got no idea where our mother, who worked as a receptionist for the last twenty years, made that kind of money.

"Maybe she robbed a bank."

Theo grins. "Maybe she was an assassin for hire."

"Hey, that's a good one and I could totally see that."

He turns to look at the will in front of us. "Are we accepting blood money?"

"It's like fifty-fifty."

"I know I shouldn't be happy about this but the house is yours now and I don't have to worry about something happening to you. It was killing me to think about leaving tomorrow and you going back to your apartment."

"The house is ours."

He shakes his head. "No. You should have the house, T. And you can finally go to school like you've always wanted."

"Yeah," I whisper, a smile teasing my lips. My life has been flipped completely on its head in the last week and as much as I would do anything to have my mom back here with me, I'm also so incredibly grateful for everything she's just done for us.

Chapter Four
Tatum

"I wish you weren't leaving," I admit as Theo drives me to work on his way out of town. He was originally supposed to leave this morning but after the shock we got yesterday, neither one of us were quite ready to say good-bye yet. Plus, we had a few new errands to run with those huge checks Mr. Wiley dropped off. Glancing over at me with a frown that matches my own, he nods.

"Believe me, I'm not looking forward to it either."

Since the moment Theo and I were born, we've truly never been alone but it sure feels like as soon as he rolls out of town, I have no one left to turn to. I lived across town from Mom but she was always here if I needed her. She was a constant in my life and never once had I imagined having to live without her. Her death and her absence in my life is a gaping hole. I can feel it with each breath I take in and push out, and I don't think it will ever be filled. It's just part of who I am now and I have to learn to live around it.

"Do you have leave saved up?" I ask, hoping he'll be able to get back home soon. He's at a shore command right now, which means no deployments so in theory, he should be able to get time off to visit.

He glances over at me and nods. "Yeah, somewhere around forty five days, I think. Why?"

"Come back soon, please." I hate how broken my voice sounds but the thought of not having Theo here anymore has tears building in my eyes and a lump lodged in my throat. I've lost my mother and I need my brother.

"You know I will, T. Everything has changed now and what's important to me is different. We have to look out for each other."

"Slacker," I tease, giving him a nudge and doing my best to crack a smile even though I feel like everything is falling down around me. "I've been doing that for years."

"I'm serious, Tate. I don't like you being alone."

I shrug, trying to play off the loneliness that's already weighing down on me. "What about you? You're going to be all alone in Charleston."

"I'll be all right," he shoots back as he rolls his eyes and I cross my arms over my chest.

"And why wouldn't I be okay? Because I'm a girl? I had the same training you did, jerk."

He laughs, holding his hands up in surrender for a second before returning them to the wheel. "You're right. I just meant that I wish I could stay."

"I know," I mutter. I didn't mean to snap at him. He pulls into the diner's parking lot and I sigh at the sight of the afternoon crowd filling the tables as he finds a spot in the back. Once the car is parked, he turns toward me and tears well up in my eyes.

"You have to be better at texting me back," I tell him and he nods.

"I will, T. And if I don't, just scream at me in your head and I'll hear you."

I laugh, sniffling as I wipe away a tear. "I wish it really worked like that."

"Sometimes I swear it does. Right before you called to tell me Mom was dead, I woke up in the middle of the night and I felt like I had to call you. Then, the phone rang."

"Yeah, and then there are other times like when we went out on a double date in high school and you brought your friend, Daryl. I was sending you 'get me out of here' vibes all night and you didn't even realize."

He starts laughing. "Actually, I did. I just wanted to see how long it would take before you hit him."

"And were you disappointed when it took two hours?"

"No," he answers, shaking his head. "It was thoroughly entertaining the whole time."

"Ass," I mutter, turning away from him to hide my smile.

"Hey, on a serious note though, there's something I want to give you."

I turn back to him and he holds out an envelope full of something. Taking it from him, I open it and gasp.

"Theo, what is this?"

"It's half of the money Mom gave me."

I thrust the envelope back toward him. "I can't take this."

He wraps his large hands around mine, stopping me from dropping the cash in his lap. "Please, sis. I need you to take it."

"It's your money, Theo. I can't."

"I have a great job, Tate, and I make more than enough money. Let me do this for you, please. There are going to be expenses for the house and I want you to finally be able to go to school. Not to mention, you could also use a car of your own."

"All of which I could do with the money Mom left me."

He meets my eyes and from just one look, I know he's not going to drop this. No doubt we could fight about it all day if we wanted to but I only have a few more minutes with him and I don't want to waste them. Sighing, I take the envelope and stuff it into my purse. I'll take it for now and maybe once he gets out of the Navy I can give it back to him.

"This is not over, Carter," I warn him and he laughs.

"Go buy a car so I don't have to worry about you walking home at night."

"I'll think about it." Glancing at the clock, I sigh. "I've got to get in there."

He nods and we both climb out of the car, meeting at the front of the hood as he wraps me up in a hug.

"Text me as soon as you get back to Charleston," I instruct him and he nods.

"I will, I promise."

"And come back home as soon as you can."

He pulls away, nodding. "You got it, T."

"Okay," I whisper, tears burning my eyes again as I bite my lip.

"Bye."

"I love you. Don't forget to text me."

He nods. "Love you, too."

Crossing my arms over my stomach, I watch him as he rounds the car and slips behind the wheel before backing up. As he puts the car in drive, he holds his hand up in a wave and I repeat the motion, feeling choked up again. He pulls out of the parking lot and I wipe away a tear, missing him immensely already. This is going to be so much harder than I thought. The idea that I have no one here is so devastating that I know I have to force it to the back of my mind for now. I have an eight-hour shift to work and I can't be crying in the customer's coffee. There are still a few minutes before my shift starts so I lean back against the building and will myself to calm down before squaring my shoulders and turning toward the door.

As soon as I walk in, it's like I never left and I hear someone squeal my name before my friend, Mia, is bolting out from behind the counter and barreling toward me. She crashes into me and I laugh as I wrap my arms around her.

"Hey, Mia."

"Oh my god, I'm so happy you're back. I missed you so much. How are you doing?"

I release her and hold my hands up. "Whoa, girl. Take a breath."

"Sorry," she breathes. "I'm just so excited."

"I gathered."

She puts her hand on my arm as her eyes soften and her head tilts. Theo and I have dubbed it the sympathy tilt and it's something we've seen way too much in the past few days.

"How are you?"

I force a smile to my face, trying to keep my mind focused on work and getting through the next eight hours. "I'm good, Mi. How are things here?"

"Oh, you know. Same old, same old." She rolls her eyes and I laugh. Working as a waitress at Sunrise Diner is only one of two jobs I currently have and the one I prefer since my boss at the gas station a couple blocks over is a total jackass.

"It can't be that bad."

She wraps her arms around my waist as we walk toward the door and go into the hallway that leads to our manager's office, the kitchen, and the walk-in freezer. "You know how it is."

I grab my timecard and meet her gaze over my shoulder, arching a brow.

"People have been especially fussy lately. One lady even tried to order sparkling water yesterday."

I snort as I hang my purse on the hook and double check that it's zipped up before slipping my card in the machine.

"She did read the menu, right? Most of our entrees cost less than ten dollars."

"That's what I said and then she complained to Roger."

Glancing past her, I see one of our managers pouring over paperwork in the little office. At the mention of his name, he glances up and I wave.

"Glad to have you back, Tate," he calls and I let out a laugh.

"Let's see if you're still saying that in an hour."

"Did I hear a feisty little redhead out here?" a voice booms from the kitchen and I roll my eyes as Mia laughs.

"See, everyone missed you."

"No," I call back, shaking my head. "You heard a woman who's gonna kick your ass if you call me little and feisty ever again."

Shaun pokes his head out from the kitchen and flashes me a wide grin. "Feisty as ever I see."

"Don't make me get my pepper spray," I warn him, a smile teasing my lips and he backs up into the kitchen, his hands up.

"Careful, boys! She's filled with hellfire, today."

Mia laughs and Roger shakes his head as I pull the level down on the machine before slipping my card back in its holder.

"And don't you forget it!" I yell back before turning to Mia. "Who's on tonight?"

"Just you and me, bestie." She slips her arm through mine and I smile.

"Perfect. It shouldn't be too bad. It is only Monday, after all."

Mia jerks away from me, covering her ears with her hands and singing to herself.

"Don't you dare jinx us, lady."

She slips through the door and I giggle as I grab my apron off the rack, slipping it around my waist and tying it neatly in the back. Once I have my ticket book and a couple pens, I meet Mia behind the counter.

"You've got this half," Mia says, motioning to one side of the diner. "And someone just sat down at table thirteen."

"Okay." I grab a menu and a roll of silverware off the counter and as I turn toward the dining room, Mia puts her hand on my arm.

"Also, if you need anything tonight, just let me know. I've got your back, girl."

I smile as she releases my arm. "Thanks, Mia."

"Don't mention it," she calls over her shoulder, balancing a tray of drinks out in front of her.

Mia started working here at the diner shortly before I did three years ago and thankfully, she wasn't put off by my standoffish behavior or resting bitch face. I've never been good at making friends since we moved around so much when I was younger but she just took control and essentially made me be her friend. When she introduced me to her two best friends from middle school, they essentially adopted me into the group. We're not super close but I'm glad that if I don't have Theo here with me, I still have them to lean on – even if they don't understand what I'm going through right now.

Shaking my head, I suck in a breath and brush away any lingering sad thoughts and slip into work mode easily enough. Thank God, too, because if I fall apart tonight, I don't know how I'll ever put myself back together. With the menu and silverware in hand, I walk over to table thirteen and flash a wide smile as I lay the menu and silverware in front of the man sitting there.

"Good afternoon, Darlin'. My name is Tate and I'll be your server this evening. Can I get you started with something to drink?" I ask in my "customer service" voice, which is sweet as sugar and annoying as hell. It helps me get better tips though and I'm not in a position to give those up. My mind drifts to the check I got yesterday and the envelope of cash in my bag. I guess that's not really true anymore.

The man in front of me glances up and I have to physically stop myself from gasping and taking a step back. He's so damn handsome in this rugged sort of way that makes me think of log cabins and sex by fire light and his whiskey eyes inspect me from head to toe before his brow furrows.

"Coffee. Black," he snaps before dismissing me with a vague hand gesture and any attraction I felt toward the arrogant bastard dies a quick death. He turns back to the menu without another word and my fingers twitch to rip it out of his hand and teach him a thing or two about common decency.

Prick.

When he glances up again, I expect him to offer me a smile or some sort of apology for his incredible douchiness but he simply arches a brow as if to ask why

I'm still standing here, breathing his air. Oh, this guy's a real piece of fucking work.

"You want anything to eat?" I ask, keeping my voice perfectly sweet because I'm afraid if I break, I'll just end up clocking him. And that would be bad for both of us. Even though I know about ten different ways I could kill this guy before he even realized what was happening, I've never once had a problem with self-control. I've always been able to keep a handle on my emotions... until now. Although, with the week I've had, I suppose that makes sense.

"I'll let you know," he mutters before turning back to the menu and I feel a growl building in the back of my throat. With a curt nod, I spin on my toes and walk away from his table, my hands balled into fists. One thing I have never tolerated well is a rude customer and this guy just took the fucking cake for worst patron of all time. Mia is leaning against the counter and when I storm past her to the coffee machine, she follows me, squealing.

"Oh my god," she whisper screams, fanning herself. "That man is hotter than the inside of a car on a summer day and he could not keep his eyes off of you as you walked away from him. He was like glued to your ass."

She smacks my butt and I laugh despite my irritation.

"Actually, he was pretty rude to me."

Her expression falls but only for a second before a slow smile stretches across her face and she claps her hands. "Uh-oh."

Roger pokes his head out of the door to the hallway. "Did I just hear someone say "uh-oh"?" he asks and I shake my head.

"Nope."

"Damn it, Tate. It's your first day back. You can't be mean to customers."

"It's about to go down," Shaun says in a deep voice through the pass through and I grin at him before turning back to Roger and laying my hand over my heart.

"Roger, I'm as nice to the customers as they are to me. It's called human decency."

"It was so nice when I had a whole week without any complaints that my waitress was a bitch."

I shrug, grabbing a mug and filling it with coffee before holding it out to him. "I suppose you could take his coffee to him."

He shakes his head and shoos me away. "Keep it in check."

Mia claps and posts up at the counter so she can watch it all go down as the guys in the kitchen gather around the pass through.

"Y'all are something else. I'm simply going to take his order."

"Hell. Fire," Shaun whispers and I laugh as he winks at me.

"You egg me on and yet you never get in trouble, Shaun."

He nods. "Uh, yeah, cause it's entertaining as hell and I don't get in trouble because I'm back here. Now, go be sweet to the customer, Tate."

Curling my lip, I turn back to table thirteen and meet golden eyes. A ghost of a smile teases his lips and I square my shoulders before pasting a smile on my own face. As I walk back into the dining room, I feel Mia following behind me and my smile quickly becomes real. There was no way she was staying at the counter. With my head held high and a black coffee in my hand, I walk back over to his table and notice him watching me out of the corner of his eye as he scans the menu. It's subtle enough that if I were anyone else, I'm not sure I would have noticed.

"Coffee, black," I snap as I set the mug down in front of him a little too forcefully. Thankfully, it doesn't spill on him. "What do you want to eat?"

He chuckles, leaning back in the booth and spreading his arms out over the entire back of the seat. Jesus, he's huge.

"I knew you were being fake," he says, his voice smug and I blink, my anger returning full force. One thing I'm not is fake.

"Excuse me?"

"Before, that sweet voice you used on me was fake."

"I think the word you're looking for," I spit, crossing my arms over my chest. "Is polite."

He laughs, flashing me a brilliant smile and my insides turn to mush. Oh, hell, what is happening to me right now?

"I meant what I said. It was fake."

Mia laughs quietly behind me and I suck in a breath, trying to calm myself before I go off on this poor unsuspecting man. He really has no idea who he's dealing with. Planting my hands on his table, I lean forward, locking eyes with him.

"Maybe it was but it's because I have to deal with douchebags like you all day long and I have bills to pay. Now, what the fuck do you want to eat?"

"Tate!" Roger yells through the dining room and I flinch as everyone turns to look at me and silence descends. I force a smile to my face, pushing off the table.

"Excuse me."

Everyone's eyes are on me as I walk into the back and trudge to Roger's office. I know that I went too far but there's just something about the man at table thirteen that riles me up in the worst way.

"What were you thinking?" Roger asks, sighing as he walks into the office behind me and I sink into a chair. "I know you're having a tough time lately but you cannot talk to customers like that."

"I know, Roger, but did you see what a prick he was being to me?"

"It doesn't matter. You will go out there and apologize to him."

Do I really need this damn job?

The thought crosses my mind for only a moment before I realize that without something to do everyday, I would lose my ever-lovin' mind and for the most part, I do enjoy this job.

"Fine," I snap, shoving myself out of the chair. I will go out there and apologize but I'm done waiting on him. Walking back to the hallway, I press my shoulders against the tile and take a few deep breaths, trying to calm down before walking through the door. As soon as I'm behind the counter, I feel his gaze on me again.

"You fired?" Mia asks and I shake my head.

"No. I have to go apologize to him and as soon as I do, will you take that table?"

"Are you sure?"

I nod. "Yeah."

Turning back to the dining room, I square my shoulders and suck in a breath before marching over to his table and pasting a smile on my face.

"Sir, please accept my apology. I'm having just about the worst week of my life and I was out of line earlier."

He arches a brow and I continue staring at him, unsure of how much more he wants from me. Finally, he sighs.

"To apologize, you actually have to say the words "I'm sorry"."

One.

Two.

Three.

Four.

Five.

"Sir," I say through gritted teeth. " I am so sorry. Please accept my apology. My behavior was incredibly rude and it's been a terrible week for me."

He nods. "It's forgotten."

"Thank you. Our other waitress tonight will be taking over for me." I turn to leave but he reaches out and grabs my hand, sending a zap of electricity down my spine. My eyes widen as I turn back to him.

"I don't want the other waitress. I want you."

I want you.

The words rattle around in my brain, conjuring up images that I have absolutely no business thinking. I can't look away from him as I search for an appropriate thing to say that won't get me fired but my mind isn't working as quickly as usual with his warm grip on my wrist.

"I'm...uh, I'm afraid that's not possible. Again, I'm so sorry." I rip my arm out of his grasp and retreat into the back as Mia follows me.

"That last part looked intense. What did he say?"

I shake my head. "Nothing important. I think he's ready to order, though."

"Okay," she chirps before practically bouncing out from behind the counter. If he didn't like my sweet voice, he's going to hate hers. That gives me a little satisfaction and I smile as I make my way back out to the dining room to check on my other tables.

One of my regulars, Devlin, walks in and I smile as he saunters up to the counter.

"Tate! You're back!"

I laugh, nodding. "I am. Where do you want to sit today, Devlin?"

"Right here is good," he answers, pointing to one of the open seats at the counter and I meet him there with a menu and silverware. Devlin is probably in his mid-fifties and handsome as can be. He's been one of my regulars pretty much since I started here, coming in a few times a week.

"So, how have you been, Dev?" I ask, propping my elbows on the counter and he grins.

"Missin' you, Darlin'."

I laugh, swatting his shoulder playfully. Devlin has always been sweet to me and even a little flirty but I know it's all in good fun. He's told me many times about the woman he loved who died and you can see it in his eyes that he'll never get over her. It's honestly a little inspiring.

"You're such a damn flirt. You want your usual today?"

"Mm," he hums, glancing down at the menu. "Bring me a sweet tea and give me a minute to look things over."

I nod. "You got it."

I spin around to get his sweet tea and catch table thirteen watching me again as Mia walks behind the counter. "Damn, that man is grumpy."

"Looks like he's got eyes for Tate," Rico, one of the other guys in the kitchen, says and I roll my eyes but don't say anything.

I pour Devlin's sweet tea and set it down in front of him as he continues studying the menu. While I wait for his order, I seat two other tables in my section and get their drink orders.

"You ready, Dev?" I ask when I get back to the counter and he nods, handing me back the menu.

"I think I'm feeling the BLT today if Shaun can hook me up with a little extra bacon."

"I got you, big man," Shaun calls out, pointing to him and Devlin smiles.

"Coming right up," I tell him and glance up as a few more people sit at my tables, quickly losing myself in work.

*　　*　　*　　*

Glancing up at the clock, I sigh. My shift ends in five minutes and I'm ready to go back to Mom's house and crash. As I scrub the counter clean, I wonder how long it will take before I can start thinking of it as my house instead of Mom's. I spent most of my childhood there so why now is it all of the sudden not my home? I feel like I can't change anything or move things because Mom will be home any minute and she likes her house the way it is.

"Looks like your secret admirer finally bailed," Shaun says and I look at him before turning toward the dining room. Table thirteen is finally empty and I sigh. He sat there through most of my shift and alternated between reading the newspaper, working on something, and watching me. He was never obvious about it but I knew each time his eyes would find me across the dining room and I spent a good part of the night wondering what his deal is. I mean, who just sits in a diner for seven and a half hours?

"Good riddance," I reply and Shaun scoffs.

"Sure, you keep telling yourself that, girl."

"Gigi just called and said she's running ten minutes late," Roger says from his spot at the counter. I sigh.

"So you need me to hang around?" I ask and he shakes his head.

"Nancy is already here and we aren't too busy so you can go ahead and clock out whenever."

Releasing a breath, I nod and head into the back before grabbing my time card and clocking out. Grabbing my purse, I say good-bye to Roger and Nancy as I head outside, pulling my coat tighter around me. I consider just going to my apartment but decide against it. I haven't been back there since the night Detective Rodriguez knocked on my door and I have no desire to go back. I'll need to find someone to take over my lease, though.

Whatever.

It's not something I want to deal with tonight.

As I walk away from the diner, I sense someone behind me just before I hear footsteps. My heart rate quickens as I reach into my bag and wrap my hand around the bottle of pepper spray.

"Tate!" a deep voice calls and I peek over my shoulder, groaning. Table thirteen.

"I was hoping you'd left."

He laughs, closing the distance between us and his golden eyes look even more intense under the glow of the streetlight.

"Do you need a ride?" he asks, ignoring my question and I shake my head.

"Nope, I'm good."

I start to back away from him and he arches a brow. "You gonna walk home at this time of night? In the cold?"

"That was the plan."

"Let me give you a ride."

I scoff. "Not going to happen."

"Please?"

"If you're looking for money, I don't have any," I announce, looking him square in the eye as the envelope full of cash feels especially heavy in my bag.

"Yeah, think I gathered that from your place of employment, Darlin'. And I've got plenty of my own money." His eyes seem sincere but it goes against everything I've ever been taught.

"Then what do you want?"

He smiles, a soft smile that strangely puts me at ease. "Just want to make sure you get home okay."

I release a breath and stare at him as I reach for the phone in my purse. On the one hand, this is exactly what the stupid girl is not supposed to do but I don't really feel like walking tonight and he doesn't feel threatening.

"Why would I accept a ride from you after you were such a dick?" I ask. I'm going to get a ride from him but there's no reason I have to make it easy for him.

He nods. "I am sorry about that. It was that damn voice and callin' me Darlin'. It really threw me off."

Oh, I see.

He's a player and the second a girl doesn't follow one of his scripted conversations, he hasn't got a fucking clue what to do with himself. It's sad, really.

Pursing my lips, I pull my phone out of my bag and unlock it, typing out a message to Mia before meeting his gaze again.

"Okay, you can give me a ride but I've just texted one of my best friends and if she doesn't hear from me in exactly thirty minutes, she will call the police. I should also mention that I have a twin brother in the Navy who will hunt you down and gut you like a fish if you try anything. Oh, and one more thing, you try to touch me at all and I'll stab your junk with the knife I keep in my purse. Are we clear?"

He bites his lip, holding back laughter as he nods. "Crystal, sweetheart. My car's this way."

I follow him as he leads me through the parking lot to a matte black Camaro that makes my heart race for a whole other reason. Since I was a little girl, I've always had a thing for muscle cars and any guy that drives one, really. There's just something about those bad boys and I'm sure my mother prayed I would grow out of it but to this day, this car gets me a little wet.

"Gorgeous car," I say, running my finger along the hood. He grins as he opens the passenger door.

"Glad you like it. Your chariot awaits." He extends his hand to the seat and I scrunch up my nose.

"Don't do that."

His brow furrows. "What?"

"That chivalry thing. You're not selling it well and I'm definitely not buying it."

He chuckles, shaking his head like he can't quite
believe the things that are coming out of my mouth and I
wonder if my brutal honesty is too much for him. I walk
over to him and brush past him as I slide into the car,
enjoying the quick intake of air and the stiffening of his
body. This is exactly what I needed after this past week.

As he closes the door, it crashes down on me –
the realization that Mom is dead, the pain I was able to
escape for a few hours and the guilt that I managed to go
even one moment without thinking of her. God, what
kind of daughter am I? Who flirts with someone one
week after their mother died?

He slips behind the wheel and I suck in a breath,
discreetly wiping away the few tears that managed to
escape. The engine rumbles to life and I run my hands
over the leather interior, appreciating the quality. All my
boyfriends in the past were hard on their cars, driving the
piss out of them, and living life to the fullest inside them
but this one is damn near show quality.

"I'm Lincoln, by the way," he says as he pulls out
of the parking lot and I nod.

"Tate. But you obviously knew that already."

"It's nice to meet you." He glances over at me.
"Where am I going?"

I rattle off my mom's address and he nods. We're
quiet for a while, my mind running with questions from
the last few days. Each time we learn something new, it
feels like a hundred more questions spill out and at this
point, I think I'd like to just grieve in peace.

"Can I ask you a question?" he asks as we near
Mom's house.

I nod. "Sure."

"Earlier, you said this has been the worst week of your life. What did you mean by that?"

Sucking in a breath, I sit up straighter in the seat and clear my throat. "Uh, my mom died eight days ago."

"Fuck, I'm so sorry," he says and I nod, fighting back tears again. It's nice but it's just something people say and no one really knows how this feels unless they've lost a parent, too.

"My dad died when I was a kid," he admits and I turn to him, surprised. "I know what it's like."

"Oh," I whisper. "It's a bitch, huh?"

He chuckles, nodding his head. "Yeah, it is."

"Does it ever get better?" I ask, not sure that I really want the answer but I've never lost a loved one before and I hate not knowing. He sighs.

"I don't know that better is the right word. Some days are easier and some days are like it just happened or I'll think of something I want to tell him before realizing that I can't."

"That's kind of what I figured," I mutter as he pulls up in front of the house.

"Nice place."

I turn and look up at the southern cottage. "Thanks, for the compliment and the ride."

"Not a problem."

Reaching out to grab the door handle, I look back at him. "Well, see you...probably never."

He laughs. "If you gave me your number, we could rectify that."

"Who said it was a problem?" I ask, smiling as I open the door and duck out of his car. When I turn to close the door, he's grinning at me and I can't help but feel like I just laid down a challenge for him. "Bye."

"Mm-hmm," he hums and that's all it takes to tell me I'm in big trouble.

Every Breath You Take

Chapter Five
Lincoln

"The National Weather Service has issued a severe thunderstorm warning for the following parishes..."

"Yeah, no shit," I mutter, leaning forward and turning down the radio as the deep automated voice starts listing parishes around the Baton Rouge area. Glancing up at the windshield, I watch the rain fall in sheets all around the Camaro and sigh. It's been pouring for the last two hours without any sign of letting up and I'm starting to worry that we're going to have a flooding problem. Sighing again, I grab my phone and fire off a text to Storm to check how many sandbags we have at the clubhouse.

Turning toward the diner window, I wonder if Tate's house will be okay when I catch sight of her in the window, standing next to a customer's table as she talks to them with a wide smile. The kind of smile that lights up her whole face and draws people in. Even out here in the car, I can see the way folks gravitate toward her and I can't say that I blame them. Since finally meeting her face-to-face last night, all I want to do is find an excuse to be near her again. The man sitting at the table in front of her reaches out and grabs her hand and I'm gripping the door handle before I even realize what I'm doing.

Blowing out a breath, I release the handle and cross my arms over my chest. She effortlessly wiggles out of his hold and backs away from the table. My mind flashes back to last night when her hand was in mine and my heart pounds in my ears as my fingers twitch to touch her again. It was only a few seconds but it shook me to my core.

Fuck.

Since the moment I first saw her in that folder Blaze gave me, I could tell there was something about her, something different, something I can't quite put my finger on but yesterday when she was right in front of me, I saw just how truly enchanting she is. Even pissed as hell and ready to rip me a new one, she's the most beautiful woman I've ever seen and if I thought I was obsessed with her before, it's nothing compared to how I feel now. I can't force her out of my head no matter how hard I try but I don't do this.

I don't get attached.

I don't develop feelings.

Except I can feel them already growing inside me and there's no way to stop them, nowhere to hide, and nowhere to run. I'm not even sure that I want to. I'm standing in the path of a tornado and my feet are glued to the concrete. All I can do is pray that this time, it doesn't destroy me.

Last night, I sat up half of the night, watching the cameras in her house and thinking of new ways I could see her. And then she gave me the perfect excuse. Glancing over in the passenger seat, I grab the ad for someone to take over her lease that I printed out. It's so perfect that I just couldn't ignore it. Glancing down at my phone, I find the ad online and email her.

From: Kodiak@devilsbikeshop.com
Subject: Apartment lease
Date: February 6, 2018 7:52:36 PM CDT
To: t_carter@gmail.com

Saw your ad and I'm interested in taking over the lease. When would you have time to show me the apartment?

Kodiak

I toss my phone back in the passenger seat and glance back up at the diner. She's behind the counter now and I smile as she pulls her phone out of her pocket and starts typing. As soon as she slips the phone back into her apron, mine dings with a new message.

From: t_carter@gmail.com
Subject: RE: Apartment lease
Date: February 6, 2018 7:55:15 PM CDT
To: Kodiak@devilsbikeshop.com

I'm free tomorrow morning. 10:30 work for you?

Tate

The sooner the better as far as I'm concerned. I'm thoroughly grossed out by how much I can't control myself when it comes to watching her on the cameras and lying to her last night when she told me about Sarah dying was hell. Pretending that I don't know things about her when I've studied her file inside and out at least a dozen times feels disgusting and I wish I knew why Blaze has me doing this.

Sighing, I type out my reply.

From: Kodiak@devilsbikeshop.com
Subject: RE: Apartment lease
Date: February 6, 2018 7:56:48 PM CDT
To: t_carter@gmail.com

Sounds good. See you then.

Kodiak

---

*   *   *   *

"Do y'all need anything else?" the waitress asks, flashing me a smile. I look around the table at the stack of pancakes I ordered along with the eggs, hash browns, toast, and bacon before shaking my head.

"No, I think we're good."

"Well, let me know if you need anything. My name is Gabby."

I nod and she lingers by the table for a second before turning and heading back to the kitchen.

"What is up with you?" Izzy asks and I glance up at her.

"What?"

She glances toward the door where the waitress disappeared. "She was totally into you and you barely looked at her."

"Just wasn't feelin' her," I lie and thankfully she buys it. My mind flashes to Tate and I glance down at my watch, eager to see her again.

Izzy tries to maneuver my plates to fit her juice glass on our little table before giving up and standing up.

She marches over to the table next to us and pulls it up to ours, giving us twice the room, as I laugh.

"Jesus. I don't know how you eat that much," she complains, eyeing my plates.

"What? I'm hungry."

In true Izzy fashion, she arches a brow and mutters, "Clearly."

"What have you been up to?" I ask as I cut into my pancakes and shove some into my mouth. She shrugs and cuts into her omelet.

"Same old."

"Breakin' hearts all over town, then?"

She giggles. "Yeah, something like that."

I met Izzy just shy of a year ago and we were hot and heavy for one night before we realized that we would be better as friends. Carly and Ali are her best friends and married to my brothers so it could have easily gotten messy and turns out, we're pretty similar when it comes to relationships. She's become a really good friend and someone I can talk to about things I would never even dream about saying to the guys.

Glancing up at her, I frown. "What's wrong?"

"Nothing," she sighs. "I just wish I could find someone who was serious about keeping things casual for once. As soon as I start seeing a guy, he wants to change the arrangement."

"It's the rule of three," I tell her and her brows shoot up.

"What's that?"

"The theory that after you sleep with someone three times, you start getting attached."

Her fork drops out of her hand and lands with a clank on the table. "So, I've got to only sleep with guys twice before finding a new one? That sounds exhausting."

"Or settle down."

"Ack," she snaps. "Take that back. Don't you put that bad juju on me. That's never going to happen."

I laugh, leaning back in my chair as I sip my sweet tea.

Izzy had a bad first marriage like me and that combined with her parents' divorce has put her off the idea forever but since seeing Tate, I'm beginning to wonder if that's really the path I want to go down.

"What the heck is on your mind?" Izzy asks, breaking through my thoughts and I snap my gaze to hers.

"Huh?"

"You just got this look in your eye... I don't know. It was crazy."

Sighing, I sit forward and set my glass down on the table before running my hand through my hair. "I met someone."

"And?"

"She's... special." Saying the words out loud feels weird but it's true and I can't deny it anymore. Tate is different from any of the other girls that I've used to fill my bed these last six years. I don't know what it means or where it's going to lead or even if it can lead anywhere but it's out there now.

"Whoa. Are you... are you in love with her?"

I scoff. "No. She's just different."

"How is she different?" she asks, tilting her head to the side as she studies me. I stare down at my plate, unable to believe that I'm about to admit this out loud.

"I don't think once would be enough."

When I glance up, we lock eyes and she stares at me for a moment, her gaze surprised. Finally, she blows out a breath.

"Okay, then."

I shake my head. "No, not okay. It's complicated."

"How?"

Sucking in a breath, I debate telling her the truth but only for a split second before realizing that out of everyone I know, Izzy is the last person that will judge me.

"I'm kind of stalking her."

"What?" she screeches, earning the attention of all the tables in our general vicinity and I hold my hands up to try and silence her as the waitress stops at our table.

"Can I get y'all anything else?" she asks, directing her question toward me as she bats her lashes.

"Seriously?" Izzy hisses. "Can you not see that we're in the middle of a very serious conversation? Got lost, lady."

The waitress huffs before stomping off and I laugh as Izzy points her finger at me.

"Oh, no, you start talking now. What the fuck do you mean you're kind of stalking her?"

I straighten the silverware next to my plate and take a deep breath. "Well, Blaze called me to the clubhouse and asked me to watch her..."

"Why?" she interjects.

"I don't know but I assumed that he had a good reason. Blaze is a good guy."

She nods. "Continue."

"So I've been following her."

"And have you actually spoken to her or have you completely lost your mind? Is this another Chris situation?" she asks, referencing Ali's stalker last year.

"No," I growl. "It's not like that and yes, I've spoken to her."

"So, now you're lying to her on top of stalking her?" When she says it out loud, I realize how hopeless it is.

"I have to come up with a way to fix this."

She lets out a humorless laugh as she leans back in her seat and crosses her arms over her chest. "I don't know that you can. When this all comes out, she's going to run far, far away from you. Unless, of course, she's also a lunatic in which case, you two are fucking perfect for each other."

"Thanks, Iz," I snap and she shrugs.

"Just telling you the truth. You are doomed, my friend."

"No, I'll find a way."

"Kodiak, I say this with as much love as possible but you look like a psycho right now."

"I know," I admit but the thought of never seeing Tate again causes me physical pain. Glancing down at my watch, I can't help but smile, relieved to know that I'll be with her again soon.

Every Breath You Take

Chapter Six
Tatum

After wiping the sheen of sweat from my forehead, I brace my hands on the open, half-packed box in front of me and sigh as I gaze around the living room of my apartment. I've been here for a few hours now and I've gotten everything I want to take with me packed up. My clothes and shoes are crammed into two boxes and thankfully, all my bathroom stuff fit into a smaller box. The three bookshelves in the living room are cleared out and all my books are safely packed away as well as all the photos off the walls. The only thing left is to decide what to do with the furniture and dishes.

Mom's house doesn't really have the storage space for them and even though I can afford to, it seems silly to pay for a storage unit when I don't really want this stuff. I don't want to be wasteful though. Sighing again, I sink into the dining room chair. I suppose maybe the new tenant can use it. It's in fairly good shape and who can say no to free furniture, right?

Grabbing my soda off the table, I take a drink and lean back in the chair, thinking over the last few years. Between my job at the diner and the gas station, I've worked at least ten hours almost every day and it's taken a toll on me. I can't remember the last time I got my hair cut and if a stylist saw my ends, she might shriek in horror. I was in high school the last time I had money to get my nails done and I haven't eaten out at a restaurant since I started working at the diner. Hell, I don't even have a damn car.

Maybe Theo was right and it's time for me to make a few purchases but spending any of that money feels wrong. I've gone so long without, that I'm plagued by indecision – half of me wanting to treat myself and the other half eager to horde it away for a rainy day. What the hell kind of rainy day requires half a million dollars though? Maybe I could afford to splurge a little and save money. I know one thing for certain, I'm enrolling in school as soon as possible.

After I graduated high school, I scoffed at the idea of going to school. I was cocky and thought I knew what I was doing when I got a job at a department store and moved out of my mother's house. Very quickly I realized that it wasn't that easy but I was stubborn and kept fighting. Just when I was about to lose everything, I met Beth. She was an escort and told me how I could make triple what I was making at the department store just by going out on dates with men. Believe me, I was appalled at first but when she explained that there was absolutely no sex involved, it seemed like the perfect solution. For three years, I went out with various men

and got paid to let them wine and dine me until one night
when Beth showed up on my doorstep with a bloody
face. One of the men had gotten angry when she told him
that she wouldn't be sleeping with him and I knew the
money wasn't worth the danger I was putting myself in.

As soon as I got her all bandaged up, I called all
my dates for that week and canceled – indefinitely. I'd
managed to save up a little money but I knew it wouldn't
last long so I quickly got to work searching for another
job and landed at the diner. Only two weeks later, it
became clear that even that wouldn't be enough so I got
the second job at the gas station. I also had to move out
of my apartment and find something cheaper, which is
how I ended up here. Releasing a breath, I look around
the room again.

I can't believe how much my life has changed in
a little more than a week. Ten days ago, I was walking
through this shitty neighborhood at night, hoping I didn't
get mugged or worse and now, I've got a beautiful house
in a safe part of town, I have money to finally go to
school and my mom is gone. It feels so wrong that every
other part of my life is looking up when she's not here to
see it but I guess that's what she wanted. She did
everything she could to take care of Theo and me for
years after she was gone. Tears well up in my eyes as the
alarm of my phone goes off and I quickly wipe them
away, pushing off the chair.

Kodiak, the man interested in taking over the
lease, will be here any minute and I need to get these
boxes down to the truck that I borrowed from Roger.
Pushing the sleeves of my long sleeved t-shirt up, I lean

down and pick up one of the lighter boxes before navigating to the door and slowly going down the steps. When I get out to the truck, I set it in the back and shove it toward the cab before dusting my hands off on my jeans. There, one down and only six more to go. My phone buzzes in my pocket and I pull it out as I step up onto the sidewalk and turn toward my door. Stepping forward, I crash right into someone and my phone falls to the pavement as I let out a squeak of surprise.

"Shit," I mutter as two large hands wrap around my arms and I look up. "I'm so... You!"

Lincoln, the man from the diner a few nights ago flashes me a lazy smile as he crosses his arms over his chest and leans against the side of the truck.

"You."

"What are you doing here?" I ask as I lean down and scoop up my phone, inspecting the screen for cracks.

"I'm here to meet someone about taking over a lease."

My head whips up and my mouth drops open. "Oh my god, you've got to be kidding me."

"I take it that's you."

"Did you do this on purpose?" I ask, flashing back to the other night when he asked me for my number. He frowns, looking sexier than any man has a right to, and tilts his head to the side.

"And how would I have done this on purpose?"

"Well," I hum, deciding to have a little fun with this. "You're clearly a stalker."

His eyes widen and he takes a step back, holding his hands out in front of him as he starts choking on nothing. "No, it's not like that."

"Dude, it was a joke, not a dick. Don't take it so hard."

My comment earns more surprised coughing that turns into a laugh and he stares at me like I'm crazy for a moment before shaking his head. With a smile slowly creeping across his face, he takes a step toward me and presses his big, hard body against mine.

"I promise you, Darlin', I don't roll like that."

My lips part and my body floods with warmth as my heartbeat races in my chest. A musky scent surrounds us and my hand trembles as I fight the urge to lean in and take a deep breath.

"Isn't that what they all say?" I whisper, my entire body aching for him to reach out and touch me again like he did at the diner. His golden gaze locks with mine as his smile grows and he trails the tips of his fingers down my arm.

"Want a demonstration?"

My mind has no trouble conjuring up images of the two of us wrapped up in sheets while he does just that and I lean into him, licking my lips just as a car horn pierces through the air. I stumble back and draw air into my burning lungs.

"So, um… the apartment?" I ask, my voice squeaking and I manage to not wince at how embarrassed I am right now. He drops his head for a moment before nodding.

"Yeah. Let's check it out."

I lead him upstairs, wondering the whole time if he's watching my ass and secretly hoping that he is. It's been a long time since I've been with someone or even liked someone so I don't really have a clue what to do. In fact, the last time I dated anyone was in high school. I'm so out of my league it's not even funny.

"So, this is it," I mumble, stepping into my apartment and the room seems to shrink as soon as he steps inside.

"It looks nice."

I shrug. "It's okay. The neighborhood is not super safe but I put an extra deadbolt on the door to combat that."

"You think a deadbolt is going to stop anyone?" he asks, arching a brow, and I square my shoulders as I meet his eyes.

"No. It just gives me an extra second to grab my gun. How about you don't worry about me and just take a look at the apartment?"

He holds his hands up in surrender and starts looking around the living room before stepping into the kitchen. "You mind if I take some pictures of the place?"

"Why? You got a girlfriend that you need to send them to?" I ask, hating myself as soon as I do. Why the hell does it matter if he has a girlfriend? It's not like anything is ever going to happen between us. When I meet his gaze again, he smiles.

"No. I'm a member of the Bayou Devils. You heard of us?"

I nod. "Yes, but I don't see what that has to do with anything."

"We help people – get them out of bad relationships, protect them if they're being stalked, save children from abusers – that kind of thing."

"Oh…"

"We're looking for a place we can take the folks we rescue."

I jump up on the counter and cross my legs. "Like a safe house?"

"Exactly like that."

"Okay. Well, go ahead and take a look around and then I'll answer any questions you have."

He nods and starts snapping photos of my living room before moving into the kitchen. I don't move as he snaps a couple before moving on to the bathroom.

"Oh, by the way, if you want the furniture, I'll leave it," I call out to him and he pokes his head out of the bathroom.

"Really? You don't want it?"

"Nope. My mom's house already has everything I need."

He nods again and disappears down the hallway to my bedroom while I try to imagine him stretched out on my queen-sized bed. Jesus, what the hell is wrong with me? I seriously haven't even looked twice at a guy since high school and now all of the sudden I'm envisioning Lincoln or Kodiak or whatever his name is spread out on my bed naked.

"The place is great," he says, walking back into the living room and it takes a huge amount of effort to keep my gaze above his belt.

"What's your name?" I blurt out and he scowls at me.

"Didn't I introduce myself at the diner?"

I nod. "Yeah, Lincoln, but in your email, you went by Kodiak."

"Oh, right. Kodiak is a nickname."

I hug my knees to my chest. "Why?"

"I'm from Alaska."

My brows shoot up. "Oh, yeah? I lived in Alaska once."

"Really? Where at?"

"Anchorage. We were only there for a few months when my brother and I were three."

He walks over to the table and sits in one of the chairs. I'm honestly surprised it doesn't buckle under his weight.

"Twins, right?" he asks and I nod.

"Yeah, his name is Theo. You have any brothers or sisters?"

He nods, rubbing his hands down his legs repeatedly. "I've got two sisters."

"What are their names?" I ask, studying him as he continues to withdraw into himself.

"Nora and Rowan."

"Pretty names," I mutter and decide to drop the subject. "So, you interested in the apartment?"

"Yeah," he answers before clearing his throat and brushing off whatever emotion crashed down on him. "I think we might be. I texted the photos to my boss and as soon as he gets back to me, I'll let you know."

"Well, you know where to find me but if I don't hear from you in forty-eight hours, I'll need to put the ad back up."

He nods, standing. "You need help getting these boxes downstairs?"

I nod, hopping down off the counter. "Yeah, that'd be great. I need to get the truck back to Roger before two."

"Who's Roger?" he asks with a slight growl in the back of his throat and I arch a brow.

"Why do you care?"

He takes a step back, shaking his head. "Oh, I don't. It's just…uh…"

"He's my boss," I say, putting him out of his misery.

"Oh, right." He turns toward the boxes and picks up one full of books. "Jesus. What the hell is in here?"

"Books," I reply, sheepishly. "Do you need some help?"

I try to grip the other side but he moves it out of my grasp, shaking his head.

"No, I got it. I don't need you falling down the stairs and breaking your neck."

My cheeks heat and I turn to hide my smile as he walks out of the apartment with the box in his hands. I grab one of the lighter ones and follow behind him, ready to get this over with. It takes us fifteen minutes to get all of the boxes downstairs and loaded into the truck. As I close the tailgate, he pulls out his phone.

"Blaze approved. Looks like I'll be taking over the lease."

I pull the truck keys out of my pocket. "Okay. How about we meet at a coffee shop on Saturday with the paperwork and I'll hand over the keys then?"

"Sounds good. Did you lock up?" he asks, pointing to the door to the apartments. I nod.

"Yep. It's all good. I'll text you the address and see you Saturday." I turn toward the truck when he wraps his hand around my arm. Sparks race across my skin and I suck in a silent breath as I turn back to him.

"I should probably get your number. You know, so you can text me."

Nodding, I grab his phone out of his hand and program my number into it before handing it back to him. "Seems like you made me a liar."

"How so?" he asks, leaning against the truck and getting closer to me. Oh, Lord, I can't take this.

"I told you that you couldn't have my number the other night and now you've got it."

He takes a step forward and his mucky smell fills the space between us. "Purely a coincidence."

"Is it?"

With a smile teasing his lips, he reaches down and grabs my hand, bringing it to his lips. His gaze stays locked on mine as he kisses my knuckles and I struggle to breathe, my heart pounding in my ears.

"See you Saturday," he promises then turns and walks away without a word.

*   *   *   *

A.M. Myers

My teeth sink into my lip as I scan the street
through the coffee shop window, watching for Lincoln's
Camaro and trying not to hyperventilate. For the past
three days, I haven't been able to stop thinking about him
or the way he made me feel when he pressed up against
me outside my apartment. And if I did find a moment
where his charming smile and alluring eyes weren't at
the forefront of my mind, he would text me and bring it
all rushing back. His messages were mostly friendly and
a little flirty, sending a rush through me each time I heard
my phone beep. As much as I'm enjoying it though, I'm
so out of my element that it's not even funny. When I
broke up with my high school boyfriend three weeks
before graduation, I had just been through the scariest
time of my life and I swore off men for a while. Once I
felt like I was ready to date again, I just wanted to wait
for someone special but it's hard to meet people when all
you do is work.

The deep rumble of an engine draws my gaze
back to the window and my lips part as Lincoln pulls into
a parking spot on the back of a sexy black chopper. God,
he's lethal. From his ripped up jeans and black boots to
his freshly fucked hair that I'm starting to think he just
wakes up with, he screams bad boy and it's definitely
doing things for me. He stands, the bike between his
thighs and I fidget in my seat, all sorts of fantasies
playing out in my mind. What the hell is wrong with me?
My mom just died and here I am, imagining straddling

his hips and losing myself for a few hours. Swinging his leg over the bike, he pulls off his helmet and runs his fingers through his hair, giving it that sexy messy look and as he glances up, he meets my gaze in the window, flashing me a smile before walking toward the door.

Butterflies zip around in my belly as he opens the door of the coffee shop and directs his gaze toward me as he maneuvers through the tables.

"I got you a coffee," I say when he reaches me, pointing to the to-go cup sitting in front of the empty chair across from me.

"Thanks." He sits down and takes a sip before humming in approval. "You remember how I take my coffee?"

"Occupational hazard, I guess."

Yeah, right.

I've never remembered another customer's coffee order unless they were a regular. It's just him. He nods, oblivious to my lie, and takes another sip before leaning back in his seat.

"So, do you have the paperwork?"

Nodding my head, I set my cup down and grab my bag off the floor, digging through it for the contract I had Mr. Wiley draw up for me and a pen. I was so focused on him that I almost forgot the reason for our meeting, which is strange since I'm so eager to be done with this apartment. I set the contract and pen on the table before turning them to him.

"I've let the landlord know that you'll be taking over the lease so he's expecting payment from you from now on. It's seven fifty a month with an eight hundred dollar deposit. February is already paid for so don't worry about that. As soon as he gets the deposit from you, he'll give me mine back."

He lays his hand on top of mine on the table. "Wait. I'll pay you for February's rent, too."

"It's not a big deal. I really just want to be done with all this."

He shakes his head, an adorable scowl knitting his brows. "I insist. It's your money and I highly doubt you've even spent a single night there this month."

"It doesn't matter," I say and sigh when I see the stubborn expression on his face. "But okay. You need to sign here, here, and here."

He takes the pen from me and signs his name in the three places I indicated before spinning the contract back to me. Our fingers brush when he hands me the pen and I suck in a breath, my head spinning from the urge to touch him again as I sign my name three times.

"Congrats. You've got an apartment," I say when I'm done, laying the pen on the table and handing him the keys. He flashes me a smile and I hand him a sticky note. "I'll get a copy of the contract over to the landlord and that's his number if you ever need anything. He doesn't come around much but he's a good guy."

He nods. "Thanks."

"Of course. Well, I guess I better get going," I murmur, searching for any excuse to stay and somehow wanting to flee at the same time.

"Hold up."

He reaches out, grabbing my hand, and I suck in a breath as the hair on my arms sticks straight up and warmth pulses over my skin. "Stay and hang out with me?"

"Oh, I…uh, I don't know about that."

"Please?" he asks, his smile turning shy and my heart skips a beat. Oh, hell…

"Why do I get the feeling that you don't use that word a lot?"

He laughs. "Because I don't but I'm saying it now."

"Can I be honest with you?" I ask and he nods. "Of course."

I bite my lip and drop my gaze to the table. "I haven't been able to stop thinking about you since the night you came into the diner but this," I motion between the two of us, "is a really bad idea."

"Why?"

"So many reasons," I whisper, a humorless laugh slipping past my lips. Nothing about this is funny.

"What if I just want to be your friend?"

I arch a brow. "Friends?"

He nods.

"It's been a while since I've been out on a date but I'm not an idiot, Lincoln. I can see exactly what you want."

"How long is a while?"

"Eight years."

He lets out a low whistle, shaking his head like he can't even comprehend what I just said. "Wow."

"Yeah, and I get the distinct feeling that you're a love 'em and leave 'em type, which I have no interest in and on top of that, this might be the worst timing ever seeing as my mom just died."

He nods and I can see the wheels turning in his head. "Look, you're not wrong about me but that's not what this is about. I remember how it felt right after my dad died and even with my mom and two sisters, it was still confusing and lonely so I just want to be here for you."

"As friends?"

He nods. "I know what you're going through and I also know how to help you when things start get to be too much."

I chew on my lip, considering his words. "And how would you help me?"

"It helps to stay busy and sometimes, just having someone to sit with you so you don't have to be alone is everything. I can be that guy for you."

The thought of having him around to lean on and turn to when the emotions are just too strong to handle is very appealing, especially with Theo back in Charleston.

"Okay, I'd like that."

He smiles, giving my hand a squeeze before releasing it and leaning back in his chair, sipping his coffee.

"I've got to ask you a question," he prompts and I nod. "Has it really been eight years since you went on a date?"

I laugh. "Not exactly but the last time I was in a relationship was eight years ago."

"Oh, I see. You give me hell for being the love 'em and leave 'em type when you're the exact same way."

"Uh, no," I murmur, a blush staining my cheeks. "It's complicated but I haven't been with anyone in eight years."

"You mean... no sex?"

Glancing down at the table, I shake my head. "No."

"Why?" he whispers, his voice bewildered and I laugh through my embarrassment. Pursing my lips, I pick at my coffee cup.

"I was a bit of a wild child in high school – anything that would make my mother lose her mind, I did it. A few weeks before graduation, I missed my period and my whole world came crashing down on me. I thought my life was over and I regretted all the stupid things I had done during my little rebellion."

"So you have a kid?" he asks and I shake my head.

"No, thankfully it turned out to be a false alarm but it scared me enough that I broke up with my good for nothing boyfriend and became dedicated to getting my life back on track."

"Okay... but that was eight years ago..."

I hear his unspoken question and nod. "For the first year or so, I made a point to stay single and focus on myself but after that, I promised myself I wouldn't jump into bed or a relationship with just anyone. He had to be special and I guess no one has ever come along."

"So you've just been living like a nun?"

I laugh, meeting his warm honey eyes. "Essentially."

"Damn. The more I learn about you, the more interesting you get," he comments and I meet his gaze, a blush rising to my cheeks as I smile.

"It's all part of my master plan to trap you with a white picket fence and two point five kids. Now, it's time to spill some of your emotional baggage," I joke and he laughs, studying me as he takes a sip of his coffee.

"What do you want to know?"

I glance to the side of our table as a couple brushes by and wait for them to get far enough away before I turn back to him. "Will you tell me what happened to your dad?"

"Shit, you're going right for the bull's-eye, aren't you?"

"You don't have to…" I start, but he holds his hand up to stop me.

"No, it's okay. And it's only fair." His smile falls away and he sets his coffee down in front of him, taking a deep breath. "My parents had this charter plane business up in Alaska, still do actually… anyway, they would take tourists on sightseeing tours and help deliver supplies to some of the smaller villages, stuff like that."

I nod for him to continue.

"My mom asked me to cover her one day 'cause my sisters had been throwing up all night long and I was pissed but I went anyway. My dad was just running supplies so it should have been an easy day. Right around the time I expected him back, his voice came over the radio, telling me that the plane had gone done and that he was losing blood fast. I called nine-one-one and talked to him until the radio went silent."

"Oh my god, Lincoln," I whisper, tears welling up in my eyes for our shared pain. "How old were you?"

"Fifteen."

A tear slips down my cheek and I quickly wipe it away. "I'm so sorry."

"Shit, babe," he whispers, his voice full of pain. "I didn't mean to make you cry."

Wiping the tears away, I shake my head. "It's okay. Everything is still so raw for me that I cry at the drop of a hat these days."

He nods, reaching across the table and grabbing my hand. "What happened to your mom?"

"We still don't know," I answer, my voice hoarse. "She was involved in a hit and run accident and Detective Rodriguez thinks the driver was drunk but there aren't any witnesses or anything."

"Rodriguez?" he asks and I nod.

"Yeah, you know him?"

He releases me and grabs his coffee, taking a sip. "The club works with him from time to time on cases."

"Oh. What kind?"

Shrugging, he leans forward, propping his arms up on the table. "It changes. Sometimes he helps us and other times, we help him. It's beneficial to both of us since sometimes, there are things that as a cop, he can't do and vice versa."

"Is the club super top secret or can you talk about it?" I ask and he laughs.

"I can talk about it to an extent. Why? What do you want to know?"

"Why do y'all do this? I mean, there are so many things you could do with your time, why go out of your way to help people?"

Nodding, he leans back and crosses his arms over his chest. "We each have our own reasons for why we do this. Each member has watched the injustice of this world and wished we could have done something to stop it. Now, we do."

"It's just so different from what I've heard about other clubs," I say and he nods again.

"It is but they weren't always like that. Back before I joined, they had their hands elbow deep in all that illegal shit."

"What changed?"

He shrugs. "I wasn't here so I only have this information second hand but it seems that Blaze, our president, got shot during a deal and another member, Henn, was set up for selling drugs and went to prison. Blaze said it was like a light bulb went off and he realized he needed to step up and be a better leader, put the club on a better path."

I lean forward and rest my arms on the table. "And what if the members didn't agree with the new direction?"

"I think at that point, everyone was getting tired of it all but I'm sure they did have a few members leave."

"How does the club survive if there's no more money coming in?"

He laughs. "You're just full of questions, aren't you?"

"I guess so."

"Well, just because they don't run drugs and guns anymore doesn't mean there's no money coming in. The motorcycle shop has been running since before Blaze changed things, which is where I work, and afterward, he also started a P.I. business."

"Huh," I hum, sitting back in my seat with my mind working in overdrive. I'm fascinated with the idea of his club and the work they do to help people who would otherwise be forgotten.

"Sorry, we were talking about your mom and kind of got off track," Lincoln says and I glance at him.

"Oh, don't worry about it. What was it you said about distracting me?"

He grins. "Glad I could help. I'm here for whatever you need."

I nod. "Thank you. It still doesn't seem real to me most of the time. My mom was bigger than life, so strong and vibrant that her dying in a car accident just seems impossible."

"It's harder when you don't know what happened."

"I've learned so much about who my mother was since her death but it's only raised more questions. I'd give anything just to have one more conversation with her." Tears sting my eyes again and I blow out a breath, looking up at the ceiling. "Sorry."

"Hey, don't apologize and anytime you need to rant, give me a call. I understand what you're going through and I want to be here for you."

Smiling through my tears, I nod. "Thank you, Lincoln."

Every Breath You Take

A.M. Myers

Chapter Seven
Tatum

"Have a nice day," I chirp, pasting a smile on my face as the grumpy middle-aged man swipes his bag of chips off the counter and grumbles something inaudible. I doubt whatever he said was anywhere near polite, though.

"Yeah, you, too, asshole," I whisper, rolling my eyes. How hard is it to just say thank you? I don't even care if you don't mean it.

"Tate," my boss, Reed, calls as he steps out of the back office. "Why don't you go stock shelves and I'll manage the register?"

Nodding, I step out from behind the counter and sigh as I walk down the center aisle and turn toward the back room. Once there, I grab a pad of paper and pen before starting at the beginning of the first aisle and making my way down its length, writing down the items that need to be restocked before moving to the end cap and the next row. About halfway through the store, I feel someone's gaze on me and glance up, catching Reed ogling my ass from his perch behind the register.

A low growl slips out of my mouth as I turn back to the shelf and try to ignore his inappropriate behavior. There was a time when I really liked this job – it was fairly easy and I was usually by myself while I worked – but six months ago, my old boss, Otis, retired and handed the reins over to his nephew, Reed. It's bad enough that Reed is a college dropout who couldn't stop partying long enough to pass his classes but turns out, he's also a bit of a perv. His advances have been getting more and more blatant in the past three weeks and I don't know how much longer I'm going to have a job.

The bell over the door rings and I peek over my shoulder as I write down another product that needs stocked. Lincoln struts into the gas station in all his bad boy, biker glory and my mouth goes dry as my pen trails off the page. Damn. It's been two days since he suggested we just be friends and already, I know it's not going to work. Not when just the sight of him is enough to melt my panties.

"Hey, Darlin'," he says, an easy grin pulling at the corner of his mouth as he walks over to me.

"Hey, yourself. What are you doing here?"

He shrugs, gazing around the store. "I was in the area and I remembered you saying you worked here."

"And?" I ask again, arching a brow as I focus on the shelf in front of me. Maybe if I keep my gaze on the bags of chips, I won't notice how his t-shirt clings to the muscles in his stomach like a second skin or how damn good he smells.

"And I wanted to see you."

"Tate, this isn't social hour!" Reed yells from the counter, his face red and I roll my eyes.

"Who's that?" Lincoln asks.

"A punk ass little bitch who thinks he's my boss."

He barks out a laugh, glancing over his shoulder at Reed as he leans against the shelf.

"Tate!" Reed yells again.

"Shut up, Reed!" I yell back before turning my annoyed glance to Lincoln. "You're going to get me in trouble."

A wicked grin lights up his face and goose bumps race across my skin. "Sounds fun."

"What do you want? If you haven't noticed, I'm a little busy here."

He stands up straight, tucking his hands into his jean pockets. "What time do you get off?"

A crude joke pops into my head and I bite back a smile as I peek up at the clock. "Ten."

"Damn," he mutters. "Well, how about tomorrow? You want to go do something?"

"This sounds an awful lot like you're asking me out on a date," I point out, moving on to the next aisle. He shakes his head.

"No, ma'am. Just want to hang out with you… as a friend, of course."

I nod, flashing him a skeptical look. "Of course."

"So?" he asks. "You free tomorrow?"

"Nope, sorry. I've got to work at the diner."

As I peek up at him, the sight of him chewing on his bottom lip makes me smile.

"What time is your break tomorrow? Could I swing by and grab lunch with you?"

Sighing, I turn to him. "You're awfully eager for someone who is just my friend. What are you really trying to accomplish here?"

"I swear, Tate," he promises, placing his hand over his heart. The black and gray tattoos on his fingers hold my attention. "I'm just trying to be a friend. Like I said, it's easier if you stay busy and I want to be here for you if you want to talk."

I study his face for a moment, soaking in the sincerity shining in his eyes, before I see Reed watching us from behind Lincoln. He looks pissed and I know he's going to make the rest of my shift hell.

"Okay, swing by the diner tomorrow and I'll have lunch with you."

If I hadn't already said yes, his bright smile alone would have gotten the job done. He leans in and presses a soft kiss to my cheek that makes my head spin.

"See you tomorrow, Darlin'."

He turns and I watch him walk out of the store before turning back to the shelf with a blush staining my cheeks.

"Was that your boyfriend?" Reed asks and I jump, glancing to the end of the aisle where he's standing.

"That's none of your damn business."

His eyes narrow. "Why don't you go be a slut on your own time, okay?"

My eyes widen as he turns, thinking he's won and I resist the urge to chuck a flashlight at his head.

"Hey, Reed," I call, using my sweet diner voice and he spins back around, a smile on his face. "Go find a bag of dicks and fuck yourself. If you ever speak to me like that again, I'm going to raise your voice a couple octaves."

Laughter draws both our attention to the door where Lincoln stands, pride shining in his eyes. Pride for me?

"Sorry, y'all. I forgot a soda."

Reed retreats back into the office, his face bright red and as Lincoln passes me, he whispers, "That was sexy as hell, babe."

Closing my eyes, I can't fight back my smile. Yeah, this whole "friends" thing isn't going to last long at all.

*   *   *   *

"Sweet Tatum, when are you going to kick all those other losers to the curb and admit your true feelings for me?" Devlin asks with a wicked smirk on his face and I bark out a laugh as Shaun and Rico whistle from the kitchen.

"What losers, Dev? You know I've only got eyes for you."

His smile grows as he places one hand over his chest and holds the other one out to me. "My girl."

123

Laughing, I refill his coffee before going down the length of the counter, refilling each cup.

"You know, Devlin," I whisper when I get back to the other end of the counter. "I hear Gigi thinks you're devilishly handsome if you ever want to turn that charm on someone who's available."

"Now, Tate, you know the only woman for me is my sweet Claire, God rest her soul."

"I'm just saying that you're a real nice guy and you should be happy."

His smile is wistful as he shakes his head. "I will be happy when I finally get to see my girl again."

"It's kind of romantic," Mia sighs as she comes up behind me and I laugh.

"Tate, you taking your break anytime soon?" Roger asks from the kitchen. I peek through the pass through and nod.

"Yeah. I'm just waitin' on someone."

Out of the corner of my eye, I see Mia's head whip in my direction. "Tatum Elizabeth Carter, do you have a date?"

"No, it's not a date. He's just a friend."

She arches a brow. "He?"

"Well, now it's getting interesting," Devlin says, folding his arms over his chest. "Seems our Tate finally met a man."

"You, hush," I scold him and he grins. I haven't said a word to anyone about Lincoln yet so there will be hell to pay when he walks in and she recognizes him but I don't even know what I would say. We're friends but also…not.

124

"Yes, he."

She turns to Devlin with a wide grin on her face. "Oh, this is about to get good, y'all."

"You're an instigator," I tell her, shaking my head as I grab a plate off the pass through and set it in front of Devlin.

"And yet you still give me plenty of ammunition."

"Oh, so it's my fault?" I ask, laughing and she nods before her mouth falls open, her gaze locked on the door. I don't even have to look. It's clear from her expression alone that Lincoln just walked in.

"Hey, Darlin'," he says. His deep voice washes over me and goose bumps race across my flesh.

"Oh, shit." Shaun laughs as I suck in a breath and spin around.

"Lincoln."

"You ready for lunch?" he asks, his gaze dropping down to my lips for a brief second before he meets my eyes again. God, I would give anything to feel him press his mouth against mine.

"Yeah," I whisper before glancing over my shoulder and yelling, "I'm going on break, Rog."

His hand pokes out of the door and he waves, giving me the go ahead so I grab two menus and step out from behind the counter.

"Follow me."

A whistle sounds behind us and I shake my head, resisting the urge to flip Mia off. It would only add more fuel to her fire and possibly make Lincoln think this lunch is more than it is. Not that I even know what it is.

After he came into the gas station yesterday, I spent most of my shift thinking of all the reasons that I should avoid any kind of relationship with him and basically it came down to two things. First, he's obviously a player and while he seems to be putting in the extra effort to woo me, I'm not naive enough to think that he'd want more than one night with me and two, with Mom's death, this is the worst time for me to be getting into a relationship. I can't deny that he affects me, though. More than anyone has in years.

"You're not going to wait on yourself, are you?" Lincoln asks as we sit across from each other in a booth and I shake my head.

"No, I'm sure Mia will be by in a second. Not like I could keep her away if I tried."

He arches a brow. "Oh? Why's that?"

"'Cause she's nosy as hell and she remembers you from the other night."

"You mean the night you verbally assaulted me?" he asks, a smile playing at his lips and I roll my eyes.

"Let's not be dramatic and you totally deserved it."

Barking out a laugh, he takes one of the menus from the table and opens it. "Did I now?"

"Yes," I reply with a nod. "I'm only mean to people who are rude to me and you, sir, were very rude."

"All right, maybe I was a little bit off that night but it's only because I was so nervous about talking to this gorgeous woman."

126

I point a finger at him, shaking my head. "If you're talking about me, stop it and if you're not talking about me, also stop it."

"Why?"

"Because if you are talking about me, friends don't talk about each other like that."

He nods thoughtfully, studying me. "And if I wasn't talking about you?"

"The chicken is good here," I answer, glancing down at the menu like I didn't just ignore his question. The truth is, I don't want him talking about another girl like that but it doesn't make me sleeping with him any less of a bad idea. "I feel like I need to get something out of the way."

He looks up. "What?"

"I'm not going to sleep with you. Ever. It's not going to happen."

Whiskey colored eyes narrow and he bites down on his full lip. "I don't know, Sugar. Forever is a long time."

"Okay," I choke out, holding my hands up. "First of all, don't ever call me Sugar again. I'm not your sugar and even if we were sleeping together, I wouldn't let you call me that and secondly, I can't be doing this with you. It doesn't matter that I'm attracted to you or that you're attracted to me because my mom just died and I'm trying to figure out where to go from here. You understand everything I'm dealing with in a way that none of my other friends do so I need you right now and this can't get screwed up by us falling into bed together."

"Look, Tate," he sighs, running a hand through his dark hair. "I'm serious about wanting to be your friend and yeah, there is obviously more between us but it's not my focus right now. Maybe someday, you and I can explore that but not right now and I get that."

He reaches across the table and grabs my hand as I gasp softly at the butterflies flapping around in my belly.

"Okay, then."

Mia steps out from behind the counter, her eyes on us, and I rip my hand away as she approaches.

"Y'all know what you want to eat?" she asks, eying me with a mischievous grin on her face and I shake my head as Lincoln orders a sweet tea and a sandwich.

"My usual, Mia," I tell her and she nods, winking at me before turning and walking away from our table.

"So, in all seriousness, how are you doing with everything?" Lincoln asks and I shrug.

"I don't know how to answer that. One minute I'm fine, the next I'm crying, and then a few seconds later I'm mad."

He nods. "Yeah, that sounds about right."

"God, I have so many questions, too," I sigh. "It's starting to feel like I didn't even know my mother."

"Like what?"

"Everything," I answer and his brows shoot up. "I know that sounds dramatic but I literally don't know anything about her anymore."

"Well, tell me about it. That's why I'm here."

I stare at him for a moment, debating how much is safe to tell him before sighing. "My mom left my brother and me a lot of money… like, *a lot*, but the thing is, when we were growing up, it always seemed like we were just scraping by."

"Did she have life insurance?" he asks and I shake my head.

"No, it wasn't life insurance. A lawyer came over to the house and presented us with checks as part of her estate. And then there were all these love letters tucked away in a box and a photo of a little boy."

His brow furrows and a feeling of contentment washes over me, knowing that he's really invested in this conversation and helping me figure this all out as a friend. I halfway expected this whole "friend" thing to be a way to get into my pants but when I speak, it feels like he's really listening and he really cares.

"Could they be from your dad?"

"I don't even know who my dad is so it's possible."

He scowls. "What do you mean you don't know who your dad is?"

"She wouldn't ever tell us."

"Are you sure she even knew?"

I don't like to think that my mother was a bit of a slut but at this point, I can't dismiss anything.

"I'll add that one to the bottom of the list. God! It's driving me crazy. We never had a normal childhood but everything that's come up since she died is just on another level."

"Why didn't you have a normal childhood?"

I sigh and meet his gaze. Normally, I would never unload this much of my past onto a person I barely know but the more I talk to him, the better I feel and something inside me, something I can't ignore, is telling me to trust him.

"As soon as Theo and I were born, my mom hit the road with us. We lived in roadside motels, bouncing from city to city every few months until we turned six and Mom brought us to Baton Rouge."

"So, she was a nomad?" he asks and I shake my head.

"I don't know why we lived like that but I doubt it. Once we settled here, she stayed in the same house until the day she died and seemed perfectly content."

"That is weird," he says, his voice trailing off as Mia approaches with our drinks.

"Your food will be right out."

"Thanks, Mia." I smile at her and when Lincoln turns to look out the window she flashes me a thumbs-up and I roll my eyes. When she leaves, I glance over at Lincoln.

"You got any Valentine's Day plans for tomorrow?" he asks and I laugh.

"What part of "I haven't dated in eight years" made you think I would have Valentine's Day plans? Why? Do you?"

"Naw, as you've pointed out, I'm not really the type."

I nod. "Right."

Even though I knew that and even though it's stupid as hell, hearing him admit that things between us could never be more than friends with benefits stings more than I would like to admit.

Chapter Eight
Lincoln

"Let's get some wine glasses and pop this baby open," one of Tate's friends says as they gather in her living room, curled up on the couches. Tate leaves the room and I watch her walk into the kitchen. She stops in front of the sink and braces her hands on the counter and drops her head.

"So fucking stupid," she mutters to herself and I can't look away from the screen, enthralled by the woman who's been haunting my dreams since the first moment I saw her. My mind drifts back to my shower this morning when I jerked off to images of her in my mind and experienced the most intense orgasm of my fucking life as my cock grows hard again. It's so much more than that, though.

Yeah, I'd do just about anything to get this sexy, bold woman underneath me but whenever I think about that being it, about ending it after one night like I always do, an unexplainable panic rises up in me. And although

I've spent a fair amount of time picturing her naked, I also imagine taking her out on a proper date. In my mind, she'll wear a dress that hugs her lush curves and teases me with all the possibilities once we get back to her house and the soft glow of candlelight will shine in her eyes as she breaks my balls about something stupid.

"Fuck," I mutter, tossing the tablet in the passenger seat of the van before glancing up at her house. I'm losing my fucking mind over this woman. It's not me and I'm in so fucking far over my head. Maybe, when this is all over, I'll finally spend a night screwing her brains out and all this shit will pass so I can get back to my life.

Grabbing the tablet again, I scroll through the cameras until I find all four girls back in the living room with full wine glasses.

"Fuck Valentine's Day," Willow, one of Tate's friends, says, holding her glass up in the air and Mia does the same.

"Here, here."

Tate thrusts her glass above her head, almost spilling it on the white couch before pulling it back down and chugging half of it. My brow shoots up and I watch her as she leans back in the couch, a frown etched into her face. What the hell is up with her tonight?

A large part of me wants to jump out of this van and run in there to make sure she's okay but I can't do that. Damn it, this is so complicated. What happens when she finally finds out that I've been lying to her and spying on her all this time? She'll hate me. The thought makes my chest ache and I rub over my t-shirt, trying to make it go away.

"Tate, what's up with you tonight?" Lexi asks and I perk up, turning the volume up all the way on the tablet.

She shakes her head. "Nothing."

"Uh, yeah right. Something is definitely wrong with you," Mia says, plopping down next to her on the couch and pushing her hair out of her face. My fingers itch to do the same and I blow out a breath.

"It's stupid."

A wry smile stretches across Mia's face. "Oh, so it's a guy then."

Tate nods but doesn't say anything. I know she's talking about me, though, and the thought that I've caused her any upset doesn't sit well with me. Or maybe it's not me. Is it possible that she's been talking to someone else, too? The thought makes me growl.

"Is it the guy you had lunch with yesterday?"

Tate pushes her hand away and grabs her wine glass off the end table, chugging the rest before setting it on the end table. "It's been so fucking long since I've felt like this about anyone and when I do, he's the worst possible guy for me."

I toss the tablet across the car and it hits the window before landing with a thump on the passenger seat. Thank God for the case Streak insisted I put on it.

"How is he the worst guy for you?" someone asks and as much as I want to turn it off, I can't force myself to reach across the van and do it.

"Yeah, I mean, I wouldn't say no to that yummy man," Mia says. "That bad boy vibe just does it for me."

"Me, too," Tate adds. "That's the problem. After high school and the pregnancy scare, I told myself when I decided to date again, I would pick a better guy. The kind of man that wouldn't lie to me or cheat on me, the kind that would treat me like his whole world."

I reach across the van, grabbing the tablet because I can't not look at her any longer.

"And this guy can't be that?"

"He's the type that never sleeps with a girl more than a couple times and calls them all "baby" or "sweetheart" because he can't be bothered to remember their names. He's the kind of guy that always got me in trouble before and I want more than that now."

Her words are spot on and they hit a mark she didn't even realize she was aiming for. I suck in a breath, fighting back the memories but they flood in anyway – reminding me why I promised myself I would never get serious with a woman again. If I close my eyes, I can still smell the scent of that little church packed full of flowers as I stood in front of family and friends, waiting for a bride that was never coming.

My phone rings, snapping me out of my daze, and I turn the volume on the tablet down so I can answer it and drop it in the seat next to me. My baby sister Rowan's name pops up on the screen and I groan.

"What do you want?" I ask, sounding annoyed despite the smile on my face.

"Well, it's nice to talk to you, too, old man. Happy Valentine's Day. You spending it with someone special?"

Rolling my eyes, I grab the tablet and watch Tate as she continues talking to her friends. I wish I knew what she was saying. "Very funny, Ro. You know that I don't do that anymore."

"Damn. I was really hoping this might be the year that a woman knocked you on your ass and made you realize what a fool you are."

I know she's teasing but the moment the words left her mouth, I pictured Tate. "Don't count on that, baby sister."

"Some day, Linc. Some day."

"Yeah, yeah. What's up with you? Did you need something?" I ask, glancing to the side mirror as a car drives past the van.

"Nope. Just wanted to talk to you. It's been awhile."

I nod. "I'm sorry. I've just been busy. How are you? How's Mom?"

"We're good, Linc. You should stop worrying so much."

Sighing, I rub my hand over my face. "Taking care of the two of you is my responsibility."

"No," she snaps. "It's not. You were a kid the same as Nora and me when Dad died. It's not all on you and besides, I'm an adult now. I can take care of myself."

"I know you can but you have to know that I'm always here for you. All it takes is a text or phone call,

Ro, and I'll be on the next plane to Alaska. I would never forgive myself if something happened to you."

She sighs. "When are you going to stop blaming yourself, Lincoln? You couldn't have known."

Tears sting my eyes and I shake my head as I ball up my fist. "Enough."

"You're right. I didn't call to fight with you. Come home soon, okay? We miss you."

"I will. I promise."

"Good. I'll let you get back to whatever you were doing then. I love you."

"Love you, too, Ro. I'll talk to you later."

Hanging up, I release a sigh and lean back in my seat as I try to stamp down all the memories that Rowan brought up before grabbing the tablet and turning the volume up.

"Boys are stupid!" Lexi shouts, holding up another glass of wine and all the other girls follow suit. There's one empty bottle laying on its side on the coffee table and the second is halfway gone already.

"Aw, hell," I mutter. Tate is going to have one hell of a hangover tomorrow. Though, the thought of nursing her back to health is appealing. With a smile teasing my lips, I scan the neighborhood again and jerk to a stop when I see a man sitting in his car behind me. From my vantage point, it seems like he's watching Tate's house as well but I can't tell for sure. I reach for the door handle before thinking better of it and grabbing my phone to snap a picture of his license plate.

Blaze still wants me watching her and truthfully, I'm not ready to give her up yet so I can't confront him out here without a damn good explanation for why I'm also sitting outside her house. One thing is for sure, though, I'm not leaving until I know she's safe.

*   *   *   *

"Hey, guys. Thanks for coming," Rodriguez says, holding his hand up in greeting as Storm and I walk into the small apartment. We've been working with Detective Rodriguez for a couple years now so when he called us for help with a case, we jumped into action. I do a quick scan of the apartment for Laney, the girl he called us here to watch over, but I don't see here.

"What's going on, brother?" Storm asks, stopping in front of the dining room table where Rodriguez has various papers and photos laid out in front of him. They shake hands and Rodriguez sighs.

"I wish I knew how to answer that question."

I point to the papers. "Lay it out for us, man."

"Two days ago, Laney came into the station and asked to speak to me. She wanted to know what could be done about the threatening phone calls she'd been getting and I started looking into it."

I nod. "And what did you find?"

"Not a lot. But I've got this feeling in my gut that there is something going on here and I just need to find it."

"Okay," I murmur, looking over his evidence. One photo grabs my attention and I pull it out, showing it to him. "What's this?"

"One of the phone calls came from a payphone a few blocks away and there are security cameras but either this guy knew about them or he just got really lucky."

I stare down at the dark grainy image of a man's figure and scowl. It's definitely weird.

"What is he saying on the calls?"

"In the beginning, nothing. He would just call her and breathe on the other end of the line, real creepy shit like that. Then, he started telling her how beautiful she was and how much he liked her outfit that day – stuff to let her know that he truly was watching her. Just before she came into the station, he called her beautiful again and said it would be a shame when he had to kill her."

"Jesus Christ," Storm whispers, rubbing his hand across his jaw as I shake my head. That's some sick shit.

"Where is she?"

"Sleeping right now but I'll wake her up before I leave and introduce you guys."

I rifle through some more papers, my mind working over the facts he's already given us. "Is there any indication that he's shown up here at her apartment?"

"Yeah," Rodriguez answers, pulling out a photo of dead flowers. "He left these for her the day she first talked to me to show his anger that she went to the cops. That's when I started staying with her. Captain doesn't want to spare the men to sit a car in front of her place which is why I called y'all."

"And because you think if he sees you leave, he'll think it's safe to come around," I point out and he nods.

"That's the idea anyway. I need proof that he's been here and I need to know who he is."

I nod. "Okay. I think we can handle that."

"There are cameras all over this building so if he shows up, we should get him on camera. Your main focus is protecting her."

"Diego?" a soft voice asks from behind us and we all spin around. Laney's eyes widen and fear flits across her face for a moment before she gets a handle on it.

"Laney, these are the guys from the club that I told you about. This is Kodiak and Storm."

I step forward, holding my hand out. "Hey, it's nice to meet you."

"You, too," she replies, straightening her spine and shaking my hand. This poor girl is scared out of her goddamn mind but she's trying so hard to be brave.

"Someone from the club is going to be with you at all times from now on, okay?" Rodriguez asks and she nods.

"I know I'm probably being a huge pain in the ass but it means so much to me that you're taking this so seriously."

He gathers up his papers from the table and walks over to her, placing a hand on her shoulder. "Laney, he threatened your life. That is as serious as it gets."

She sucks in a breath and nods.

"I'm going to dig into this case as much as I can and call me if you need anything, okay?"

She nods again. He pulls away and heads toward the door before turning back to us. "Call me if you run into any problems."

"We'll take good care of her," Storm assures him and he nods again before leaving. He closes the door behind Rodriguez and locks it before glancing at me with a raised brow.

"What the hell was that about?" I ask. Rodriguez seemed more involved than usual and I have to wonder if he's got something going on with Laney. Storm shrugs.

"If I had to guess, I'd say he's sleeping with her."

I sigh and walk over to the chair in the corner before sinking into it. It isn't ideal since Rodriguez will have a harder time being objective but I really don't care if he is sleeping with her as long as he's honest with us.

"Can I ask you a question?" I say to Laney as she sits on the sofa. She nods.

"You and Rodriguez... are you a thing?"

She smiles. "Yes."

"All right, then," Storm grumbles, sinking into the other side of the couch as Laney frowns.

"Is that a problem?"

I shake my head. "Nah, sweetheart. We were just curious. If we're going to protect you, it helps to have all the information, you know?"

"Yeah, I understand," she agrees before her teeth sink into her bottom lip. "Do y'all mind if I watch TV?"

"It's your house, Darlin'. Do whatever you like and we'll be here to keep you safe."

She turns on the TV and I pull my phone out of my pocket, a photo of Tate greeting me as soon as I unlock my screen. Fighting back a smile, I pull up the feed from her house and search through the cameras before I find her lying in bed, reading. Fuck, that might be even sexier than the time I peeked in on her getting undressed. Yeah, it happened. Don't fucking judge me, though. I'm only a man. I need to see her again.

Closing out of the cameras, I pull up our texts and send one to her.

Me:
You free this weekend?

I go back to the camera and watch her place her book on the bed as she grabs her phone. When she reads my message, she smiles and if I wasn't sitting with Laney and Storm right now, I would jump up and do a fist pump. My phone vibrates in my hand and I click on her message.

Tate:
Why?

Me:
Do you always have to be difficult?
I want to take you up to my cabin.

"Dude," Storm says and my head whips up, already listening for danger before I realize that he's smiling.

"What?"

He starts laughing. "You're so fucking screwed."

"What the fuck are you talking about?"

Dropping his head back, he laughs harder before mimicking me on my phone with a wide goofy smile on his face. "I'm talking about you with your nose buried in that phone, texting a girl."

"You have no idea what I'm doing on my phone," I scoff.

"Sure, I don't. I was only the exact same way a year ago when I met Ali and now look at me," he says, holding up his left hand where his wedding ring sits.

"What's her name?" Laney asks and I scoff again.

"There's no girl."

Storm turns to Laney and points to my face. "You see that face right there, sweetheart?"

She nods.

"That face means there's definitely a girl."

My phone vibrates again and I roll my eyes before glancing down at it.

Tate:
I don't know about that.
It sounds an awful lot like a romantic getaway.

Me:
Just as friends, scouts honor.
It will help you get your mind off things.

"Now, you see that grin on his face?" Storm asks and I glance up to see both of them studying me with smirks.

"Yeah," Laney answers him.

"That grin means he's head over fucking heels in love with her and the best part is he doesn't even realize it yet."

"Shut the fuck up," I snap, grabbing a throw pillow from behind my back and chucking it across the room. "You don't get to weigh in on these things anymore."

"Why? 'Cause I'm married to the most incredible woman you've ever met? I think that makes me a goddamn expert on that stupid ass look you're sportin'."

My phone vibrates in my hand and I ignore him as I glance down.

Tate:
Okay, but just know that I'm bringing my
Taser and knife so you better not try anything.

Me:
You won't regret it, Darlin'.

Every Breath You Take

Chapter Nine
Tatum

I Don't Dance by Lee Brice starts playing on the radio as I creep down what I assume is Lincoln's driveway. Trees line either side of the road, so thick that I can only see about ten feet or so into the forest before everything becomes muddled. My heart skips a beat as I scan the gravel road in front of me, looking for an opening, and I slam on the brakes, gripping the steering wheel tight. I'm asking for trouble by agreeing to this but when he texted me yesterday to invite me, I couldn't think of a good enough reason to say no. Now, as I inch closer to the address he gave me, every single reason why this is a terrible idea runs through my mind.

I shouldn't be here.

My dream from this morning, one in which Lincoln pressed me up against the kitchen counter and knocked a plate to the floor as he kissed me like it was his saving grace, fills my mind and I shift in my seat – needing relief that I'm not going to get anytime soon.

What the hell was I thinking? This whole thing would be a hell of a lot easier if I weren't so damn attracted to him. But, of course, I am. A part of me thinks I only like him this much because I've forbidden myself from acting on it. Like, maybe if I hadn't, I wouldn't find him as appealing. Or maybe if Mom hadn't just died, I wouldn't be feeling so attached to a man I just met but I can't help but think that he understands me in ways that I don't even understand myself yet. My entire world has just shifted and he knows what that looks like from the other side while I'm still muddling through it.

"It's going to be okay," I whisper to myself, the shakiness of my voice betraying me. I shake my head and suck in a breath. No, it has to be okay. I've laid out clear boundaries for our friendship and he agreed with me so what does it matter if we'll be sharing a space for forty-eight hours? We can control ourselves and act like adults. Besides, Lincoln was right. I do need to get away from my life for a little while. Living in Mom's house is stressful. I constantly feel like I'm going to open up a box or dig around in a closet and discover another secret that she kept hidden from Theo and me. And the more I learn about all the lies, all the secrets, the angrier I get.

Nodding, I ease my foot off the brake as *Losing Sleep* by Chris Young starts playing on the radio. Ugh. What is with all these sappy songs today? Leaning forward, I switch the station and *Lips on You* by Maroon 5 fills the car as the trees open up, revealing a quaint little lake with a red A-frame house on the far side. I can just make out the outline of Lincoln standing in front of a grill and I lick my lips, unable to stop myself.

A.M. Myers

Okay, so I'm not going to sleep with him but does that mean that I can't appreciate how damn fine he looks in his black wife beater and jeans? Black and gray tattoos fill both his arms and I find myself wishing I were closer so I could study each one. He glances up at the sound of the car I borrowed from Mia rolling over the gravel road and he flashes me a smile as he waves. Butterflies take flight in my belly and I take a deep breath as I round the lake and park in front of his house.

"Hey, you made it," he calls, setting a pair of tongs down before sauntering over to me. I'm so fucking screwed.

"Yeah. Nice place." I nod to the house and he turns to it.

"Thanks. It's my little piece of paradise. You hungry?"

My stomach growls and I nod. "Very."

"Well, come on. I've got steaks on the grill and they are just about done."

I grab my bag out of the back seat before following him over to the grill, where he also has a fire pit and a couple tables set up.

"Seriously," I say, sitting down and setting my bag on one of the tables. "This is really nice. It's so peaceful out here."

"Told you this is just what you needed."

Smiling, I nod. "This might be the only time in the history of ever that you're going to hear this from me but you were right."

147

"Shit…" he drawls, barely holding back a laugh. "I feel like we should watch the skies for swarms of locusts."

I bark out a laugh and grab a stick from the ground before chucking it at him. "I'm not that bad."

"Naw, you're not bad at all." His gaze heats before dropping to my lips and my belly clenches as my heartbeat pounds in my ears. Time seems to stretch between us and out here in the middle of nowhere, it's so easy to forget everything that's happened in the past few weeks and all my reasons for resisting him.

The growling of my stomach breaks our trance and he turns toward the grill. "You want to eat inside or out?"

"It's so beautiful today so let's eat outside."

He nods. "Sounds good. Hang tight and I'll go grab our plates."

I stand up and glance toward the house. "Oh, I can help you."

"Nope," he replies, his voice strained and I scowl. "You just stay here and I'll be right back."

Turning, I watch him as he jogs up to the house and yanks open one of the sliding glass doors before disappearing inside and I plop back down in my seat, wondering what happened. My phone vibrates in my pocket and I grab it, smiling at Theo's name on the screen.

"Hey, what are you doing?" I answer, a feeling of contentment washing over me as I stare out at the water.

"Just got off work. What about you?"

I glance back at the house. "Hanging out with a friend."

"Mia?" he asks and I shake my head.

"Nope."

"Willow?"

I laugh. "You don't know him."

"Him?" he asks, his voice instantly shifting to protective brother mode and I roll my eyes, lean back in my seat, and close my eyes.

"Yes, Theo. Him."

"What's his name? Where did you meet him? Give me his social security number."

"Oh, for fuck's sake. You're insane."

The little growl on the other end of the line makes me smile even as I roll my eyes again. "I'm serious, T. Who is this guy? You didn't mention anyone to me when I was there and you've got money now. You need to be careful that he's not using you."

"Theo!" I shout through my laughter. "I haven't even spent any of that money so I don't think men are suddenly looking at me like I'm their sugar mama."

"I'm worried about you," he grumbles as the sound of the screen door opening behind me catches my attention. I glance over my shoulder and watch Lincoln as he walks down the steps with a pile of plates and silverware in his hands. "Hey, I gotta go. We'll talk later, okay?"

"Don't think this is over, Tate!" he yells into the phone as I hang up, giggling at his reaction. Back in high school when I was getting into trouble, Theo was always stressing over where I was and who I was with but it's not something he's had to think about in a long time. Not that he has to now anyway. Lincoln and I are just friends.

"You want any help?" I ask as he fumbles with one of the steak knives and he glances up, glaring at me.

"I got it. You just sit your pretty ass there."

My brow arches. "You better watch it unless you want a repeat of our first meeting."

"Maybe I do. You're not as scary as you think you are."

I scoff and hop up from my chair. "You'd be singing a different tune if you emptied my purse right now."

He studies me for a moment, trying to decide if I'm telling the truth and I almost want him to do it just so I can see his face when he pulls out the Taser, knife, and pepper spray. Not to mention the pistol I stowed in the glove box of Mia's car.

"I never know if you're serious or not about the weapons."

Crossing my arms behind my back, I flash him an innocent smile. "Why don't you take a peek?"

My stomach growls again and he shakes his head. "Why don't you get some food and tell me why you feel like you need to carry around multiple ways to defend yourself?"

Sighing, I take a plate from him and go to the grill where I grab the tongs and put one of the steaks on my plate.

"What's in the tin foil?" I ask, eyeing the shiny little pouches on the grill.

"Potatoes and veggies."

I grab one and set it on my plate before walking back over to the table and sitting down as Lincoln passes me. With him behind me at the grill, I take a deep breath, mentally reminding myself that I've got this before he walks back over and sits across from me.

"So, how was your Valentine's Day?" he asks as I cut into my steak and I picture two nights ago when the girls and I went through five bottles of wine and spent hours bashing the men in our lives – including the one staring at me now.

"Uh…uneventful. You."

He nods, staring at his plate. "Same."

Something is off with him tonight but I can't quite place my finger on it. "What the hell is wrong with you?"

"What?" he asks, his head snapping up.

"You're being weird. What's going on?"

Shaking his head, he finishes chewing before setting the fork on his plate and sighing. "Sorry. It's just… uh, not a good day."

"Why?"

"Forget it, it's nothing," he says, waving his hand through the air like he might be able to physically push whatever is bothering him away.

"Hey," I snap and his head jerks up, his gaze meeting mine. A quiet gasp slips past my lips at the pain etched into his face and I stand up, rounding the table and straddling the bench next to him. "You can talk to me, Lincoln."

Reaching forward, I lay my hand on his face and he sucks in a stuttered breath.

"I'm sorry, Tate. I thought if I invited you here, maybe it wouldn't be so hard but I guess I was wrong."

I scowl, searching his face for answers. "What wouldn't be so hard? Please just talk to me. I'm your friend."

I scoot closer to him and he glances up at me.

"Tomorrow is the nine year anniversary of my little sister's death."

Tears flood my eyes in an instant as I gasp and squeeze his hand. "Oh my god, Lincoln. I'm so sorry."

"It's something that's always in the back of my mind, you know? Something that always haunts me."

I try to put myself in his shoes and imagine what it would be like if I lost Theo and the pain is unbearable. Honestly, I don't know how I would survive.

"What was her name?" I ask and he quickly wipes away a tear.

"Nora."

Our knees touch as I scoot closer to him and I take his hand in both of mine. "Will you tell me what happened to her?"

"Just…uh, please don't think less of me."

I shake my head. "Why would I ever think less of you?"

"Because it's all my fault."

"What happened?" I whisper. I don't believe that it was actually his fault for a minute but I know hearing me say that wouldn't help him right now. He sucks in a breath and nods.

"Right after Nora graduated high school, she met this guy, Ben. I did the usual big brother thing and he

seemed like an all right guy so I was cool with them
dating. Eight months later, Nora decided to end things
and Ben lost it. I didn't know it at the time but he'd been
stalking her for months, begging her to take him back
and it didn't matter that she ignored him because he just
kept at it." His voice breaks and I wish I could wrap him
up in a hug but I want him to finish his story first.

"About two months later, Nora started dating
someone new and that's when Ben really went off the
deep end. For the first time, she was scared of him and
what he was capable of so she came to me for help. At
the time, I worked two jobs to help support my family
and I always intended to look into it but I never got the
chance because Ben killed her and her new boyfriend."

"Lincoln," I whisper, tears running down my
cheeks. His hand trembles in mine and I can't hold back
anymore. I wrap my arms around him. "I'm so sorry."

"I understand if you want to leave," he murmurs
and I squeeze him tighter, shaking my head. How could I
possibly leave him?

"I'm not going anywhere and her death was not
your fault. I'll say it as many times as you want me to but
I get the feeling it wouldn't do any good."

"I should have been there for her, Tate. Taking
care of them after Dad died was my responsibility and I
failed her."

Imagining myself at fifteen, I don't know how I
would have handled everything I'm dealing with now
and the full weight of the pain he's been carrying around
for years crashes down on me. Pulling back, I cup his
cheek and turn his face toward mine.

"I'm so sorry."

His brow furrows as his eyes search mine. "What are you sorry for?"

"All this time, all I've been focused on is my own pain. I was so blinded by it that I couldn't see how much you still carry around every day. I've been a shitty friend but my eyes are open now and I see you, Lincoln. I really see you."

He sucks in a breath and his gaze drops to my mouth for a second before he leans in and plants his lips on mine. I'm frozen for a moment and then a big, strong arm wraps around my waist and pulls me into his lap. All bets are off. His hand slips into my hair as he flicks his tongue against the seam of my lips and nothing else in my life has ever felt this…right. In this moment, I don't care that he's the wrong guy for me and I don't care about the promise I made to myself all those years ago because I'm lost in him.

"Lincoln," I whisper, rocking my hips over the growing bulge in his jeans and he groans, gripping me tighter. At the firm touch of his hand, I sigh and my lips part in invitation as I grab the back of his neck. A large hand presses against the bare skin on my back and my body arches into his, aching with a need unlike any I've ever felt before. Pulling back, I look down into his eyes and I know that I'm not going to stop this. Not tonight, despite any consequences I'll face in the morning.

Or maybe, just maybe… we could be more.

"Fuck," he growls, shutting his eyes as he pushes me away from him. "You should leave."

A.M. Myers

Before I can say anything, he picks me up, deposits me back on the bench, and stomps up to the house. As the screen door slams shut, tears burn my eyes and I hate him for doing to me what I always knew he would.

No, he doesn't get to have this power over me.

He doesn't deserve my tears.

My hands tremble and anger racks my body as I stand up, swinging my leg over the bench before marching over to the other table and ripping my bag off it. Pain throbs in my chest and I suck in a stuttered breath as I turn toward the car and practically sprint to it before throwing myself behind the wheel. The fall is coming. I can feel it building inside me and the crash is going to be spectacular. God, I was so stupid. From the start, I knew better than to get involved with Lincoln but with my mother's death, I leaned on him and I didn't even realize that I'd begun to need him. I always knew better and yet, I still went there.

The first tear slips down my face and I grit my teeth as I start the car and slam it into reverse, flipping around way faster than I should before flying back down the way I came in, pounding my fist on the steering wheel. So, so stupid. It takes every ounce of self-control I possess to not turn this car around and taze Lincoln just on principle. I was vulnerable with him in a way that I never am with any one else and he rejected me as soon as I was ready to give him everything. It burns more than I care to admit. Not to mention, I'm truly alone now. The only friend I had who understood the emotions that rock through me on a daily basis just walked away from me.

On second thought... renewed anger surges through me and I slam on the brakes before flipping around on the narrow gravel road. As I ease my foot off the brake, I reach into my purse and grab my Taser, flipping it on so it has time to power up. Fuck this asshole for thinking he can play me after I let him in. I don't do that shit with anyone and I fucking trusted him. When I get to the house, I put the car in park and jump out with the Taser in my hand. My heart pounds in my ears and my knuckles hurt from balling my hand up as I stomp up onto the porch and pound on the door.

It flies open and he looks surprised for a moment before he scowls. "I'm sorry, Tate. I can't do this..."

I press the end of the Taser to his beefy arm and hold it there as his body seizes and drops to the floor like a goddamn rock, still twitching.

"Fuck you, motherfucker," I snarl before spinning on my heel and marching back down the stairs to the car and climbing inside. He's struggling to get up as I flip the Taser off and put the car in reverse again, flying out of the driveway. Serves him fucking right. Don't play games with a girl that knows endless ways to cause you pain.

As I drive closer to the city, my mind drifts back to the kiss and fresh tears well up in my eyes, irritating the hell out of me. I'm not a crier. I don't do shit like this but here I am, bawling like a baby because a damn guy rejected me. But, then again, I've never experienced a kiss like that either. It was damn near poetic and I can't stop myself from wondering what it means.

"Don't fucking go there," I growl to myself, glancing in the rearview mirror and wincing at my red, puffy eyes.

I spend the rest of the drive to my house focusing on not thinking of anything and it's harder than I imagined it would be. For some reason, my brain wants to torture my heart tonight and the look on Lincoln's face just before he leaned forward and destroyed everything between us keeps popping into my mind.

Pulling into the driveway, I slam the car in park and grab my purse and bag out of the passenger seat before climbing out and trudging up the front walk. When I reach the front door, I fumble with my keys for a moment before noticing the note taped to the door with my name scrawled on the front. Scowling, I rip it off and unfold it.

LAUNCELOT
Yes, look, it's true that children are punished for the sins of their fathers. That's why I'm worried about you. I've always been straightforward with you, so now I'm telling you what I think. Cheer up, because I think you're going to hell. There's only one hope for you, and even that's a kind of illegitimate hope.

JESSICA
What hope is that, may I ask?

157

LAUNCELOT

You can hope your father isn't your real father. Maybe your mother fooled around, and you aren't the King's daughter.

JESSICA

That really is an illegitimate hope. Then I'd be punished for the sins of my mother.

LAUNCELOT

In that case I'm afraid you're damned by both your father and your mother. When you avoid one trap, you fall into another. You're in trouble either way.

It's in modern text but I recognize the scene from *The Merchant of Venice* by William Shakespeare that my high school drama program put on when I was a junior. The only other change is when it says, "King's Daughter". The original line was "Jew's Daughter". My scowl deepens as I study the note but there's nothing that stands out about it, nothing special. The hair on my arms raises and I glance over my shoulder as I slip the key into the lock, eager to escape from the feeling of someone's eyes on me. As I twist the deadbolt, unlocking the door, a car door slams and my hand is in my purse before I know it, gripping the knife tightly.

Mrs. Saunders across the street waves to me when I turn and I force a smile to my face, still on edge, and my mind racing with the possibilities of what this note means. And in the back of my mind, I can't help but think it's one more thing to add to the growing list of questions my mother left behind in her wake.

Every Breath You Take

A.M. Myers

Chapter Ten
Tatum

Sighing, I watch the customer walk out of the gas station with his soda before plopping down on the little stool tucked away behind the counter and cross my arms over my chest. I spent the whole weekend analyzing that note, trying to figure out what it really means and its implications for me but I'm as lost as I've been since the moment my mother died. And I can't help but feel like I'm being watched now. I searched the surveillance cameras set up around the house but whoever taped the note to my door was as average as they come and he kept his face covered.

My gaze flicks to the windows surrounding me and I shudder as my phone rings. Slipping off the stool, I grab it out of my bag and make sure Reed isn't looking before pressing it to my ear.

"Hello?"

"Hey, T. What are you up to?" Theo asks and I let out a relieved breath. I've been so fucking paranoid since that note showed up so it's nice to talk to him.

"Not much. Just at work."

"Oh, do you need to go?"

I shake my head, scanning the empty parking lot "Naw, I can talk for a minute. What's up?"

"I just wanted to see how you are. My twin sense was tingling."

I snort, slipping out from behind the counter and ducking into one of the aisles. "Your twin sense is broken then."

"Or you're lying."

"I don't think that's it," I lie, the high pitch of my voice betraying me.

"Start talking, Tate," he orders and I sigh. I don't want to tell him about the note because he will just freak out and there's nothing he can do from all the way in Charleston.

"It just this guy." It's not a total lie and honestly, Lincoln has been haunting my dreams these past few days.

"Wait. The guy from Friday night? What the hell did he do to you? Tell me the truth, Tate. I'll call my chief and get in the damn car right now."

"Slow your fucking roll, Theodore," I say as I roll my eyes. God, he's so overprotective. "Do you honestly think he could do anything to me that I didn't want him to do?"

"Then why are you upset?"

A.M. Myers

Sighing, I rub my fingers into my temple. "Because he kissed me."

"And...you didn't want him to...?"

"No, I wanted him to but after he kissed me, he just said "fuck" and "you should go" before stomping into his house."

"I see," he replies and I can tell he's trying not to laugh. "And then what happened?"

"Then, I marched up to his door and tased his big, stupid ass before leaving."

He starts laughing and he's so damn loud that I have to pull the phone away from my ear.

"Of course you did. You better be careful or someone's going to call the police one of these days."

"Why?" I cry. "I don't run around in the streets laughing and tasing innocent civilians. If I tase someone, there's a damn good reason and they know they deserve it."

"I'm just sayin', sis."

"Tate!" Reed calls from the office and I shrink down the aisle, covering my mouth and the phone with my hand.

"Hey, I gotta go. My boss just yelled for me."

"Call me later, okay? I love you."

I nod. "I love you, too."

Hanging up, I slip my phone in my pocket and walk to the office, arching a brow as I stand in the doorway.

"Yeah?"

He tosses a notebook at me. "I need you to go in the back and do inventory."

"On it," I reply, snagging a pen off his desk. Maybe I should point out that this is his job but I'd prefer to be in the back room today. I haven't been able to shake the feeling that someone is watching me since I started my shift two hours ago.

Once in the back room, I start going through the shelves and my mind drifts to Lincoln. I hate myself for it but I kind of miss him. Before Friday night, he would send me at least one text a day asking me how I was doing but my phone has been painfully silent since I drove away from his house. I guess I can't be surprised though. If he wasn't already thinking about ditching me, tasing him probably sealed the deal.

Whatever.

I don't need him.

"So, Tate," Reed says and I gasp, glancing up to find him standing in the door. "I was thinking about what you said to me last week. It was very disrespectful."

"And?"

He takes a step toward me and I wish I had my trusty Taser in my pocket right now. "And I can't have my employees speaking to me like that."

"Maybe you should act like our boss instead of a prick, then."

Another step closer and he wags his finger at me, chuckling. "See, there's that mouth again. Why keep flinging barbs at me when I can think of such better uses for it?"

My brow arches and anger surges through my veins. "You mean like filing a police report on you for sexual harassment?"

"Who would believe you? I mean, with your past and all..." He trails off and my mouth pops open. "You see, one of my buddies used your services once and when he came in here to see me, he recognized you. I gotta say, though. You look better than any hooker I've ever seen."

"I'm done," I snap with a deadly smile on my face as I shove the notepad into his hands. This job is not worth the fucking trouble. I try to slip past him but he reaches out, wrapping his hand around my arm and I react without a thought, clocking him in the side of the head with my free hand. He blinks in shock and stumbles but doesn't release me so I stomp on his foot with the heel of my boot and he shrieks in pain as my arm falls out of his grasp.

He limps after me as I jog to the counter and grab my bag from under the register. When he comes toward me again, I slip the knife out of my bag and hold it out in front of me. His hands shoot up in surrender and I circle around him until my back is to the door.

"You can't just walk away from me, bitch," he snarls and I smile, backing away from him.

"Fucking watch me, pervert."

When I get to the door, I slip outside and walk to Mia's car, keeping a firm grip on the knife until I'm safely inside with the doors locked. Sighing, I glance up at the gas station and relief washes over me knowing that I'll never have to come back here.

* * * *

"Thanks for letting me borrow the car," I say to Mia, handing her the keys as we walk into the restaurant where we're meeting Willow and Lexi for lunch.

"No problem. What did you need it for?"

Sighing, I shake my head. "Lincoln invited me to his cabin over the weekend."

Her eyes light up but she doesn't get a chance to say anything as the waitress approaches us.

"Hi! Just two?" she asks.

"No, we've got two more coming."

"We're here," someone says from behind me and I peek over my shoulder as Willow and Lexi walk up to us. Turning back to the waitress, I nod and she grabs four menus before instructing us to follow her. The girls are all whispering about something and giggling but I can't be bothered to even pay attention. Not after this past weekend and yesterday when I quit at the gas station.

The waitress leads us to a table and sets a menu down in front of each chair as we all circle it, plopping down in a seat.

"Can I get y'all something to drink?" she asks.

"Coke, please," Lexi says and the waitress nods before turning to Mia.

"Sweet tea."

She turns to me. "Just a water, please."

"And I'll get a coffee," Willow chimes in and the waitress flashes us a smile before turning to leave. Once she's out of ear shot, all three girls smile at me.

166

"So…uh, Mia tells us that you went to Lincoln's cabin over the weekend," Lexi says and I grimace. During our anti Valentine's Day get together, I spilled the beans about Lincoln – everything from how I am attracted to him but he's just a friend to how I'd maybe like to be something more.

"I went up there Friday night but left shortly there after and he and I are done."

They share a look before Mia lays a hand on my shoulder. "Sweetie, what happened?"

"Don't y'all have some juicy boy gossip of your own that you could share instead of me?"

Lexi grins. "Yes, we do but we're talking about you right now."

My phone starts rattling on the table and Mia snatches it up before I have a chance to.

"Ooh, look who it is." She turns the phone to me and I glare at Lincoln's photo on the screen. "Maybe we should we ask him what happened."

"Fine, I'll tell you. Just give me my phone."

She hands it over and I sigh, fiddling with the silverware on the table. "So, I went up there Friday and we started having dinner outside but I could tell he was upset so I asked him what was wrong. After he told me, he kissed me."

Frowning, Willow glances around the table at the other girls. "I'm sorry, back up. Why was he upset?"

"That's his business," I tell her, shaking my head and she nods.

"Okay, and then he kissed you?"

I nod.

"How exactly does that relate to the two of you being done?"

The waitress comes back with our drinks, saving me for another minute as she sets them down in front of us.

"Are y'all ready to order?" she asks and Lexi shakes her head.

"We still need a minute."

She nods and walks away from the table as three sets of eyes turn back to me.

"Continue," Mia prompts and I sigh, my mind replaying the scene from Friday night and I swear I can still feel his lips pressed to mine.

"When he finished kissing me, he started cursing, told me to leave, and stormed into the house."

Everyone's eyes grow wide and they all glance at each other before turning back to me.

"He just left you outside?"

I nod. "Yes."

"And what did you do?" Mia asks cautiously because... well because she knows me.

"Got in my car and started driving away..."

"Oh, thank god," she breathes, placing her hand over her heart.

"...before I decided to turn around and tase him."

Willow starts laughing, Lexi shakes her head, and Mia gasps.

"Jesus Christ, Tate. You can't just go around tasing people."

My brow furrows and I shoot a glare in her direction. "Why does everyone keep saying that to me?

The asshole made me feel like I could open up to him, share my pain with him and hope for something more for the first time in a long time and I'm the bad guy for shocking him?"

"Well, it's a little dramatic," Lexi interjects and I roll my eyes.

"I didn't shoot him, okay? And I could have because I had a gun in the glove box but the situation didn't warrant it. Don't act like I'm some crazy deranged person. The punishment fit the crime."

"For fuck's sake," Mia whispers, turning to her menu and flipping it open. "Normal people don't go around tasing people for things, Tate."

"Well, maybe they should. Folks would be less likely to be assholes if there was a threat of tasing."

Willow chuckles under her breath. "So, I take it you haven't heard from him since?"

"Nope. And I don't expect to."

"He just called you," Mia snaps, pointing to my phone and I shrug.

"So? I didn't answer and I won't answer. He's dead to me."

"Well, rest in peace to your non relationship then," she says, holding her glass in the air and I do the same before taking a sip of water.

"I wouldn't write him off just yet," Lexi points out and I shake my head.

"I already have and I'm focused on other things."

Mia leans back in the chair and crosses her arms over her chest. "Like what?"

"Like talking to Roger about getting more hours at the diner and getting registered for college."

"Tate," Lexi exclaims, looking bewildered. "How the hell are you going to work more hours at the diner, work at the gas station, *and* enroll in school? When will you sleep?"

"Oh," I murmur, thinking back to yesterday when I stormed out of the store and quit my job. I also haven't told the girls about the money my mom left me either. The only person I shared that with was... Lincoln. "I quit at the gas station."

"Why?"

I suck in a breath. "I didn't have much choice when Reed cornered me in the back room and tried to blackmail me into giving him a blowjob."

"Oh, fuck," Mia whispers.

"Shit," Willow says and Lexi shakes her head. Mia grabs my arms and turns me to face her, her eyes wide.

"This is important, Tate. Did you kill him?"

I laugh, shaking my head. "No. Because I told you, I'm not some deranged person. Y'all have no faith in me."

"No, sweetie. I have infinite faith in your abilities to defend yourself. I worry about your temper sometimes though."

Shrugging, I shake off her grip and grab my water, taking a sip. "Whatever. No one's died yet."

She turns to the group with those wide eyes again. "Yet. She fucking said "yet". I feel like I need to ground you from your guns or something."

"Stop it," I scold through my giggles. I've been in a sour mood for the past three days but only twenty minutes with my girls has turned that all around. "Tell me all about your love lives now."

As Willow launches into her latest dating adventure, I sit back in my seat and let my gaze roam around the table to each girl as a smile forms on my face. Yeah, they may not understand what it feels like to lose a parent but these girls are my rocks and they are here for me unconditionally so fuck Lincoln. I don't need him.

Every Breath You Take

Chapter Eleven
Tatum

Stepping out onto the screened in porch off the dining room, I sink into one of the wicker chairs and let out a sigh as I bring my coffee cup to my lips. There's a chill in the air despite the bright morning sunlight piercing through the old oak trees out in front of the house and birds are chirping sweetly above my head. It's almost idyllic.

The phone rings for the sixth time in the last hour and I sigh, glancing through the open door into the dining room. The call has come in every ten minutes on the dot since seven this morning and I'm quickly losing patience with whoever is on the other end of the line. The machine picks up and since it's just past the door, I can hear everything when the heavy, creepy breathing starts up again.

At first, I thought it was maybe a wrong number or the caller had a bad signal but when the next call came ten minutes later, I was less convinced that that was the case. By the time the phone rang for a third time, I knew it was intentional and meant for me. Maybe it's just a prank. In fact, it doesn't seem like a childish thing Reed might do but my mind tends to go darker than that and I can't help but wonder if it has anything to do with the note taped to my door the other day.

When the phone stops ringing, I stand with my mug in my hand and walk back into the house, making sure the door is locked behind me before grabbing my pistol off the dining room table and stomping back to Mom's bedroom. Theo and I avoided her room when we started going through her things and it wasn't until the note showed up that I ventured in here but since then, I've been spending a lot of time in the safe room.

I open the closet door, revealing the tiny space she used to store her clothes. Pushing them to the side, I go to the back wall and press on the hidden control panel. With a little pressure, it pops right out and as soon as I enter the code, the door swings open, revealing a long L-shaped room. There's TVs along one wall and I flip them on, watching as the video feed from the cameras fills the screens. When I was a wild, crazy teenager, I hated that Mom had cameras all over the house and could see what I was doing all the time but now I understand it. This room is where I've felt safest since that note showed up. Something that comforts and annoys me to no end.

The doorbell rings and I jerk out of my thoughts, glancing up at the screen that shows the front door. Lincoln rocks back and forth, his hands shoved in his pockets and I sigh, wondering if he's here to bitch me out about tasing him. Honestly, I'm surprised it took him this long. A heavy sigh slips past my lips and I set my coffee down on the desk, grabbing the pistol and tucking it into the waistband of my jeans.

Might as well hurry up and get this over with.

Stepping out of the closet, I close the outer door but leave the hidden door open for a quick escape. Not that I think Lincoln will truly hurt me but it makes me feel better to have multiple plans in place when everything feels so off balance. When I get to the living room, his gaze locks with mine through the glass on the front door and I suck in a breath, those damn butterflies taking flight in my belly again.

"What do you want?" I yell.

"Open the door, please."

I arch a brow, slowly approaching the door. "You mad?"

"For tasing me? Yeah, I'm a little fucking mad, Tate."

Rolling my eyes, I unlock the door and open it, propping my hand on my hip. "You deserved it."

"Are you kidding me? Have you ever been tased? That shit hurts. How did I deserve that?"

"Uh, well, first of all, yes I have been tased. And you deserved it because you're playing fucking games with me. Stupid move on your part, really."

He growls and I narrow my eyes into a glare.

"I'm not playing games."

Like I'm going to buy that.

"What do you want, Lincoln?"

He takes a step back, rubbing the back of his neck as he clear his throat. "I want to talk to you."

"What could we possibly have to talk about?" I ask. I think after Friday night, everything is pretty fucking clear.

"Can I just come in, please?"

I shake my head. "Naw, you're good there."

"Goddamn it, Tate!" he roars and my eyes widen as I watch him start pacing in front of the door, my hand twitching to grab the gun behind my back. "Why does everything have to be so damn difficult with you?"

"It doesn't... as long as you do what I want."

His gaze snaps to mine and he balls his fists up before turning away and slowly blowing out a breath.

"I don't want to lose you."

Releasing the door, I cross my arms over my chest. "I think that ship has sailed."

"Don't say that."

"We can't go back to being just friends," I tell him and he nods, turning back to me. The two of us being friends was a terrible idea from the start with how attracted we are to each other. It was always doomed to end the way it did.

"I know."

I scowl. "So what are you saying?"

Whiskey eyes meet mine and I suck in a breath at the heat raging in his gaze. He takes a step toward me and I love and hate how weak he makes me feel.

"I want more."

"No, you don't. You said yourself that you're not a relationship guy."

"There's a lot you don't know about me," he whispers, closing the space between us and reaching up to cup my cheek. My eyes flutter closed and I lean into his touch, completely at his mercy. "Shit happened and my life fell apart. I haven't been in a relationship in six years and I had no intention of ever being in one again but you make me want to try, Tate. You make me hope for things I thought I had no business hoping for anymore."

"Oh," I whisper, opening my eyes and meeting his gaze.

"Yeah, oh."

My teeth sink into my lip. "So, more then? A real relationship?"

"Nothing would make me happier."

"I swear to God," I murmur, tears burning my eyes as I shake my head. "If you're playing me again, I will kill you."

He chuckles, nodding. "I know you will, Sweetheart."

Leaning in, his lips hover above mine and I lose my train of thought for a second before I press on his chest and he pulls back, scowling at me.

"If we're going to do this, we need to lay all our cards on the table."

He studies me for a moment before nodding. "Okay."

"Come on in, then," I whisper, my hands shaking with nerves. There are still things about me and my past that Lincoln doesn't know and I honestly have no idea how he'll take them. He steps into the house and I scan the street as I shut the door and lock it again.

"You want some coffee?" I ask, turning to face him and he nods.

"That sounds good… you know how I like it."

I am reminded of the first day we met in the diner and I smirk as I brush past him. "I'm gonna dump it on your lap if you're not careful."

"Eh, I don't think you will," he calls after me and I laugh.

"And here I thought you knew me better than that already."

Peeking over my shoulder, I catch his shudder just as the phone starts to ring and I sigh. I brace my hands on the counter and close my eyes, counting to ten in my head as I feel Lincoln step up behind me.

"You gonna get that?" he murmurs and I shake my head, snapping up and grabbing a mug off the open shelving by the sink.

"Nope."

The machine picks up as I pour his coffee and heavy breathing fills the room.

"What the fuck is that?" he growls, marching over to the machine and reaching out to grab the phone.

"Don't!"

He glances up at me, his face set in a glare. "What the hell is going on, Tate?"

"I don't know. It's just a prank call or something. They've been coming all morning."

His eyes widen before he walks back over to me and crosses his big arms over his chest. "That doesn't sound like a prank call."

"Okay, so it may be… my boss from the gas station."

His jaw ticks. "And why would he be calling you like that?"

"Because I quit?" I suggest and his eyes narrow. "After, I pulled a knife on him."

"Jesus Christ," he breathes, pinching the bridge of his nose. "Any particular reason that you pulled a knife on him?"

I shrug. "He tried to blackmail me into giving him head and when I said no, he grabbed me and wouldn't let go."

"Motherfucker," he snarls, looking toward the machine as the message finally cuts off. He clenches his jaw and he balls his fists, looking ready to murder someone.

"Hey, it's okay because I took care of it."

"Yeah?" he asks, turning back to me. "And what if he decides to take this further and shows up here?"

I laugh, picturing just how that would go down. Reed wouldn't even know what hit him. "Oh, I wish he would."

"You're terrifying," he tells me, a smile teasing his lips and I grin.

"Only if you cross me so, you know… don't do that."

He nods, grabbing his coffee out of my hand and turning toward the dining room table. "Noted. You ready to talk?"

"Yeah," I answer, sucking in a breath and grabbing a fresh cup of coffee for myself. "Let's do this."

We sit across from each other at the table and I pull the gun out of my waistband, setting it down between us. He arches a brow and I shrug, smiling at him.

"So, what is it that you wanted to talk about?" he asks and my stomach does a little flip.

"Uh… you know how I told you about the pregnancy scare in high school?"

He nods. "Yes."

"Well, that was really only the start of it. I moved out right after graduation because I was rebellious and wanted to be on my own but it was way harder than I ever thought it would be. I was struggling to make ends meet when I met Beth. She was working as an escort and told me all about how much money I could make…"

"Are you saying you were a hooker?" he asks, shock filling his voice and I glance down at the table, twisting my fingers together. Why do I even care so much what he thinks of me?

"Not exactly. I never had sex with anyone but I did get paid to go out on dates with them."

"So, in the coffee shop, when you told me that you'd been waiting for someone special, was that a lie?"

I shake my head. "No. Those dates, they weren't real. I was there for companionship and they could talk to me about anything they needed to get off their chests but that was it. As soon as the date was over, I didn't speak to them again unless they booked another date and I never even kissed anyone."

"Why did you quit?"

180

"One day, Beth showed up at my apartment, beat to shit. Apparently, her date didn't get the memo about the no sex thing and when she told him, he lost it. I rushed her to the hospital and she was there for three days. By the time she was discharged it just wasn't worth it to me anymore."

He stares at me as he lifts his coffee cup to his mouth and I wring my hands together under the table, fighting my urge to get up and run into the kitchen. "Did your mom know? Does your brother?"

"No and I would prefer that Theo never finds out. It's not a time in my life that I'm proud of but I was too determined to make it on my own without my mother's help. Please tell me you don't think I'm a terrible person?"

With a quick shake of his head, he reaches across the table and grabs my hand. "No, Tate. I think you are one of, if not the strongest person I've ever met in my life and I certainly can't judge you for your past when you haven't judged me for mine."

"Why haven't you been in a relationship in six years?" I ask and he sighs, scrubbing his face with his free hand.

"I suppose turn about is fair play, huh?"

I nod.

"After Nora died, I was lost and I met this girl, Tara, who made me feel sane again. Looking back, all she did was give me a place to hide and pretend like I was fine again but at the time, she felt like my saving grace so I asked her to marry me."

I suck in a breath and try to pull my hand away but he refuses to release me.

"On our wedding day, I was standing at the altar, waiting for her to walk down to me when my mom walked into the church and told me that Tara had run off with my best friend."

Her loss, I think and try not to look smug as he continues his story.

"Anyway, I kind of lost it after that, packed up everything I owned and threw it in the back of the Camaro. I left town and just traveled all over the country for two years until I landed in Baton Rouge and I promised myself that I would never get close to anyone again."

"You and I are so alike it's a little scary," I say and he smiles as the phone starts ringing again. Sighing, he glances over his shoulder.

"What are you going to do about that?"

I shake my head. "I don't know yet. I've been kind of hoping that he'd get bored."

"And if he doesn't?"

Shrugging, I squeeze his hand. "Then, we'll deal with it."

"I like the sound of that. Do I get official boyfriend privileges now?"

Boyfriend.

My mind spins at the mention of the word and I suck in a breath, meeting his warm golden gaze.

"About that... I do want this but I need to take it slow. I'm not just going to jump into bed with you because you used the word boyfriend or say you want more."

He smirks, leaning back in his chair. "Shit. I knew you wouldn't make this easy on me."

"Yeah," I muse, standing up from my chair as the machine picks up and I silence it as I pass by before sitting down in Lincoln's lap. "But it will be so worth it."

Leaning in, I thread my fingers through his dark hair and press my lips to his as he lets out a low groan that shoots straight to my neglected core. Damn, resisting him is going to be one hell of a challenge but I'm determined to do things right this time.

Every Breath You Take

Chapter Twelve
Lincoln

Where the fuck is she?

I frantically flick through each video feed, searching for movement or a shock of red hair but I come up with nothing. Glancing up at the house, I sigh. I watched her walk in the front door ten minutes ago and after going through her mail and deleting more weird messages from the answering machine, she went into her mother's room and disappeared. The only reasonable explanation is that she's in the closet but I can't, for the life of me, figure out why. When I first started following her, I went through each room in her house so I could see the layout in my mind and the closet in her mom's room is so small, I don't even know how she fits in there.

The phone rings and I go back to the bedroom camera, waiting with bated breath and sure enough, a few seconds later, she appears at the bottom of the screen and walks out of the bedroom.

What the fuck?

When she gets to the dining room, she sets a
piece of paper down on the table and I squint at the
screen, trying to read it but it's impossible.

"Hey, Theo," she answers, leaning back against
the wall. "Yeah, I'm doing all right. How are you?"

Putting the phone on speakerphone, she sets it on
the dining room table and walks to the fridge.

"I'm fine, T. Same as always. But I'm worried
about you," Theo says, his voice barely audible and I
turn the volume up on the tablet. Tate laughs.

"Why are you worried about me?"

"I don't know. I just have this feeling."

Tate walks back into the dining room with a glass
of sweet tea in her hand and sits down at the table.

"Are you sure you're not confusing worry with
indigestion?"

"Tatum," he growls and she laughs again. "I'm
serious."

"So am I, Theo. Everything is good here." Her
teeth sink into her bottom lip, which I've learned recently
is a sure sign that she's lying. She picks up the paper and
stares at it for a second, worry on her face. I've got to see
that damn note.

"Well, you do sound better."

Dropping the paper to the table, she smiles.
"That's because I am."

"Any particular reason?"

Her smile grows and I'm glued to the screen, my
heart pounding in my chest.

"Yeah, actually. You remember the guy I told
you about?"

He laughs. "The one you tased?"

Fucking perfect.

How many other people did she tell?

"That's the one. He showed up at the door the other day and we're giving things a real shot."

"Whoa, this is huge, T."

"I know but it feels so right."

Shaking my head, I turn down the volume. I'd love to sit and listen to her tell her brother about me but I can't stand the guilt eating away at me. Not when she sounds so happy because that's all I want for her and I can't brush away the sinking feeling that I'm going to ruin her.

Focusing back on the paper, I try to read it again but it's just too damn small. I toss the tablet down and grab my phone, dialing Streak's number.

"Streak's Technical Support. How can I help you today?" he answers with a bored tone and I bark out a laugh.

"I need you to zoom in on one of these cameras, smartass."

"Which one?"

I roll my eyes. "The one Tate is in. I need to see what that note on the table says."

"On it," he murmurs, the sound of typing filling the line and I grab the tablet, watching as it zooms in on the note but it's too blurry to make out.

"Can you make that any clearer?"

"Nope, sorry. You'll have to go inside to get a look at it."

I sigh. "Okay, thanks."

He hangs up and I lay my head on the headrest, staring up at Tate's house and debating if I should go see her. It's not that I don't want to because I do, badly, but I hate lying to her. I've never been a dishonest person and these secrets are eating a hole through me each time I'm near her. Two days ago when I showed up on her doorstep, all I could think about was doing whatever it took to get her back and if I didn't have to lie to her, I would be totally comfortable with being in a relationship for the first time in six years but this whole situation is complicated. We ended up spending the whole day together, watching old TV shows and her favorite movies. It was a cool way to learn all the little things about her that I'm dying to discover. Afterward, I made dinner for us and she was a totally different woman. She's still quick to break my balls but she's letting me in – in ways that she didn't before – and there's this sweetness to her that doesn't feel fake like it did the night we officially met. Honestly, I'm addicted.

Our relationship is on shaky ground though and I'm the only one that knows it. One wrong move from me, one thoughtless comment could make this whole thing blow up in my face and it's something that I can't even imagine.

"There's got to be a way out of this," I whisper, my anger with Blaze growing. He's gotten more irrational as the weeks have gone by and I'm at the end of my rope. Besides Streak, no one else in the club knows what I'm doing every day and if Tate ever finds out, she'll kill me. Although, I'd rather be dead than watch her walk away from me.

The thought stuns me and I blow out a breath, the gravity of it crashing down on me. I've spent so long avoiding feelings of any kind and then here comes Tatum Carter, knocking me on my ass and swallowing me up in her orbit. It started with the photo but meeting her, getting to know her – it sealed my fate and I can't walk away now. If this ship is going down, I'm going down with it.

"Shit," I grumble, reaching for the door handle because I can't stay out here any longer. Not with my girl only fifty feet away from me. Opening the door, I climb out and a car in the side mirror catches my attention. I spin around and as I shut the door, the same car from Valentine's Day pulls away from the curb before flying past me. Adrenaline surges through my veins and I watch his taillights until he turns left, disappearing from my sight.

What the fuck is going on here?

"Lincoln?" Her sweet voice calls to me and I take a moment to just let it soak in. I don't know how much longer I'll get to keep her so every moment has to be cherished. Turning toward her house, I barely hold back a laugh as she crosses her arms over her chest and arches a brow.

So damn sassy.

"Hey, babe."

"What the hell are you doing in the street?"

My mouth pops open and I realize that I have no excuse to give her. "Uh, this guy was just sitting in his car. I don't know… it seemed weird."

"Or maybe he was just looking up directions, you crazy man."

It's my turn to cross my arms and pin her with a stare. If she thinks for one second that I would ever let something go instead of investigating it, she's lost her damn mind. I'll never do that again.

"Or they were a creep and had no business being in this neighborhood."

She rolls her eyes and turns back to the house before peeking over her shoulder. "Well, are you done searching for the boogeyman or do you want to stand out there and get hit by a car?"

"Are those my only two choices?"

"Yes," she yells, turning back to face me and leaning against the railing of her porch.

"I guess I choose you then."

Her smile is blinding and my heart skips a beat as I stare up at her. I can't help but grin as I jog up her front walk and wrap my arms around her. God, I fucking love her attitude.

"Smart man," she whispers, leaning in to me and I meet her halfway, claiming her lips in a kiss that ignites every cell in my body. Fuck, she's everything. My poison and medicine, heaven and hell, fire and ice all rolled up into a body that was made to fit against mine. That's the crux of it all. She was made especially for me and in the end, I'm going to destroy us both with my lies.

"Mmm," she hums, pulling away from me with a dazed look in her amber eyes and I want to throw my fist in the air because I put that look on her face. The

A.M. Myers

caveman in me wants to show the world that she's my girl.

"You have plans today?" I ask and she blinks before meeting my eyes.

"Not exactly."

I tilt my head and scowl. "What does that mean?"

"Um… I have a couple things I want to go do but you don't have to go with me if you don't want to."

She tries to wiggle out of my grasp and I pull her closer, shooting her a look. "Babe, if you're there then I want to be there."

"You keep saying shit like that and I'm going to fall in love with you," she whispers and my heart stalls as a smile stretches across my face.

"Sound like a fucking plan to me."

We just stare at each other for a moment before she drops her gaze and shakes her head.

"All right, let me go get ready and then we can go."

Reluctantly, I release her and watch as she heads toward the stairs. "Where are we going?"

"I want a tattoo," she calls down to me and I arch a brow as I slowly approach the dining room table where the piece of paper from the video still sits.

"What are you gonna get?"

"I don't know yet."

Laughing, I grab the note and read through it once before scowling. It looks like lines from a script or something but I've never heard of it. I flip the paper over and find Tate's name written on the front with a piece of tape folded over the edge. The floorboard above me

191

creaks and I pull my phone out of my pocket and snap a picture to send off to Streak. If anyone can figure out what this means, it's our boy genius. By the time Tate walks back into the room, the note is back on the table and I'm inspecting some of the photos on the wall.

"You look just like your mom," I say.

"Yeah, people used to call me her mini-me."

I point to the guy in the photo. "Is this your brother?"

"Yep, that's Theo."

"He doesn't look anything like y'all."

She walks up behind me and slips her hand in my back pocket as she stares at the photo. "I know. I always wondered if he looks just like our dad."

"Do you want to find him?" I ask, wondering if that's something Streak could do for me. She shrugs.

"I don't know. I've always wanted to know who he is but I don't know if I'd want to meet him. I mean, he's had twenty-five years to give a damn about Theo and me so should I really bother worrying about him?"

I wrap my arm around her and pull her into my side, loving the feel of her next to me. "Maybe he doesn't know about you."

"That's possible, too." She pulls away and clears her throat. "You want some sweet tea or something?"

"Sure, baby."

Turning, I watch her walk into the kitchen, the gentle sway of her hips conjuring up images of the two of us spending the whole day in bed. I respect her need to take things slow but damn, that doesn't mean it's easy.

Especially not when I've been imagining what it will feel like to sink into her since the moment we first met.

She walks back out with two glasses of sweet tea and sets one down in front of me before trying to turn away but I grab her and deposit her in my lap. She scoffs.

"You know I have plenty of chairs, right?"

"But why waste one when you can just sit on my lap?" I ask and she laughs.

"They're chairs. You can use them more than once."

I shrug. "So? You'd still be all the way over there instead of right...here," I whisper, trailing my hand up the bare skin of her thigh until I get to the hem of her shorts. Her eyes flutter closed and she releases a breath as she drops her head back, exposing the side of her neck. Leaning in, I press my lips against her skin and a soft moan slips past her lips and straight to my cock.

"Fuck, Tate," I hiss and she wiggles her ass with a giggle.

"It's your own damn fault."

Growling, I wrap both arms around her and squeeze until she starts to squeal.

"Oh my God, let me go before you break me!"

Her words hit me straight in the chest and I turn away as I loosen my hold. "So, tattoo time, then?"

"Yes, please," she says with a smile and I know it doesn't matter how many times I have to lie to her because I'll come back for that smile alone every single time.

*   *   *   *

Streak:
It's from the Merchant of Venice.

Me:
Shakespeare?

The buzz of the needle drowns out the other noise around us and I glance up, meeting Tate's eyes as she smiles at me.

"Everything okay?"

I nod. "Yeah, sweetheart. Just club stuff."

She nods and I get up from my seat to check out how her tattoo is coming along. When we first rolled up to From the Ashes Tattoos, the shop that Blaze's son owns, she was insistent on getting one for her mom but she couldn't decide what she wanted so she went with the letter "T" with a little two up in the corner for her and Theo. It's actually pretty damn cute.

My phone buzzes again and I pull it out.

Streak:
Yep.

Me:
What the fuck does it mean?

The buzzing stops and I glance up as her artist, Kenny, grabs some paper towels and squirts it with soap before rubbing it over her ink.

"Hey, is Nix here today?" I ask and Kenny shakes his head.

"Naw, he took the day off to spend with his family."

I nod and Tate turns to me as he pulls out the plastic wrap and covers her skin with it.

"Who is Nix?"

"Blaze's son. This is his shop."

"Follow me and I'll get y'all checked out," Kenny says and I help Tate off the table before slipping my arm around her waist and leading her up to the front.

"That will be one hundred."

Releasing Tate, I grab my wallet but Tate snatches it out of my hand.

"I am perfectly capable of paying for my own tattoo," she snaps and Kenny smirks as she hands him a wad of twenties.

"Thanks, guys," Kenny says, laughing and I nod at him as we turn toward the door.

"Can I have my wallet back now?" I ask and she glares up at me.

"I don't know. Are you going to try to pay for anything else?"

Chuckling, I open the door for her and guide her toward the car. "I feel like the correct answer here is no."

"Then say it."

"I can't," I answer with a laugh and she lets out a huff of annoyance.

"And to think Theo was worried you were going to use me to be your sugar mama."

I bark out a laugh, stopping her on the sidewalk and turning her to face me. "What? Exactly how much money did your mom leave you?"

"Um," she murmurs, biting her lip. "Almost half a million dollars."

My eyes widen and I let out a low whistle as I start leading us to the car again. Well, there's one more plot twist in this confusing story. When she said her mom left her money, I'd figured it was a few thousand not enough to buy a new house outright. My phone buzzes just as we reach the car and I pull it out as I open Tate's door for her.

Streak:
Based on what it says and the fact that it was left for her...
I'd say someone is threatening her.

Me:
I'll talk to you in twenty.

As soon as I drop Tate off at home, I'm going straight to the clubhouse to see what Streak knows and confront Blaze again. It's time for all the secrets to end. I shut her door and jog around the hood before slipping behind the wheel and firing the engine to life.

"I've got to run to the clubhouse and deal with some shit. You just want me to take you home?" I ask and she nods as I pull away from the curb.

"Yes. Thanks for hanging out with me today."

I grab her hand, lacing our fingers before I bring it to my lips and kiss her thumb. "Anytime, baby. You like your tattoo?"

"Yes," she replies, her grin growing as she glances down at her forearm. "It's perfect."

I kiss her hand again. "I'm glad."

She turns on the radio and changes the station until *Smile* by Uncle Kracker starts pouring out of the speakers. Grinning, she turns it up and turns to me as she sings along with the song, capturing my full attention. A grin splits my face as I watch her sing and just be silly, something that I get the feeling Tate doesn't do all that often but it's fucking adorable and in a moment, I realize that this girl already owns my heart.

By the time we pull up in front of her house, she's already belted out two more songs and I might as well go out and buy a ring today because I'm never walking away from her. I don't care if she finds out everything and chops my balls off, I'll still beg for her to take me back and I'll spend every day of the rest of my life making it up to her.

"All right, I suppose I better let you go," she says, pouting as she turns down the music and I laugh.

"What if I promise to come back later?"

Her face lights up. Man, I'd do anything to see that look on her face.

"Yeah?"

I nod.

"Okay, I suppose I'll release you then but tell Blaze that if he doesn't give you back, I have no problem going in guns blazing and stealing you myself."

I laugh, reaching across the car and brushing my thumb over her cheek. "I'll be sure to pass that message along."

"Make sure he knows how scary I am, too," she orders, looking anything but scary and I laugh again.

"You got it, Sweetheart."

With a curt nod, she leans across the Camaro and I claim her lips, thrusting my hand into her hair and wishing I didn't have to go. This is important, though. It's time to end all the secrets and lies if she and I are ever going to have a real chance.

"Bye, baby," she whispers against my lips and I smile.

"I'll be back before you know it. Now, get inside."

Rolling her eyes, she opens her door and climbs out of the car before leaning down and meeting my stare. "Don't think that just because I kiss you now that you can tell me what to do. I'll still tase you."

I laugh. "Noted."

"Text me when you're on your way back."

I nod and she winks at me before shutting the door and walking away from the car. My gaze is glued to her as she walks up the front steps and I swear she's putting a little extra swing in her hips to tease me. When she glances over her shoulder and laughs, I know I was right. Once she's safely inside her house, I pull away from the curb, my knee bouncing against the steering wheel as I drive to the clubhouse.

Based on all our previous conversations, I know Blaze isn't going to want to tell me the truth but I'm not leaving until I get some answers. I care too much about Tate to settle for however much time I have until this thing blows up in my face. My mind drifts back to the note on Tate's table and I scowl, gripping the steering wheel tighter. Something deep down in my gut is telling me that she's in danger but unless Blaze is ready to divulge some details I don't know how I'm supposed to protect her.

There are few bikes in the parking lot as I pull into the clubhouse and I park my car in my usual spot before jumping out and heading inside. Smith waves as I storm past him toward the stairs, eager to see what Streak has on this whole situation. His door is open as I approach the end of the hallway and he glances up when he hears me coming.

"Shut the door and sit down," he instructs, pointing to the chair by his desk. I do as I'm told, shutting and locking the door before going to his desk.

"What do you have?"

He sighs and turns one of his three computer screens to face me. On the screen is the photo I sent him of the note next to a web search. "Okay, so the note in Tate's house is a modern version of the original scene but it's essentially the same except for one thing."

"What?" I ask.

"Right here," he starts, pointing to part of the note. "Where it says King's daughter is wrong. The actual line is Jew's daughter."

"And you think this is a clue?"

He nods. "I do, but I couldn't tell you what it means."

"Yeah, you're not the one who can give me answers," I growl and his brow arches.

"Do I even want to know?"

I shake my head. "Did you see anything on the cameras? Like who dropped off the note?"

He presses a couple buttons before an image from the camera on the front porch of Tate's house pops up. "This is the best I can get you. He kept his face hidden the whole time and he's about as average as they get."

"Shit," I hiss before slapping his shoulder and standing up. "Thanks, man."

"Yeah, you got it."

As anger racks my body, I slip out of his office and go back downstairs before heading straight for Blaze's office. I barge in without knocking and he glances up from the paperwork in front of him.

"You and I need to chat," I growl, slamming the door shut and his eyes widen before he stands up and puffs out his chest.

"Boy, I don't know who the hell you think you are but you will not talk to me like that."

I shake my head. "I'm done playing your games. I want to know why I'm watching Tate and I want to know now."

"No," he snaps, turning away from me and I lose it, grabbing a pencil off his desk and chucking it at the wall. Instead of falling to the floor, it sticks in the wood and he turns to me with wide eyes.

"Why do you have me watching her?"

His gaze narrows and the office is silent as he studies me for a moment before his eyes widen.

"Oh, fuck." He collapses in his chair and blows out a breath. "You fucking fell in love with her, didn't you?"

"Yeah, and? What does that matter now?"

Bewildered, he stares at his desk for a moment before sighing. "Nope. I'm taking you off this. I'll get Storm or Chance to watch over her from now on."

Rage bubbles up inside me and I slam my fist down on the desk. No one is taking me away from my girl. "No, you will not. You started this and I'm going to finish it."

"I'm your president!"

"I don't give a shit. She's mine now. You hear me?"

With wide eyes, he nods because he knows what this means. I've officially claimed her with the club and she's mine. No man can come between that, not even Blaze.

"Sit down, son. If you're going to be with her, there are some things you need to know."

Every Breath You Take

Chapter Thirteen
Tatum

Ain't No Rest For The Wicked by Cage the
Elephant blares through the speakers in the living room
as I dance around the kitchen in a tank top and boy
shorts, getting ready to make popcorn. I wiggle my hips
as I pour the kernels in a stockpot, add in a little oil, and
cover it with a lid. Once the stove is on, I dance over to
the cupboard and grab a couple glasses and the pitcher of
sweet tea out of the fridge, setting both on the counter as
I go back to the stove and grab the handles on the pot,
giving it a good shake. My cheeks hurt from smiling so
much but I can't help it. I can't remember the last time I
was this happy and as strange as it feels, it's also
amazing.

Once the popcorn is done popping, I pour it into a
bowl and dance over to the couch. Lincoln should be
back soon and I have Road House cued up on the TV.
The last time he was over, we spent the whole day
watching my favorite movies so it only seems fair that

we watch his this time. Glancing down at my bare legs, I wonder if I should put some pants on before grinning. I may not be ready to have sex with him yet but that doesn't mean I can't tease. Besides, I'm not opposed to hitting third base to take the edge off for both of us. My phone buzzes from the couch and I walk around to the front, setting the popcorn down on the coffee table so I can grab it.

Lincoln:
Sorry, babe. Shit's running long and I'm not going to make it over tonight.

I toss the phone down on the couch with a frown just as it lights up with another text. Sighing, I grab it again.

Lincoln:
Rain check?

Staring at his message, an idea hits me and I smile as I tap my camera app and hold the phone above me, snapping a photo of my body.

Me:
Fine but just know that this is what you're missing.

A.M. Myers

Me:
Also, I'll be watching Road House all by myself.

A few seconds after I press send, my phone rings and Lincoln's picture pops up on the screen as I laugh.

"Yes?" I answer, still giggling as I turn the music off.

"Are you seriously going to watch Road House half naked?"

I fall back onto the couch and cross my legs in front of me. "I really am. Shame you're missing it."

"Fuck, babe," he groans and I can just imagine him running his hand over his face in frustration – something he does quite often around me. "Just thinking about that is making me hard."

"That sucks since I was considering letting you get to third base tonight, too."

"Jesus Christ," he breathes. "You can't say shit like that to me when I'm in a clubhouse full of guys."

"Well, you should have come over."

He sighs on the other end of the line and an ache forms in my chest. He only left a few hours ago and I already miss him like crazy.

"If I could get away, I would, babe."

"I know. I'll let you get back to whatever you're doing. Just call me tomorrow, okay?"

"Count on it."

We say good-bye and when I hang up, I sigh and toss the phone next to me on the couch. Never in my life did I think I would be one of those clingy girls but I can't

205

help it with him. When it comes to him, I'm greedy as hell.

Glancing down at my new tattoo, I run my fingers gently over the raised ink and smile as I remember the drive back to the house. I can't remember the last time I was that silly around someone and it felt good to just let go. Lincoln makes me feel safe and I wasn't scanning the street, searching for signs of danger or running through defensive moves in my head. Besides Theo, he may be the only person I can just be myself with.

Lincoln is my escape, my safe place to land and it concerns me how quickly I'm falling for him. It's like as soon as I let down my guard, he rushed in and stole my heart right out from under my nose and it makes me wonder if I could have been happy long before now. If I had just let someone in, given them a chance, would things have turned out different? Shaking my head, I realize I don't want things to change because I think, maybe, Lincoln is the prize for all the years of waiting for the right man to come along.

The house phone rings and I glance over my shoulder before standing up and walking around the couch to grab it off the table, Theo's number flashes on the screen and I smile.

"Hey, little brother," I answer, biting back a smile and I'm greeted with a growl.

"Tatum, don't start shit with me when I'm nine hundred miles away."

I laugh, walking around the couch and sinking into it. "What are you going to do about it, Theodore?"

"I'll take time off just to come down there and kick your ass," he taunts and I throw my head back and laugh.

"Do it. We should have a sparring match like we used to and this time I won't be afraid to hurt your fragile little face."

"You're such a goddamn pain in the ass," he mutters and I giggle.

"Whatever. You love me. What are you up to?"

"I just got off work. What are you up to?"

"Nothing, really. Just getting ready to watch a movie."

"Fun. Oh, hey, do you have any idea why my forearm was burning today? It feels like I got a sunburn but there's nothing on my skin."

"Shut up." I laugh, shaking my head. "You're such a liar."

We may be able to communicate differently than other people but there's no way in hell he felt me getting my tattoo today.

"Yeah, you're right. Lincoln sent me a photo of you getting it done."

I jerk up, blinking. "Wait a minute. What do you mean Lincoln sent it to you?"

"He texted it to me," he says like that somehow explains everything when it literally explains nothing.

"You guys are texting?"

"Yeah. I got his number after you told me about him and I gave him the brother talk."

Groaning, I drop my head into my hands. "No, you did not."

"Yes." He laughs. "I did. Don't worry; he was cool about it."

"I'm going to block you on his phone the next time I see him," I warn and he laughs again.

"Don't do that. Besides, I didn't get to do the whole brother thing very much lately. Not since high school."

"Did you feel like it was one of the big things missing from your life?"

"Maybe I did."

Sighing, I lean back into the couch. "Well, I'm glad I could help your dreams come true."

"Don't be a smartass." He laughs but it quickly turns into a yawn. "So, what did you permanently mark your body with?"

"T squared," I answer.

"Aw, you got a tattoo for me?" he teases and I wrinkle my nose up.

"Keep it up and I'll get it covered up with a donkey for you," I warn and silence greets me.

"A donkey? Why?"

"Smartass... duh."

He yawns again. "Oh, you're so funny."

"Hey, go get some sleep and call me tomorrow, okay?"

He mumbles something before saying, "Yeah, that sounds like a good idea. Send me a picture of your new tattoo, okay?"

"I will," I promise before saying good-bye to him. Once he hangs up, I toss the house phone next to my cell and sigh as I grab the remote and start the movie.

Grabbing the bowl of popcorn off the coffee table, I settle into the couch and pop a kernel in my mouth when the phone rings again. Rolling my eyes, I grab it and press it to my ear.

"What did you forget, Theo?"

"Taaaaatuuuum," a creepy, high-pitched voice sings on the other end of the line and my stomach sinks like a rock as a chill races down my spine. I sit forward, spilling popcorn on the carpet as I toss the bowl to the coffee table. "Are you there, Taaate?"

The voice sounds like something straight out of every horror movie I've ever watched and my hand trembles as I press my fingers to my lips, trying not to cry. My gaze flicks to every window in the living room and the sensation that I'm being watched intensifies.

"Who is this?" I ask, my voice shakier than I would like.

"Walls have ears," the voice coos and my chest aches as my heart races in my ears. "Doors have eyes… Trees have voices."

"Who the fuck is this?" I cry, standing up and scanning each window again.

"Beasts tell lies. Beware the rain. Beware the snow. Beware the man you think you know."

"Who is this?" I roar, anger replacing some of my immediate fear but the only response is the hollow, high-pitched laughter that will haunt me for the rest of my life.

Every Breath You Take

Chapter Fourteen
Tatum

Sighing, I drop my keys onto the entry table and lock the front door behind me, the sensation of being watched still following me around from last night. I wasn't able to shake it all morning at work and it's even worse now that I'm back here. I do a quick scan of the room and once I'm sure that everything is exactly how I left it, I'm able to breathe a little easier. As I walk into the kitchen, the phone rings and I jump, my hands shaking as I grip the handle on the fridge and wait for the answering machine to pick up. I let out a breath when it does and Theo's voice fills the line.

"Hey, T. I was just calling to check in. Call me back later, okay?"

He hangs up and I open the fridge, grabbing a bottle of water before I retreat to Mom's room and slip into the closet. Once I enter the code and the hidden door swings open, I rush inside and shut it behind me as relief crashes over me. I glance over at the pillow and blanket on the couch where I slept last night and sigh before going over to the desk and wiggling the mouse to wake up the computer.

I feel like the last twelve hours have taken years off my life and I'm eager to do a little research on the quote my mystery caller said to me last night. I type it into the search engine and wait as results pop up on the screen. After a few clicks, I find a book called *Incarceron* by Catherine Fisher that the quote is from. From what I can tell, the book itself doesn't have any relevance to me or the caller. The more I read, the more I think that it just had to do with that specific quote which opens up a whole other lists of questions.

Beware the man you think you know.

How many men in my life does this apply to? Right now, the possibilities are endless or maybe this is all just a sick game. Maybe the quote was meant to throw me off my game and it means nothing at all. Blowing out a breath, I scrub my hand over my face and lean back in the office chair. I'm not ruling out anyone at this point. My mind drifts back to my shift this morning and the chill that rushed over me when Reed walked in with a few friends and sat down. Thankfully, he wasn't in my section but I could feel his eyes on me the whole time. This seems too sophisticated for him, though. Then again, what do I know? Maybe under all that shit personality, he's actually smart. It's also entirely possible I don't even know this person at all. With all the secrets that have been revealed since Mom's death, I don't have the slightest clue which direction to look in.

My phone buzzes on the desk and I sigh as I pick it up. Lincoln's picture pops up on the screen and I smile.

"Hey you," I answer.

"Hey, Sweetheart," he replies and just the sound of his voice is enough to take away some of my stress. "You busy today?"

"Nope. I just got off work. Why?"

"I'm cashing in my rain check. How soon can you be ready?"

I glance at the clock on the computer. "Two-ish. I need to take a shower since I literally just walked in the door."

"Okay, you go get ready and I'll be there in an hour."

Once we hang up, I push out of the chair and leave the safe room, instantly feeling vulnerable again before I remind myself that I'm okay. The call last night really scared me but that doesn't change who I am. If anyone decides to come after me, I am perfectly capable of defending myself. Not to mention the numerous guns hidden all over this house.

I've got this.

Feeling stronger, I jog upstairs and strip out of my uniform before slipping under the hot spray of the shower and closing my eyes. An image of Lincoln pops into my mind and I smile as I wonder what he's got planned for us today. I was so upset when he didn't come over last night but in hindsight, I'm glad he didn't. If he'd heard that call, he would worry and I was certainly in no state to calm him down either. The more I think about it, the more I think that has to be another prank –

like the heavy breathing. The horror movie voice, the weird poem, and the evil laugh – all of it is part of an elaborate mind game and I refuse to play anymore.

With renewed resolve, I rush through the rest of my shower and get dressed before scribbling a note to remember to change the house number. I smirk. He can't call if he doesn't know the damn number.

"Shit," I mutter, glancing up at the clock. I only have twenty minutes until Lincoln gets here and I need to dry my hair and put on makeup. Turning on the radio, *Your Song* by Rita Ora spills out of the speaker and I dance back into the bathroom and grab my hair dryer, losing myself in the music and the task at hand.

When I'm ready, I take one last look in the mirror before grabbing the remote, switching the music off and heading downstairs. As soon as my foot hits the bottom step, someone knocks on the door and I glance up, grinning when I see Lincoln on the other side.

"Perfect timing," I say as I swing the door open and his gaze travels down my body before meeting my eyes.

"You look fucking gorgeous, babe."

I glance down at the ripped black jeans and white t-shirt I put on, feeling every bit as gorgeous as he says I am. "You are very easy to please, sir."

"Naw, I'm not," he murmurs, holding his hand out to me and I take it, letting out a squeak of surprise when he pulls me into his arms and presses his lips to mine. His kiss is liquid fire and I moan, reaching up on my tippy toes to wrap my arms around his neck as his arms lock around my waist. My fingers rake through his hair and he groans against my lips as I rock my hips into his. We stumble back into the house and my back meets the cool wall as his tongue teases the seam of my lips.

"Open up for me, Darlin'," he whispers, his minty fresh breath caressing my skin and I comply immediately. Our tongues tangle together and it takes the kiss to another level as I whine. I can't get close enough to him to satisfy this need rocking through my body and I'm about to chuck my rule about not sleeping with him out of the window when he pulls back and clears his throat.

He meets my eyes, his bright and filled with fire as his chest rises and falls rapidly. My core clenches and I press my hand against the wall for support when his tongue pokes out and slowly runs along the length of his bottom lip, licking up every last taste of me.

"We should go," he whispers and I nod because I'm afraid if I open my mouth, I'll tell him we should stay. I have my rules for a reason and it won't be long before I give in to this incredible force between us but not today.

He holds his hand out for mine again and I take it, smiling when he laces our fingers together and leads me toward the door.

"So, where are we going?" I ask and he smiles.

"It's a surprise."

I stop, tugging on his arm when he keeps walking. He glances back at me. "I don't like surprises."

"Well, we're going to help you grow today," he answers with a laugh and I scowl at him. "You can give me that cute as shit look all you want, baby, but I'm not tellin' you where I'm taking you."

Arching a brow, I rip my hand from his and cross my arms over my chest.

"That's the way you're going to play it?" he asks and I nod. "All right, then."

He shrugs before stepping forward and grabbing me behind the knees. I'm half-way over his shoulder by the time I realize what he's doing and I hit his back with my fists.

"Put me down, you giant!"

He smacks my ass. "You gonna stop being a brat?"

"Yes," I huff. As much as I don't want to give in, I want to be carried out of the house like a child even less and he fucking knows it. He sets me back on my feet and takes my hand in his before leading me out of the house to his car.

As we pull away from the curb, I turn to him and smile. He glances over at me and laughs, shaking his head.

"No way, Darlin'. Don't think you can be cute and get me to ruin the surprise."

"You know, I've got my Taser. I could just torture it out of you," I tease and his gaze flicks to my bag.

"Seems like not a very bright idea since I'm driving the car."

"Fine. I'll be patient."

He grins. "See. Was that so hard?"

Rolling my eyes, I settle into my seat as he turns on the radio and reaches across the car to grab my hand. Truthfully, I don't really care where we go since I just want to spend time with him but old habits are hard to break and I'm not exactly versed in letting other people run the show. It's something to work on, I guess.

"Oh, I know where we're going," I say a few minutes later when we turn down the road to Lincoln's house and he grins.

"Figured I owed you a redo for the weekend I messed up."

I squeeze his hand. "You didn't mess anything up."

"You tased me for nothing then?" he asks, humor in his voice and I shrug.

"Okay, so maybe you messed up a little bit, but look," I hold up our intertwined hands, "it all worked out."

"Yes, it did. You know when I kissed you that night was the first time I realized I had real feelings for you."

My gaze narrows and I laugh. "Oh! So, that's why you freaked out."

"Yep," he answers. "Kissing you shocked me more than the Taser."

I place my hand over my heart. "That might be the sweetest thing anyone's ever said to me."

"Don't joke."

"No," I say, shaking my head. "I'm serious. That Taser packs one hell of a punch and besides, kissing you kind of knocked the wind out of me, too."

Our eyes meet across the car and he smiles before turning back to the road.

"Now I've got to know," he muses as he pulls into his driveway. "Have you really been tased?"

"Yeah. My mom insisted that Theo and I experience it ourselves if we were going to carry them around to protect ourselves."

His eyebrows shoot up. "Wow. Your mom was..."

"Intense?" I interject. "Yeah."

The trees open up, revealing Lincoln's house and the pristine lake in front of it and I sigh. It's so peaceful out here that you can just forget everything and truly relax.

"Was she like that all the time?" Lincoln asks as he puts the car in park in the garage and I nod.

"Pretty much. She was a complicated woman."

"Wait there and I'll come get you," he instructs as he opens his door and I roll my eyes.

"What did I say about that chivalry thing?"

He pins me with a stare. "Your ass leaves that seat before I get there and I'll spank it."

"I might like it," I shoot back and he grins.

"Noted."

He rounds the back of the Camaro and opens my door, holding his hand out to me and I grab it as I stand up. We leave the garage and go up to the porch. I turn and look out at the water as he digs in his pocket for his keys, peace settling over me. This is exactly what I needed after that creepy phone call last night and sleeping in the safe room.

"Tate?" Lincoln asks and I spin to find him waiting for me with the door open. "You okay?"

I nod. "Yeah, sorry. My mind started to wander."

Taking his hand, I let him pull me inside the house and I gasp at the gorgeous, rugged interior that matches him so perfectly. The wall that faces the lake is full of windows, flooding the room with light and I picture curling up on the sofa on a cool day and reading a book.

"This is amazing," I tell him and he smiles.

"I forgot you didn't get to see the inside last time. Do you want the tour?"

When I nod, he grabs my hand and starts leading me through the house, pointing out various rooms. The middle of the house is one large open space that houses the living room, kitchen, dining room, and office and there's a master suite on either side. The office is in the corner by the hallway and sectioned off by three large logs that go to the ceiling. It's packed with bookcases full of books and I grin as I run my fingers along the titles.

"You like to read?" he asks and I nod.

"Do you not remember the boxes of books you hauled down from my apartment for me?"

He sighs. "Ah, yes. How could I forget? I nearly put out my back."

"You did not, you liar." I laugh, smacking his ass and he growls, spinning me around and wrapping his massive arms around me.

"Careful, Darlin'."

"Why?" I ask, heat creeping up my cheeks as I quietly gasp for air. "I think I can handle you."

"Why don't we test out your theory?" he whispers, leaning in until his mouth hovers above mine and I reach up on my tippy toes just as his phone rings and he closes his eyes, letting out a breath. "I'm sorry. Just give me a minute."

He pulls his phone out and presses it to his ear.

"Yeah?"

His gaze snaps to me.

"Right now?"

Worry creases his forehead and I step forward, laying my hand on his arm.

"No, I can't."

He nods.

"Yeah, let me know."

When he hangs up, I tilt my head in question and he sighs.

"Sorry, babe. Club business. Did you already eat lunch?"

I nod, wishing he'd share what's going on with me but I understand the need for secrecy with the work that they do. If his silence keeps someone safe, I'll deal with it.

"Yeah, I ate before I left the diner."

"We can start with the movie then. I'm pretty sure I still owe you for last night as well."

"Sounds good, but I'm not stripping down to my underwear. That was a one time deal and you missed it."

"I think I might be able to talk you into it."

I shake my head. "Don't count on it."

He laughs, throwing his arm over my shoulders as he leads me to one of the bedrooms. There's a king-size bed against one wall and it faces a huge TV mounted on the wall.

"We're going to watch in here?"

"Yeah. It's impossible to have a TV in the living room with all those windows. Why? Is that going to be a problem for you?"

He's got a wicked grin on his face and I turn away from him, examining the bed and trying not to picture the two of us naked on it. Oh, hell… How am I supposed to spend two hours sprawled out on a mattress with him? My willpower is never going to last.

*　　*　　*　　*

"Watch your step," Lincoln whispers in my ear with his hands clamped over my eyes and a shiver races down my spine at his warm breath on my neck. I was right about my willpower not lasting long and it only took ten minutes for me to shed my pants and curl up between Lincoln's legs. It's not my fault, though. I just hate pants. After our movie, we laid in bed and made out like a couple teenagers but thankfully, things didn't get past heavy petting. Or not thankfully… I don't know anymore. When it comes down to it, I already know that what Lincoln and I have is special so why am I still waiting? I guess the truth is that I'm scared. It's been a long time since I've been with anyone and while I was once very promiscuous, that's not who I am anymore.

"There's a ledge right here," he says against the shell of my ear and a breathy moan slips past my lips before I can stop it. I wrap my fingers around his wrist and step forward gingerly, feeling for the ledge and stepping over it. Once things cooled down between us, Lincoln started making us dinner and banished me to the room so he could set up yet another surprise. I was serious earlier when I said I didn't like surprises but a girl could get used to this. Especially with a man like Lincoln.

"You ready?" he asks and I nod.

"Yes."

He presses a kiss just below my ear and all my nerve endings spring to life. "When I pull my hands away, you can look, okay?"

I nod, breathless. "Okay."

He pulls his hands away and my eyes flutter open, drawing a gasp out of me. Candles line the railing of the front porch and he brought one of the tables and a bench up from the yard.

"Just one bench?" I ask, eyeing the blanket strewn over the edge. He grins.

"You've lost your damn mind if you think I'm letting you get more than an arm's reach from me."

I glance down at my bare legs. "Do you have neighbors?"

"Do you really think I would have brought you out here in your sexy little panties if I did?" he asks,

A.M. Myers

wrapping his arms around my waist and gripping my ass cheek. "Mine."

I wrinkle my nose. "Don't go all caveman on me."

"Don't act like you wouldn't like it," he whispers, leaning in and claiming my lips as I sigh. Damn it. For being such a strong independent woman, he sure makes me weak.

My stomach growls and he pulls back and points to the bench.

"Sit."

My brow arches. "Excuse me?"

"I said, sit."

"Oh, I heard you, macho man. I was giving you a second chance to change your answer. Don't order me around like a dog or you'll see how big of a bitch I can really be."

His lips twitch as he fights back a smile and I growl. "Even worse than the Taser?"

"Yes, even worse than that."

Rolling his eyes, he lets out a dramatic sigh and gestures to the bench. "Would you like to sit down now, dear?"

"Don't be a smartass," I hiss, grabbing his face in my hands and glaring at him He barks out a laugh and wraps his arms around my waist, lifting me off the ground as he walks over to the bench and sits down with me sitting across his lap.

"Beast," I grumble and he laughs again.

"You want the blanket, babe?"

I nod, a shiver racking my body. "Yes, please."

223

As he wraps the blanket around his shoulders and swallows me up in it, I look up at the stars as peace settles over me. Not once since we got here have I thought about all the shit at home.

"Thank you," I whisper, laying my head on his shoulder. "This is exactly what I needed."

"Everything okay?" he asks, handing me one of the pork kabobs he whipped up for dinner. I sigh and nod.

"Yeah. You don't need to worry about me. I can take care of myself."

He cups my cheek, guiding my gaze to his. "Well, I do worry about you because I don't know what I'd do if I lost you and you saying you can handle it does nothing to ease my concerns. Spill."

"It's just more of those prank calls," I admit, picking at my dinner and he studies me for a moment before sighing.

"Let me handle it, baby. The guys and I will pay a little visit to Reed and put an end to this. I hate seeing you so stressed."

I shake my head. "I don't want him to know that he's getting to me. I'm stronger than this."

"Tatum," he growls and my head jerks up as I meet his eyes. "You are, without a doubt, the toughest, most badass woman that I've ever met but you're still human. It's okay if this bothers you."

"If he just came at me, I could deal with him no problem but I hate the mental games."

"We'll handle it, okay? I'll take a few guys over there and we'll put the fear of the devil into him." He grins at his own joke and I laugh.

"Did you practice that one?"

He shakes his head. "Naw, it just came to me."

"It was good," I answer with a grin but my mind is back on Reed and the phone calls. Maybe I should just let Lincoln handle this. I mean, what's the point of having a big strong biker as a boyfriend if he can't scare the shit out of little asshats from time to time.

"I'll think about it, okay?"

He nods, holding a cube of potato in front of my lips. "Good. Now, eat before it gets cold."

I grab the potato from his fingers with my teeth and the hunger in his eyes intensifies as he meets my gaze. With his eyes locked on mine, he starts trailing his hand up the inside of my thigh and I suck in a breath.

"I think we need to save this food for later," I whisper and he nods.

"Couldn't fucking agree more, Darlin'."

Every Breath You Take

Chapter Fifteen
Tatum

We crash through his bedroom door, a mass of fumbling hands and desperate, crazed kisses as he slams me against a wall and braces his hand next to my head. His knee shoves between my thighs and I hook a leg around his hip as he groans, scraping his hand down my skin. Shivers rack my body and he groans, gripping my thigh as he pulls me closer but it's still not close enough and I'm beginning to think I'm not going to be happy until his cock is seated inside me.

"I'm going to fucking destroy you in the best fucking way, baby," he whispers, his nose nuzzling into my neck before he presses his lips to my skin. My core clenches and I arch my back, rubbing my breasts against his chest.

"We're not having sex. That's still off the table."

He jerks back, looking equal parts confused and ravenous. "Then what are we doing?"

"Anything else," I breathe, trying to convey the urgency that I feel pumping through my body with each rapid beat of my heart. My nerve endings spark, sending electric currents across my skin as a wolfish grin spreads across his face.

"I can get down with that."

Both hands dip under my t-shirt and span across the entire width of my back, making me feel so small but also so protected as he claims my mouth again, his tongue hungry for another taste of me. My nipples pebble and ache as they brush against the material of my t-shirt. I wish it was his broad chest instead. Balling his shirt in my hand, I tug on it, trying to get it over his head but he's too damn tall. He laughs, letting his hands fall away from my body long enough to reach behind his head and rip the shirt off. All his tattoos come into view and I suck in a breath as my fingers skate over his skin.

"You keep touching me like that and I'm going to lose control, baby," he warns and I smile.

"Who said that was a bad thing?"

The thin white t-shirt is torn over my head and he pulls me against his large body as his lips find mine again, need pouring out of both of us. The air is thick with it, enveloping us in a world where he and I are the only two people who exist. There's nowhere I have to be, no one to see because everything begins and ends with the two of us losing ourselves in each other for the rest of the night. His hands fist my hair and he kisses me so hard that I'm convinced he's breathing for me.

"I'm going to spend hours eating your sweet little cunt, Tate, and only when you lose count of the amount of times you've come will I let up."

I shudder, my pussy clenching as I grab his forearms. "Lincoln."

"You want to know the best part of living out here?" he whispers, leaning in and dragging his lips down my neck. I shake my head. "I can make you scream as loud as I want to and no one will ever hear you. Are you going to scream for me?"

"Yes," I breathe out, squeezing my eyes shut and mentally begging him to kiss me.

"You promise?"

I nod. "Yes, I promise. Make me scream."

Growling, he wraps his arms around my ass and lifts me into the air as I squeal. My legs wrap around his waist as he turns and carries me over to the bed where he lays me down and presses his lips to my belly, just above my panties.

"I can smell you already, gorgeous. Are you wet?"

Gripping the comforter beneath me, I nod. "Yes."

He runs his hands up the inside of both my thighs before parting them and I hold my breath, my entire body tense as I wait for the touch I so desperately need.

Please.

Touch me.

A soft kiss presses against my thigh, just above my knee, and I jump as a whimper slips out of my mouth. He chuckles.

"Is that not what you want, Tate?"

I shake my head. "No and you know it."

"Do I?" he asks, laughter in his voice and I growl. He's playing games with me and my restraint is about to snap. "Why don't you tell me what you want?"

I sit up and grab his chin, forcing his gaze to mine. "I want you to rip my panties off and eat my pussy until I scream your name."

Just because it's been a long time since I've been with anyone doesn't mean I've ever been one to shy away from telling a man what I want. Lincoln's eyes close as if he's in pain and he lets out a low groan that sends goose bumps over my skin.

"Jesus Christ," he breathes and when his eyes pop open again, there's an inferno staring back at me. "Hope you know what you just started."

I don't get to say another word as he shoves me back on the bed and hooks his fingers into my panties, tearing them from my body before he drops to his knees next to the bed.

"Lincoln," I moan, eager for his touch. He grabs my leg and pulls me closer to the edge before trailing his fingers down the sides of my sex. "What are you doing?"

He laughs. "Did you really think I was going to just give you what you want without teasing you first?"

I growl, earning another laugh out of him as he drags his thumb over my clit and I jolt on the bed, sucking in a breath.

"Do that again."

"This?" he asks, repeating the move and I moan.

"Yes, that."

He repeats the move – back and forth – again and again until I'm writhing on the bed and whimpering his name. Just when I think I can't take anymore, he slips a single digit inside me, pumps a few times before pulling out, and going back to my clit. He follows the pattern for what feels like forever as he slowly builds me up to what I know will be a blinding orgasm.

"You are magnificent," he whispers and my heart skips a beat as I glance down at him. He smiles as a vibrating sound fills the room and I scowl but don't get a chance to ask what it is before he's pressing a bullet against my clit.

"Oh my god!" I yell, my body jerking from the sensation and he groans.

"You are so fucking wet," he murmurs as his finger dips inside me again and I start to tremble. Pressure builds in my belly and I know I just need a little bit more to let go.

"Please, Lincoln."

"Please what?" he asks, looking smug as hell as he meets my eyes. When our gazes connect, I know I can't hold it back anymore.

"Don't stop. I'm going to come."

He presses the vibrator harder against my clit before moving it in a circle and I gasp as my hips shoot off the bed. When he does it once more, I cry out, my body shattering with a blinding orgasm that I can feel through every inch of my body.

"Oh my god, that was…" I murmur after he tosses the vibrator on the bed next to me and I catch my breath.

"Oh, Tate." Lincoln laughs. "I'm only getting started."

I arch a brow. "Getting started with what?"

"Worshipping you until the sun comes up."

I smile. "I can get down with that."

"I've been absolutely crazy about you since the moment I first laid eyes on you," he says, moving on top of me and settling between my thighs.

"I hated you so much that day but I think it's only because from the second you looked up at me, you affected me more than anyone else ever had."

"Same, babe."

My brow wrinkles and I glance to where he threw the vibrator on the bed. "Uh… Lincoln?"

"Yeah?"

"Why do you have a vibrator?"

He glances at it and starts laughing. "Bought it the other day for you."

"You bought me a vibrator? Did you assume you'd get lucky tonight?"

He shakes his head. "Naw, baby. It was just a gift but I would be lying if I said I didn't imagine you using it in front of me."

Heat floods my body and my heartbeat pounds in my ears as I imagine spreading my legs in front of him and using my new toy.

"Come here," I whisper. "And take your shorts off."

Grinning, he shoves his shorts and boxer briefs down his legs before lying next to me on the bed and trailing his fingers over my skin. The gentle touch drives me crazy and I shiver. His fingers slip between my legs again and skate over my clit as he presses his lips to mine and I wrap my hand around his impressive length, sucking in a breath. Jesus, there's no way that thing is going to fit inside me. He shudders as I stroke him back and forth, a low groan spilling out of his mouth.

"Fuck, baby. I'm never going to last if you keep doing that."

I shrug, still stroking him. "We have all night, right?"

"Yeah," he whispers with a devilish grin. "We do."

*　　*　　*　　*

Images of last night flit through my mind on repeat as I yawn and refill coffee cups at the counter. A blush creeps up my cheeks as I remember Lincoln with his head between my thighs as I screamed his name so many times that my voice is a little hoarse this morning. In fact, I completely lost count of the number of times he made me come but my body is achingly satisfied this morning. So much so that I almost couldn't drag myself out of his bed. Although, that could also be because we didn't sleep much either. I was able to sneak in an hour or two before I would wake up again with his mouth or hands all over my body.

"Good night?" Mia asks, nudging me and I blink, turning to look at her.

"Huh?"

"I asked if you had a good night but I think I already know the answer," she teases, laughing and my cheeks heat further. It's been so long since I've done anything with a guy that it probably is written all over my face.

"Leave her alone," Nate, one of the cooks, adds. "She looks happy."

I glance back at him through the pass through. "Don't I normally look happy?"

"If this is you happy," he says, motioning to my face. "Then, I'm going to go with no."

Turning back to the dining room, I mull over his words. I guess if I really think about it, I wouldn't say I was happy before. Not that I was sad or depressed or anything but I just existed. I was so focused on just getting to the next day or getting to the day when all my worries would be behind me that I wasn't really living my life. And then Lincoln walked into the diner and changed all that.

"Hey, Darlin'," a gravelly voice says and I turn, grinning as Lincoln's eyes drop down to my lips.

"Hey, what are you doing here?"

He shrugs. "Came to pick you up after your shift and I was kind of hoping you'd spend the day with me."

"Okay, but only because it'd be really awkward right now if I said no."

He barks out a laugh and holds his hand out to me. I take it and let him pull me closer. "Really? Is that the only reason?"

"The only one that comes to mind," I whisper, distracted by his tongue trailing across his bottom lip.

He leans in and I repeat the move before I realize what I'm doing. His lips brush my ear and I fight to keep my eyes open as goose bumps race across my flesh. "So, you haven't spent all morning thinking about last night or how mind-blowing it will be when I finally take you?"

"Nope," I whisper, my hands trembling as I picture just that. He pulls back, grinning, as he releases my hand.

"Oh, okay. You about done?"

It takes me a full three seconds to register his question and I turn to the counter where Roger is pouring over the books to find Mia, Nate, Roger, and half the customers staring at me. I blush and Mia grins.

"Hey, whatever you're doing, dude," she calls to Lincoln. "Keep doing it. I've never seen her this happy."

I glare at her before turning to Roger. "Do you need me to stick around?"

He checks his watch. "No, you're good to go."

I slip back into the hallway and take off my apron before grabbing my bag and meeting Lincoln in the dining room. His smile makes my heart skip a beat as I slip my hand in his and I can't believe I almost didn't let this happen. How could I have ever walked away from him? From us?

"So, what do you want to do today?" I ask when we get out to the parking lot and he shrugs.

"I was going to ask you."

He opens the door to the Camaro for me and I slip inside before watching him walk around the front of the car. There is one thing I've wanted to do lately but it's a little silly and I'm not sure he'd want to. He climbs behind the wheel and glances at me as I bite my lip.

"What?"

"Well," I muse, pursing my lips. "There is something I want to do but it's kind of silly and you may not want to."

"What is it?"

"Well, when Mom, Theo, and I were traveling," I say, unable to think of a better word to call my nomadic first years. "We would get bored in the hotel rooms so Mom started buying us board games and it kind of became a tradition for us. It's been a long time since we played and I was just thinking about it this morning."

His brows furrow. "You want to play board games?"

"Yeah. Is that stupid?"

"No, not at all. Actually, I have an idea." He pulls his phone out of his pocket and starts texting someone. Leaning across the car, I try to peek at what he's saying but he hides it from me with a grin on his face. "Just wait. It's a surprise."

"I thought we went over this last night and again this morning when you cooked me french toast. I don't like surprises."

He chuckles, still hiding the phone from me. "Aw and see here I thought you were coming around to the idea."

"I have no clue what gave you that idea."

I cross my arms over my chest and he just grins as he continues typing away. When he's finally done, he puts the phone back in his pocket and fires up the Camaro. As he pulls out of the parking spot, I glare at him.

"Are you really not going to tell me?"

He laughs. "You'll find out soon enough, baby. How was your morning?"

Sighing, I tell him about work, which was fairly uneventful, and he tells me about some bike he's working on. As we pull up in front of the house, I scan the area, looking for both whatever surprise he's planning this time and still unable to shake the habits my mother instilled in me. The door to the Camaro opens and he scowls at me.

"What are you doing?"

I shake my head, climbing out. "It's stupid."

"Tell me anyway," he insists, taking my hand as he shuts the door and I sigh.

"When we were younger, Mom had us play this game whenever we left the place we were staying. We would have to scan the room and memorize where everything was. When we came back, she would quiz us and if we got it wrong, we had to do push-ups and wall sits."

He glances down at me, his eyes wide. "Wow. That's...intense."

"Yep, it was and even now as an adult, I do it without thinking."

Every Breath You Take

"I suppose that was the point of it though, wasn't it?" he asks and I nod as I unlock the front door.

"You're not wrong but it's a pain in the ass. Especially when I can't remember how I left the damn curtains. It'll bother me all night long."

He blows out a breath and shuts the door behind us. "You know, I half thought you were exaggerating when you told me about your childhood."

"Nope," I snap, letting out a humorless laugh. "I could also knock you out before you even realize what's happening if I wanted to but I won't."

"What did you train in?" He sits at the dining room table and I go into the kitchen, grabbing two mugs and turning the coffee maker on.

"Boxing, Jiu Jitsu, Judo, Krav Maga... If you can think of it, we probably did it for a little bit. When Theo and I turned twelve, Mom made us choose three to focus on."

"And you chose?"

"Krav Maga, Kickboxing, and Jiu Jitsu."

He leans back in his chair and crosses his arms over his chest. "So what you're saying is you could kick my ass anytime you wanted to?"

"Yeah. Not to mention the number of guns hidden in this house."

"Where?" he asks, glancing around him and I grin.

"Oh, I'm not telling you that but I will say, right now you're sitting no more than thirty feet from two."

His eyes narrow on me and I finally see it sinking in. He finally understands what I've been talking about

238

this whole time with the questions about my mom. "And how close are you to a gun?"

Grinning, I reach into the hidden cubby next to me and pull out the 1911, showing it to him before slipping it back into hiding.

"Jesus."

I laugh as he shakes his head. "See, baby? The Taser wasn't that bad at all."

"You're terrifying," he whispers, standing up and stalking over to me. "And gorgeous, magnificent, enchanting, and so many other big words that I can't think of right now because all I can think about is kissing you."

I grin as he lowers his lips to mine and the moment we connect, I sigh, feeling more at home than I ever have anywhere else. This is the kind of feeling that I could get used to, lose myself in, and despite what my mind is telling me, it doesn't scare me. Lincoln is quickly becoming my everything.

A knock at the door has us pulling apart and I'm reaching for the gun behind me when he stops me.

"It's Storm and Chance and their old ladies."

I scowl. "Why?"

"Because you wanted to play board games and these guys are my family."

"Oh," I whisper, a smile creeping across my face as I drop my hand. "Okay."

He plants a kiss on my forehead before going into the living room and opening the door.

"Thanks for coming, y'all," he says, holding the door open as I creep out of the kitchen, suddenly nervous. These people are important to Lincoln and I've never been all that good with first impressions. I just hope I don't make a total ass out of myself.

"You must be Tate," someone says as a gorgeous blonde walks over to me and wraps me up in a hug. I meet Lincoln's eyes across the room and beg for mercy as I hug her back.

"Yeah, that's me."

"Well, I'm Ali," she says, taking a step back as a man with dark hair and piercing gray eyes wraps his arm around her, "And this grumpy bastard is Logan. Or Storm, whichever works. I'm so happy to meet you."

I force a smile to my face. "It's nice to meet you, too."

"He didn't tell you we were coming, did he?" the other blonde asks as the man at her side smirks.

"Uh, no."

"Jesus, Kodiak," Ali groans. "You can't just spring things like this on a girl. Fucking cavemen, all of you."

I laugh and she flashes me a smile as the other blonde steps forward and holds out her hand. "I'm Carly and this is Chance."

"It's really nice to meet you guys."

"So," Chance says, clapping his hands. "What are we playing?"

"Strip poker?" Lincoln asks, a mischievous grin on his face.

"Not a fucking chance," Storm growls and I laugh as Lincoln steps up beside me and wraps his arm around my waist.

"Let me go grab the games." I walk into the hallway and Lincoln follows behind me.

"So, in hindsight, maybe I should have warned you."

"You think?" I hiss. "That was maybe the most awkward I've ever been in my life. I don't make a good first impression, Lincoln. People need time to warm up to me."

He laughs, pinning me to a wall as he brushes his nose over mine. "I thought you made a fantastic first impression with me."

"Yes, well, you're insane," I whisper with a giggle and he grins as he leans in and kisses me.

"Dude, I thought we were here to play games, not watch you make out with your girlfriend," someone grumbles and we both turn to find Storm and Chance standing in the entrance to the hallway.

"I've had front row seats to your disgusting love fest for the past year so you don't get to complain," Lincoln tells them and Storm rolls his eyes.

"The games are in there," I say, pointing to the dreaded closet. Thankfully, Theo and I managed to get it cleaned up when he was here or we'd never get to them.

Lincoln plants a kiss on my cheek before turning to the closet. "Go wait with the girls; we'll get the games."

Nodding, I slip into the kitchen and stop in the doorway to the dining room. "Y'all want some coffee or sweet tea or something?"

Ali smiles up at me. "Some sweet tea would be amazing."

"No, it fucking wouldn't," Storm snaps, walking out of the hallway with a couple games in his hand. I scowl as Ali sighs. "You can't have the caffeine."

"Logan, if I have to tell you one more time that some caffeine is okay, I'm going to lose it."

Carly grins, folding her arms over her chest as she watches them banter.

"Why wouldn't she be able to have caffeine?" Chance asks, following behind Storm.

"Kitten," Storm growls, ignoring everyone else. "Don't push me on this."

"No, Logan. You don't push me on this or I will murder you before this baby is born."

My mouth falls open as the rest of the room falls silent, every pair of eyes on Ali and Storm. Lincoln drops the games on the table and starts laughing so hard that he has to grab onto the chair to stay upright.

"Oh, shit, you're so screwed," he teases Storm through his laughter and Chance joins him.

"Imagine if it's a girl," he adds, nudging Lincoln and they both start laughing harder as Storm rolls his eyes and Ali beams.

"It's going to be a boy," he grumbles and the boys laugh harder, tears building in their eyes.

"It's so going to be a girl and she's going to be just as pretty as her Mama," Carly says, getting in on the fun and Storm plops down in a chair, losing all the color in his face.

"Fuck. I'm going to have to buy some guns."

Lincoln wraps his arm around my waist and pulls me closer. "You can have some of Tate's."

"Don't go giving away my guns!" I yell, shoving him and he just keeps laughing.

"Wait, wait," Storm hollers, holding his hands up. "How many guns do you have?"

"In this room?" I ask and five pairs of eyes widen on me. "Three."

"Jesus," Chance breathes out and Lincoln beams down at me.

"She could also kick your ass without breaking a sweat so be nice to her."

Rolling my eyes, I grab the deck of cards off the table and hold them up. "Y'all want to keep cataloging all my weapons or should we play some cards?"

The girls wander into the kitchen to get snacks and drinks and as I grab the other deck of cards and start shuffling them together, Storm slaps Lincoln on the back and whispers, "She's a keeper, brother."

His eyes meet mine and he smiles. "I know."

Every Breath You Take

Chapter Sixteen
Tatum

"I brought you donuts!" Mia yells as I open the
door and grab the bakery bag off the seat before I climb
into the car. Opening the bag, the scent of sugar and
bread hits my nose and I moan, my stomach grumbling.

"Thank you. I'm starving." Pulling out a maple
bacon donut, I take a bite and my eyes roll back in my
head as I let out another moan. "It's so yummy."

She laughs as she pulls away from the curb.
"What was that? I couldn't understand what you said
around half the donut in your mouth."

"It's not half," I mutter with a scowl as I glance
down at the two thirds left in my hand. "Besides, I'm
hungry. I didn't get breakfast this morning."

A mischievous grin stretches across her face.
"And why is that? A little too busy with a certain biker to
worry about sustenance?"

"No," I shoot back, a blush staining my cheeks.
That's a lie. Ever since Sunday night when he took me

over to his house, Lincoln and I haven't been able to keep our hands off each other. We still haven't had sex but I've experienced more orgasms in the last four days than I did for the two years I was having sex in high school.

"You are such a little liar," she teases, her gaze flicking between my face and the road. "Lincoln's been giving it to you good, huh?"

I shake my head. "We, uh… we haven't had sex yet."

"What?" she shrieks, her eyes wide. "How the hell have you not jumped that man? And what the fuck are you waiting for?"

"I don't want to be just another girl to him."

She pulls up to a stoplight and turns to me. "Sweetie, you're not. He made things official with you *after* you tased his ass. That man is yours."

I laugh as she turns back to the steering wheel and the light turns green. "I'm just not ready yet."

"Why?"

"I don't know." I shrug. "I guess I'm just nervous. It's been a really long time for me."

"Yeah," she sighs, nodding. "I get that. Just don't wait too long, okay? 'Cause you'll keep building it up in your head and making it harder than it needs to be."

"I thought being hard was the whole point," I say with a mock scowl and her mouth drops open as her gaze flicks in my direction. I smile.

"Oh my god, for such a prude, you're a little pervert."

I bark out a laugh as we pull into the store's parking lot.

"What are we looking for in here?"

Mia blushes. "Well, I need a dress."

"For?" I ask, polishing off my donut as she pulls into a space and parks the car.

"I kind of have a date."

My eyes widen and I smile. "That's great, Mia. Anyone I know?"

"Uh…" she hums and I arch a brow. Oh, this just got interesting. "Shaun."

"Shaun? From work?"

She nods and I beam as I picture it in my head. It's not all that far fetched and she looks really happy about it.

"Yeah. We've been dancing around each other for the better part of a year and I finally had enough and asked him out."

We climb out of the car. "Wow. I'm impressed. Where is he taking you?"

"I have no idea. He just grinned and told me to wear something cute when I asked him what his plans were."

I hook my arm through hers as we walk toward the store. "We are going to find you something to knock his freaking socks off."

She's bristling with nervous energy and I smile to myself as we walk into the store and we're blasted with air-conditioned air. Mia had a pretty steady boyfriend until six months ago when he left her without much of an explanation. She was absolutely heartbroken so I'm glad to finally see her moving on. And Shaun is a good guy so no worries there.

"So," she says, releasing my arm to grab a shirt and hold it up. "Besides never leaving the bedroom, how are things with Lincoln?"

It's my turn to blush as I glance down at a shirt to hide my face. "Good. Really good, actually."

"Look at you. I don't think I've ever seen you this happy."

I meet her eyes. "I don't think I've ever been this happy. He's… incredible."

"Oh my god, your face right now… are you in love with him?"

I suck in a breath and fight back a smile. "I think I am."

"Tate," she whispers, grabbing my shoulder and pulling me into a hug. "I'm so fucking happy for you."

"Me, too," I mumble, tears stinging my eyes but for maybe the first time in my life, they're happy tears instead of sad ones. I don't know if it was timing or the desperate situation I found myself in when Lincoln and I first met but all the stars lined up perfectly for us and I'm head over heels in love with him. He stole a piece of me the moment he glanced up from that booth and our eyes met. In that moment, I was his even if neither one of us knew it yet.

"Let's find you something to wear to knock him on his ass, too," she says, pulling away and turning toward the racks. "And don't worry about paying. I've got it."

"Oh, you don't have to do that."

She glances over her shoulder and rolls her eyes. "Why do you always have to argue with me? I want to do this for you."

"It's just… I can afford to pay for it myself now." Turning to me, she scowls. "How?"

"After my mom died, a lawyer showed up to the house with a check for Theo and me. Apparently, she had money tucked away for us."

"How much money?" she asks, her brow arching as she crosses her arms over her chest.

"A lot." When she motions for me to continue, I sigh. "Almost half a million each."

"What?" she shrieks, drawing the attention of everyone else in the store. I paste a smile on my face and wave them off before glaring at her.

"Shh."

"Sorry," she whispers. "But, what the fuck? Where did she get that kind of money?"

I shake my head. "I don't have a clue."

"And you didn't tell me?"

"How the hell do I just drop that into conversation one day? Oh, hey, by the way, my mom was loaded and left her money to me."

She nods. "Exactly like that would have worked."

"I'm sorry, Mia. It's all been a lot to process."

After studying me, she sighs. "Any other secrets you've been keeping from me?"

Pursing my lips, I look away from her and she slaps my arm with the back of her hand.

"Spill now."

"It's just these prank calls I've been getting. I'm almost sure that it's just Reed being a dumbass but they're starting to get to me." Relief washes over me as soon as the words leave my mouth. I don't like to admit it but the calls are really starting to bother me, especially since they just keep coming. I've lost count of how many times my mystery caller has sung my name over the answering machine in the past week.

"Why would Reed do that?" she asks and I roll my eyes.

"Because of the way I quit."

Her eyes widen and she grabs my arms, shaking me a little. "Tate, you promised me that you didn't hurt him."

"Uh… no. I promised you that I didn't kill him and that is true but he grabbed me when I was trying to leave and I punched him."

"Anything else?" she asks, releasing me and planting her hands on her hips. I shrink back.

"I may have also pulled a knife on him but I mean, I didn't cut him or anything."

"Jesus Christ, Tate," she breathes, shaking her head. "This is what I've been saying to you. It's dangerous."

"What would have happened if I hadn't been able to defend myself, Mia? He could have raped me or worse. I refuse to back down and make myself small to support these fragile fucking egos. Besides, Lincoln thinks it's sexy."

"Or he's scared you'll gut him like an animal if he says any different," she mumbles and I laugh as I poke her in the ribs.

"Shut up, jackass. Lincoln offered to take the guys to have a chat with Reed and I might just let him."

Laughter bubbles out of her. "Oh, to be a fly on the wall when that goes down. Reed will probably piss himself."

"One can only hope," I add and we giggle together as I pull out my phone and send a text to Lincoln.

Me:
You know that Reed thing we talked about?

"Did you just tell him to do it?" she asks, trying to read the screen. I nod.

"I'm about to."

Beaming, she turns back to the rack of clothes. "Perfect. Now, let's find us some hot dresses."

We start sorting through the racks, occasionally grabbing a hanger and holding it up for each other but nothing feels right. As I reach for a little red flowy number, the hair on my arms stand on end and I can't shake the feeling that I'm being watched. I glance around the store as my phone buzzes with a text.

Lincoln:
Yeah, I do.

Me:
Will you handle it for me?

After pressing send, I blow out a breath and shake out my arms as I turn back to the clothes. It has to be just because I was talking about the whole Reed situation. As I start looking through clothes again, the sensation intensifies and I turn toward the large windows lining the walls, searching for anyone out of place but nothing stands out.

God, I'm losing my mind.

"So, speaking of money, what are you going to do now that you have some?" Mia asks and I turn back to her, shrugging.

"I'm not sure actually. I had a meeting with a school counselor yesterday but things have changed for me."

She scowls. "How so?"

How haven't things changed?

"When I wanted to go to school to become a nurse, it was only because it was a stable, well-paying job not because I loved it. Now, my options are wide open and I don't know what to do."

She nods thoughtfully as my phone buzzes.

Lincoln:
Oh, it'll be my pleasure, Darlin'.

Lincoln:
You free tomorrow night?

Me:
Thank you and yes.

"What do you love to do, Tate? Like really, really love," Mia asks and I glance up from my phone.

"I don't know. Read?"

She scoffs. "Yeah, don't I wish I could get paid for that."

"I actually really like working at the diner if it paid better."

She nods, humming. "You could always go for a manager position the next time one opens up."

"Yeah, I guess," I whisper as a chill twists down my spine. God, why can't I shake this? It was the same thing yesterday as I walked through the campus after my meeting with the counselor. I felt like I had eyes on me constantly and I didn't feel safe again until I was in Lincoln's arms.

My phone buzzes and I glance down.

Lincoln:
The club is having a family bbq.
Wanna go?

I smile at the message, loving that he wants to introduce me to the people important to him. Mia is right about him – he's mine.

Me:
Absolutely.

"I'm going to go try this on," Mia says, holding up a little black dress and I force a smile to my face. "Want to come with me?"

My gaze flicks around the store again and I shake my head. "No, I'll wait out here but show me before you take it off."

"You got it." She bounces back to the dressing rooms with a grin on her face and I suck in a breath. As much as I would like to escape from this feeling, the thought of getting trapped back there with no exit is even more terrifying.

Turning back to the racks, I pull out a red dress that would barely even cover my ass and my phone buzzes. Sighing, I set the dress back and glance down.

Unknown:
Oh, not that dress, Darling.
It would clash with your gorgeous hair.

My hands tremble and I read the message three more times before it sinks in that someone is truly watching me. With tears burning my eyes, I type out my reply.

Me:
Who is this?

I turn back to the dresses and try to focus but my mind is solely focused on the phone in my hand as I wait for it to vibrate. An emerald green dress catches my eye and I pull it out, examining it as the phone buzzes.

Unknown:
That green would look stunning on you.

Me:
Who the fuck is this?

The room feels like it's closing in on me as I look up, scanning the rest of the store for anyone with a phone. A few people glance in my direction but no one looks out of place. My heartbeat thrashes in my ear and black spots dance across my vision. I grip the rack and close my eyes, drawing a fortifying breath before opening them again and turning toward the dressing rooms. Mia walks out of the first one and smiles as she does a little spin in her dress.

I gulp in air and force what I hope is a convincing smile to my face as I give her a thumbs-up.

"Shaun's jaw is going to drop."

She moves to the mirror and runs her hands down the front of the dress. "You think? I was kind of wanting something with color."

"What about this?" I ask, holding up a chunky coral necklace and she beams as she spins around and takes it from me.

"Yes, this is perfect. Oh, and they have a matching bracelet." She holds the necklace up to her body and I nod.

"You look gorgeous."

"I'm so excited," she squeals, doing a little dance on the pedestal. "What about you? Did you find anything you like?"

I shake my head. "No, we should go check out a different store."

"Okay, just let me change and pay for this stuff." She retreats back into the dressing rooms just as my phone buzzes.

Unknown:
Beware the man you think you know.

Chapter Seventeen
Tatum

"You nervous?" Lincoln asks, grabbing my hand as he pulls the Camaro into the clubhouse parking lot. Classic rock blares through two large speakers set up by the door and people mill around the grill, drinking beers and laughing. I suck in a breath and nod.

"A little. I want them to like me."

He flashes me an easy grin and grabs my hand, lacing our fingers before he brings it to his lips. "They're going to love you, baby."

"If you say so." Butterflies flap around in my belly as I look out over the parking lot.

"Hey," he says, nudging my chin with his finger. "I do say so. Don't stress it. You've already won Ali and Carly over and that's probably the hardest part. Oh, and if you get a chance, ask the guys to tell you how they got their names."

I smile and nod, feeling a little bit better but I don't know why I'm surprised. That's just what Lincoln does for me. He makes everything better. My mind drifts to last night and the unsettled feeling that haunted me into the early hours of the morning while Lincoln slept peacefully in my bed. After Mia and I went to the second store, I didn't get any more texts but that didn't make the feeling of being watched go away. If anything, it made it worse because I didn't know if he was there or not. I'm also beginning to wonder if this is really Reed's doing.

"Did you handle that Reed thing?" I ask as we climb out of the Camaro and he nods.

"Yeah. Storm, Chance, Smith, and I took care of it last night."

I nod. "How did it go?"

He chuckles, meeting me at the back of the car and wrapping his arm around my waist. "Uh, let's just say he won't be bothering you again."

"What time did you go over there?"

He stops, scowling down at me. "Why?"

"Just wondering."

"Did you get another call?"

I shake my head. "Just a text but it was earlier in the day."

"It was probably before we went over there, then. Have you heard anything from him since I got to your house last night?" he asks, his brow furrowed and I shake my head.

"No."

"Okay. You let me know the second something else happens, okay? It's my job to take care of you."

I scoff, shoving him as I roll my eyes. "I don't need you to take care of me. I'm terrifying as you like to point out."

"Don't fight me on this," he grumbles through a smile as he wraps his arms around me and pulls me into a kiss. A moan builds in my throat and I grab the back of his neck as I reach up on my tippy toes, trying to get just a little bit closer to him. Whistles pierce the air around us and we pull apart as Lincoln holds up both middle fingers.

"Go up to your room!" Chance yells from his seat by the fire. Carly smiles from his lap, flashing me a subtle wave.

"Tate!" someone yells and I glance up as Ali runs over to me.

"Alison!"

She stops mid-step and we both turn to see a very pissed Storm stomping over to her.

"No running."

"Logan James Chambers, if you don't ease up, I'm going to go live at the cabin until this baby is born. Do you hear me?"

He growls at her. "Keep pushing me, Kitten. I'll haul your ass inside and spank it raw, pregnant or not."

"Oh, whatever," she mumbles, rolling her eyes but I can see the smile teasing her lips as she turns back to me and gives me a hug.

"I'm so glad you could make it."

"Me, too."

She hooks her arm through mine and pulls me away from the boys. Lincoln lets out a small noise of protest but I peek over my shoulder and flash him a smile.

"Are you hungry?" Ali asks. "We've got hot dogs and hamburgers."

"Yeah, I'll grab some food here in a minute."

She nods. "Oh, let me go around and introduce you to the guys. First up, we have Blaze; he's in charge of all these toddlers."

I laugh and extend my hand. "Hi, it's really nice to meet you."

"You, too," he mumbles, shaking my hand as his gaze bores into me like he's just seen a ghost but Ali either doesn't notice or chooses not to acknowledge it.

"And this here is Smith."

Smith stands and grabs my hand before kissing it, making me giggle. "My lady."

"Dude," Storm groans from his chair and all the other guys laugh.

"Keep your lips off my woman!" Lincoln yells and I beam at him as my cheeks heat. It's the first time he's ever said something like that and it does crazy things to my hammering heart.

"This is Moose," Ali says, pointing to another handsome man with a beard. Jesus, are all these guys ridiculously good looking? Is that a requirement for this club?

"Nice to meet you," Moose says from his seat with a kind smile and I nod.

"And that is Fuzz and Streak," she says, pointing to two men sitting on top of a picnic table.

"Hey," one calls while the other nods in my direction and I hold up a hand to wave.

"Uh, hey, y'all. Thanks for inviting me."

Lincoln grabs my hand and pulls me into his lap before handing me a beer.

"Tate, you've got to settle a bet for us," Smith says and I nod as I take a sip of my drink.

"Okay, what is it?"

Lincoln starts laughing and I flash him a confused expression before turning back to Smith.

"Last night, Kodiak bet us that you would have no less than three weapons on you when you came tonight. I said one, at the most."

Beer shoots through my nose as I laugh and start to cough as Lincoln rubs my back.

"Uh," I hum, wiping at my nose. "Going anywhere with only one weapon is as bad as going with none."

"Aw, shit," he whines. "Did I just lose fifty bucks?"

"Wait," Moose interjects. "We've got to see proof."

Lincoln's body shakes underneath me as he loses it and I fight back a smile as I set my beer down on the arm of the chair and open my purse. First, I pull out the Taser and show it to them before digging out the can of pepper spray. Smith lets out a low whistle when the knife comes out next.

"That's only three," Storm points out and I nod, lifting up my pants leg to show them the pistol in my ankle holster.

"Jesus," someone whispers and I laugh.

"You just made me a whole lot of money, baby," Lincoln whispers in my ear and I grin at him.

"Glad I could help."

I glance around the circle as half the guys step forward to toss fifty-dollar bills at Lincoln and I catch Blaze staring at me again. He doesn't look away when he meets my gaze and I shift in Lincoln's lap.

"Wait, there's one more bet," Lincoln points out and Smith groans, tapping his beer bottle against his head.

"I don't even doubt the second one now and I don't want to lose any more money."

I arch a brow. "What was the second one?"

"Kodiak said you tased him," Fuzz says with a smirk and I laugh, nodding my head.

"Uh, yeah. I did."

"Why?"

I shrug. "'Cause he was being a dick."

Hoots and hollers rise up around us.

"Oh, she's going to fit right in," someone says and my heat skips a beat because for the first time in my life, I really do feel like I belong here. My skin crawls with the sensation of being watched again and I glance toward the grill where Blaze is still staring at me, his face white and his eyes filled with pain. What the hell is with this guy?

Smith stands up and trudges over to us before dropping another fifty in Lincoln's lap.

"Thanks, Tate," he grumbles and I shrug.

"Play stupid games, win stupid prizes."

Moose snorts out a laugh and slaps Smith on the back as he plops back down in his seat and chugs his beer.

"Now, I'm told that I need to ask y'all the stories behind your names?" I ask, glancing back at Lincoln as he grins. Moose groans and the guys start to laugh.

"What's wrong, Moose? Don't you want to tell Tate how you got your name?" Chance asks and he shakes his head.

"Naw, I'm good."

"Well, I'll tell it," Smith says, launching into a story about a girl who knocked Moose out with a tranquilizer dart in an attempt to kidnap him and when he went down, he started moaning like a moose.

The entire circle falls into hysterics and my belly aches by the time we finally calm down.

"That story gets better every time I hear it," Ali says, wiping at her eyes.

Moose grumbles and takes a sip of his beer. "Speak for yourself."

"What about you, Smith?" I ask and he shrugs.

"That's just my name, same as Chance. Fuzz was a cop in a previous life, Streak is the luckiest son of a bitch you'll ever meet, Kodiak used to be a moody bear but not so much since he met you and the same goes for Storm since he met Ali."

"And Blaze used to like to set fires," Lincoln says and I glance toward the grill, scowling when I find two blue eyes still locked on me. Finally, he blinks and turns away from us before stomping into the clubhouse. No one else even notices but I glance back at Lincoln, who just shakes his head. What the hell is going on?

"Tate, come dance with us," Ali says, holding her hand out to me and I smile as I take it and let her pull me off Lincoln's lap.

"Just don't bounce too much," Storm grumbles and she rolls her eyes before arching a brow.

"Not even on your…"

"Watch it," he snaps, cutting her off and I laugh as she wraps her arm around my waist with a victorious grin on her face. Carly, Ali, and I move away from the boys a little bit, closer to the speakers as *Bohemian Rhapsody* by Queen starts playing. Ali starts out singing the first part and when she stops, I pick up where she left off, really getting into it as they laugh. After a few minutes, they sit down at one of the picnic tables and I join them.

"So, what do you do, Tate?" Carly asks.

"Uh, I'm just a waitress."

Ali shrugs. "Hey, no harm in that. If you're doing what you love, it doesn't matter what anyone else thinks."

"I wouldn't say that I love it but I like it and it pays my bills. I'm actually thinking about going to school, though."

"For what?" Ali asks, leaning back and propping her arms up on the table. Gravel crunches as someone walks up behind us and we all turn as Storm slams a bottle of water down on the table.

"Drink."

She rolls her eyes again. "For fuck's sake, Logan."

"Drink," he repeats, pointing to the bottle and she nods as she grabs it.

"Man, he's bossy," I point out as he walks away and she laughs, shooting water out of her nose.

"Oh, you've got no idea. Don't worry, though. He'll get his later for being such an ass tonight. He's been especially uptight since we found out I'm pregnant." She places a hand against her belly and I smile, imagining that for myself one day.

"How far along are you?"

"Only about six weeks which is why I've been trying to convince her to get pregnant with me," she says, nudging Carly who sputters out a laugh and holds her hands up.

"Uh, no. I think Chance and I are good on the baby front for a while."

The guys drop off three plates of food for us before going back to the grill and we chat as we eat. I've never been all that good at making new friends but with Ali and Carly, it's easy to just be myself and they seem to like me. As I turn to glance at Lincoln, I see Blaze watching me from his seat by the fire and I scowl.

"What's the deal with Blaze?" I ask and both girls turn to look at him.

"What do you mean?"

I shrug. "I don't know. He's just been watching me all night long."

"Don't let it bother you," Ali urges. "Logan says that something has been off with him lately and he's just grumpy."

"So he doesn't hate me then?"

Carly shakes her head. "No way. I don't think Blaze hates anyone. He may look mean but the man's a big teddy bear."

"Speaking of bears... How did you and Kodiak meet?" Ali asks and I laugh, remembering the first time he came into the diner.

"Uh, I was his waitress and he was rude to me so I pretty much told him to go fuck himself."

Both girls burst out laughing and the guys glance in our direction before turning back to the fire.

"That's just perfect," Ali mutters, shaking her head. "I swear, it's what these guys need most of the time."

I giggle. "What? Someone to put them in their place?"

She nods and starts talking about how ridiculous the guys can be, which has me in stitches by the time Lincoln approaches the table.

"Hey, baby. You about ready to get out of here?"

I turn to him and smile. "Yeah."

"It was so nice to see you again," Ali says, standing up and giving me a hug. "Get my number from Kodiak and we'll hang out sometime, okay?"

I nod. "Yeah, that sounds great."

Lincoln leads me back over to the fire where all the guys are. "Hey, we're heading out."

"Great to meet you, Tate," Moose calls from his chair, holding his beer up and I nod.

"You, too."

Smith jumps up and gives me a hug that makes Lincoln growl. "Don't be a stranger, okay?"

"I think that's enough," Lincoln snaps, peeling Smith away from me and I grin at the knowing look in his eye.

"Thanks for inviting me," I say to the whole circle. "It was great meeting all of you."

We turn to leave and Lincoln slips his hand in mine, lacing our fingers together as we walk toward the car.

"Tate!" someone calls and I glance over my shoulder to see Smith waving to me. "When Kodi fucks up, I'll be right here waiting, baby."

I start laughing as Lincoln spins around and flips him off.

"You're damn lucky I don't break your neck tonight, Lucas," he growls and a few of the guys laugh.

"Lucas?" I whisper and Lincoln nods.

"His first name."

My Heart Will Go On by Celine Dion starts playing and I glance back again to see Smith waving his phone over his head with his eyes closed.

"Come back to me, Tate!" he yells and Lincoln sighs as I giggle.

"Jesus, he's drunk tonight."

Turning back toward the Camaro, I drop my head back and yell, "Good-bye, Smith!"

"Get down before you fall in the fire, dumbass!" someone else yells and I laugh, feeling more carefree than I have in weeks.

"Did you have fun?" Lincoln asks as he opens my door and I nod, turning to face him with the door between us.

"Yes. This is amazing. Thank you for bringing me." Leaning up on my tippy toes, I press my lips to his and he groans as his fingers slip into my hair.

"I've got to get you home," he whispers against my lips, urgency in his voice and I nod before slipping into my seat. He closes my door and jogs around the back of the Camaro before getting behind the wheel. As we pull out of the parking lot, I glance in the side mirror and watch the scene behind me. It was exactly what I always imagined having a big family would feel like and it hits me that I don't want to lose any of this.

We spend the rest of the ride to my house in a comfortable silence with our hands clasped between us and in my mind, I'm imagining an entire life with Lincoln. For the first time, I'm thinking of this as long term because the truth is that I'm completely and totally in love with the man sitting next to me and I'm ready for more. I'm ready for all of it.

When we pull up in front of the house, Lincoln parks the car and instructs me to wait while he jogs to open my door. Hand in hand, we walk up the front walk as butterflies flutter around in my belly. Tonight is the night. I'm done waiting for some sign that this is right because I already know that it is. Lincoln is the one I've been waiting for.

When we get to the front porch, I turn to face him and grip his shirt, pulling him to me as I press my lips to his. He lets out a low groan as his arms wrap around my waist, pulling me even closer as I slip my arms behind his neck. Stumbling in the dark, he moves us to the side of the house and my back presses against the doorbell. It rings from the other side of the door and I pull away as I start laughing.

"Sorry," he murmurs. "Where were we?"

I lean in, letting my lips brush his. "Right about here, I think."

He kisses me, mutters "Keys," and kisses me again as I slip them into his hand. As he pulls back to focus on getting the door unlocked, I press my lips against his neck, loving the scratch of stubble on my lips as I breathe in his rugged scent. He groans and flicks his hips against me.

"Fuck, that feels good."

Smiling, I lick a slow path up the side of his neck before nipping at his ear. "Unlock the door, baby."

"I'm fucking trying but that is a little distracting."

I giggle and blow a stream of cold air across his neck. He shudders in my arms with another groan.

"I don't want to wait anymore, Lincoln. Tonight, I want you to make love to me."

He groans, planting his fist on the side of the house as his cock jerks against my thigh.

"Baby," he breathes. "Give me two seconds to get this fucking door open and then it's on."

I nod and press gentle kisses against his neck as he slips the key into the deadbolt and unlocks the door.

Once we're in the house, he slams the door shut behind us and locks it again, not even bothering to turn on the lights as he kicks his shoes off on the way to the stairs. His fingertips scrape up my thigh as he pulls my dress up and over my head, leaving me in only panties as I fumble with his belt.

He releases me to pull his shirt over his head and I trail one hand down his stomach as my mouth waters.

"Keep looking at me like that, Darlin', and tonight is going to be a whole lot rougher than I intended."

I meet his eyes. "Good. That's how I want it."

"Fuck," he hisses, slamming me up against the wall in the hallway and slamming his lips on mine as I pull his hair, urging him on. "Get my pants off."

I grab his belt and unhook it as he bites into my neck and my eyes flutter closed, heat flooding my body.

"Pants, baby," he growls, his hands seemingly all over me at once like he can't get enough. Forcing myself to focus, I manage to undo his belt and shove his jeans over his hips before they fall to the floor. He steps out of them and effortlessly picks me up, turning toward the stairs.

"Wait," I yelp and he pauses. "I moved rooms. I'm down here now."

I point to my mom's old bedroom and he nods, quickly changing direction and charging through the door before tossing me on the bed.

"Shit, condoms," he mutters, looking back to the hallway where he left his pants and I laugh as I point to the bedside table. I didn't think it would happen tonight

but I was prepared for whenever it did happen. He
marches over to the table and grabs one out of the drawer
before standing in front of me and holding out his hand. I
take it and he helps me to my knees as he molds me to
his body and wraps his arm around my waist.

"I never stood a chance against you," he
whispers, leaning in and pressing a soft kiss against my
lips. I thread my fingers through his hair as I pull back.
"What I feel with you, for you, I never thought I would
love someone like this."

Tears burn my eyes. "You love me?"

"Yeah, baby. I fucking love you, think I have
since the moment I first saw you."

I beam, pulling him in to another kiss as I work
up the courage to admit my feelings. As he leans back, I
sigh. "I love you, too, Lincoln. You're everything that
I've been waiting all these years for and at this point, I
don't know what I'd do without you."

It's so weird how you can go through most of
your life and be so self-sufficient and then you meet
someone and in the blink of an eye, they are an integral
part of who you are – like you were never truly you or
whole until the moment your eyes met theirs.

"We'll have time to talk about all this later but
I'm just letting you know now that I'm never walking
away from you. You are my everything and I have no
future if you're not in it," he whispers.

Our lips meet in the space between us, no one
leading the kiss this time as we fall back onto the bed
with him on top of me. He kisses down my jaw to my
neck before planting kisses across my chest and I arch

off the bed, begging for more. I grab his hand and move it to my breast, earning a grin from him as his fingers squeeze my flesh and I sigh.

"Lincoln," I pant, my clit pulsing with need and my entire body aching for more. "Panties off."

"Yes, ma'am," he chants, moving between my thighs and licking his lips as he slowly peels the lacy material down my legs before tossing it over his head. Leaning in, he kisses the inside of my thigh and I jerk beneath him, mentally screaming at him to move a little higher.

"You need something, baby?" He chuckles and I moan, lifting my hips off the bed.

"Please, Linc. I need it."

He groans. "Fuck, I love hearing you beg, baby."

Spreading my legs, he kisses my thigh again before flicking his tongue over my clit softly. I sigh, gripping the sheets underneath me as he keeps a slow steady pressure with his tongue.

"Lincoln," I moan, slipping my fingers into his hair. He groans and the sound vibrates across my flesh, earning another moan from me. He starts with long slow drags of his tongue before taking a break and switching to short, fast flicks to my clit. Each one sends me climbing to a glorious release before he changes it again and I'm practically back at square one.

I yank his hair in frustration and he chuckles before sucking my clit into his mouth. I cry out, arching off the bed, and he pushes me back down as he slips a finger inside me.

"Fuck, baby. You're soaked."

I nod. "Why don't you do something about it?"

"Yeah?" he asks, standing and shoving his boxer briefs down his legs. His hand wraps around his impressive length and my sex clenches as I watch him stroke the shaft. "This what you want?"

"Yes." The word comes out as a desperate whisper and I reach for him. "Please."

Growling, he grabs the condom off the bed and tears it open, his molten gaze locked on me as he slides it on. My heart hammers in my chest as he settles between my thighs and gazes down at me.

"Hey, Tate," he whispers and I nod.

"Yeah?"

Leaning in, he kisses me so softly, so reverently that I almost cry before pulling away. "I love you."

"I love you," I whisper with a nod as the head of his cock presses against my entrance and he slides inside. I gasp, gripping his arms as he slowly works himself inside me and when his hips meet mine, he strokes my face.

"Okay?"

I nod. "It's just been a while."

"Don't worry, baby," he whispers, inching out of my pussy before slowly sinking back in. "I'll take care of you. Always."

"Linc."

At the sound of his name on my lips, his eyes close and he groans, thrusting forward a little harder. My legs wrap around his waist and all bets are off. He grabs my hands and pins them to the bed over my head with one hand while the other grips my hip. He pulls out and sinks into me again and again, hitting the perfect spot each time he drives forward that it doesn't take long before I'm trembling beneath him.

Pressure builds in my belly and I moan, managing to wiggle one hand free to cling to him. He releases the other and my fingers dig into his back as a powerful orgasm washes through me.

"Oh, fuck," I cry, throwing my head back and lifting my hips off the bed as my pussy clamps down on him. Dropping his head to my shoulder, he groans, his muscles tensing as his cock jerks inside me. Our panting is the only sound in the room until he pulls back and meets my eyes. Happiness bubbles out of me and I have no other choice but to start giggling and he joins me, shaking his head as he presses his lips to my forehead.

"I hope you weren't planning on getting any sleep tonight, Sugar," he murmurs and I'm so happy that I don't even object to the name.

Chapter Eighteen
Tatum

Staring at my reflection in the mirror, I fight back a smile as a blush creeps up my cheeks and my gaze cuts to the large tub in the corner where Lincoln and I had sex a couple times last night. Closing my eyes, I can almost still feel his hands on my skin and I let out a sigh as I open them again. The woman staring back at me looks like me but better like a Tatum 2.0 – brighter eyes, a permanent smile on her face, and so in love with the most incredible man on the planet that it shines through every pore. This is what pure happiness looks like. I've never seen it on my own face before but it looks damn good on me and I know I'll fight to the death to hang onto it.

Biting my lip, I peek around the bathroom door and grin at the sight of Lincoln stretched out across my bed on his stomach. He's naked as a jaybird and the sheet has fallen enough to show off his pert ass that I just want to grab. My mind replays last night again and I shake my head as I watch him. I still can't believe this is my life now when only a month ago, everything was falling down around me and I'm never going to take that for granted.

"Why are you just standing there staring a me?" Lincoln asks, his voice thick with sleep as he peeks one eye open.

"I was just thinking how sexy you looked sprawled out in my bed."

He flashes me a lazy grin as he rolls to his side. "Yeah? Why don't you come over here and prove it?"

"You're insatiable." I laugh, shaking my head. I lost count of how many times we had sex last night and my poor vagina needs a damn break.

He nods. "I'm never going to get enough of you, Tate."

"Well, I was actually thinking I'd make you some breakfast first and then we can come back to bed."

His stomach growls and he nods. "Mm, yeah. That sounds good. Is it cool if I jump in the shower first?"

"Of course." I step out of his way and he swings his legs to the side of the bed before scrubbing his hand down his face. When he hops up, he barrels toward me and I squeal as he picks me up and claims my lips.

"Good morning, gorgeous," he whispers as he pulls back.

"Back at you, handsome. You feelin' pancakes or french toast this morning?"

He purses his lips and I giggle. God, he's just so damn cute. "Pancakes sound good but let me take you out for breakfast."

"You sure you don't want to stay in?" I ask, wiggling my eyebrows and he laughs, squeezing me tighter.

"Yeah, I want to take my girl out for breakfast and then we'll come back here and spend the whole day in bed. How does that sound?"

I nod. "Perfect."

"You want to get in the shower with me?" he asks as he sets me back on my feet and I shake my head as I pat his chest.

"If I did that, we would never get to breakfast and I'm starving."

Grinning, he reaches for the tie on my robe. "Let me just get a peek then."

"No." I slap his hand away and he laughs, grabbing my hand and pulling me back into his body like he can't stand to be away from me.

"I love you," he whispers, flicking my nose with his and my heart skips a beat as I close my eyes and nod.

"I love you, too." My stomach growls and I smack his bare ass. "Now, go get in the shower."

"Okay, okay," he concedes, holding his hands up and letting me back away from him. Before he disappears behind the bathroom door, he blows me a kiss and my grin grows. Damn, my cheeks hurt from smiling so much but I don't think I even care.

As the water starts running, I turn away from the bathroom door and yawn.

"Coffee," I mutter to myself as I head toward the bedroom door. When I step into the hallway, my foot hits something and I glance down, shaking my head as I scoop his jeans off the floor. Glancing up, I giggle at the trail of clothing from the front door to my bedroom. I guess we weren't all that concerned with tidiness last night.

I tuck the jeans over my arm and walk into the kitchen, depositing them on the island before I turn toward the coffee maker and turn on the radio. Take On Me by A-ha starts playing and I dance around the kitchen as I set the coffee maker up. I should find a few minutes to call Theo back today since I haven't spoken to him for a few days and I want to talk to him about coming for another visit. I'd really love to introduce him to Lincoln.

A beeping sound cuts through the music and I turn it down as I spin around and inspect the kitchen as I wait for the beep to come again. When it does, I turn to the sound and spot Lincoln's cell phone laying on the floor in between the bedroom and kitchen. The notification light is going crazy and I roll my eyes as I trudge over to it and scoop it up off the floor. I press the button on the side to wake it up. If nothing else, I'll just turn it off so it stops annoying me.

Before I can do anything, an image appears on the screen and I freeze, my mouth popping open as I stare at it, my mind screeching to a halt. I don't know how long I stand here, staring at the image before I suck in a breath and glance up at the camera in the corner of the kitchen. When I turn back to the phone, I take a step to the left and watch in horror as the image moves also.

Spinning toward the camera, I watch the image of me spin also and shake my head.

How? How does Lincoln have the live feed from the cameras?

And why?

Why is he watching me?

There has to be a reasonable explanation for this, right? I know him. He wouldn't do... whatever this is to me. Right?

He knows so much about my past but the one thing I never told him about was the cameras or the safe room so how did he even know they were there?

And how long has he been watching me? Since we started hanging out? Since we first met? Before that even?

The implications crash down on me and I struggle to breathe as I move to the counter and plant my hand on it. After the past three weeks and last night, I don't want to jump to conclusions but nothing is adding up and I feel more in danger than I did in the store when I was receiving those messages. Could that have been Lincoln, too? Is this all just a big game to him?

My breathing becomes labored and tears sting my eyes as I think over the past few weeks. Is he really behind all of this? It makes perfect sense and absolutely no sense at the same time but with everything I know and all my training, I have to assume these things aren't a coincidence. My chest aches and I gulp in a breath, willing myself not to cry as tears sting my eyes. This can't be happening. Not when I thought I had finally found my happiness.

Was this a joke?

Does he even love me?

Glancing down at the phone, I back out of the camera and notice a folder labeled Tate. I shouldn't click it because it will only bring me heartbreak but I have to know. I click on it, holding my breath as multiple files pop up. The first one I click on has general information on me – name, date of birth, height, weight, hair color – that sort of thing and a quiet sob bubbles out of me.

"No," I whisper, shaking my head. "No, no, no."

The next file I click on is all about Theo and anger floods my system. It's one thing to come after me but it's another thing all together to go after my brother - one that I will not stand for. The next file is all about Mom but there isn't much information there and I sigh as I click the next one and suck in a breath. It's a photo of Theo and I sprinkling Mom's ashes on the beach and it tells me everything I need to know. This has been a set-up from the beginning.

Dropping the phone on the counter, I close my eyes and let the pain swallow me up for a moment as my heart shatters in my chest. All the dreams I built up in my head vanish like footprints in the sand and just when I think I'm going to break under the burden of my heartache, I stop. I let the anger replace the pain, shutting down anything that doesn't serve a purpose in this moment. Lincoln, if that even is his real name, made one grave mistake when going after me and that was choosing me in the first place.

The love I felt for him turns to hate and I finally understand that old saying about there being a thin line between the two as I reach into the cubby next to the sink and pull out the 1911. The water turns off in the bathroom. I plant my feet and aim the gun at the bedroom doorway, gripping tightly to my anger. All this time, all the fear I felt whenever the phone rang, it's all been him and it pisses me off as much as it worries me. What are his intentions?

Beware the man you think you know.

The saying runs through my head again, like it has so many times since that first call came in, but this time, I understand it perfectly. The seconds tick by in agonizing slowness and my mind races through scenarios. Will he freeze when he sees the gun? Will he charge me? The thought of shooting him, of watching a bullet rip through his body makes my stomach roll and a tear slips down my cheek before I wipe it away, baring my teeth. Why the fuck do I care if I shoot him? He's done nothing but lie and manipulate me since before we even met. He's playing games with my heart and he's going to lose.

"Hey, baby, do you know where…" His words trail off when he glances up and notices the gun in my hand, aimed at his chest. "Tate, what are you doing?"

"Was it fun?" I hiss, my hand shaking. He frowns and takes a few steps toward me. "Don't move."

He freezes, holding his hands up. "Was what fun, baby?"

"This." I motion between the two of us. "Was this fun for you? Did you just hang out with the guys and have a good laugh over what an idiot I am?"

"Sweetheart," he whispers, stepping forward again. "I don't know what you're talking about."

I grab the phone off the counter and back away from him before tossing it in his direction. "I'm sure this will clear it up."

He catches it effortlessly and glances down at the screen, his eyes going wide and the color draining from his face.

"Baby, no," he whispers in horror. "You don't understand. You have to let me explain."

He takes another step toward me and I cock the gun.

"I don't have to do anything. Everything I just saw makes things perfectly clear for me."

"It's not what you think," he pleads and it all just sounds like excuses to me. I roll my eyes.

"Don't give me that tired line. You've been caught red-handed, Lincoln. The game's up and I'm not your pawn anymore."

He takes a few steps and I arch a brow in warning.

"Please, Tate," he pleads, his voice cracking as he folds his hands behind his head and his gaze wanders around the room.

"Get your shit and get out."

He shakes his head. "You have to hear me out. Please, I can explain everything."

"I've made myself perfectly clear," I say, my chest tightening as my hands tremble and a sob builds in the back of my throat. "If you don't leave, I will shoot you."

"Tate, baby, I love you so much. Please just let me explain."

Hearing him say he loves me is the final nail in his coffin and rage barrels through me as I drop my aim to his thigh and fire. He roars in pain, clutching his leg as he falls to the kitchen floor. Turning away, I grab the phone and dial nine-one-one before pressing the phone to my ear.

"911, what is your emergency?" the operator asks and I turn to face Lincoln.

"Yes, I need the police, please. There's a man in my home and he's been stalking me."

Typing fills the other end of the line. "And where is this man now? Are you safe, ma'am?"

"Yes," I whisper, tears building in my eyes. "I'm safe. He can't get to me anymore."

Every Breath You Take

Chapter Nineteen
Tatum

My eyes burn from a lack of sleep as I drop my coffee mug onto the counter and grab the pot, pouring the rest of its contents into my cup. I scowl. Did I really drink this whole thing already? Sighing, I lean back against the counter and scrub my hands over my face. After the police carted Lincoln off last night and I'd given my statement, I locked myself in the safe room but even that wasn't enough to calm me down. Not when every time I close my eyes, I see Lincoln, lying in bed next to me with a sleepy smile on his face.

"No," I hiss, dashing away a tear that managed to escape before I was able to lock down my emotions. I will not cry for this bastard.

He used me.

He played me.

He lied to me.

None of it was real.

That's what I just need to keep reminding myself
until this crushing ache in my chest goes away. Yawning,
I push off the counter and grab my coffee before trudging
back to the safe room where Mom's box of letters is
spilled out across the desk. Sitting down, I pick up the
one in front of me and start reading.

*Days like today, I get so mad at you, S. Mad that
you felt you had to run away from me to hide your pain
and mad that you felt you couldn't lean on me when it
was too much for you to handle. I know that's not fair but
I was right there with you. I lost something, too, and
then, I lost you as well.*

Sighing, I toss the letter down and shake my
head. How many people did my mother hurt and for what
reason? It had to be a damn good one, right? All I've
been able to find in these letters is cryptic and mysterious
– like they were edited to exclude anything that could
give me some answers. And I'm eager for answers.
Especially after I solved one mystery in my life last
night.
"Tate?" Theo's panicked voice echoes through
the house and my mouth pops open as I jump out of the
chair and run to the door.
"Theo?"
He pokes his head into the bedroom and I barrel
out of the closet, crashing into him and wrapping him up
in a hug as relief surges through me.
"What are you doing here?"

A.M. Myers

He releases me and takes a step back as he inspects me. "Lincoln called me last night and told me to get my ass to Baton Rouge as fast as I could. What's going on, T? Are you okay?"

"Lincoln," I snarl, spinning away from him and marching back into the safe room before I throw myself in the office chair. He scowls as he follows behind me.

"Why are you in the safe room?"

I shrug. "Because it feels safe."

"And why wouldn't you feel safe, Tate?" he asks, his voice taking on a hard edge as he perches on the edge of the couch. I meet his gaze and a sob rips through my lips before I can stop it. His eyes widen and he jumps up, pulling me out of the chair and into his arms.

"I fucking knew something was going on with you. Why did you lie to me?"

I shake my head. "I didn't think it was a big deal and I didn't want to worry you."

"You need to tell me everything," he insists, wiping a few tears from my cheeks and I nod as I pull out of his grip and sit back down.

"You should sit."

He moves back to the couch and I suck in a breath before spilling my guts to him, starting with the phone calls and the note that was taped to the door.

"And you think that was Lincoln all along?" he asks and I nod. He sighs. "I don't know, T. Why did he call me yesterday?"

My chest aches as I tell my brother everything that happened in the last forty-eight hours and when I finish, he jumps up and slams his fist into the wall.

Every Breath You Take

"Motherfucker," he seethes, pacing back and forth across the floor. "And you shot him?"

I nod. "Yeah."

"Good. Serves the bastard right."

As I watch my brother pace in front of me, I scowl. "Why did he call you though?"

"He wants me to bring you over to the clubhouse."

I scoff, spinning away from him. "Well, how fucking nice for him but if I see him again, I'm putting a bullet in his chest."

"He said it has to do with Mom."

I freeze and spin to face Theo. "What the fuck does he know about Mom?"

"Only one way to find out," he answers with a shrug and I only have to think it over for a second before I nod. Lincoln knows exactly how to get me there because he knows how desperately I want answers.

"Fine, let's do it."

Standing up, I open up the gun safe and grab my ankle holster, propping my foot up on the couch so I can put it on.

"What are you doing, T?" Theo asks, his voice full of humor and I shoot him a glare.

"If you think I'm showing up there without weapons, you've lost your fucking mind."

He laughs, crossing his arms over his chest. "Are we going to have a shoot-out with a biker gang?"

"Club," I snap, unsure why I'm defending them. "They are a club and no. I might shoot Lincoln again for good measure, though."

He nods, watching me as I slip the pistol into the holster at my ankle before grabbing another one and threading it through my belt.

"And what if there's a good explanation for all of this?"

I sigh, nodding my head. "I'm not willing to rule out the possibility that there's a reason he was watching me but inserting himself into my life, making me fall in love with him, and sleeping with me? He has no fucking excuse there."

And let's not even get into the note and phone calls.

"I'm sorry that the first time you decided to try again, it turned out like this, T."

My lip wobbles as I redo my belt and grab a gun. "You have nothing to apologize for, Theo."

"I wish I would have been here. I would have seen him for who he really is."

I shake my head, patting his shoulder. "I love you, but I don't know that you would have. He fooled me. I was imagining a future with him and the whole time he was playing me."

"I warned him about breaking your heart," he whispers, balling his fist up and I pat his shoulder again as I stick a knife in my boot.

"Let's get this over with and then we can focus on spending some time together. How long are you here for?"

He shrugs. "That depends on what happens at our meeting, I suppose."

I nod and wait as he puts a holster on before we head out to his car. As soon as we start driving toward the clubhouse, my nerves start to take over and my hands shake. Sucking in a breath, I steel my shoulders and focus on my anger, using it to shield me through this meeting. So what if I'm going to see him again? He doesn't get to affect me anymore, not after all the mistakes he's made.

"We're here," Theo says as he slows the car and pulls into the clubhouse parking lot. My knee bounces and he glances over at me. "You going to be okay?"

"Yep."

He points to my knee. "You sure about that? You're usually more steady than this."

"Well, this is real not just a simulation so yeah, I'm a little jittery."

It also might have something to do with the pot of coffee I drank.

We pull into a spot and my stomach flips as I open the door and step out, sucking in a breath. Just like in the kitchen yesterday, I shut down everything but the anger I need to face Lincoln again and slam the door closed. Blaze walks out of the clubhouse with Smith and Storm on his heels and Theo and I meet him halfway.

"Thank you for coming," he says and I nod.

"Why are we here?"

He sighs. "We'll go over all that inside. I just need Smith to check you for weapons."

"I have weapons and I'm keeping them," I assert, meeting his blue eyes.

"I'm afraid I can't take that risk, Tate. I understand you're angry and I can't put my guys in danger."

I bark out a laugh, turning to Theo, whose gaze is scanning the area. "You know I'm mad? Understatement of the fucking year and do you really think I need my weapons to defend myself?"

"No one here wants to hurt you, Tate," Blaze assures me and I sneer at him.

"It's a little late for that, I think."

"Let her keep them," a voice calls out from the door to the clubhouse and I stiffen as Lincoln hobbles out, pain etched into his face.

"Oh, how fucking gracious of you."

"Baby, please," he pleads, anguish in his whiskey eyes and my heart stutters as white-hot pain pierces my chest.

"You call her that again and I'll shoot your other leg, motherfucker," Theo snarls, taking a step forward with his hand on his gun.

"Enough!" Blaze shouts and everyone turns to look at him as silence descends on the parking lot. "Tate, you can bring one weapon in."

Fuming, I turn back to the car and open the door before propping my leg up on the seat and pulling the pistol out of my ankle holster. I toss it down on the seat before grabbing the Taser out of my back pocket and setting it down next to the gun. As I slam the door and walk back over to Theo, I catch sight of Smith smiling at me but I look away. No matter how much I like these guys, I don't know who I can trust here.

"Follow me," Blaze says, turning and walking back toward the clubhouse door like he's leading a death march and my hands shake with nerves as my mind runs wild with questions. I don't even know where to begin with why we're here because Theo and I know nothing of our mother's past. We could be walking into anything right now.

Inside the clubhouse, the rest of the guys mill around, talking quietly to each other and sipping beer, and when we walk in a few of them offer me a smile. I spot Ali and Carly in the back corner, talking, and when Ali waves, I ignore her, turning back to stare straight ahead of me. Blaze leads us into a room with a long rectangular table and everyone else, except Ali and Carly, file in behind us. A vaguely familiar man sits on one side with his arm around a little brunette with a kind smile and Blaze points to the two chairs across from them.

"Please have a seat."

Theo and I sit down as the guys line up along the back wall and the wall across from me. Lincoln posts up right in front of me so that when I look up, I have no choice to lock eyes with him. Not that his pleading expression is going to do him any good. I do not easily forget or forgive.

"What are we doing here, Dad?" the man across from me asks and I recall when Lincoln took me to get my tattoo. He said the owner was Blaze's son, Nix, but I was sure I didn't meet him that day. Why does he look so familiar then?

"I was just about to get to that, kid."

Theo squeezes my hand and I glance over in his direction as he mouths, "Okay?"

I nod and he gives my hand another squeeze as Blaze sits at the head of the table and sighs.

"Nix, I'd like you to meet Theo and Tate Carter, your brother and sister."

Gasps fill the room and my eyes widen as I feel Theo's hand clamp down on mine. My head feels fuzzy as I stare at the man across the table, trying to put the pieces together.

"What?" Nix asks, turning to look at Blaze. "What the hell do you mean they are my brother and sister?"

"Their mother, Sarah, is… was your mother, too."

With wide eyes, he stares down at the table, his jaw ticking.

"You need to keep explaining, Dad."

Blaze sighs. "I first met Sarah, your mother, in 1986 when she moved to Baton Rouge to go to school and we hit it off right away. God, she was mesmerizing and I fell in love with her the very moment I met her. From that day on, we were inseparable." The love and devotion still shining in his eyes for our mother is so real, so potent that I have no choice but to believe him. I can see the pain of losing her splayed out across his face and it's another one of those moments when it hits me how little we really knew about her.

"A year later, we found out we were pregnant with twins."

Theo and I look at each other with wide eyes. The math doesn't work out for us but there's only one man sitting across the table from us so I have no idea what to think.

"Wait," Nix says, sitting up straight. "What the fuck are you saying?"

Blaze's eyes shine with unshed tears and my stomach sinks as I hold Theo's hand a little tighter. "I'm saying that you are a twin but your brother died during delivery."

Theo squeezes back and our eyes meet, both of us trying to imagine how empty we would feel without the other and tears well up in my eyes. I turn back to Nix, watching as he drops his head into his hands.

"I had a brother?" he asks, his voice faint and I want to go over to him and give him a hug but I stay rooted to my seat.

"Yes, you did."

"And my mother, was she really a club whore like you always said?" He looks up, meeting Blaze's eyes with an anger that I recognize.

"What? You called our mother a whore?" Theo snarls, standing up but I pull him back down, shaking my head. Now is not the time.

"She wasn't. She was the love of my life."

Nix blows out a breath, still shaking his head like he can't process any of this. I don't blame him since I'm struggling myself.

"Why did she leave us?" he asks.

"When we lost your brother, she broke down and she just couldn't get over it. She said she needed to go away for a while and I would have done anything she needed me to do."

"So you just let her leave? Why didn't she come back?"

Blaze turns to Theo and me. "This is where you come into the story. While your mother was traveling around, she met a man named Dominic King. King was and still is a notorious crime boss in Chicago and not the kind of man you mess with. Before she even realized what was happening, she was swept up in that world."

I scoff. "Seemed to be a common problem for her."

"She was in pain, Tate, and she didn't care about anything because her baby was dead."

"One of her babies," Nix cuts in and I nod in agreement.

"Look, I'm not defending all her choices and you all have every right to be fucking pissed about all this but you need to know everything."

"Fine," I snap. "How did we end up back here in Baton Rouge?"

"When she found out she was pregnant with the two of you, she knew that she couldn't let you be raised in that world so she ran but before she did, she managed to get her hands on evidence that would put Dominic King away for a very long time and a boatload of money."

Theo and I share a look.

Seems we took blood money after all.

"And that's why we stayed in hotels and moved so much?" I ask and Blaze nods.

"Y'all were on the run from him."

"So, what changed?" Theo asks, the hard set of his eyes giving away nothing.

"When the two of you were five, Sarah knew that she couldn't keep doing this for the rest of her life so she arranged a sit down with Dominic and made a deal with him. As long as he stayed away from the three of you, she would never turn the evidence over to the authorities."

"He just let us go?"

Blaze nods. "You've had people from his organization watching over you through the years but you never knew they were there and as far as I can tell, he kept his word."

"Then why are we here?"

"Because your mother's death opened a door and Dominic has decided to walk through it. He wants the evidence back and he wants the two of you."

"Stop," I say, standing up and pulling Theo to his feet with me. "I need somewhere to talk to my brother alone."

"Kodiak, take them to my office."

I point to him and shake my head. "Anyone but him."

"Smith," Blaze says as Lincoln's face falls. I turn away from him and Smith leads us to the next room over.

"Can I just say, none of us knew anything, Tate," he whispers and I nod.

"I can see that. It's okay. I don't blame you."

He nods and shuts the door behind us as I lock eyes with Theo.

"What the fuck is happening?" I whisper scream and he shakes his head.

"I feel like my brain is exploding. We have a brother and our dad is a criminal and our mother... Jesus, our mother is the best goddamn liar in the fucking world."

I shake my head, plopping down in the chair in front of the desk. "My head is spinning. I don't know how much more I can hear."

"I know but I think we need to hear everything," he says, crouching down in front of me and grabbing my hands.

"How much more could there possibly be?"

He shrugs. "Only one way to find out."

After sucking in a breath, I stand and he takes my hand as we march out of the office and into the room where everyone else is gathered. It's eerily quiet as we sit down and Theo gives my hand a squeeze. The other side of the table is empty and I glance over my shoulder, searching for Nix and the brunette but they're gone.

"Is there anything else we need to know?"

"Look, Tate," Blaze sighs. "I just want to apologize for the way I handled things. Since her death, I haven't been in a good place and I haven't been thinking clearly."

I study him for a moment before nodding. "I can understand that but if you'd just come to me in the first place, this could have been so much simpler."

"I've been keeping life altering lies from my son for his entire life. There is no simple in this situation."

"Then why do it?"

He sighs, running his hand over his face. "Because it's what she wanted and I would have done absolutely anything for her. She got it in her head that if Dominic ever knew about Nix or me, he would hurt us as a way to get back at her and maybe he would have, I don't know."

"What did you mean when you said Dominic wants the two of us?" Theo asks and Blaze nods.

"One of the biggest things that pissed Dominic off when your mother ran was the fact that she took the two of you. You're his blood and his legacy and to a man like that, it means everything."

"Are we in danger?"

Blaze runs a hand over his face again. "I don't know if he'll hurt you but I think he wants you back in Chicago with him and he won't mind forcing the issue if he has to. It's why I had Kodiak watching you."

"We are not talking about him," I hiss, my gaze flicking in his direction for only a second before I look back to Blaze.

"Tate, please, I'm fucking sorry," Lincoln says from his place against the wall and before I even realize what I'm doing, I have the knife out of my boot and I stab it into the table.

"Shut up."

A chuckle and a whispered, "Damn" comes from somewhere in the back of the room but I'm too busy directing my death glare at Lincoln to turn and look who said it.

"I would like Kodiak to stay with you until we sort all this out."

I scoff. "Not fucking happen…"

"Done," Theo cuts me off and I turn to him with wide eyes.

"What the fuck?"

He offers me an apologetic look. "I need to know you're safe when I go back to Charleston."

"We're just trying to keep you safe, Tate," Blaze adds and I turn to him.

"Congratulations. Do you want a goddamn medal?"

"It's what your mother would want me to do."

I shake my head. "Don't you dare talk about what my mother would want. She spent her entire life lying to us and she doesn't get a say now that she's dead."

"Kodiak is staying with you and that is the end of the discussion," he growls before standing up and heading toward the door.

"Might want to invest in some Kevlar for him, then," I call and Smith snorts out a laugh in the back of the room. Meeting Lincoln's eyes across the table, I know I'm in for a rough time until this is cleared up but I will never forgive him for what he did to me.

Every Breath You Take

Chapter Twenty
Lincoln

Grabbing my bag out of the back seat of the Camaro, I climb out of the car and stare up at Tate's house, sighing as I try to work up the courage to walk up there and knock on the door. My mind drifts back to the last time I was here, watching the woman I love more than anything break in front of me as all my lies crashed down around me and the piercing ache that's been plaguing me since that morning intensifies. I would do just about anything to be able to go up there and wrap my arms around her right now but if I tried, I'm much more likely to get tased or shot... again.

God, what the hell was I thinking lying to her?

I knew there was no way it could end well but I just kept pushing forward because I couldn't bring myself to walk away from her. I still can't. Just seeing her in the clubhouse two days ago, filled with the magnificent fire of hers that I love so much, I know I'll fight to win her back until I take my very last breath.

Although, knowing my girl, it could take that damn long. My leg aches as I take a step and I fight back a smile. Even when her heart was breaking right in front of me and I hated every decision I had made over the last month, she had me enraptured.

But that happens anytime she walks into a room.

Shaking my head, I round the car as my phone starts ringing. Glancing down as I pull it out of my pocket, I silence it when Blaze's name pops up on the screen, anger barreling through my system. I take responsibility for my part in all this but it doesn't change the fact that if Blaze had just manned up in the beginning and told everyone the truth, I wouldn't be in this position. I understand he's in pain but his judgment was off. We count on him to look out for all of us, something he hasn't done since Sarah died because he's been swallowed up by his grief.

The front door opens as I reach the top step and Theo steps forward, crossing his arms over his chest. I stop, meeting his gaze.

"Thank you for coming," he grunts and I nod.

"Of course. I'd do anything for her."

He shakes his head, taking a step toward me. "No, there is none of that shit. You are the first man she's trusted, maybe ever, and you shredded her heart so you are here to keep her safe and that's it."

"I can't walk away from her."

He steps up to me, getting in my face with the same look Tate gets when she's pissed. "You better figure it out or I will put you in a box. I'm not playing around and you better not either."

"I get that you're trying to protect her, Theo, but she is the love of my life and I'm never going to stop trying to win her back."

He lets out a sardonic laugh, taking a step back as he shoves his hands into his jean pockets. "The love of your life, huh? Man, if this is how you treat someone you love…"

"I made a mistake," I admit, glancing up. My eyes meet Tate's in the foyer. Her expression is vacant as she stares at me and I realize just how much work I have to do to get her back. I would rather she rage and scream at me right now. "Tate…"

She arches a single brow before slowly turning and walking back to the couch where she flops down and grabs her book. I will her to look up at me, just once to let me know that I've still got a fighting chance but her gaze stays locked on her book, looking completely unaffected by my presence. Hopelessness weighs down on me as I rack my brain for a way to express my remorse.

"I'm serious," Theo says, dragging my attention back to him but it's half-hearted as I keep glancing over at Tate, hoping to catch her looking at me. "You will not hurt my sister again."

I nod. "You're right, I won't but not because I'm going to leave her alone. I will win her back and I'll spend the rest of our lives making this up to her."

He scoffs and rolls his eyes. "You know what, Dude. You do you. Right now, Tate is five times scarier than I could ever be. It's your fucking funeral."

"I'll be all right."

"Yeah," he muses, nodding. "Or you'll be dead. I know which one I'm hoping for."

Without another word, he turns back into the house and stops in front of the couch. "Hey, T, I've got to get on the road."

She smiles and my chest aches like a bitch. I wish she'd smile at me like that.

"I know. Please drive carefully in the dark, okay? And call me as soon as you get back to Charleston."

He nods. "I will."

She stands up and they wrap their arms around each other, seemingly in their own little world as they say good-bye to each other. Finally, he pulls away and grabs his bag from the floor.

"Hang in there, 'kay? And call me the second anything happens. I'm going to be a nervous wreck worrying about you."

She rolls her eyes. "Right back at you. Just because you're in Charleston doesn't mean he won't come looking for you."

"I can take care of myself," he assures her and she growls at him.

"If you didn't have to leave right now, I'd kick your ass for saying that."

He laughs, giving her another hug before he walks to the door and turns to me.

"Lincoln."

I nod. "Theo."

"Hope I don't see you again," he states, flashing a smile that doesn't reach his eyes but I ignore it. Fighting with Theo will only make it harder to work things out with Tate.

She walks him to the door, watches him get in his car and drive away before shutting the door and locking up for the night. She turns and walks past me like I'm not even here, sitting down on the couch again. As she opens her book, I study her, wondering how I can break through her icy exterior.

"Tate?" I call to her and she glances up, an expectant expression on her face. All I can do is stare at her with my mouth hanging open for a moment before I get control of myself. "Can we talk?"

"About?" She glances back down at her book and turns the page as I run my hand through my hair. Who is this woman?

"Us. I want to talk about us."

She meets my eyes again and the rage shining back at me almost makes me stumble back. Theo was right – she's terrifying right now.

"There is no us." She stands up and tosses her book down on the coffee table. "I'm going to bed. Lock the back door, please."

"Tate!" I yell at her retreating back, but she doesn't even acknowledge me as she disappears into the bedroom and shuts the door behind her. Collapsing in the dining room chair, I bury my head in my hands and try to force myself to think. How the hell am I going to fix this?

Sighing, I stand up and go into the kitchen, locking the back door before I work my way around the house, checking each and every window to make sure it's locked up tight before I pull the curtains closed. There's no need to make this any easier for her father. Once I'm convinced that everything is secure, I drag my tired body over to the couch and rub my thigh.

Jesus. Getting shot, no matter how minimal, really takes it out of you. I've spent the last four days feeling like an old man as I hobbled around the clubhouse and this is just a flesh wound. Of course, none of the guys were willing to help me either since they are all firmly on "team Tate", as Smith put it. I'd gladly take another bullet to the thigh just to get her to talk to me, though. My phone rings and I dig it out of my pocket.

"Hey, Rodriguez, what's up?"

He sighs. "Just wanted to let you know that I took care of everything for you."

After Tate shot me and the police carted me off to the hospital in handcuffs, I called Rodriguez and explained everything to him. He pulled some strings and was able to make it all go away. It should be easy since Tate probably won't pursue pressing charges now that she knows the truth. Or maybe she will. What the hell do I know?

"Thanks for that, man. I owe you."

"Yeah, well, I'm gonna call that favor in now. I want in on this case."

I glance down the hallway to Tate's closed bedroom door. "Why?"

"I handled her mother's car accident and I need to know what y'all do."

I nod, sighing. "All right. I'm sure Blaze will appreciate the help. Just give him a call tomorrow but tread lightly. This whole thing is complicated and personal for a lot of people."

"How's Tate?" he asks and I drop my head to the back of the couch.

"Fucking furious."

He laughs. "Yeah, she didn't really seem like the shrinking violet type when I met her."

"You have no idea, dude," I tell him, barking out a laugh as I try to imagine Tate ever being shy or timid.

"All right, I'll give Blaze a call tomorrow and get up to speed."

I nod. "Sounds good. Talk to you later."

After we hang up, I pull up the camera feed on my phone and click on the master bedroom. Tate's curled up under the blankets in the middle of her bed and as far as I can tell, she's out cold. Unable to stay away from her any longer, I kick off my boots and creep down the hallway to her room. I hold my breath as the door slowly opens, revealing her serene face bathed in moonlight. Yep, she's passed out. Lord knows, if she were still awake, I'd be missing half my face by now.

Letting out a breath, I sneak into the room and pull the chair in the corner closer to the bed before sitting down and propping my chin in my hands. What the fuck am I going to do here? It already feels helpless, the walls she's built around her heart too high to climb but what other option do I have? I'm not capable of leaving her, of giving up on us. My stomach knots as I think about all the things I've done wrong since meeting her and I hate myself for the choices I made. Looking back now, I don't even know what I was thinking. If I had just been honest with her from the moment I learned the truth, everything would be different between us now.

Her full lips are parted in sleep and my entire body aches to lean forward and press my mouth to hers, just for a little taste to get me through the rest of the night. I miss her so fucking much that it feels like half of me has been ripped away and my mind drifts to the night before everything fell apart. I picture her creamy skin under my hands as I made her come again and again, my name falling from her lips in complete bliss. In my mind, I can see her, bathed in the moonlight like she is now, riding me with her hands in her fiery hair and her perky tits bouncing in my face. I let out a low groan and freeze as she shifts.

A noise from outside has my head snapping up to the door and I strain my ears, trying to hear anything else but the house remains eerily quiet. Sighing, I pull my phone out and bring up the cameras, flipping through each of them and when I find nothing, I lean back in my chair. I could go investigate but I refuse to leave her all alone. In fact, we should really have two people here at all times. I make a note to talk to Blaze about it tomorrow as I grab the pistol out of her bedside table and settle into the chair for the night.

* * * *

Laughter draws my attention toward the table where Tate is talking to Smith and sharpening a few of her knives. I'm half convinced she's doing it just to fuck with me but it doesn't matter. I shoot them a glare, pissed that he gets to see her smile and make her laugh while all I get is her hatred. I can't blame her for it when I'm the reason for this tension between us but I still don't like it. She's mine – her smile, her laughter – it all belongs to me and I fucking miss it more each second I'm locked up in this house with her. When I close my eyes, I can still see it – the special smile that she only shared with me – and I want it back so badly that I'm barely resisting the urge to walk up to her and shake her. I want to scream at her to talk to me, yell at me, hit me, or shoot me again because I'd be happy with anything other than the indifference or snarky comments directed at me this morning.

"I've got to go to the clubhouse. You good here, brother?" I ask, my gaze flicking to Tate but she ignores me, focused on sharpening her knives. Smith meets my eyes and nods.

"Yeah, man. We're cool." He gives me a thumbs-up and I roll my eyes at the ridiculous "Team Tate" t-shirt he showed up in this morning. He's just egging her on and loving every fucking minute of it. Finally, Tate glances up at me, her gaze warring between rage and disinterest.

"I don't know why you're so fucking worried about Smith. He's not the one inspiring me to cause bodily harm."

Her gaze flicks to my injured leg and I take a step back as she smirks, turning back to her knives.

"Just go, brother. I'll keep her safe," Smith assures me and her heavy sigh makes me smile. Every time someone insinuates that she's not capable of defending herself, she gets so damn mad and ready to fight anyone to prove them wrong.

"All right. I'll be back later."

"Oh," Tate whispers. "Please do hurry back."

I grit my teeth at the sarcastic tone of her voice as I nod at Smith and yank the door open, ducking outside before she can hurl more insults at me. I almost prefer the indifference from yesterday but when she woke up this morning and found me sleeping in the chair next to her bed, she was pissed. I woke up on the floor with the gun pointed in my face after she kicked the chair over.

Sighing, I climb behind the wheel of the Camaro and fire her up, loving the deep throaty rumble of the engine. I take one last look at the house before pulling away from the curb. When I agreed to keep her safe, I knew winning her over again wouldn't be easy but I greatly underestimated how stubborn she is. And how angry she is. I also get that, though. She and I are so alike that it's easy to put myself in her place and if the roles were reversed and she spent all our time together lying to me, I don't know how I would forgive her. She opened up a part of herself to me that she had kept shielded from the rest of the world for so long and I abused that privilege. I know that and I also know winning her back won't be as easy as saying I'm sorry or bringing her flowers. Her trust in me is broken and I need to fix that.

Problem is, I'm not sure how.

When I pull into the clubhouse parking lot, I spot a few bikes lined up out front and I'm glad that everyone else is out today. Even though I just left her, I'm eager to get back. Sure, she'll still be throwing insults and threatening to maim or murder me but I'll stand there and take it all for her.

I park the Camaro near the door and climb out as Storm walks out into the parking lot. He spots me and nods.

"I'd be careful in there if I were you."

"Yeah?" I ask. "Why's that?"

He chuckles. "Ali is fucking pissed at you for screwing things up with Tate and she's less cute kitten and more angry cougar these days."

"Did you just call your wife an old woman?" I ask, scrunching up my brow and his head whips up as he shoots me a death glare.

"No, I fucking did not and if you tell her that, I'll hold 'ya down while Tate enacts whatever punishment she's got planned for you."

"Asshole," I mutter and he laughs.

"What did you think would happen when you lied to her, Kodiak? A woman like that does not just forgive and forget."

I sigh, running my hand through my hair. "Yeah, I know that and I guess I wasn't really thinking. Blaze asked me to do him a favor and before I knew it, everything was going to shit."

"And now what? You're going to convince her to give you another chance?"

I paste a grin on my face. "Or die tryin'."

"Good fucking luck," he mutters, swinging his leg over his bike and I nod as I turn toward the door to the clubhouse. Fuzz is behind the bar when I stroll in and he nods before turning back to Ali, who glares at me. I spin back toward the door as her voice rings out through the room.

"Oh, no, you don't! Get back here."

Wincing, I spin back to face her. "Yeah? Something I can help you with, Ali?"

"Don't you try to be cute with me, Kodiak," she snaps, getting up in my face as she slaps my arm. "What the fuck were you thinking? That girl is fucking perfect for you."

"I know she is," I agree, rubbing my arm where she hit me.

"You love her?"

I nod. "Absolutely."

"You want to live your life without her?"

I shake my head, my heart stalling at the thought. "No. Not a second of it."

"Okay," she sighs, studying me for a moment. "I suppose I forgive you then but you'd better fix this. I liked her."

"She liked you, too, and I'm working on fixing it."

She nods, satisfied with my answers, and turns back to the bar as I head for Blaze's office and knock on the door.

"Come in."

I open the door and step inside before collapsing in the chair in front of his desk.

"How is it going over there?" he asks and I scoff.

"She's filled with the rage of a thousand suns," I answer and he laughs before a wistful expression crosses his face.

"I couldn't believe my eyes when you brought her to the barbecue. I knew she looked like Sarah but the two could have been twins."

I nod, crossing my legs. "Ah, so that's why you were so weird that night."

"Yes. It was like going back thirty years."

"I hope you know that I intend to make her my old lady someday," I say and he lets out a surprised laugh as he grabs a bottle of bourbon out of his desk.

"Yeah, good luck with that. I've been running this club for a long time and dealt with some scary fuckers but I wouldn't take on that woman. I like my balls right where they are."

I laugh before letting out a sigh. "I'm just a glutton for punishment, I guess."

"Just be careful, yeah? I know I let you down when I asked you to do this but it's turned into a real mess." He holds up an empty glass, offering me a drink, but I shake my head. I don't want to be here that long anyway.

"Do you have any news?"

He nods. "Yeah, actually. Dominic King crossed the Louisiana state line last night around midnight. If I had to guess, I'd say he's already here in Baton Rouge."

"Okay," I whisper, thinking over the moves we could make. "We going to wait for him to reach out?"

"I think that's best. Once he realizes that he can't get to Tate, he'll be in contact."

"About that, we need two people at the house at all times."

He nods. "Keep Smith with you and make sure you keep everything locked up at all times. One slip-up will be all it takes to lose her."

"I'm not going to let anything happen to her."

"Let's hope not," he mutters, turning away from the desk and sipping his drink. I stand and walk out of his office with determined steps. There's no need to hope. I'll take another bullet, this one to the chest, before I let anyone near her.

*   *   *   *

"I'm exhausted," Smith says and I glance over at him. "I think I'm gonna go pass out."

"You can sleep in Theo's room. It's the room right at the top of the stairs," Tate informs him with a smile. He nods and shoves himself off the couch.

"Night, y'all."

"Goodnight, Luke," Tate calls, not even sparing me a glance as she turns back to the TV where *Vikings* is playing. Sighing, I focus back on the screen but I can't focus on the show. Not when she's so close to me and still so goddamn far away.

"Tate?"

She arches a brow but doesn't turn to look at me.

"Could we finally talk, please? I know how angry you are, baby, but there's got to be a way we can work this out."

Sighing, she meets my eyes. "What is there to work out, Lincoln? You lied to me and used me as a favor to Blaze. Now we can both move on."

"I don't want to move on. I know I lied to you and trust me, I hate that I did but everything I felt and everything you felt, that was all real. Hell, I wasn't even supposed to make contact with you but once I saw you, I couldn't stay away."

"Really?" she asks, vulnerability creeping into her eyes and I sit forward, wishing I could pull her into my arms.

"Yes, baby. I defied Blaze's order because there was just something about you that called to me. You were made for me."

Her lip wobbles and her eyes shine with unshed tears as I hold my hand out to her, praying that she'll take it. It feels like the heavens are shining down on me when she slips her hand into mine, standing up from the loveseat. Slowly, I pull her to me and into my lap, keeping an eye on her expression as hope wells up in my chest.

She straddles my legs and places her hand on my chest, right over my heart and peace settles over me as I suck in a breath.

"I miss you," she whispers, so quiet that I almost don't hear her. I wrap my arms around her waist and pull her closer.

"I miss you, too, Tate."

Leaning down, she cups my face in one hand as her lips hover above mine and she meets my eyes, silently asking if I'm good with this but I'll never deny her. I close the space between us, claiming her lips and groaning as she melts into me. My cock springs to life and I fist her hair, taking control of the kiss as I flick my tongue against the seam of her lips.

"Open up for me, baby."

She sighs, giving me exactly what I want and I groan again when the taste of her favorite spearmint gum meets my tongue. She moans, grinding on my lap as she grips my shirt in her fists and I thrust up off the couch, desperate to remove the layers between us.

"If you don't want this, you gotta stop me now," I warn her and she shakes her head.

"Don't stop."

And just like that, it's on. We're a flurry of hands and frantic kisses as we both peel out of our clothes and the next thing I know, Tate is wrapping her hand around my bare cock. I groan, my head falling back on the couch as I suck in a breath. She straddles my legs again and lines the head up with her entrance before slowly sinking down.

"Fuck," I hiss as her warmth envelops me and I grab her hips, digging my fingers into her flesh. Fisting a handful of her hair, I pull her lips down to mine and kiss her hard before pulling back just enough to whisper, "Ride me, gorgeous."

She moans, pulling back and grabbing her tits as she bounces on top of me at the perfect tempo. Not too fast and not too slow but just enough to drive me out of my fucking mind. Just when I think that I'm going to lose it, she pauses and leans forward, kissing me so softly that my entire body goes lax. With a firm grip on the back of my neck, she teases me with her tongue and starts rocking her hips – slowly, seductively – and I feel a tingling at the base of my spine.

"Shit, I'm gonna come, baby."

She shakes her head. "I'm not there yet."

Reaching down between us, I find her clit and circle it with my thumb as she lets out a moan.

"Yeah, do that," she says and stops moving her hips as I work her closer and closer to orgasm. Her head falls back and her chest rises and falls rapidly in front of me as she grips my shoulders, lost in a world of pleasure. She starts to tremble and I know I'm close so I start to pull away, wanting to finish with her.

"No, don't stop," she cries and I press my thumb against her clit again. Not like I could ever deny her anything she wants. I circle the sensitive nub again and again as I pinch her nipple and she screams as her pussy constricts around my cock. I let out a low groan and reach for her, ready to throw her down on the couch and fuck her senseless but she pushes away from me and stands up.

I frown but before I can reach for her or ask her what she's doing, a shock rolls through my body and every muscles locks up to the point of agony. I look up at her, trying to understand what the fuck is happening when I see the Taser pull away from my skin.

"Motherfucker," I hiss and she smirks.

"Now you know what it feels like to be used and lied to, Lincoln."

As I slowly regain control of my body, she walks away from me in all her naked glory and slams the bedroom door shut.

Chapter Twenty-One
Tatum

"So, what happened last night?" I hear Smith ask from the front seat of the Camaro as I pretend to sleep in the back. Emma and Nix invited the whole club over for a barbecue and although I was reluctant to go, I wasn't given much of a choice since Lincoln's been a little pissy today. I smirk.

"What are you talking about?" Lincoln asks.

I peek my eye open just enough to see Smith shrug.

"I don't know. I thought I heard y'all talkin' last night."

Lincoln glances in the rearview mirror before sighing and shaking his head. I don't think he saw me watching him.

"Naw, man. We didn't talk."

"You sure? 'Cause I could have sworn I heard y'all."

"What the fuck are you trying to get at, Smith?"

Smith starts laughing. "Streak sent the camera feed to my phone, too, dumbass. I watched the whole thing."

I bite my lip to hold back my giggle as Lincoln growls.

"What the fuck do you mean you watched the whole thing?"

"I mean," he replies, getting himself under control. "I watched the two of you go at it like rabbits as soon as I went upstairs and I saw her tase your stupid ass before she walked away. That had to hurt like a bitch."

"I could give you a demonstration so you'd know for sure," Lincoln snaps and Smith laughs again, holding up his hands.

"Naw, man. I'm good. When are you going to give it up though?"

My heart pounds in my chest as I wait for Lincoln's response. Last night turned out to be more real than I intended it to be. I wanted to get back at him; I wanted him to know how much he'd hurt me but I never intended to let him see past my defenses. I never once intended to admit that I missed him so much it was hard to function sometimes.

"Never. I'm never going to give up on us."

Smith sighs, looking out of the passenger window for a second. "I don't know, brother. Sometimes you've just got to cut your losses. There may be too much damage here."

"I don't believe that for a second. What I feel with her… I've never felt it before and it's something I won't feel with anyone else so I'm never giving up on that."

Oh, hell, why does he have to say things like that?

"She might never forgive you."

I open my eyes and find Lincoln staring at me in the rearview mirror. "Then I'll spend every day of the rest of my life trying to win her back because there's no one else on this earth for me."

"It's really too bad you couldn't figure that out before you ruined us," I snap, hoping he doesn't pick up on how half-hearted it is. Truthfully, each day I'm warming up to him more and more. I'm still pissed as hell and nowhere ready to forgive him but I can't confidently say I'm through with him either. In those few weeks we were together, despite the multitude of lies he told, he also managed to steal my heart and mark me as his and if I walk away now, it will be with an empty chest.

"Good morning, sleeping beauty," Smith says, smiling at me and I roll my eyes.

"You're lucky I don't pluck your eyes out for watching me have sex, Lucas," I tell him and he has the decency to look embarrassed. He rubs the back of his neck and nods.

"Yeah, sorry about that."

I shrug. "You should ask Lincoln to describe what it feels like to be tased so you can make a more informed decision next time."

Lincoln flicks an annoyed glance to the mirror.

"You wouldn't do that to me," Smith says with little confidence.

"Wouldn't I?"

"We're here," Lincoln growls as we pull down a dirt driveway that opens up to a large plantation house that takes my breath away.

"Jesus, they live here?" I whisper and Smith nods.

"Yeah, Nix bought it for dirt cheap and fixed it up."

Lincoln parks the car next to a few bikes and the boys climb out first before Lincoln leans the seat forward and helps me out. I tuck the shoebox under my arm as I turn toward the house.

"What's that?" he asks, pointing to the box and I glance down at it as I tuck it closer to my side.

"Something I need to show to Nix."

Lincoln nods and wraps his arm around my waist as we head for the house. Flicking an annoyed glance over my shoulder, I sigh. He leans closer, his lips brushing my ear.

"After what you pulled last night, I'm done playing nice, Tate. You and I are going to work this out but I'm not your damn punching bag anymore."

Damn, why does that turn me on?

"We'll see," I murmur and his grip on my hip tightens.

"You're just going to have to come to terms with the fact that I fucking love you and I'm not going anywhere."

"Tate!" the brunette from the clubhouse says as she comes walking out of the house and I freeze. "Sorry. I never introduced myself the other day. I'm Emma, Nix's wife."

"Oh, it's really nice to meet you." I hold my hand out for her to shake but she ignores it, going in for a hug.

"It's so nice to meet you officially. I know this whole situation is... unorthodox but you're family so if you ever need anything, just holler."

I nod. "Okay, I will."

"Here, why don't you put your stuff down and I'll introduce you to a few people," she says and I scan the yard.

"Actually, I was hoping to talk to Nix first. There's something I need to show him," I reply, holding up the shoebox and she nods, turning toward the house.

"You'll find him down at the dock. He wasn't all that thrilled that I invited everyone over today with things so tense between him and Blaze."

I nod in understanding. "Have they talked at all?"

"Blaze has showed up here everyday and they go outside and talk until they start yelling. Then, Nix barrels inside and Blaze peels out of here on his bike so tensions are still a little high."

Nodding, I excuse myself from the group and round the back of the house, spotting Nix at the end of the dock. As I get near the water, he glances back at me.

"Sorry, I hope you don't mind but I wanted to talk to you for a bit."

He studies me for a moment before nodding. I sigh as I walk out onto the dock and sit next to him.

"What a fucking mess, huh?" he says, staring out at the water and I laugh.

"Yeah, you could say that. It's been one thing after another lately."

He nods, looking a little lost. "What was she like?"

"Our mom?"

"Yeah."

I sigh, thinking over my words before explaining my childhood to him – the moving around, the drills, the training – and when I finish, he blows out a breath.

"Sounds…intense."

I nod. "Yeah, it was but she did try to give us some normal. We used to have family game night and we went to the zoo in every city we stopped in when we were running."

"There is so much shit I want to ask her and now I'll never get the chance to," he muses and I grab the shoebox.

"That's why I brought this. Theo and I found it while we were cleaning out her stuff. There's a photo of a little boy in here that I'm almost certain is you along with every report card you ever got."

He glances over at me. "Can I see it?"

"Sure." I hand it to him and he takes the lid off, setting it next to him on the dock. "Oh, there's also love letters from your dad, I think."

"You think?"

"Well." I shrug. "They are only signed "M" and I don't know his name but it seems fairly likely that they are from him."

"His name is Malcolm," he says, pulling out the photo and shaking his head. "This was my kindergarten picture."

He starts going through the letters and report cards in the box and I sit next to him silently, only speaking to answer any of his questions. Finally, he sighs and sets the box down next to him.

"This is all fucking insane. I spent my whole life thinking my mom was a club whore that wasn't capable of taking care of a kid and I was cool with that. I understood why she wasn't around and now I find out it was all a lie."

"If it makes you feel any better, I'm still learning new things about her all the time. Until we were in that room at the clubhouse, I had no idea who my dad was because she wouldn't tell me. I didn't know I had another brother. You and I are in the same boat so I'm always here if you want to talk."

He glances over at me and smirks. "There is one question I want to ask you."

"Go ahead," I say with a nod.

"Is it true you shot Lincoln in the leg?"

I bark out a laugh and nod. "Um, yep. That's true. Although to be fair, at the time, I thought he was some kind of psycho or something."

"Naw, I heard the whole story from Fuzz. Seemed like he got what was comin' to him."

I smile and point over my shoulder. "I think Smith still has some extra "Team Tate" t-shirts if you want to show your support."

"I just might do that," he says, laughing as he turns back to the water. We sit in silence for a few seconds before he turns to the house. "We should probably get back in there. I'm sure Em will have food ready soon."

He starts putting things back in the box and after setting the lid on top, he hands it to me. I shake my head.

"No, you should keep it."

His brows furrow. "You sure?"

"Yeah. I've already read them all and she was your mom, too."

He nods, placing his hand on top of the box as he sighs. "Thank you. I know I probably haven't been handling any of this well but it's pretty cool to finally have a brother and a sister."

"I couldn't agree more," I tell him, smiling. "Our parents are super fucked up but Theo and I got you out of this whole thing and I'm grateful for that."

He smiles and helps me up before we walk back up to the house together before he joins the guys and I step into the house in search of the girls. Ali, Carly, and Emma all glance up when I walk in.

"How'd your talk go?" Emma asks and I smile.

"Good. I think."

"Nix is a straightforward guy. If you think it went well, then I'm sure it did."

I nod, glancing out into the yard where the guys are gathered and Lincoln catches my eye. He laughs at something Smith says and my chest aches something fierce. I miss the way things were before I knew everything and there's been so many times in the last week that I've wished I could go back.

"You know," someone says, stepping up beside me and I turn as Ali flashes me a smile. "It's okay to forgive him."

"It's not in my nature," I tell her and she snorts out a laugh.

"Yeah, I've kind of picked up on that but you should try anyway. Lincoln is a good man – the kind that would never make this mistake again."

I scoff, watching him as he raises the beer bottle to his lips. "He lied to me."

"Oh, trust me, honey, I know. I already read him the riot act once for what he did to you but I also know he didn't mean anything by it. He was torn in half by his loyalty to the club and his love for you – something that no one could have predicted."

"He still should have told me the truth and he had so many chances to."

Carly steps up on my other side and sighs. "It's not that simple. This club – they're a family – and he would take a bullet for any one of those guys just as they would take one for you simply because Kodiak loves you. That's not an easy thing to betray and I'm sure that it haunted him everyday."

"Both Carly and I," Ali adds, "have been through some shit and the entire club stepped up for us without a moment's hesitation. They've taken us both in as family and loving one of these men means that you won't always know what's going on but you have to trust him.

He lies to you to keep you safe or to keep someone else safe."

"Say he had told you the truth," Emma says and we all turn to face her. "When he first met you, if he had spilled his guts, would you have ever let him into your life?"

I shake my head. "No, I don't think I would have."

She gives me a look that screams "exactly" and I sigh as I turn back to the window, wondering if I'll ever be able to handle Lincoln lying to me regularly even if it was to save someone.

*　　*　　*　　*

"Tate, it's not safe to be out here," Lincoln growls, stepping out onto the screened in porch and I grab the pistol out of my lap, holding it up for him to see.

"I just needed a little fresh air."

He sighs, sinking into the chair next to the door as he studies me. "Did you have fun at the barbecue?"

"Yeah," I murmur, a soft smile gracing my face. "It was really nice to spend time with everyone."

"You seem different."

I meet his gaze and shrug as I remember the talk I had with the girls. "Maybe a little bit. Can I ask you something?"

Shock blankets his face and he stares at me for a second before slowly nodding. "Of course."

"How much did you know when you started following me?"

"I... uh, I knew your name and Theo's name. I knew what you looked like and all the basic information like your address. And that your mom had died."

I think back to the morning I found the camera feed on his phone and the photo of Theo and me on the beach. "That picture you had, where we were spreading Mom's ashes. Was that when you started watching me?"

"Just about," he answers with a nod and I sigh.

"When did you learn everything?"

"Tate," he whispers, leaning back in his chair as he shakes his head.

"I want to know."

Sighing, he stands up and pulls his chair closer to mine so our knees are touching. "The night that I had to bail on Road House."

"Oh," I whisper, sucking in a breath. "And you never once thought to tell me?"

"Baby, I almost told you every fucking day. It was killing me but there was nothing I could do. I couldn't betray Blaze and I couldn't walk away from you either."

I narrow my eyes. "You keep saying that but no one forced you to do any of this."

"I'm not trying to put the blame on anyone else," he says, grabbing my hand and wrapping it between both of his. "I wish I could explain the way I felt when I first saw you. It was like someone punched me in the gut and it didn't take long before just watching you wasn't enough. And once I met you face-to-face in that diner, there was no walking away for me. It didn't matter that I had avoided relationships for years or that I have a shit ton of baggage I carry around with me because what I feel for you is bigger than all that."

Tears sting my eyes as I watch him, searching for the right answer. "You made me fall in love with you and then you tore me apart in a single second. I don't know how to let that go no matter how much I want to."

"But you do want to?" he asks, hopeful for the first time since this all went down. I shrug.

"I don't know."

He nods, the hopeful expression still on his face. "That's okay. I'll keep working to make this up to you, Tate. I'm never going to stop. I'm never going to walk away. My love for you is stronger than my mistakes."

I nod, turning away from him as I wipe away a tear and stare out at the night sky.

"I do have one more question," I prompt, glancing back at him and he nods. "Why the phone calls? Was it part of some game? Did you need me to truly believe I was in danger so when all this was revealed, I'd take it seriously?"

His brow furrows. "Are you talking about the creepy breathing calls?"

"Yes, among others."

"Baby, that was never me. I thought you said it was Reed."

I blow out a breath and lean my head back on the chair. "I thought it was but when I found the video feed on your phone, I thought it had been you doing that, too. I mean, the whole "beware the man you know" thing seemed obvious."

"What the fuck are you talking about?"

Sighing, I grab the gun and push out of the chair as he releases my hand. "Follow me."

We step inside and he closes the door behind us, making sure it's locked up tight before he turns to me. I walk through the kitchen, to my bedroom, and go to the closet, pushing the clothes to the side.

"Where are you taking me?"

I grin as I glance over my shoulder at him. "You'll see."

I press on the number panel and hear a quick intake of air behind me as it pops out and I enter the code. The door springs open.

"What the fuck?" he whispers as I step inside with him hot on my heels. "This is where you were hiding when I couldn't find you on the cameras?"

I laugh, imagining him freaking out when I'd gone missing. "Yes. I started spending a lot of time in here after the first phone call."

"Right," he says as I sit down in front of the computer. "What were you saying about that?"

"Hang on, I'll pull it up." I click on the folder where I have all the important video saved and click on one where the answering machine picked up.

"Taaaaaatteeee," the voice says and a shiver works its way down my spine just like the first time. "Are you there, Tate?" It waits a few seconds before continuing. "Walls have ears. Doors have eyes. Trees have voices. Beasts tell lies. Beware the rain. Beware the snow. Beware the man you think you know."

There's a few seconds of heavy breathing before the maniacal laughter that's tormented my dreams since echoes through the safe room.

"Jesus Christ, baby. Why didn't you ever tell me about this?"

I roll my eyes, leaning back in my chair. "I don't know if you've noticed, Lincoln, but my mother raised me to be pretty self-sufficient. I don't like asking for help."

"Yeah," he scoffs, crossing his arms over his chest. "I noticed. Is there anything else?"

Sighing, I show him the note that was taped to my door and he reads it before meeting my gaze. "Does this have any meaning to you?"

"Besides the obvious threat, it was a play I performed in high school."

"King's daughter," he muses, staring back down at the note. "Dominic King."

I nod. I'd reached the same conclusion after Blaze told us all the truth. My mind drifts to a man I've never even met before as I watch Lincoln study the note.

"Is he really that bad?"

He glances up. "Who? Your father?"

I nod and he scoffs.

"You haven't googled him yet?"

I shake my head, glancing at the computer screen. "I've been too chicken."

"Wait here," he growls, tossing the note down as he storms out of the safe room and disappears into the living room. Glancing up at the camera feed, I watch him walk over to his bag and rip a folder out of the side pocket before turning back to the bedroom. He barges into the safe room again and slaps the folder down in front of me.

"That is your father."

I grab it and flip it open, my mouth dropping at the first newspaper article's headline: *Family of Four Killed in House Fire.*

"Are you saying he did this?" I ask, whipping my head in his direction and he nods with a grim expression on his face.

"No," I whisper, turning back to the folder and flipping through more articles, each one worse than the last.

Man Skinned Alive
Woman Killed in Acid Attack
Missing Child Suspected Dead

"How could someone do all this?" I whisper, tears burning my eyes and Lincoln grabs the arms of the chair and spins it to face him.

"Dominic King will do anything to the people who betray him and even their families aren't safe from his wrath."

I shake my head as a tear streaks down my cheek. "Just like me."

"No, baby," he says, kneeling in front of me. "You are nothing like this man."

"I… I shot you in the leg because you hurt me. I tased you over a misunderstanding and again just to cause you the same pain I was feeling. I'm a monster."

"No," he growls, fisting my hair. "I don't ever want to hear you talk like that again. Before me, had you ever hurt anyone?"

I shake my head. "No."

"Okay, then. I deserved this," he says, pointing to his leg. "And I don't care. Do it to me again. Hit me, tase me, shoot me; as long as you're mine, I'll take it all."

"That's sick. We're sick," I whisper and he smiles, leaning forward and pressing his forehead to mine.

"So be it, baby. If loving you makes me a little sick, I don't give a shit because I also think loving you makes me a better man and I'll take that trade any day of the week."

Chapter Twenty-Two
Tatum

"This is not up for discussion!" Lincoln yells from the bedroom and I laugh as I stomp away from him in a pair of shorts, pulling my diner t-shirt over my head. It's actually quite admirable that after being shot and tased twice, the man still has balls left to challenge me.

"I don't know who the fuck you think you are, Lincoln Paul Archer, but you don't get to tell me what to do. Not when we were together and definitely not now that we are split up."

"Goddamn it!" he roars and I pick up my pace when I hear the pounding of his boots running after me. Ducking into the kitchen, I'm certain I have him beat but when we both enter the living room at the same time, I skid to a stop. With a huff, I turn back to the kitchen and pretend like I'm going back to the bedroom before I double back and book it for the front door. I'm almost there when I feel his arms wrap around my waist and lift me up in the air as I scream.

"I said no," he growls, pinning my back to the wall and I grit my teeth.

"I don't give a shit what you said."

"Uh, morning, y'all," Smith mutters, walking down the stairs with sleep still in his eyes. "What's going on?"

"She's trying to go into fucking work," Lincoln snarls and I roll my eyes. It's not like I'm walking into a lion's den and besides, they could watch me there just as easily as they could here.

"Y'all can just sit in a corner booth and watch me there," I say, trying to placate them.

Smith shakes his head. "It's not a good idea, Darlin'."

"Whose side are you on?"

"Whichever one keeps you alive." He walks into the kitchen and heads straight for the pot of coffee I made this morning.

"You want something to do, baby?" Lincoln asks and I narrow my eyes at him. "Why don't you cook us some breakfast?"

"Oh, shit," Smith whispers, turning to face us as I glare down at Lincoln. He probably expects me to whip a gun out of my waistband for that comment but sadly, none are within reach.

"Really? That's your solution? Let's get the little woman in the kitchen where she belongs?"

His eyes widen and he shakes his head as I pull my arm back and punch him in the adam's apple. He releases me in an instant and I land on my feet as he stumbles back and coughs.

"Not your brightest idea, dude," Smith mutters as he sits down at the dining room table and pulls out his phone as he smirks. "I'm gonna get Fuzz to grab some donuts for us."

"Are you laughing at your own joke right now?"

He glances up at me, unable to hide his laughter. "What? It's funny. Getting donuts is the perfect job for a cop."

"Oh my god," I whisper, rolling my eyes as he glances back down at the phone and sends the text. Glancing around the living room, I realize Lincoln is gone and I sigh.

"I think you hurt his ego."

I turn to Smith. "His ego is fine. Have you ever been punched in the throat? That shit hurts."

"Maybe he just realized that you are allowing us to keep you here because if you really wanted to leave, we'd both be unconscious and you'd be out the door."

I put my finger over my lips and furrow my brow. "Shh. Don't spill my secrets."

"Why don't you ease up on him? He's just trying to protect you."

I sigh, sinking into the seat across from him. "And going about it all wrong. Would you ever allow someone to pick you up and push you against a wall? Men tend to think they can pick women up and toss them around as long as they are protecting them. The only difference here is I'm perfectly capable of defending myself."

"Well, shit," Smith mutters, staring down at his coffee.

"If I promise to stop, will you stop punching me or tasing me?" Lincoln asks from behind me, his voice hoarse. I turn to him and nod.

"Include me in the conversation from now on instead of barking orders at me and yes, I will refrain from physically assaulting you."

He nods, rubbing at his throat as he sits next to me and grabs my hand. "You can't go into work. There are too many points of entry and it would be impossible for us to keep our eyes on you constantly."

"I reiterate that I am perfectly capable of defending myself."

He sighs, squeezing my hand. "Please do this for me, Tate. I would lose my mind if we lost you and I need you to work with me on this."

"Okay," I whisper, nodding at him and he smiles as he leans toward me. Just before his lips are about to touch mine, I put my hand up and shake my head.

"Still not together."

He sighs, leaning back in his chair. "Stubborn ass woman."

"Caveman," I shoot back at him and he bares his teeth at me, making my pussy clench with need.

Oh, shit.

The doorbell rings and all three of us turn to stare at it for a second before Lincoln stands up.

"Expecting anyone?" he asks and I shake my head.

"Check the cameras," he orders Smith and Smith digs his phone out of his pocket, flicking through a few camera angles.

338

"Whoever it was is already gone."

I stand up and take a step toward the door before Lincoln grabs my arm and shakes his head.

"He just said no one is there," I protest but he just shakes his head again.

"Go check all the windows and doors to make sure they're locked. I did it an hour ago and they were all good. I'm keeping Tate with me," he says over his shoulder, completely ignoring me. Smith stands up and walks into the kitchen as Lincoln pulls a gun out of his waistband. I reach under the table and grab the gun out of the holster bolted under the top. He glances over at me and rolls his eyes.

"All good," Smith says, walking back into the living room and Lincoln nods, glancing back at me.

"Stand back."

I roll my eyes as he unlocks the door and pulls it open. Just like Smith said, the porch is empty and something falls into the house as Lincoln pulls the door open further. He scoops it up before slamming the door shut again and locking both deadbolts.

"It's got Tate's name on it," Smith says, ripping it out of Lincoln's grip and I inspect it as he hands it to me. I suck in a breath as I peel it open. Inside is a photo of my mother and a blonde woman I don't recognize. Frowning, I glance in the folder and spot a little piece of paper folded up at the bottom. I pull it out and unfold it.

You owe me a life.

My hands tremble and I suck in a breath as I meet Lincoln's eyes before glancing back down at the photo in my hand. The photo is from years ago, my mother's face bright and worry free in a way that I had never seen her and I turn to the blonde, searching my mind for a connection but I come up empty.

Lincoln steps forward, gently taking the note and photo from my hand before he glances down at them.

"Fuck," he hisses after reading the note. As he hands them off to Smith, he wraps his arm around my waist and pulls me close, giving me the comfort I need right now.

"Hey," he whispers, getting my attention and I peek up at him. "It's going to be okay. I'm not going to let him anywhere near you."

I nod, cuddling closer to him as I try to steady my breathing. After what Lincoln showed me and the research I did afterward, I can honestly say that my father terrifies me. There is no length he won't go to, no boundary he won't cross, and I understand all the things my mother made Theo and me do. I understand the drills and the training and I'm so thankful for them now but I can't help but feel like I carry around the same evil he does – like somewhere deep down inside me is a person who's capable of the terrible things he's done.

"I need to call Blaze," Lincoln says, pulling back to look at me. "I'll put it on speakerphone so you can give your input, too."

I nod, grateful that he's really listening to me and we all congregate around the table as he dials Blaze's number, puts the phone on speakerphone, and sets it in the middle of the table.

"What's going on, Kodiak?" Blaze answers and I sink into the chair as the guys follow suit.

"Someone just dropped a folder off at Tate's house."

"What's in it?" he asks, apprehension filling his voice.

Lincoln glances over at me and grabs my hand as calm washes through me. "A photo of Tate's mom with someone else and a note that says, "you owe me a life"."

"Shit. Did you see who dropped it off?"

Smith shakes his head, looking annoyed. "No, they were gone by the time we checked the cameras, boss, but I'll go back and look at the feed beforehand."

"Good. In the meantime, I think we need to get Tate out of there."

Lincoln nods. "I agree."

"Well, I don't," I cut in. My house was designed to keep me safe from Dominic King and I tell him that.

"I understand that, Tate, but he knows you're there and it's only a matter of time until he gets in. It's just a house. I want you to come down to the clubhouse."

The thought of being under the same roof as Blaze right now is not appealing and I shake my head. "I don't think so."

He sighs. "Look, I get that I'm not your favorite person but this is the safest option."

"How is it safe? That will be the next place he looks for me and how the hell are we going to stop him? I'm not running from this man for the rest of my life."

"No one is suggesting that you do, baby, but the clubhouse is safe," Lincoln says.

I shake my head. "Nowhere is safe. He's been following me for who knows how long and I'm sure he knows all the moves I can make before I even make them."

"Wait, what do you mean he's been following you?" Blaze asks, an edge in his voice and I sigh before telling him about the note, phone calls, and text messages.

"Goddamn it," he growls. "Kodiak, this is the kind of shit I needed you to watch out for."

"Yeah, well, I didn't find out until last night," he fires back, giving me some major side-eye and I shrug. Mom always taught me to only depend on myself and that's not going to change now.

"She's right," Smith says, watching me. "If he's been following her, he knows everywhere she could go hide."

"We could go to my place," Lincoln suggests.

I scowl at him. "How is that any better?"

"No, wait, that could work," Blaze says, ignoring my question as Lincoln turns to me.

"When I bought that property, we used it to house girls we were moving so I have the entire perimeter covered with motion detectors. It's not much but it will give us a little bit of a head start if he does show up there."

The squeal of brakes pierces through the silence and I flinch as both men jump up and rush to the windows, guns drawn.

"It's just a mail truck," Smith calls and I release a breath as Lincoln turns back to me and we lock eyes. The plea in his gaze wins me over and I sigh as I nod.

"Okay, I'll go to your house."

*   *   *   *

Morning sunlight streaks across the room, warming my skin as I stretch and curl up with Lincoln's pillow. Mist hovers over the lake and I would love to just sit out there for a few hours if I could bring myself to leave this bed. Two big arms wrap around me and pull me into his naked heat. I take a moment to savor the comfort of his touch and his manly scent surrounding me before I jerk away. He growls, pulling me back to him.

"Don't."

I roll my eyes. "You, don't."

Silence greets me and I scowl as I grab his hand and try to pry him off my body but it's no use. He's got an iron lock on me and the only way I'll get free is to hurt him and I've promised to no longer do that. Last night when we arrived at Lincoln's house, Smith took one of the bedrooms, leaving the other for Lincoln and me. I was ready to just sleep on the couch but he refused – saying it was safer if I slept in a bedroom. After a little arguing, he assured me that he would stay on his side of the king-size bed but clearly, that didn't happen.

"Let me go, Lincoln," I order and feel him shake his head against my back as his arms tighten around me again. I smack his forearm. "Can't...breathe."

"Just let me pretend for a few more minutes, baby," he whispers and I sigh as I flop back down on my pillow.

I flick an annoyed glance over my shoulder. "Thought you were going to stay on your side of the bed."

"I think we both know I was lying when I said that," he mumbles and I wiggle in his arms again.

"Let me go."

With a huff, he releases me and I roll over in bed to face him. He cracks an eye open and smiles, reaching out, brushing his thumb over my cheek. It feels so damn good even though I know it shouldn't. God, this wouldn't be so hard if I didn't miss him.

"Morning, baby."

I shake my head. "Don't call me that."

"Tate," he breathes, frustration lacing his tone and I sigh right along with him.

"How many times do I have to tell you that this is over before you'll believe me?" I ask, motioning between the two of us.

"Ten times..." he says and I arch a brow. "Every day for the rest of our lives."

"Lincoln," I growl, flopping to my back and throwing my arm over my eyes. Because of all my years of avoiding relationships, I really am inexperienced and I think that's part of the reason that, before I learned of his deception, I trusted Lincoln so completely. In my mind

344

he was the one man who would never hurt me but then he did and I don't know how to move forward from that.

"How many times do I have to apologize for this?"

"Ten times everyday for the rest of our lives," I snarl in annoyance and he nods.

"Done."

I shake my head, pointing a finger in his face. "No. I wasn't serious."

"You know what," he prompts before rolling on top of me. I buck my hips, trying to get him off but he's too damn heavy. "Listen to me. Yeah, I lied to you and I kept things from you but that doesn't change the fact that the moment you walked into my life, I fell head over heels in love with you."

"It changed everything."

He shakes his head, reaching across to the bedside table and pulling something out before slamming the drawer shut again. Sunlight glints off the diamond ring in his hand as he holds it out in front of me. I suck in a breath.

"I bought this one week after I met you because right from the jump, I knew you were it for me. I played it cool with anyone who asked but I was already planning a life with you and I know I screwed up by lying to you, Tate, but I never meant to hurt you. If anything, all I ever wanted was to keep you safe."

"You didn't mean to hurt me and yet, I'm still hurt. Am I just supposed to be okay with that?"

He nods, grabbing my hand. He sets the ring in my palm before wrapping his hand around mine and forcing it closed. "I know you're hurt, baby, and you have to admit that it's not all my fault. Yeah, I hid things from you and I lied to you but this mess was coming for you whether I was here or not. This is on you now and you have a choice to make."

"What?"

"You can either forgive me and put this ring on your finger. I can't promise to never screw up again or unintentionally hurt you but I do promise that I'll be right there by your side, fighting for you and fighting for us until my very last breath. We'll face any challenge together and I'll spend every second of my life loving you with every piece of me."

I swallow as a lump builds in my throat. "What's the second option?"

"You can become your mother. You can toss this ring in the trash and spend the rest of your life loving a man that you can never be with. The choice is yours."

"What happened to you never walking away from me?" I ask, my voice wobbling as I think about losing him forever. White-hot pain pierces my chest.

"I'll always love you, Tate, and if you choose to toss this ring away, I'll never be with anyone else because I've found everything that I've ever wanted in you but you were also right when you said that this is a little sick. I'm not your punching bag but I'll be everything else to you for the rest of time if you let me."

Without another word, he climbs off me and walks into the bathroom. I watch him until the door closes and a soft sob bubbles out of me as I think over what he just said. When faced with those two choices, I don't know how I could ever possibly choose living my life without Lincoln in it. Yeah, he lied to me but I'm not ready to walk away from him either so I need to find a way to put this behind me.

The bathroom door opens and I glance over as he walks out in a pair of jeans hanging loose on his hips. "You want some breakfast?"

"Um… yeah," I whisper, blinking at him. How does he look so unaffected, like that entire conversation never happened? "Are we going to talk about this?"

He shakes his head. "I've said everything I need to say. You can put the ring on when you're ready or give it back to me. Like I said, the choice is yours. Now, get dressed and come eat."

Swiping his shirt off the end of the bed, he walks out of the bedroom and I suck in a breath as I watch him before glancing down at the ring in my palm. It's gorgeous and my fingers itch to put it on but I need to wait. I need to be sure that I can forgive him before I decide. Sighing, I set it down on the bedside table and lay my hand over it as I climb out of bed and slip my jeans on before wandering out into the living room.

Lincoln is at the counter, stirring something in a large mixing bowl as steam rises from the pan on the stove.

"Please tell me you know how to cook," I say, sliding onto one of the barstools and he grins over his shoulder.

"Guess you're just going to have to wait and see."

I shake my head, grabbing the newspaper and opening it. "I don't think I like this game."

"And what game would that be?"

"Is it edible or not?" I quip and he laughs as his phone goes off next to me. He peeks over his shoulder again.

"Shit. Can you see what that is for me?"

I nod and grab the phone before unlocking it. An image of my kitchen fills the screen and in the top corner, I spot movement and gasp. He whirls around, leaving his bowl and spoon abandoned as he moves behind me. A figure dressed in black creeps into my kitchen from the back door and my hand shakes as I watch him move through the house.

"Fuck," Lincoln hisses, checking his watch. "Maybe if I drive fast, I can get there before he leaves."

He takes off for the bedroom and I watch the man pull a pistol out of an ankle holster and the glint of metal at his back tells me he's got at least one more. The thought of Lincoln alone in my house with him shakes me to my core and I jump down off the stool. As I march past Smith's door, I pound on it and grab my boots from the living room floor where I left them last night.

Lincoln comes barreling out of the bedroom as I'm digging a few guns out of the couch that I stashed there last night and he stops when he sees me.

"What the hell are you doing?"

I scowl at him as I grab my ankle holster and start putting it on. "I'm going with you."

"Like hell you are."

"Don't you dare try to stop me, Lincoln. I am fucking going with you."

He shakes his head, storming past Smith's door and pounding on it. "It's not happening, Tate. Get it out of your gorgeous little head right now."

The bedroom door flies open and Smith steps out, rubbing his eyes. "What the fuck is with all the yellin'? It's early as hell, y'all."

I glance at the clock and smirk. It's actually almost eight but I've learned that Smith is a bit of a night owl since he's been staying with us and he doesn't like to be woken up before ten.

"Someone's in her house. I'm gonna go check it out," Lincoln barks and Smith snaps to attention. "You stay here with her."

"Fuck no!" I scream, pointing at Lincoln from across the living room. "Smith, don't let him go there alone. It's not safe and I'm going with you."

"No, you're not, baby. I'll be back soon, okay?"

Smith drops his arm as Lincoln steps in front of me and presses his lips to mine. I melt at his touch and my heart pounds in my ears as he kisses me like he's saying good-bye. When he pulls away, he mouths, "I love you" and I reach for him only to be stopped by Smith again.

Lincoln walks out the door and I stare after him, my chest aching and my hands shaking. Images of him lying in a pool of his own blood with a bullet hole in his chest fill my mind and the pain in my chest intensifies. No, I have to go with him. He needs me there.

"Please, Luke. Let me go with him."

He shakes his head. "I can't do that, Darlin'."

Panic claws at me, thinking of all the ways my father's thug could hurt the man I love and I spin, stomping back toward the bedroom. I spot my bag on the floor and I reach inside, pulling my Taser out and turning it on before slipping the strap of the bag over my shoulder. Just as I turn to leave the room, the ring catches my eye and I stare at it for a second before walking over to the nightstand and picking it up. Lincoln's right. If I don't let this go and move forward with him, I'll spend the rest of my life regretting it. With a smile teasing my lips, I slip it on my left hand and turn toward the door, trudging out of the bedroom.

"Sorry, Tate. I can't let you go," Smith says as I walk back out into the living room. He offers me a sympathetic look and I nod, hiding the Taser behind my back.

"I understand, Smith. And I hope you'll understand why I have to do this."

He scowls as I press the Taser to his skin and he drops to the floor, his muscles locked as he jerks from the force of the volt. Leaning down, I press a kiss to his cheek.

"Please don't hate me."

I stand back up and step over him, grabbing the Camaro's keys off the counter before I race outside, eager to get back to my man.

Chapter Twenty-Three
Lincoln

Fuck!

I skid to a stop in the driveway and pull my phone out of my pocket, scrolling through my contacts once before dialing Rodriguez's number. I would call one of the guys but Rodriguez may come in useful if I manage to get to Tate's house before this asshole takes off. I'm being overly optimistic in hoping that it's Dominic when I'm sure, in reality, he probably just sent one of his goons to do his dirty work. I'm sick and tired of this prick coming for my girl and I want to get him out of her life as soon as possible.

"Yeah," Rodriguez answers in a clipped tone.

"Hey. It's Kodiak. Someone is breaking into Tate's house right now and I need you to meet me there," I say as I swing my leg over my bike and slip the key into the ignition.

"On my way."

He hangs up without another word and I fire the bike up, checking the cameras again on my phone. The guy is taking his damn time, looking through each drawer in the kitchen and I have to wonder just what he's looking for. It's clear that Tate's not there so why doesn't he just bail out? I shove the phone back in my pocket. Gravel flies behind me as I peel away from the house, flying down the driveway way faster than I should be but I can't help it. Not when all I can think about is the fact that if I hadn't convinced Tate to come stay at my house, she'd be there with this prick right now. She'd be in danger and the thought makes my stomach turn as I tighten my grip on the handlebars. I speed up, my anger propelling me to move faster. I need to get there before he leaves. I need to end this.

But how?

How the fuck do I stop Dominic King from coming after my girl? I had multiple fantasies about killing the son of a bitch with my bare hands before Blaze pointed out that it would only put Tate in more danger. King has racked up so many enemies over the years and at this point, he's the only thing keeping them from coming after Tate. He protects her as much as he hurts her but that doesn't mean I'm going to stand idly by while he tries to take what's mine. It will be a cold day in hell before I willingly let my woman leave with that man.

My thoughts drift to only twenty minutes ago when she and I were in bed together and my stomach rolls as my mind races. I have no fucking idea if showing her the ring and putting the ball in her court was a good idea or not but it felt like my only option. Since everything fell apart, all I've done is apologize and tell her that I would always be here and that was clearly not working. If I allowed it to continue, she probably would have taken her anger out on me for the rest of our lives. She's that goddamn stubborn. Fuck, what if she really decides to walk away from this, from us? No, I can't think like that. What she and I have is real and hopefully, with this little push from me, she'll realize it, too.

I turn onto Tate's street and the roar of my bike echoes off the houses surrounding me as I spot Rodriguez's car parked on the curb. When I pull up behind him, he steps out and inspects the front of the house, a stern look on his face. After pushing the kickstand down, I turn off my bike and pull my phone out again, scanning the cameras. Each one is empty and I flip to the last one pointed at the back door, jumping back as his mask covered face fills the screen.

"Jesus, fuck," I hiss, jumping as my heart hammers away in my chest. "Back door."

The man stares right into the camera, his baby blue eyes devoid of any life as he lets out the same demented cackle I heard over Tate's answering machine. I jump off the bike and pull the gun out of my waistband as Rodriguez holds his arm out in front of me.

"I'll take the back. You cover the front," he whispers, pointing to the open front door and I nod, tucking the phone back into my pocket. As Rodriguez rounds the back of the house, I creep up the front steps, each one creaking under my weight and I flinch, the sound of each breath filling my ears as my shaking hands hold the gun out in front of me.

"Get it together," I whisper to myself as I step into the house and scan the living and dining room. Both are empty and I take another step, my finger hovering over the trigger and I strain my ear, listening for any sound that could give him away.

"Clear," Rodriguez calls from the back door and I blow out a breath as the top stair creaks behind me. I spin around, my finger pressing down on the trigger before I catch sight of red hair and my arm falls to my side.

"Are you fucking shitting me, Tate?" I hiss, walking over to her and grabbing her arm. "What the fuck are you doing here?"

She rips her arm out of my grasp and presses her lips to mine. "If you thought for one second I was letting you come here and face my demons alone, you don't know me at all."

God, I fucking love this woman.

I love her fire.

I love her sass.

But most of all, I love the way that she can't stop loving me even though she may want to right now.

"All clear," Rodriguez says, stepping into the room. His eyes fall on Tate and he nods as he fights back a smile. "Tate."

"Detective Rodriguez."

I turn to Rodriguez. "You sure he's gone?"

"He is. He bailed out my bedroom window while y'all were charging the doors."

"Fuck," I sigh. "I really wanted to get my hands on him."

"What good would it do?" she asks with a shrug. "He's likely just one of my father's goons."

I cup her chin and force her gaze to mine. "He broke into your house and I can't stop thinking about what would have happened if you had been here so I don't care who he was; I still want to get my hands on him and teach him to never come near you again."

"Lincoln," she whispers, a smile lighting up her face as she grabs my hand. The glint on her ring finger catches my attention and time seems to stop as I stare at it, not quite believing what I'm seeing. Holy shit, it worked. My mouth pops open and she follows my gaze before grinning.

"Oh, yeah... about that..."

"Are you for real right now? You're going to marry me?" I ask as my heart stutters in my chest and my mouth goes dry.

She nods. "If you'll still have me."

"Fuck yes," I growl, wrapping my arms around her and lifting her into the air as I press my lips against hers. She giggles, threading her fingers through my hair and it's the sweetest damn sound I've ever heard in my life. She's mine now. Forever.

"I love you," I whisper against her lips and she smiles.

"Turns out, I love you, too. And I'm sorry that I'm so stubborn and unreasonable. I was so worried about you when you left and I realized that I don't want to spend another minute of my life without you."

"And you'll never have to."

She giggles again and pulls back as I gently set her back on her feet. "I can't promise to make it easy for you."

"You wouldn't be the woman I'm madly in love with if you did," I answer, holding the back of her head and pulling her lips to mine again. Rodriguez clears his throat behind us and we pull away as Tate blushes.

"Sorry. Got a little caught up," I admit. He shakes his head.

"No worries and congrats to both of you. You're good for each other."

I grin, looking back at my girl. "We have to tell the guys."

She nods and I scowl, remembering that I left Smith to watch over her.

"Wait. Where's Smith?"

She purses her lips and looks away from me as Rodriguez starts laughing.

"Tate," I prompt and she sighs.

"I kind of tased him."

"Tate," I growl, pinching the bridge of my nose as she cuddles under my arm and presses her hand to my stomach.

"I'm sorry but he wouldn't let me leave. I had to get to you."

I roll my eyes and stare down at her. "He was protecting you like I asked him to."

"Yeah," she muses, biting her lip. "We're going to have to get him a really good present to make up for it."

"How did I get roped into this?" I ask, laughing and she holds up her left hand, now adorned with my ring, as she reaches up on her tiptoes to press a kiss against my lips. "I didn't realize my marriage proposal came with apologies to my friends."

"Sorry to break up this love fest but you should see this," Rodriguez says, grabbing a piece of paper off the dining room table. I take it from him and blow out a breath as I read it.

I want my daughter
Monday
Sunrise Diner
2 p.m.

"Ready to meet your old man?" I ask, handing the note to her and her hand trembles slightly as she nods.

"Let's take it to the club and see what everyone else thinks."

My brows shoot up in surprise and she glances over at me, rolling her eyes.

"Don't look at me like that. I'm not going into this alone so I'll need support from y'all if I decide to face him."

I shake my head. "I don't like it."

"I don't either but it may be our only option."

Every Breath You Take

Chapter Twenty-Four
Tatum

"Lincoln," I moan, stretching out next to him in bed as he presses his lips to the bare skin between my shoulder blades and I cuddle closer to him, craving the warmth of his embrace. He pulls the covers up over us and kisses my shoulder.

"Morning, Darlin'."

I smile, peeking over my shoulder at him. "Good morning."

"Have I ever told you how fucking hard it makes me when you moan my name?" he asks, accenting his point by pressing his rigid cock against my ass. I giggle and shake my hips, teasing him a little more and he growls as he grips my hip. "If you're not careful, I'm going to take you again, wife."

"I'm not your wife," I point out as I turn away from him and wiggle my ass again. His fingers tighten on my hip as he leans forward and slowly kisses a path up my neck. My nipples pebble and I arch my back, pinning his cock between the two of us.

"Not yet but as soon as this day is over, we're setting a date in the very near future."

"Oh, really?" I ask, glancing back at him with a quirked brow and he nods.

"Don't even think of fighting me on this. I'm not waiting a minute longer than I have to."

I roll over to face him and palm his cheek. "You're getting very bossy. Afraid I'm going to change my mind?"

"No, not anymore. You made your choice and now you're stuck with me until the day I die. You're just lucky I didn't drag you to a courthouse the second you said yes."

I push away from him and scoot back on the bed as I fight off a grin. "And what if I run from you?"

"I'll chase you," he growls, baring his teeth as he lunges at me and wraps his arms around my waist. I giggle, pretending to fight him. "I'll never let you get away now."

He rolls on top of me and slips a hand between my thighs. "Are you still wet for me, baby?"

I nod as his fingers sink into my pussy. This would be round three in as many hours and neither one of us can seem to get enough of each other but that's been par for the course since I accepted his ring. He's been insatiable and I might be even worse. Unless we've been at the club going over what to do about my father, we've been here in this bed making up for lost time.

"Fuck, Tate," he groans as he starts fingering me and I moan, arching my hips off the bed as my eyes flutter closed. His hand wraps around my throat and my eyes spring open. "Eyes on me always, baby girl."

"Lincoln," I whimper, our gazes locked together as he brings me to the point of release with his fingers alone. Just when I think I'm going to topple over the edge, he stops and pulls out of me. "No!"

"Tell me what you want."

My gaze drops to his cock and I reach forward, wrapping my hand around it as I stroke it back and forth. His eyes close for a second as he groans. When he opens them again, they are filled with fire and he leans down, sealing his lips over mine in a kiss so hot it could burn down this whole house as he pulls my hand away from his length. As he pulls back, he grabs my hips and flips me to my belly. He straddles my hips and grips my ass cheeks, spreading them apart as he presses the tip of his cock against my entrance. My entire body tenses in anticipation and I suck in a breath, holding it in my lungs as I wait for the sweet ache of him driving into me. He leans over me, his lips brushing against my ear and a shiver winds down my spine.

"You want my cock, baby?"

I nod, wiggling my ass against him. "Yes."

"Can you say please like a good little girl?"

"No," I hiss. He pulls away and I cry out at the loss as he laughs. "Okay, please."

"Please what?" he asks, leaning over me again.

"Please give me your cock."

He groans and slips inside me, giving me that delicious ache I've been craving. "With pleasure, Darlin'."

I moan, gripping the sheets in front of me as he holds himself inside me and sucks in a ragged breath, his grip on my ass tightening.

"Jesus Christ. You feel incredible."

He rocks his hips but I need more. "Lincoln, fuck me, please."

"Tate," he groans, leaning over me as one hand grips the back of my neck. "I fucking love those dirty words coming out of your pretty little mouth but what you and I do is not fucking. It never has been."

"I need you to move," I plead, my body aching and he growls in my ear as he pulls back and sinks into me again.

"Like that?"

I nod. "Yes, please."

He keeps a firm hand on the back of my neck as he moves to his knees and sets a steady pace, rocking in and out of me with just enough speed to drive me out of my mind.

In…

Out…

In…

Out…

"Lincoln," I gasp, arching my back more and he slaps my ass before gripping it with a growl. The bite of his fingernails in my skin sends a shiver down my spine as my core clenches around him.

"Tell me what you want and I'll give it to you."

"Harder."

He pulls back and hits the perfect spot as a wave of pleasure washes over me. I cry out, dropping my head to the mattress as I moan, "More."

He does it again and again, hitting that spot over and over as pressure slowly builds inside me and I claw at the sheets in front of me, needing more.

"Faster," I command. The hand on the back of my neck moves to my hair and he fists some of it as he leans over me and kisses my neck.

"Greedy girl, aren't you?"

"Yes," I whisper, silently praying that he'll give me what I want, what I need. My body aches, desperate for the release that is just out of my grasp and just when I think that he's going to torture me some more, he picks up the pace, slamming into me repeatedly. Tension coils inside me again and I squeeze my eyes shut, gripping the sheets so hard that my hands ache.

"Don't stop," I breathe out and he ignores my request, pulling out of me as I cry out. He flips me to my back and hooks one leg over his shoulder as he lines himself up at my entrance and drives forward. I gasp, my hips arching off the bed as I grip his forearm.

"Eyes on me, Tate," he whispers and I peel my eyes open, meeting his just before he leans down and seals his lips over mine. Using the same pace as before – hard, fast, and relentless – he quickly reignites the orgasm I was chasing and my fingernails dig into his skin as stars explode behind my eyes and I rip my lips away to scream his name.

"Fuck," he groans, grabbing my face and slamming his lips back on mine as he continues thrusting, chasing his own release and wringing every last drop from mine in the process. Slipping my fingers into his hair, I give it a tug and he groans, tensing above me as his cock jerks.

"Lincoln," I whisper and he lets out a long groan that sends a shiver straight to my toes before collapsing on top of me. His breath brushes over my clammy skin as he struggles to catch his breath and I close my eyes, a smile lighting up my face.

"Look how gorgeous you are," he says and I peek up at him, unable to wipe the smile from my face.

"Thank you."

He frowns. "For your orgasm?"

"No," I say, laughing. "For being even more stubborn than I was."

He smirks, brushing his thumb over my cheek. "Sweetheart, it's easy to be stubborn when you know you're right."

I roll my eyes and scoff as I push him off me. He laughs, pulling me into his arms – the only place I want to be for the rest of my life.

*   *   *   *

Sucking in a breath, I stop in front of the full length mirror and run my hands down my front, trying not to stare at the pistol on my ankle or the other one on my hip. I also have two knives and the Taser with me but my hands are still shaking something fierce. It's not everyday a girl meets her dad for the first time. Not to mention the whole evil crime boss thing that I'm trying not to think about. All my life, my mother prepared me for this moment and I still feel woefully unqualified to take on the man who's been silently haunting my life since the moment I took my first breath. Lincoln steps up behind me and wraps his arms around my waist as he meets my gaze in the mirror and presses his lips against my neck.

"You can still back out of this, baby. No one here would blame you."

I glance out at my bedroom where most of the club hovers, each man looking nervous and irritated by the situation. When Lincoln and I took the note to the club five days ago, they were all adamant that I didn't meet with Dominic but I knew then, as I still do now, that he won't leave until he speaks to me. I could run and I could hide but eventually, he'd catch up to me. Alone with my thoughts for the past few days, I've wondered if this is exactly how my mother felt when she struck her deal with him all those years ago and I wish she was here to tell me what to do.

"You know I can't," I whisper and he scowls as he pulls me closer and shakes his head.

"Please, Tate. We'll find another way."

I spin in his arms and cup his cheek as I shake my head. "There is no other way. You and I have a life to start together and we can't do that if we are on the run from Dominic King. We deserve more than that."

"Maybe he's right," Nix says from the doorway of the safe room and I sigh.

"Guys, I appreciate the protectiveness but the longer he's here, the more danger we're all in. Especially you, Nix."

He shakes his head. "Don't worry about me."

"Are we ready to go?" Rodriguez asks, sticking his head in the room and I nod as I suck in a breath.

"Yeah, let's do this."

I can feel Lincoln's reluctance as he grabs my hand and we walk out to the van with the rest of the guys. Smith opens the back door for me and I offer him a smile that he doesn't return. He's still a little mad at me about tasing him and he was one of the loudest voices objecting to this plan. I just hope that after all this is over and everything turns out fine, he can forgive me because he's become a really good friend over the last week and a half and I don't want to lose him.

Rodriguez, Lincoln, Nix, and Smith file into the van and sit around me as we pull away from the curb and I clasp my hands together, hoping no one will see how badly they're shaking. If Mom saw me right now, she'd be pissed that I was letting an opponent get in my head but meeting Dominic King feels a little bit like meeting the boogeyman.

"Okay, here's the plan," Rodriguez says, pulling everyone's attention over to him. "Tate, I want you to sit in one of the middle tables along the wall, preferably by a window."

I nod. "Okay."

"I'm going to be seated in one corner and Fuzz," he explains, pointing to Fuzz in the front seat, "will be in another corner. Everyone else will wait outside."

"I don't fucking think so," Lincoln growls and Nix nods in agreement. Rodriguez sighs.

"You either go along with this plan or I send you back to the clubhouse with Blaze."

Blaze also really wanted to be here today but we all knew it would be a terrible idea with his history with Dominic and we couldn't risk Dominic learning about Nix.

"No fucking way," Lincoln snaps, squeezing my hand tight. "I'm going in there with her."

"Babe," I whisper and he glances over at me. "If you go in there with me, it's going to change the whole tone of this meeting and we won't accomplish what needs to get done today."

He blows out a breath, running his hand through his hair. "I don't like it."

"It's the way it's got to be," Rodriguez tells him. "But I'll keep your girl safe, okay?"

"He better not touch a single hair on her beautiful fucking head, you get me?" he asks, narrowing his eyes on Rodriguez, who simply nods in understanding. I'm just about to berate them for being cavemen when I notice the diner up ahead and suck in a breath.

"Show time."

"Last chance, Tate," Lincoln urges, holding my hand over his heart. "If you want to walk away, tell me now."

I roll my eyes, pressing my palm flat against his racing heart. "Is this going to become a regular thing for you? If so, I'm gonna need to find someone else to be with me when I give birth to our babies."

He grins, pulling me closer as the van pulls into the parking spot in the back of the lot. "How about this... march your sexy little ass in there and handle your shit, baby girl. But if you get even one scratch, I'm going to whoop your ass all over this fucking lot."

"Better," I whisper, a shiver skating down my spine as I lean forward and kiss him.

"Ugh," Nix mumbles, turning away from us. "Some things I just don't need to know."

"Fucking please," Smith whines, rolling his eyes. "You and Emma couldn't keep your damn hands off each other. Still can't."

Rodriguez snaps his fingers in front of us. "Can we focus, please? Fuzz is already inside and posted up in one corner. I'm going now. Tate, you give it five and come in after us. Remember what I said."

I nod and watch as he climbs out of the van, subtly scanning the lot before he walks toward the door and slips inside. He sits in the corner opposite of Fuzz and Mia bounces over to him, a wide smile on her face.

"Just be smart, okay?" Nix says and I nod, grabbing his hand and giving it a squeeze.

"I will. I promise."

Lincoln sinks back into the seat and sighs. "I fucking hate this."

"Just think, after today, you and I can have a normal relationship."

He scoffs. "Does normal include you tasing me?"

"I don't know. I guess it depends on how much you piss me off."

He laughs, slipping his hand into my hair as he pulls me onto his lips. When he pulls back, he brushes his thumb over my bottom lip and smiles. "I love you."

"I love you, too." I kiss him again before pointing a finger at Nix. "You both stay in this van, you hear? I can't be worried about you and watching out for Dominic at the same time."

They both roll their eyes.

"Yeah, we hear you."

I nod and give Lincoln one last kiss before opening the door and stepping out into the Louisiana sunshine. My stomach rolls as I scan the parking lot and approach the front door, wondering if he's here already. How stupid am I for not even looking at a picture of him? Truthfully, though, I didn't want to know what he looked like. I didn't want to put a face to the monster.

"Tate!" Mia squeals as soon as I walk in the door and I grin, bracing myself as she rushes toward me and hugs me.

"Hey."

"What are you doing here? I thought you were on house arrest or something," she says and I laugh. When the guys insisted that I have constant protection, I had to ask Roger to divvy up my shifts between the other waitresses and I told him I wasn't sure if I was coming back.

"Not really. I'm actually meeting someone so I'm just going to hang out at a booth, okay?"

She nods. "Of course. Take whichever one you want."

As she turns back toward the counter, my gaze flicks to one corner where Fuzz is sitting in a booth with his back to the wall. I choose a table in the middle, just like Rodriguez suggested and let out a breath as I sink into my chair.

"Coffee?" Mia asks, holding out a mug and I nod. She sets it in front of me and fills it up before propping her hip against the table. "So, what's going on with you? I haven't talked to you in forever."

"Oh, I know. It's been really crazy and I'd love to tell you all about it but I don't have much time right now."

She nods, glancing toward the door. "Sure. You want anything to eat?"

"No, I'm good with the coffee."

She nods and turns back to the counter again and I try not to focus on the awkward vibe hanging between us as I take a sip of coffee and almost choke on it.

"Creamer," I whisper to myself, grabbing a few from the bowl Mia set down and pouring them into my mug. My hands shake violently as I try to focus on drinking my coffee and I wonder how long it will take for Dominic to show up. He's probably the type of man that likes to make people wait while he makes an entrance and I roll my eyes, irritated already.

The minutes tick by painfully slow and when I finish off my coffee, I motion to Rodriguez that I'm going to go to the bathroom. He nods and I push back my chair, feeling a little off kilter as I turn toward the bathrooms but I force myself to press on. I just need to stop, take a breath, and splash some water on my face so I can get this meeting over with.

Stumbling into the bathroom, I stop in front of one of the mirrors and brace my hands on the sink as I suck in a breath. My world spins and I shake my head, my heart rate spiking in fear. Something is wrong. I glance back up at the mirror and gasp at the familiar face smiling back at me.

"What are you..." I whisper, my voice trailing off as I become weightless and darkness descends over me.

Every Breath You Take

Chapter Twenty-Five
Tatum

"Taaaatuuuuum," the same voice from my nightmares whispers in my ear and warm breath trickles over my skin as a violent shiver racks my body and I let out a whimper. *This isn't real*, I think to myself again and again as I slowly fade into consciousness. My head hurts along with the rest of my body and I fight through the haze to recall my last memory but come up empty. Where am I? "Are you awake, my sweet little Tatum?"

I suck in a breath as a chill blankets my skin, waiting for the laughter that always comes next but I'm met with silence. My chest aches and a tear falls from the corner of my eye. I peel open my eyes, hissing at the bright spotlight directly above me as pain ricochets around my brain. I try to cover my eyes but my hands won't move and I glance up, holding back a scream when I see the white metal bedframe my hands are tied to. Biting my lip, I jerk on the rope and the bed rattles against the wall.

The high-pitched laughter that I know so well fills the room and my gaze snaps to the darkness surrounding me, searching for the source but it's impossible to see past the harsh light above me. Light peeks through little slats in the wall and the smell of rotting wood fills my nose as I try to figure out where I am. It's not much to go on but it's something. Footsteps scrape along the floor and I suck in a breath as the room seems to close in on me and a figure steps out of the shadows. I gasp.

"Devlin?" I ask, scowling up at the man I've known for the past three years as he stalks toward me, victory filling his gaze. Images of his face appearing behind me in the bathroom mirror flit through my mind and I shake my head, my mind struggling to process what's happening. "What are you doing?"

"Oh, sweet Tate," he coos, stalking around the twin bed as he stares down at me. I glance down and realize that he got me down to my bra and panties before securing me to the bed and I jerk my arms again, wishing I could cover myself. "There's just so much you don't know yet but by the time we're finished here, I promise you'll never forget."

"So you're going to let me go?"

He smiles. "Eventually, but first I need your help."

"Of course, Devlin," I whisper, trying to reason with him. Once, when I was younger, Mom made Theo and me watch documentaries about what to do if you're abducted. At the time, I thought it was stupid but now it's all coming back to me and I'm thankful for it. "What can I do to help?"

"I've always liked you, Tate," he muses, shaking his finger at me. "From the first moment I started watching you, I liked your spunk and resourcefulness. Of course when I finally met you in person, you were just as sweet as can be. It's really a shame that things between us have to end like this."

My mind spins with everything he just told me and I don't know which comment to address first. I meet his gaze as my lips part. "You... You've been watching me?"

"Oh, yes. For many years now. I first arrived in Baton Rouge during your freshman year of high school."

I shake my head, disappointed in myself for being so damn oblivious. "Why?"

"Because I work for your father, dear."

Gasping, I tug on the ropes, trying to put space between us as he laughs and clamps a hand down on my leg.

"Don't do that, Darling. We wouldn't want you to get hurt."

My heart races in my ear as I try to connect the unhinged man in front of me with the one I've gotten to know these past few years and it just doesn't make sense.

"Why did he send you?"

He shrugs. "To keep tabs on you. He wanted to know who his children were and that they were okay and he entrusted me with that."

"So then why are you doing this, Devlin?"

He smiles. "Ah, now there's the million dollar question. Do you remember when I told you about the love of my life?"

"Claire?" I whisper and he nods.

"Yes, my sweet Claire. She was my everything."

I nod. "She died, right?"

"Yes," he hisses, rage twisting his features as he stares down at me. "But that was only part of the story. Would you like to hear the rest?"

"If I listen to your story, will you let me go?" I ask, hoping against hope that I can reason with him somehow. He chuckles.

"I'm afraid not, sweet girl. People have to pay for the pain they caused me and that's why you're here."

"How did you get me here?"

He shrugs. "It wasn't all that hard. Mia is easily distracted and once her attention was on something else, I slipped something in your coffee."

"And how did you get me out of the diner?"

"Ah, now that was a little more difficult but I managed to get you out of the window and into my car."

I nod, meeting his gaze as my stomach flips. "Will you tell me about Claire?"

"I first met her when my family moved in next door. We were twelve years old and the second I saw her, I knew one day she'd be my wife."

"What happened?"

He meets my gaze as rage fills his eyes and he leans forward, wrapping his hand around my throat. My mouth pops open and I wonder if he's going to kill me here. "Your mother and father happened."

"Please don't hurt me, Devlin," I whisper and his gaze instantly softens as he pulls his hand away from my throat. He tilts his head to the side as he brushes his fingers along my cheek, moisture building in his eyes.

"I wish I didn't have to, Tate, but like I said people need to pay for what happened to my Claire."

I swallow past the lump in my throat and remember the tips I learned in the documentary all those years ago.

Put your captor at ease.

Keep your dignity.

Be a good listener.

"What happened to her, Devlin?"

He closes his eyes as if the memories are too much to bear as he sucks in a breath. "After your mother left Dominic and he learned about you and your brother, he became despondent and many of the people close to him were worried about what he'd do."

"Did you work for him back then?"

He nods. "I wasn't in the inner circle like I am now but yes, I worked for him. I had just turned twenty-one and I was getting ready to ask Claire to marry me when Dominic decided that if he couldn't have you and Theo, he would have another child. And the woman he chose to give him what he wanted most was my Claire."

"Oh," I whisper, tears filling my eyes as I imagine the worst. I know what kind of man my father is.

He nods. "Yes, it shocked and devastated us both but Dominic King is not a man you can say no to, not if you want to live, so even though she didn't want to, she agreed to marry him."

"I'm so sorry, Dev." I don't know what else to say to him and he may not believe me but I really do feel a great deal of empathy for him and Claire. I can't imagine being ripped away from Lincoln like that.

"On their wedding night," he continues, ignoring my apology. "Dominic was eager to start trying but Claire was still a virgin and she was understandably nervous. Dominic didn't care. He forced her down on the bed and planted his seed in her five times before the sun came up the next morning."

A tear streaks down my cheek and my hands tremble. "Devlin…"

He holds his hand up to stop me and I clamp my mouth shut as he stands and stares down at my semi-naked body.

"He did all this because your mother left and she stole you and your brother away from him so today, you will pay for her sins," he snarls, anger filling his eyes as he inspects me and I tug on the ropes again, praying to a God I'm not sure I believe in.

"Please, no, Devlin."

Without uttering a word, he pulls a knife out of his back pocket and climbs on top of me, straddling my waist. I buck my hips as much as I can with my arms and legs secured to the bed and he arches a brow as he presses the knife to my throat.

"Stop," he orders and my body falls back to the bed, my heartbeat thrashing in my ears. "This is happening. You cannot stop it and if you fight me, I will make it worse. Do you understand?"

I feel numb as I nod my head, resigning myself to my fate. He climbs off me and disappears into the shadows only to reappear a few seconds later with a camera on a tripod.

"We're going to make a little video for daddy. How does that sound?"

I turn away from him, another tear falling from my eyes. My soul is screaming in my ears, beating her fists against my rib cage to escape from the hell that I can feel approaching me with each passing second.

Devlin climbs back on top of me and grabs my bra, cutting it straight down the center as I suck in a stuttered breath. I've spent most of my life believing something like this couldn't happen to me because of the training my mother forced upon me and now that it's happening, it all feels like a waste. What was the point of it all if I can't defend myself now when I need it most?

She would be so ashamed of me.

He moves down the bed and cuts both sides of my panties before pulling them away and groaning.

"I've been watching you since you were just a girl but I can't deny that you've turned into a stunning woman, Tate."

I bite back a scream and try to focus on this morning when Lincoln and I were wrapped up in each other and I was certain life couldn't get more perfect. Devlin climbs off me and stands next to the bed as he starts to undress. I squeeze my eyes shut and only open them again when he lets out a low groan. His cock is in his hand and his eyes trace my curves as he strokes himself and licks his lips.

"This is such a strange feeling," he murmurs. "I'm attracted to you but I'm also sorry that I have to do this. I'm going to enjoy and hate it all at the same time."

Shut up, a voice in my head screams as I turn away from him and look at the camera.

He climbs on top of me again and uses the knife to free one leg as I clench my teeth and hold back a curse. If he'd freed both legs, I'd have a fighting chance but I'm sure he knew that. The hopelessness of the whole situation crashes down on me. He's been planning this for a while and he's studied me even longer than that so I'm sure he's thought of every scenario.

Devlin throws my leg on his shoulder and leans forward, opening me up as he spits on my pussy and presses his cock against my entrance. My chest feels heavy as I squeeze my eyes shut again and wait for the nightmare I know is coming. He thrusts forward, burying himself inside me and pain pierces through me as I cry out, pulling on the ropes.

"That's it, sweetheart," he whispers in my ear. "Look right in that camera and tell Daddy how awful it is."

I shake my head, keeping my eyes shut tight. He may have me at his mercy right now but there's no way in hell I'm giving him anything he wants. With a firm grip on my thigh, he pulls back and drives forward again, groaning as another wave of pain washes through me.

My mind shuts down and my body goes numb as I open my eyes and stare at the light above me, images of Lincoln flashing through my mind. I cling to them as Devlin continues tearing me apart from the inside out, stripping away pieces of me that I know I'll never get back.

"I'm so sorry, Tate," he groans, his hand grabbing my tit as he speeds up, chasing his release in my agony. "If you want to blame someone for this, blame your mother. She's the reason this is happening to you."

"No, it's not," I bite out. "You had a choice and you chose wrong."

He shakes his head, burying his face in my neck as his thrusts get more frantic and tears pour down the side of my face.

"They have to pay," he chants again and again. He kisses my neck and I buck against him, unable to take another second of this. He grabs my face and forces it toward the camera. "Tell Daddy how much it hurts, baby. Tell him how much his actions are killing you."

He groans and his cock twitches, spilling inside me and I close my eyes and a deep, painful sob breaks free.

* * * *

Morning sunlight peeks through the slats in the wall and birds chirp outside, mocking me with their cheerfulness, as I lay naked with my hands and legs still tied to the bed frame. Everything feels tight and my stomach grumbles as another hunger pang hits me. I think I've been here for about fifteen or sixteen hours but I can't be sure. I spent most of the night begging Lincoln to find me and save me but I think I've given up on that at this point.

The door opens and Devlin wheels a tray in, smiling at me. "Good morning, Tate. How are you feeling?"

"Go to hell," I mutter, turning away from him. I don't care about following the rules anymore. The rules got me raped and I see now that there is no distracting Devlin from his mission.

"I was hoping we could talk some more."

I turn back to him as he perches on the edge of the bed. "What is there to talk about?"

"Oh, my dear, you only know half the story and you are not done paying penance."

I glance at the tray and see a scalpel, a needle, and a thick black thread. My gaze flies to his and he smiles with a remorseful look in his eyes.

"What more do you want?"

He folds his hand in his lap and sighs. "After their wedding, Dominic spent months trying to get Claire pregnant, months of forcing himself on her to breed her like cattle, and it finally worked. After six months, she learned she was pregnant but his happiness didn't last long. Just a couple weeks later, she miscarried and Dominic was furious. He beat her senseless and left her for dead, which is where I found her."

I watch him as he speaks, unwilling to add anything more to the conversation.

"I carried her to her room and nursed her back to health for a few days. When Dominic came around again, he mistook my love for devotion to him and he promoted me – put me on her personal guard detail. I spent the next few years listening as your father raped and beat the woman I loved with my whole heart on a daily basis."

"I'm sorry, Devlin," I whisper. Despite what he's done to me and the hatred I feel toward him, his story is still heartbreaking and I understand the rage he feels for my father.

He forces a smile. "Do not apologize. It got better when Claire and I finally gave into our love. We had to start sneaking around behind Dominic's back but it was worth it to me. My Claire was different than before Dominic got ahold of her and there were parts of her that were broken but we both found a little bit of happiness again."

"But it couldn't last," I whisper, pointing out the obvious and his lips flatten into a straight line as he nods.

"That is correct. Right after your father asked me to come here to watch over you and your brother, he heard rumors that someone had been sleeping with Claire. I obviously wasn't there to witness it but I heard that there was a full on inquisition. Claire and I had been careful, though, and no one knew about us which only served to piss Dominic off further. When he couldn't find answers elsewhere, he locked Claire up in the basement for three weeks and tortured her for several hours everyday."

"How do you know this?" I ask, wondering how much of this story is actually true if he was here in Baton Rouge.

"I called to check in once a week. The other guards usually answered and they liked to chat." He clenches his fists. "I had to sit down here and listen to the pain and agony he was subjecting Claire to everyday but she never broke. She never gave up my name."

I nod. "And?"

"And he finally lost his patience and killed her," he snarls through gritted teeth and I suck in a breath. It's what I expected but still somehow shocking to hear. "Which is why you now have to pay for your father's sins."

I glance over at the tray. "What are you going to do to me?"

"Dominic systematically tore my girl to shreds. He broke her and so I'm going to break you and sew you back together again. For the rest of your life, you will be a physical representation of the one I lost."

The instruments on the tray rattle as he reaches for the scalpel and I jump, sucking in a breath as the room spins. He pulls a remote out of his pocket and points it at the camera set up at the edge of the bed.

"The camera is rolling again so make sure you show him what he's done to you."

I close my eyes, my lip wobbling and my hands shaking as I wait for the pain to come and then I feel it. There's pressure against my shoulder followed by a sharp burning sensation that claws its way down my arm. Gasping, I open my eyes and look over at my shoulder as

Devlin pulls on a pair of gloves and grabs the needle and thread. He starts humming the tune of *Don't Worry, Be Happy* by Bobby McFerrin as he threads the string through the needle and I stare at him in horror.

The whole thing is bizarre and I wonder if I drifted off to sleep at some point in the night. Is this just a dream? Or am I really living this moment?

Devlin grabs a piece of gauze off the tray and dabs the incision in my arm as I hiss and try to pull away from him. Arching a brow, he grabs my arm and shoves the needle through my skin as I whimper. It burns the entire time he's pulling the thread through and the room spins as I try to focus on my breathing. I can't pass out. I have to remain conscious and ready to flee if I get the opportunity.

When he finishes stitching up the first cut, he grabs the scalpel and positions it adjacent to the first cut before slicing away from it. I writhe on the bed, screaming as pain radiates all the way to my fingers and tears leak out of my eyes. He continues humming the song. He grabs the gauze again and repeats the process from before.

When I'm stitched up, he starts again. Time and time again, he tears through my flesh as my stomach flips and the room spins around me. I don't notice the camera anymore, screaming through each cut as agony rocks through my body.

"Please, no more," I choke out when he gets to my wrist and he sighs, reaching up and cupping my face with the bloody glove.

"Even though your pain causes me such pleasure, I am sorry that it's you on the receiving end of this. You are the one thing on this earth your father cares about and I can't stop. Not until he experiences my anguish."

He moves the scalpel to my chest and cuts across my collarbone as I scream and darkness creeps in on my vision. As the needle starts piercing my skin, Lincoln's smiling face pops into my mind and I wonder if I'll ever see him again. I spent so much time pushing him away and now, I'd give anything for a few more seconds just so I could tell him how much I love him.

Chapter Twenty-Six
Lincoln

Night is falling, covering the city in darkness and we've officially passed the twenty-four hour mark since Tate was taken right from under our noses. Thinking back to yesterday, I rub my fist over my chest, trying to ease the ache that's been tormenting me since I realized she was gone. Fuck, what if she's really gone for good? My knee bounces and I scrub my hands over my face, imagining my life without her in it and it takes every ounce of strength I have not to break down in front of everyone. I don't deserve her. It was my job to protect her, same as Nora, and I failed them both so miserably that I don't deserve any happiness in my life. Maybe, if we get her back, I should just walk away. Each time I play that scenario in my head, though, my heart shatters in my chest and just when I think that this can't hurt any more, it does. It's an endless loop of pain but everything I deserve.

It's so fucking selfish but I can't let her go. Tate is every fucking thing that's good in my life and I can't do this without her. I can't go back to the way I was before she walked into my life. Looking up at the ceiling, I promise God that I'll be better – a better man, a better partner, a better protector – if only he'll bring her back to me and give me a second chance. Or third chance, I suppose.

Rodriguez walks into the clubhouse and stops short when he sees me sitting on the couch. He's been at the station, trying to get a lead on my girl but when his face falls, I know he wasn't successful. I surge to my feet and storm across the clubhouse, pinning his back to a wall. "You fucking promised me, Rodriguez! You said you would keep her safe and now she's vanished into thin fucking air!"

"I know, Kodiak. I'm so sorry," he whispers, hanging his head.

"You're sorry," I sneer, taking a step back from him. "What fucking good does that do me?"

"Hey," Streak says, slapping his hand on my shoulder. "We won't rest until we find her."

I shake my head, ripping my shoulder out of his grasp. "Yeah? How are we going to do that? We have fucking nothing!"

I turn away from him and walk across the clubhouse before turning back and running my fingers through my hair. "She could be in motherfucking Chicago by now!"

I meet Nix's eyes across the clubhouse as he holds Emma in his lap and his face falls, the loss of his sister weighing down on him. Glancing around the room, everyone mirrors his expression. Smith is sitting at one of the tables with his head in his hands and Blaze is posted up at the bar, nursing a glass of bourbon – just like I found him after Sarah's death. In her short time with us, my girl has wormed her way into all our hearts and none of us will be the same without her. Collapsing into a chair, I bury my head in my hands and fight back tears.

I've already lost too much in my life – first, my father and then Nora – and I have no idea how I'll survive this one. If she's gone, she's taking me with her.

God, why didn't she listen to me?

Why didn't I insist that I go in there with her?

That's the worst part. I knew better and I went against my better judgment to make her happy. Now, I'd just be thrilled to have her here with me – pissed or not. The door to the clubhouse opens and I half-heartedly look up, my eyes widening as Dominic King strolls in with two armed guards behind him. Guns come out all over the room, all aimed at him as he holds his hands up and arches a brow.

"Put them away, boys. I come in peace."

Blaze stumbles off the barstool and growls low in his throat. "You motherfucker!"

He balls his fists up and I flick a look at Moose, who grabs Blaze and wrestles him back into his seat before he can charge Dominic and make a tense situation even worse.

"What the fuck are you doing here?" Nix asks and Dominic turns to him, smiling.

"Ah, you must be Phoenix. How nice to finally meet you after all these years," Dominic says and I glance at Smith, who looks equally confused. We were all under the impression that Dominic had no idea who Nix or Blaze were.

"You know me?" Nix asks, standing up from the couch and moving his wife behind him.

Dominic chuckles. "Of course I know who you are. I've always known. When your mother came to me to make her little deal, I had a stipulation of my own. You see, she was taking my children from me so I told her she could never reconnect with you."

"And if she did anyway?" I growl, my finger itching to pull the trigger as I keep my gun aimed at his head.

"Then I would kill Nix and her precious Blaze."

Blaze roars, trying to jump off the barstool again but Moose keeps him contained, whispering something in his ear.

"You bastard," Nix hisses and Dominic just grins like he was paid a compliment.

"Now, who is this lovely creature behind you?"

Emma tries to step out from behind her husband but Nix holds her back.

"None of your goddamn business," he growls and Dominic laughs as he turns to me. There's an evil glint in his ice blue eyes and my mind races as I try to figure out why he's here.

"You must be the man who's been sleeping with my daughter…"

My lip curls back in a snarl. "I'm her fiancé."

A.M. Myers

"We'll see about that. I brought you a little present." He holds up a DVD case and I scowl. "You have somewhere we can watch this?"

"Moose, take Blaze to his office. Fuzz and Chance, hang out with Dominic's friends here," Storm orders, taking over as acting President while Blaze is incapacitated. "Everyone else, guns down."

I slowly lower my gun, my heart pounding in my chest as I wish I could just put one between his eyes but that's not who we are – not anymore.

"Kodiak, lead him to the TV room," Storm orders and I glance over at him as he nods, a stern expression on his face. I slip the pistol back in my jeans and meet Dominic's gaze.

"This way."

I turn toward the TV room with Smith at my side. Dominic falls in behind me with Nix and Emma behind him and I wonder where he's keeping Tate and what the hell this little visit is about. When we get into the room, Dominic strolls to the front and turns to all of us.

"First off, I need to make it clear that I didn't take Tatum nor did I give the order to have her taken."

I cross my arms over my chest. "Then who has her?"

"My associate," he answers with a sigh. "He was sent down here many years ago to watch over my children and report back to me. I always kept my promise to Sarah but I had to know that they were okay. When you do what I do, you make a lot of enemies."

Scoffing, I glance at Smith, who is glaring daggers at Dominic. I knew he and Tate had grown close

391

while he was helping me watch over her but I didn't realize how close until she went missing.

"I've also done some digging since I've been here and I think there's a large possibility that Devlin, my associate, is also responsible for Sarah's death."

"Why?" Nix asks.

"I don't know why yet but I assure you, I will find out." Darkness blankets Dominic's face and I know that I would rather be anyone else than Devlin right now.

"What about the DVD?" I ask, gesturing to the case he still holds in his hand. He sighs and nods.

"I received the first video first thing this morning and I'll warn you, it's not easy to watch." He walks over to the DVD player and slips a disk in. An image of my Tate fills the screen. She's completely naked, sprawled out on her back with her hands and legs tied to a bed frame as a man I recognize from the diner straddles her body. I stumble forward and grip the back of the couch in front of me.

"No."

"I've been watching you since you were just a girl but I can't deny that you've turned into a stunning woman, Tate," he rasps, his voice going husky and my stomach rolls as tears build in my eyes and rage simmers in my veins.

No

No

No

"Jesus fucking Christ," Smith whispers as Devlin climbs off the bed and starts undressing as he stares down at Tate's naked body. I don't want to see this but I can't catch my breath to tell him to turn it off or look away. I need this – need to know what happened to her, what she went through even if it feels like I'm being shredded right where I stand.

"This is such a strange feeling," he murmurs. "I'm attracted to you but I'm also sorry that I have to do this. I'm going to enjoy and hate it all at the same time."

"Enough," I choke out and Dominic shakes his head.

"No, not yet."

Tate turns toward the camera as he climbs on top of her again and the defeated look in her golden gaze fucking kills me. I turn toward the wall and rest my forehead against it, struggling to draw air into my lungs. My hands shake and tears burn my eyes as visions of slicing this motherfucker open and spilling his guts on the floor assault me.

The sound of Tate crying out pulls my gaze back to the screen and a tear spills down my cheek as I watch him take her as she pulls on the ropes.

"That's it, Sweetheart," Devlin whispers. "Look right in that camera and tell Daddy how awful it is."

"Enough!" I roar, slamming my fist into the wall and Dominic nods, turning off the video. "Where is he?"

Dominic smiles. "We'll get to that. First, there's one more video to show you."

"No, I can't," Nix chokes out, jumping to his feet and marching out of the room. Emma follows him, laying a supportive hand on my arm as she passes me and I suck in a stuttered breath as I wait for the next video to load.

"This video is one he was filming as we rolled up on him."

I take a step forward. "She's safe?"

"Yes."

"Why the fuck didn't you lead with that?" I growl, balling my fists and taking another step forward. He points to the screen where another image of Tate pops up.

"Because you needed to see this."

Before I can argue, he presses play and the sound of Tate screaming fills the room. My stomach rolls and my heart stops as I watch Devlin drag a scalpel down her arm, slicing her open before he grabs a needle and thick black thread and starts stitching her back together again.

"Why?" Smith breathes and I glance over at him as tears build in his eyes. He presses his fist to his lips and closes his eyes, shaking his head like he can somehow erase the images we just saw but I know there's no way in hell I'll ever forget it.

"Turn it off," I bark and Dominic nods, pausing the video before folding his hands in front of him as he flashes me an expectant look. "Where is he?"

He smiles. "I was hoping you'd feel that way."

"I don't know what kind of sick fucking game you're playing but I want five minutes alone with this son of a bitch."

Dominic holds his hands out with the sick smile still on his face. "I'm merely presenting you with an opportunity. Do you want my blessing to marry my daughter or not?"

"She's not yours to give away," I snarl as I take a step toward him. Who does this motherfucker think he is? He is the entire reason that this has happened to my girl and he has the fucking gall to come in here and act like I owe him something. Dominic takes a step toward me.

"I suppose you're right but you can't really think I'm going to allow you to marry her if you can't take care of her."

"The only reason she's in that bed is because of you."

He waves his hand through the air, dismissing me. "The point is, you have a chance to avenge her pain. Do you want to take it?"

"You have him?" I ask, watching him warily. He nods.

"Oh, yes. I've got Devlin and I'll deal with him if you're not man enough to handle it but what would she think if you didn't end the monster who spent the last twenty-four hours torturing her?"

I nod. "Let's go."

"Kodiak," Smith breathes and I shake my head. He'll never understand – not unless it's the love of his life lying in a bed being tortured.

"Stay out of this, Smith."

"Tate wouldn't want this," he growls under his breath and I suck in a breath. The night she learned the truth about the kind of man her father is pops into my mind and I remember how horrified she was that he was a part of her. Dropping my head, I sigh as my mind wars with my heart. Images of what that animal did to her replay in my head and I want to hurt him even a fraction of how much he hurt her but Smith is right. Tate wouldn't want me to become her father. Shaking my head, I turn to Dominic.

"I would love nothing more than to sink a blade into his gut a couple hundred times but Smith is right, that isn't what Tate would want."

Dominic laughs. "As far as I've heard, Tate is as fierce as some of my best men."

"She is," I say, turning back to the image of her on the screen and my chest aches. "But she's also good and pure in a way that you'll probably never understand. Besides, she already has one murderer in her life and you brought all this trouble down on her head so it's only right that you clean it up."

"What do you know of it?" he scoffs and I glare at him.

"I know that as that animal was forcing himself inside her, he wanted her to plead with *you* for rescue. Don't act like this isn't on you."

He takes a step toward me. "Know your place, you little punk."

"My place is by her side," I assert, squaring my shoulders and meeting his gaze. "Now, where is she?"

Dominic studies me for a moment, a wry smile stretching across his face. "You know, I could just take her and go back to Chicago right now. You would never see her again. So maybe you should try to be a little respectful to your future father-in-law."

"And I could kill you right now," I assert, taking
a step forward as my hand hovers over the gun in my
waistband. "Where is she?"

He sighs. "Baton Rouge General, but don't think
this is over."

"That's where you're wrong," I snarl, turning and
walking out of the room without waiting for a response.
Everyone files outside, including Nix, Emma, and
Rodriguez, and I nod to them as I jump on my bike and
fire it up. I don't wait for anyone else as I peel out of the
parking lot and no one stops me. They'll catch up
eventually but I'm getting to my girl now. Pulling down
on the throttle, I speed up, racing through a yellow light
as a car horn bellows. They can go fuck themselves.
Nothing is stopping me now.

When I pull up in front of the hospital, I park my
bike in a spot and jump off before running through the
door. I spot a nurse and I sprint to the desk she's working
at.

"I need to find my fiancée. She was brought in
here a little while ago."

She nods. "Name?"

"Tatum Carter."

She types something before glancing up at me
with a sympathetic expression and my heart stalls.
Please tell me she's okay.
She has to be okay.
"Second floor. Room 208."

I nod. "Thank you."

Turning away from the desk, I decide to take the
stairs instead of waiting on the elevator and people shoot

me looks as I race past them but I don't give a fuck. No one in this hospital is as important as my girl. Once I get to the second floor, I find a sign and race down the hallway until I skid to a stop in front of room 208.

Sucking in a breath, I step forward and my pulse spikes when I see her lying in the middle of the bed with wires and tubes all over her. Her arm is covered in bandages and a tear slips down my cheek as I walk forward and grab her hand.

"I'm so sorry, baby," I whisper, kissing her hand and willing her to open her eyes. Apart of the bandages covering her left arm, she doesn't look too worse for wear but from all the work I've done with the club, I know all the hard work is still in front of us. I will stand by her through it all, though. "Eyes on me, gorgeous. You don't get to leave me anytime soon."

Chapter Twenty-Seven
Tatum

"Where are you at, baby?" a familiar voice says, pulling me toward the light as darkness clings to me, trying to pull me back under its warm embrace. My entire body aches and I try to remember why. An image of Devlin slicing me open with the scalpel fills my mind and I cry out. Or, at least, I think I do but no one seems to notice. "I'm missing you something crazy and I need you to come back to me, Darlin'."

I try to reach for him but my arm doesn't budge. More memories flood my mind – I was fading in and out of consciousness as the door to the room burst open and then I was in someone's arms. There were people calling my name and pain, so much pain that I couldn't stand it anymore. I whimper. Someone grabs my hand and a sense of peace settles over me.

Oh, I'd know that touch anywhere.

"Tate? Can you hear me, baby?" he whispers, one hand cradling the side of my head as he brushes his thumb over my forehead. I try to squeeze his hand but my fingers won't work and I let out another whimper. "Eyes on me, gorgeous."

Fighting against the darkness, my eyes flutter open and I wince at the bright fluorescent light filling the room. Where am I?

"Hey," the voice whispers and I turn my head to the side, my heart pounding when Lincoln comes into view.

"Lincoln." My voice is weak and it cracks as I force the word through my lips but his face lights up as he brings my hand to his lips and kisses it.

"There she is."

I try to sit up but pain floods my body and I squeeze my eyes shut again as I realize just how dry and uncomfortable my throat is. "Ow."

"What do you need?" he asks, gently setting my arm back on the bed as he stands and I glance at the cup on my bedside table.

"Water."

He nods, grabbing a pitcher and filling the cup with water before setting it back down and helping me sit up a little bit. I hiss as pain swamps me again and he murmurs apologies as he raises the head of the bed. When I'm finally comfortable, he grabs the cup again and helps me take a sip of water.

"Thank you," I whisper, my throat still feeling dry but it's better than before. He nods, setting the cup down and sitting in the chair again as he grabs my hand and presses it to his forehead.

"Thought I almost lost you."

I shake my head, smiling through the constant pain now throbbing through my arm. "Lincoln Paul Archer, I'm never leaving you."

"Damn right you're not," he forces out as he looks up and brushes away a tear. My heart breaks for him as he stands and presses a kiss to my lips. When he pulls away, he flashes me a smile that melts my insides and I let the peace I feel with him radiate over me before memories start rushing back to me.

"Oh, Lincoln," I gasp, fighting back tears. I know I have to tell him what happened to me and I have no idea how he'll react.

"Hey," he whispers, running his hand over my hair. "What is it, sweetheart?"

"I have to tell you... He did things..."

He shakes his head, giving my hand a squeeze. "You don't have to tell me anything, Tate. I already know."

"How?"

Gritting his teeth, he looks away from me for a second before his gaze drifts back to mine and he sighs. "Your father showed up at the clubhouse and showed us the video Devlin made."

"You saw?" I ask in horror as tears burn my eyes. He nods.

"Yeah, baby, I saw and I don't care, if that's what you're thinking."

I shake my head. "I don't really know what I'm thinking yet."

"That's okay, too," he says with a nod and I stare at the wall for a moment, trying to play catch up. Turning to look at him, I suck in a breath.

"Do you know where he is now?"

He arches a brow. "Devlin? Or your father?"

"Both."

Shaking his head, he sighs and kisses my hand again like he can't get enough of me. "If I had to guess, I would say that Devlin is dead and who the hell knows where Dominic is."

"What happened?"

He meets my gaze. "What do you remember?"

"I remember the scalpel carving through my skin," I whisper, turning to look at my bandaged left arm. "And I remember Devlin humming *Don't Worry, Be Happy* as he stitched me back together."

"Jesus, baby," he hisses, closing his eyes as his jaw clenches. "Is that all?"

I shake my head. "I was fading in and out of consciousness and I think someone broke the door down but after that it's just flashes of stuff that don't make sense."

"It was your father. He rescued you from Devlin and then the hospital staff found you dumped on the ground out in front of the emergency room door."

"He just left me here?"

He nods. "I assume he had to get Devlin somewhere secure and then you know the rest."

"I can't believe he showed up at the clubhouse," I whisper, wishing I could have been there to witness that.

"There's one more thing you should know, babe."

I turn back to him, nodding. "Dominic is fairly certain that Devlin was responsible for your mother's death."

"Oh," I spit out, staring up at the ceiling. I'd like to say that I'm surprised but after everything else I learned, I'm not. His anger and pain was eating away at him for a long time and in the end, it took control over everything else.

"Do you know why he went after you?" Lincoln asks and my head falls to the side.

"Dominic didn't tell you?"

He shakes his head. "I get the feeling he didn't know."

"He still doesn't," a voice says from the doorway and I stiffen as a handsome man with salt and pepper hair and an impeccable suit walks into the room.

"Dominic, I assume?"

He smiles and I can actually see how easy it would be to fall for his charming act. "You can call me Dad."

"I won't," I answer, pressing my lips into a thin line.

"Dominic, what are you doing here?" Lincoln asks. My father barely even spares Lincoln a second glance as he strides into the room and sits on the edge of my bed by my feet.

"I told you this wasn't over."

"Don't you think you've caused enough trouble?" Lincoln growls and Dominic dismisses him with an eye roll. Rage twists through my belly and I narrow my eyes into a glare.

"What do you want?"

Chuckling, he pats my foot and I immediately want to pull it back. "I'm here to check on my daughter, of course."

"Yeah, right. Why don't you tell me what you really want?"

He adjusts his sleeves. "Tell me why Devlin took you."

"You're the one who rescued me. Why don't you ask him?"

"I am. A thank you is not necessary, by the way..."

"Good. Because I wasn't going to provide one. Do you have Devlin now?"

"I do," he replies with a nod as he studies me with amused eyes.

"Then ask him."

He sighs, crossing his arms over his chest. "He's being annoyingly tight-lipped about his reasons for acting so crazy. It doesn't make sense. He's always been such a good soldier."

"Claire," I reply, watching his response. His eyes widen and I watch as the truth slowly dawns on him.

"Oh... All this over a girl? What a grave mistake on his part."

Anger surges forward in me seeing his total lack of compassion or remorse. "Really? That's all you have to say? He only did to me what you did to her."

"He knew what he was doing by going after you and now he'll pay the price."

"How did you know where I was?"

404

He shrugs. "Devlin never intended to survive this so he didn't bother to cover his tracks. It took me no time at all to find him."

"You're going to kill him?" I ask, unsure how I feel about it. A part of me really felt for Devlin but after what he did to me, I'd feel so much safer knowing he was no longer walking this earth.

"Unless you want to, my dear."

I shake my head. "I'm not you."

"Yes," he muses, his gaze flicking all over my face. "I can see that now, although I do hear that you have a bit of my temper. You know, you could always come home with me."

Lincoln stands up as his grip on my hand tightens. "I don't fucking think so."

"I am home," I answer, meeting my father's gaze. "And from now on, I don't want to see or hear from you again."

He nods, standing from the bed as he straightens his suit. "I understand, Tate. I will never claim to be a good man because I'm not but for you, my darling daughter, I would go to fucking war and don't you ever forget it."

"The difference is, I would never ask you. Get out of my life and don't come back."

He sighs. "Children never appreciate their parents until it's too late. If you ever need me, all you have to do is call."

He tosses a card down on the bed and walks out without another word as Lincoln scoops it up.

"Want me to rip it up?"

Sighing, I hold my hand out for the card and he gives it to me. There's a huge part of me that wants to rip it into a million pieces but something stops me.

"Are you okay, babe?"

I shake my head. "I don't even know how to answer that question."

"You wanna talk about it?"

I meet his gaze and hold my hand out for his. "No. I don't want to give Devlin's pain or anger any more life – especially when I have such a fantastic future to look forward to with you."

"Sounds like a pretty good plan to me."

"I'm glad that you've finally learned to just give me what I want," I shoot back with a smirk and he laughs.

"Fuck, I love you, baby. The next seventy years with you are going to be interesting as hell."

I shrug, lying back in the bed as I squeeze his hand. "Would you want it any other way?"

"Darlin', as long as I get you, I'll take it however I can get it."

Epilogue
Six Months Later…

A cool sea breeze drifts in through the open sliding glass door and I smile, turning back to the full length mirror and running my hands down the gauzy fabric of the dress. It's a simple design but I fell in love with it as soon as I saw it and I know it'll make Lincoln lose his mind with the deep V and the open back. My hair is curled and pinned back as Ali secures little white flowers with bobby pins. Her belly bumps me and I laugh.

"Watch where you're swingin' that thing."

She growls. "Don't start with me, woman. It's hot as hell, my toes look like sausages, and this baby won't stop kicking my bladder."

"Well, sit down," I instruct, gently walking backward toward the bed as she holds a piece of my hair. As I sit on the edge of the bed, she sits behind me and sighs as she gets back to work.

"You look stunning, Tate. If he weren't already barefoot, you'd knock Kodiak's socks off."

I catch sight of the scars on my arm and collarbone and sigh. Maybe I should have gotten a dress with sleeves. "I hope so."

She follows my gaze and pokes the back of my head with a bobby pin. "Knock it off. You're gorgeous and Kodiak is one lucky bastard."

"Ow," I mumble, rubbing my head. Physically, I healed from Devlin's attack fairly quickly but the emotional side of it still haunts me daily. Of course I don't know what I'd do without Lincoln. He wakes up each morning and the first thing he does is kiss every scar on my body, telling me how beautiful I am. If it wasn't for him, I don't even want to imagine where I would be.

After I was released from the hospital, Lincoln took me home and promptly moved in. Neither one of us was willing to be away from the other after we almost lost it all and I still needed a lot of help as I healed. Rodriguez came by a few days after we were settled in and delivered the news that they'd found Devlin's body on the edge of town. They also found journals detailing all his plans at his house so as far as the police department was concerned, the case was all wrapped up with a tidy little bow. I thought I would find some peace in knowing who killed my mother but I don't. Instead, I'm still haunted by the type of man my father is but I suspect that's something I'll have to learn to live with.

"Knock, knock," someone says and I smile as Theo opens the door and pokes his head in. When he sees me on the bed, he sucks in a breath and a wide smile stretches across his face. "You're beautiful, T."

"Thanks, little brother."

He growls. "The only reason you're going to get away with that is because it's your wedding day."

"Uh, Tate?" I glance across the room as Carly ducks in through the sliding glass door. "I don't want to alarm you but there are some dark clouds rolling in."

"I'm done, you can get up," Ali says, patting my shoulder. I stand and make my way across the room, pulling the sheer white curtain back to peek outside. She's right. Dark, ominous clouds are rolling in toward the beach and I can't help but smile. For some reason I can't explain, it feels like Mom is with us here, which is the whole reason Lincoln and I decided to get married in Grand Isle where everything started for us.

"It's perfect," I whisper.

"Well, perfect or not, unless you want to get rained on, we should do this now."

I nod, turning back to her. "You and Ali head down to the beach and get the guys ready, okay?"

Carly nods as she flashes me a smile. "I'm on it. Come on, preggo."

"When I finally catch you, I'm smacking you for that comment," Ali growls, struggling to climb off the bed. Theo rushes over and helps her up. "Thank you."

The girls leave and Theo throws his arm around my shoulder, smiling down at me. "Ready to do this?"

"More than ready," I answer with a nod.

"Me, too. After today, you won't be my problem anymore."

I roll my eyes and give him a little shove. "You're not getting rid of me that easily, Teddy."

"I told you to never call me that again," he gasps and I laugh as I take one last look in the mirror, tucking one of the little white flowers behind my ear. When it came to the wedding, Ali kind of took over and I was happy to let her since I don't know the first thing about planning a wedding. Honestly, if it had been up to me, Lincoln and I would have been at the courthouse months ago but now that we're here, I'm glad she convinced me to let her plan things.

"Let's go get me married," I say, turning to Theo and he holds his arm out, allowing me to hook mine through it as he turns toward the sliding glass door. *Speechless* by Dan + Shay begins playing and I smile as Theo pulls the curtain back and we step out. All the guys, Rodriguez, Carly, Ali, Nix, Emma, and Mia are lined up on either side of our makeshift aisle and they all turn toward me but my gaze is solely focused on the man waiting for me by the water.

His smile lights up his face and his gaze never leaves mine as I slowly close the distance between us, my heart pounding and tears welling up in my eyes. A part of me can't believe this is real – like maybe this is all just a dream and I'll wake up any moment with only a figment of this happiness lingering in my heart. He bites his lip as his gaze drops down my body and warmth floods my system as my pulse spikes.

God, how did I ever get this lucky?

"You're stunning," Lincoln whispers after Theo passes my hand to him and a blush creeps up my cheeks. "I love you."

"I love you," I reply, staring up at him and the minister clears his throat.

"Shall we get started?"

Smith scoffs. "You'd better before we all get wet."

"Yeah, maybe we should just jump right to the vows," Storm says, glancing out at the ocean as the clouds roll closer.

"It's fine with me if it's all right with you two," the minister answers, glancing at us and I nod at the same time Lincoln does. "All right, then. Lincoln and Tatum have prepared their own vows so I'll let them take over. Lincoln?"

Lincoln clears his throat and pulls a slip of paper out of his khaki pants. "Tate, my gorgeous girl, I wasn't looking for you when you walked into my life. In fact, I would even say I was actively avoiding what you represented but all it took was one look, one smile, the sound of your laugh and I was a goner. All my reasons for running didn't matter anymore because running was no longer an option. You took me, a broken down man, and made me feel whole again. With you by my side, I know I can take on the world and for you, I would in a heartbeat. No one would ever say that you're easy…" Chuckles ring out around us. "But you are emphatically worth it. Every time. I love you more than any words could express so I hope you'll give me the next eighty years to prove it to you."

A tear slips down my cheek and he grins as he reaches out and wipes it away.

"Tate?" the minister prompts and I pull the slip of paper out of the top of my dress. Lincoln's gaze zeroes in on my cleavage and I roll my eyes, snapping my fingers in front of his face as everyone laughs. He meets my gaze again and blows me a kiss.

"Lincoln," I breathe out, resisting the urge to roll my eyes at him as I recite my wedding vows. "I waited for you for so many years and along the way, I think I stopped believing in you – not you specifically – but I lost faith that you were out there, waiting for me. I lost faith that you and I would ever find each other and then you walked into my diner and pissed me the fuck off." The minister coughs through his surprise as the guys laugh. "Even in that very first moment, you broke through my barriers and affected me like no one else ever had and I started to hope again. The road hasn't been easy but it's shown me the kind of man you are – one I can depend on, one I can build a future with – and I have faith again. Faith in you, in us, and faith that no matter where I go, you'll always come for me because even when I was pushing you away, you never gave up on me. I love you with every piece of my soul and I'm so lucky to spend this life with you."

The minister steps forward and smiles at us. "Do you have the rings?"

Lincoln digs them out of his pocket and hands them over as thunder cracks right above our heads. I duck and glance up at the sky, hoping we get a few more minutes before the heavens decide to open up on us. The minister hands the rings to us and we slip them on each other's fingers at the same time, grinning like little kids.

"By the power vested in me by God and the state of Louisiana, I now pronounce you husband and wife. You may kiss your bride," he calls as the wind picks up and our guests cheer and yell as Lincoln pulls me into his arms and claims my lips in a kiss that screams ownership.

Another crack of thunder sounds over our heads and the skies open up, pelting us with rain as everyone starts running back to the cars. I pull away from Lincoln and meet his gaze as I start laughing. I pull away from him and lean my head back as I spread my arms out and let the rain wash over me.

"You're crazy!" he yells over the rain and I meet his eyes again as I shrug.

"Get used to it, husband."

Growling, he grabs me and throws me over his shoulder as he marches across the beach back toward our room.

"What are you doing?" I yell and he smacks my ass.

"I made you a promise, Mrs. Archer."

"And what promise is that?"

He steps into our room and closes the sliding glass door before he slides me down his body. "Have you forgotten already? Eighty years starts tonight."

"Oh, that promise," I whisper, grinning up at him as he wraps his arms around me. I shove the straps of my dress off my shoulders and it pools at my feet. "Get to it, then."

Flashing me a wolfish grin, he runs his hand down my side and leans in, his lips hovering over mine. "Yes, Ma'am."

The End.

Like me on Facebook:
https://www.facebook.com/authoram
myers/

Or sign up for newsletter to make
sure you never miss a release:
http://eepurl.com/cANpav

Every Breath You Take

Other books from A.M. Myers

The Hidden Scars Series

- Hidden Scars:
https://www.amazon.com/dp/B014B6KFJE
- Collateral Damage:
https://www.amazon.com/gp/product/B01G9FOS20
- Evading Fate:
https://www.amazon.com/gp/product/B01L0GKMU0

Bayou Devils MC

- Hopelessly Devoted:
  https://www.amazon.com/dp/B01MY5XQFW
- Addicted to Love:
  https://www.amazon.com/dp/B07B6RPPPV
- It Ends Tonight: TBR: September 2018

Standalones

- It Was Always You: TBR Dec. 2018

Every Breath You Take

About the Author

A.M. Myers currently lives in beautiful Charleston, South Carolina with her husband and their two children. She has been writing since the moment she learned how to and even had a poem published in the sixth grade but the idea of writing an entire book always seemed like a daunting task until this story got stuck in her head and just wouldn't leave her alone. And now, she can't imagine ever stopping. A.M. writes gripping romantic suspense novels that will have you on the edge of your seat until the end. When she's not writing, you can find her hanging out with her kids or pursuing other artistic ventures, such as photography or painting.

Every Breath You Take

A.M. Myers

Every Breath You Take